EMPEROR TSOTUGA'S MAGIC FAN

From his ragged sleeve, Ajendra produced a large painted fan. "This," he said, "was made for the king of the Gwoling Islands by the noted wizard Tsunjing. By a series of chances too long to bore Your Imperial Majesty with, it came into the unworthy hands of this inferior person."

The Emperor was not impressed. "It looks like any other fan. What is its power?"

"Simple, O superior one. Any living thing that you fan with it disappears."

"And whither go the victims," the Emperor asked, interested.

"One theory of my school is that they are translated to a higher dimension, coexistent with this one. Another, holds that they are dispersed into constituent atoms, which however, retain such mutual affinities that they can be reassembled. Would you like to see a demonstration?"

"Very well, good wizard," the Emperor replied. "Just be careful not to wave that thing at us."

The Critically Acclaimed Series of Classic Science Fiction

NOW AVAILABLE:

The Best of Stanley G. Weinbaum
Introduction by Isaac Asimov

The Best of Fritz Leiber
Introduction by Poul Anderson

The Best of Frederik Pohl
Introduction by Lester del Rey

The Best of Henry Kuttner
Introduction by Ray Bradbury

The Best of Cordwainer Smith
Introduction by J. J. Pierce

The Best of C. L. Moore
Introduction by Lester del Rey

The Best of John W. Campbell
Introduction by Lester del Rey

The Best of C. M. Kornbluth
Introduction by Frederik Pohl

The Best of Philip K. Dick
Introduction by John Brunner

The Best of Fredric Brown
Introduction by Robert Bloch

The Best of Edmond Hamilton
Introduction by Leigh Brackett

The Best of Leigh Brackett
Introduction by Edmond Hamilton

The Best of Robert Bloch
Introduction by Lester del Rey

***The Best of Raymond Z. Gallun**
Introduction by J. J. Pierce

***The Best of Murray Leinster**
Introduction by J. J. Pierce

***The Best of Jack Williamson**
Introduction by Frederik Pohl

***The Best of Lester del Rey**
Introduction by Frederik Pohl

***The Best of Hal Clement**
Introduction by Isaac Asimov

***The Best of James Blish**
Introduction by Lester del Rey

****COMING SOON FROM DEL REY BOOKS***

THE BEST OF

L. Sprague de Camp

Introduction by
POUL ANDERSON

A Del Rey Book

BALLANTINE BOOKS • NEW YORK

To Poul and Karen Anderson: skaal!

A Del Rey Book
Published by Ballantine Books

Library of Congress Catalog Card Number: 77-26949

ISBN 0-345-25474-0

Manufactured in the United States of America

First Ballantine Books Edition: May 1978

Cover by Darrell Sweet

ACKNOWLEDGMENTS

Contents

L. Sprague de Camp—Engineer and Sorcerer

As a student of the myriad ways of man, L. Sprague de Camp has from time to time looked upon his own society with the same objective eye he uses on peoples whom geography or history make strange to most of us. He himself does not seem to find them very alien—and he has encountered many at first hand. Though he knows more about cultural differences than most professional anthropologists, his basic judgment appears to be that human beings everywhere and everywhen are much the same at heart: limited, fallible, tragi-comic, yet endlessly interesting. So in the civilizations of antiquity or among more recent "primitives" he sees engineers and politicians not unlike ours, while among us he discovers taboos and tribal rites not unlike theirs. The insight has directly inspired at least one story and added philosophical depth as well as occasional piquant ironies to most of the others.

Therefore I wonder what he thinks of this curious custom we have of prefacing a collection of one writer's work with the remarks of a colleague. It strikes me as especially odd when the former is senior to the latter, and senior in far more than years. That is, I was a boy when L. Sprague de Camp's first stories were published; I spent a decade being awed by his erudition and captivated by his ability to tell a story, none of which has changed since. When I began to write professionally myself, it became clear, once I was hitting my stride, that there was a considerable de Camp influence on me, though I will never match him in any of those areas he has made uniquely his own. In short, what the deuce am *I* doing introducing *him?*

The sole rationale that comes to mind is this. De Camp belongs to that generation of writers whom John Campbell inspired to create the golden age of science fiction and fantasy, beginning about 1937 when he took the helm of what was then called *Astounding Stories.* Critics be damned, it was the golden age in all truth, when people such as Isaac Asimov, Lester del Rey, Robert A. Heinlein, L. Ron Hubbard, Malcolm Jameson, Henry Kuttner (especially as "Lewis Padgett"), Fritz Leiber, C. L. Moore, Ross Rocklynne, Clifford D. Simak, George O. Smith, Theodore Sturgeon, A. E. van Vogt, Jack Williamson, and more and more either appeared for the first time or, for the first time, really showed what they could do. De Camp stood tall in this race of giants. Gifted new writers have made their considerable marks on the field throughout the years afterward, but the excitement—the sense of utterly green pastures suddenly opened—will never come again. Comparison to the Periclean and Elizabethan periods may strike you as overdrawn, but you might think of jazz in its heyday, or quantum physics in the 1920's and '30's, or cosmology and molecular biology today.

The era was brief, choked off—though not overnight—by America's entry into World War Two. A number of key creators found that they had more urgent business on hand than writing stories. They included de Camp.

Hostilities having ended for the time being, he returned to his proper business and had much to do with pulling science fiction out of the dismal state into which it had fallen. Besides *Astounding* as of yore, he was an important contributor to numerous other magazines in the field. The publication of science-fiction books, not as rare one-shots but as a regular thing, was being pioneered then, and his became landmarks. Of all this, more anon.

However, he began increasingly to write other things. These included some grand historical fiction but became primarily nonfiction, with emphasis on science, technology, and the history of these. Factual material, accurately and vividly presented, was not new to him—he had written it from the start of his career—but soon it comprised the overwhelming bulk of his output. I don't know whether to regret this or not. On the one hand, we have doubtless lost a number of marvelous yarns; on the other hand, we do have these perfectly splendid books about elephants and ancient engineers and H. P. Lovecraft and dinosaurs and. . . .

Luckily for us, of recent years L. Sprague de Camp has from time to time been coming back to storytelling, especially to fantasy. (He is also pleasing aficionados with light verse and familiar essays, but these are of less immediate interest to a reading public starved for honest narratives in which real things happen to persons one can care about.) And thus we arrive at a justification for this foreword: the fact that many younger folk may not be acquainted with his fiction, and in any event will not know what a towering figure he has been—and is—in the field of imaginative literature. The present book, which spans most of his career, ought to remedy that. If you haven't read a de Camp tale before now, you have a treat in store, and I am here to tell you so.

Second, since an anthology can hold but a limited part of an author's work, you might allow me to steer you onto other things, as well. What follows will not be a bibliography or a scholarly study, but just a ramble through a few of the good memories, literary and personal, that Sprague has given me. A lot will be omitted; I should not take up space which could be used for an extra story. But perhaps you will get a better idea of his achievement and of what to watch for in bookstores and libraries than you would from something more formal.

As I have remarked, he began writing nonfiction early on. Indeed, his very first published work was an important book, still in print and once cited in a Supreme Court decision, whose self-explanatory title is *Inventions, Patents, and Their Management.* Not being an inventor of anything except occasional recipes, I must confess to never having read this. However, in my teens I was delighted and enlightened by the articles he wrote for *Astounding,* pieces like "The Long-Tailed Huns" (on urban wildlife), "The Sea King's Armored Division" (on Hellenistic science and engineering), and "Get Out and Get Under" (on the history of military vehicles). The subjects demonstrate the range and depth of his interests; the titles indicate the humor with which he made the facts sparkle.

That humor became an emblem of his in science fiction, doubly welcome because it has always been in short supply there, and in fantasy, where it matched the funniest things ever done in a field which has nurtured a lot of sprightliness. His humor was often called "wacky," but I think that's the wrong word. De Camp constructed his stories every bit as carefully, with the same respect for fact and logic, as he did his nonfiction. (He still does, of course.) Much of the laughter came from the meticulously detailed working out of the consequences of a bizarre assumption.

For instance, in the short novel *Divide and Rule,* extraterrestrial conquerors have imposed a neo-medieval culture on Earth as a way of keeping the human race from uniting to overthrow them. The story opens with Sir Howard van Slyck, second son of the Duke of Poughkeepsie, riding along in chrome-nickel armor, puffing his pipe, near the tracks of the elephant-powered New York Central. Upon his plastron he bears the family arms—which he calls a trademark—consisting of a red maple leaf in a white circle with the motto "Give 'em the works."

In another short novel, *Solomon's Stone,* there is a parallel universe in which Earth is inhabited by those people whom we daydream of ourselves as being. The mind of the shy, bookish hero is transferred to the body of the alter ego he had always supposed was purely imaginary, a French cavalier like d'Artagnan. Practically every man is big, muscular, and handsome; every woman ravishingly beautiful. New York is a wild conglomeration of ethnic types, ranging from the Siegfrieds in Yorkville to a Middle Eastern sultan complete with harem (who in our world is really a bachelor clerk at the YMCA). With so many aggressively *macho* toughs around, society is pretty chaotic, though a government of sorts does exist and even maintains a small army, which consists almost entirely of generals and is commanded by the only private it has.

In the classic Harold Shea stories, written in collaboration with the late Fletcher Pratt, we are taken to a whole series of universes where various myths or literary works are strictly true. For example, in "The Mathematics of Magic," Shea finds himself in the world of Spenser's *The Faerie Queen*. At one point, traveling through a forest with the virginal Belphebe, he encounters the Blatant Beast, a monster that will devour them unless it is given a poem it has not heard before—and in such an emergency, the single poem he can think of is the luridly gross "The Ballad of Eskimo Nell." Magic works here, by strict rules of its own, and at another point Shea seeks to conjure up a unicorn for a steed—but he doesn't phrase the spell quite clearly enough, and gets a rhinoceros instead. I needn't go on, for happily the first three of these stories are again available, collected together as *The Compleat Enchanter*.

Nor does space permit me to give more examples of this particular source of de Campian humor. It isn't necessary anyway; you can find plenty for yourself in the stories gathered here, in which you will also note an equally important source of humor, character.

De Camp's people are never stereotypes. They are unique and often think and act in ways that are funny. Like Molière or Holberg, de Camp observes them with a slightly ironic, basically sympathetic detachment, and then tells us what he has seen. We laugh, but all too often we recognize ourselves in them.

The humor, and oftimes the pathos, of character became particularly evident in the postwar "Gavagan's Bar" stories, also written in partnership with Pratt. Gavagan's Bar is a friendly kind of neighborhood place, whose steady customers all know one another, and the genial bartender, Mr. Cohan (Co*han,* if you please), does his best to keep it that way. But people do come in who have the strangest tales to tell, and sometimes a breath of that strangeness blows through the establishment itself. "These little whiskey fantasies," as critic Groff Conklin called them, usually evoke very gentle laughter.

Indeed, offhand the postwar stories of de Camp's seem rather different from the prewar ones: more serious, frequently downright somber. However, this is not true. There has been a shift of emphasis, as might be expected of a writer who is not content to repeat himself endlessly but, instead, keeps experimenting and developing. Yet recent stories have had their wit, and early stories had their gravity.

His first major piece of fiction, the novel *Genus Homo,* in collaboration with the late P. Schuyler Miller, contains comic moments but is essentially a straightforward tale of a busload of travelers—the believably ordinary kind you meet on a Greyhound—who end up in the far future, when mankind is long extinct save for them, and apes have evolved to intelligence. Though the conclusion is hopeful, the narrative does not pretend that the opening situation is anything but catastrophic, and tragedies as well as triumphs occur.

Another early novel, *Lest Darkness Fall,* illustrates this combination of qualities still better. It is, in a way, de Camp's answer to Mark Twain, whose Connecticut Yankee started modern technology going in Arthurian Britain with the greatest of ease. Martin Padway is scholarly, even a little timid, but a highly knowledgeable man. This much was necessary for the author to postulate, else his protagonist would soon have died a messy death, after being hurled back to Ostrogothic Italy of the sixth century A.D. Nevertheless, Padway has a terrible time as he struggles to introduce a few things like printing, which may stave off the Dark Ages he knows will otherwise come. He never does manage to make gunpowder that goes *Bang!* instead of *Fizz-zz.* His most successful innovations are the simplest, like double-entry bookkeeping or an information-carrying line of semaphores. Here de Camp was at his most rigorously logical.

The book is full of hilarious scenes. For instance, when Padway catches a bad cold, his main problem is how to avoid the weird remedies that well-meaning friends try to apply to him. Yet when war breaks out, its horrors are quietly described; we are not spared.

Thus the stories of later years represent no mutation, but rather a steady evolution.

The tales of the *Viagens Interplanetarias* are, in fact, quite like their predecessors. These are straight science fiction—so much so that de Camp does not permit his characters to exceed the speed of light through "hyperspace" or any similar incantation, but confines them to the laws of relativistic physics and the nearer stars. That, though, gives the same scope for exotic settings and exciting adventures that Haggard found in the then unmapped parts of Africa. The humorous possibilities are fully realized; an example in the present collection is "The Inspector's Teeth." Likewise realized are the possibilities of derring-do—and, occasionally, pain and bitterness.

The historical novels show the same meticulous care throughout and the same general line of development, from the comparatively light-hearted *An Elephant for Aristotle* and *The Dragon of the Ishtar Gate* (my personal favorite) to *The Golden Wind,* which holds a poignant depiction of what age can do to a man and how the spirit can rise above that.

As I have said, de Camp came more and more to specialize in nonfiction, fine stuff and highly recommended but outside the purview of this essay. It may have been Conan the Cimmerian who finally lured him back to a reasonable productivity of stories. If that is true, we have much to thank Robert E. Howard for, over and above the entertainment he gave us in his own right.

When the creator of the original Mighty Barbarian died, he left behind him a heap of unfinished manuscripts, some involving Conan and some which could be adapted to the series. Perhaps mostly for enjoyment, de Camp undertook to complete the work with collaborators Björn Nyberg and Lin Carter. The enthusiastic rediscovery of Conan by the reading public may have surprised him. I don't know. What I do know, and what matters, is that since then he has increasingly been writing original fantasy. You'll find a few of the shorter pieces here. *The Goblin Tower* and *The Clocks of Iraz* are two rather recent novels. Let us hope for many more.

I have already admitted that this foreword is not going to be anything like a proper survey of the de Camp canon. Still, I would like to mention anew certain of his incidental writings—essays, reviews and criticisms, verse, aphorisms—which have appeared over the years in such places as the magazine *Amra* or his anthology *Scribblings*, to the pleasure of smaller audiences than they deserve. Unless a major publisher has the sense to gather these together, you may never see them; but they should be mentioned as showing yet another dimension of his versatility.

In person, L. (for Lyon) Sprague de Camp is a tall, trim man of aristocratic appearance and bearing—aristocratic in the best sense, gracious and kindly as well as impressive. More than one woman has confided to me that she tends to swoon over him, but he remains content with his lovely wife of many years, Catherine, with whom he has collaborated on books as well as children.

Born in New York in 1907, he studied at Caltech, MIT, and Stevens Institute of Technology, and held down a variety of jobs until he went into full-time writing. As a Navy reservist, he was called up in World War Two and did research and development (alongside Isaac Asimov and Robert Heinlein), which was a substantial contribution to the Allied cause.

His vast fund of information comes not only from omnivorous reading but from extensive traveling. This isn't just through the tourist circuits, but into strange places hard to reach. He doesn't brag about it, but if you can get him to reminisce, it makes great reading or listening.

By the time this is in print, he will be past his seventieth birthday, but he doesn't look or act it—and, what the hell, Goethe wrote the second part of *Faust* in his eighties. Long may L. Sprague de Camp go on, to the joy of us all.

Poul Anderson
Orinda, California
June, 1977

Hyperpilosity

"WE ALL KNOW about the brilliant successes in the arts and sciences, but, if you knew all their stories, you might find that some of the failures were really interesting."

It was Pat Weiss speaking. The beer had given out, and Carl Vandercook had gone out to get some more. Pat, having cornered all the chips in sight, was leaning back and emitting vast clouds of smoke.

"That means," I said, "that you've got a story coming. Okay, spill it. The poker can wait."

"Only don't stop in the middle and say 'That reminds me,' and go off on another story, and from the middle of that to another, and so on," put in Hannibal Snyder.

Pat cocked an eye at Hannibal. "Listen, mug, I haven't digressed once in the last three stories I've told. If you can tell a story better, go to it. Ever hear of J. Roman Oliveira?" he said, not waiting, I noticed, to give Hannibal a chance to take him up. He continued:

"Carl's been talking a lot about that new gadget of his, and no doubt it will make him famous if he ever finishes it. And Carl usually finishes what he sets out to do. My friend Oliveira finished what he set out to do, also, and it should have made him famous, but it didn't. Scientifically his work was a success, and deserving of the highest praise, but humanly it was a failure. That's why he's now running a little college down in Texas. He still does good work, and gets articles in the journals, but it's not what he had every reason to suspect that he deserved. Just got a letter from him the other day—it seems he's now a proud grandfather. That reminds me of my grandfather—"

"Hey!" roared Hannibal.

Pat said, "Huh? Oh, I see. Sorry. I won't do it again." He went on:

"I first knew J. Roman when I was a mere student at the Medical Center and he was a professor of virology. The J in his name stands for Haysoos, spelled J-e-s-u-s, which is a perfectly good Mexican name. But he'd been so much kidded about it in the States that he preferred to go by 'Roman.'

"You remember that the Great Change, which is what this story has to do with, started in the winter of 1971, with that awful flu epidemic. Oliveira came down with it. I went around to see him to get an assignment, and found him perched on a pile of pillows and wearing the godawfullest pink and green pajamas. His wife was reading to him in Spanish.

" 'Leesten, Pat,' he said when I came in, 'I know you're a worthy esstudent, but I weesh you and the whole damn virology class were roasting on the hottest greedle in Hell. Tell me what you want, and then go away and let me die in peace.'

"I got my information, and was just going, when his doctor came in—old Fogarty, who used to lecture on sinuses. He'd given up general practice long before, but he was so scared of losing a good virologist that he was handling Oliveira's case himself.

" 'Stick around, sonny,' he said to me when I started to follow Mrs. Oliveira out, 'and learn a little practical medicine. I've always thought it a mistake that we haven't a class to train doctors in bedside manners. Now observe how I do it. I smile at Oliveira here, but I don't act so damned cheerful that he'd find death a welcome relief from my company. That's a mistake some young doctors make. Notice that I walk up briskly, and not as if I were afraid my patient was liable to fall in pieces at the slightest jar . . .' and so on.

"The fun came when he put the end of his stethoscope on Oliveira's chest.

" 'Can't hear a damn thing,' he snorted. 'Or rather, you've got so much hair that all I can hear is the ends of it scraping on the diaphragm. May have to shave it. But say, isn't that rather unusual for a Mexican?'

" 'You're jolly well right she ees,' retorted the sufferer. 'Like most natives of my beautiful Mejico, I am of mostly Eendian descent, and Eendians are of Mongoloid race, and so have little body hair. It's all come out in the last week.'

" 'That's funny . . .' Fogarty said. I spoke up: 'Say, Dr. Fogarty, it's more than that. I had my flu a month ago, and the same thing's been happening to me. I've always felt like a sissy because of not having any hair on my torso to speak of, and now I've got a crop that's almost long enough to braid. I didn't think anything special about it . . .'

"I don't remember what was said next, because we all talked at once. But when we got calmed down there didn't seem to be anything we could do without some systematic investigation, and I promised Fogarty to come around to his place so he could look me over.

"I did, the next day, but he didn't find anything except a lot of hair. He took samples of everything he could think of, of course. I'd given up wearing underwear because it itched, and anyway the hair was warm enough to make it unnecessary, even in a New York January.

"The next thing I heard was a week later, when Oliveira returned to his classes, and told me that Fogarty had caught the flu. Oliveira had been making observations on the old boy's thorax, and found that he, too, had begun to grow body hair at an unprecedented rate.

"Then my girl friend—not the present missus; I hadn't met her yet—overcame her embarrassment enough to ask me whether I could explain how it was that *she* was getting hairy. I could see that the poor girl was pretty badly cut up about it, because obviously her chances of catching a good man would be reduced by her growing a pelt like a bear or a gorilla. I wasn't able to enlighten her, but told her that, if it was any comfort, a lot of other people were suffering from the same thing.

"Then we heard that Fogarty had died. He was a good egg and we were sorry, but he'd led a pretty full life, and you couldn't say that he was cut off in his prime.

"Oliveira called me to his office. 'Pat,' he said, 'You were looking for a chob last fall, ees it not? Well, I need an asseestant. We're going to find out about this hair beesiness. Are you on?' I was.

"We started by examining all the clinical cases. Everybody who had, or had had, the flu was growing hair. And it was a severe winter, and it looked as though everybody was going to have the flu sooner or later.

"Just about that time I had a bright idea. I looked up all the cosmetic companies that made depilatories, and socked what little money I had into their stock. I was sorry later, but I'll come to that.

"Roman Oliveira was a glutton for work, and with the hours he made me keep I began to have uneasy visions of flunking out. But the fact that my girl friend had become so self-conscious about her hair that she wouldn't go out any more saved me some time.

"We worked and worked over our guinea pigs and rats, but didn't get anywhere. Oliveira got a bunch of hairless Chihuahua dogs and tried assorted gunks on them, but nothing happened. He even got a pair of East African sand rats—*Heterocephalus*—hideous-looking things—but that was a blank, too.

"Then the business got into the papers. I noticed a little article in *The New York Times,* on an inside page. A week later there was a full-column story on page 1 of the second part. Then it was on the front page. It was mostly 'Dr. So-and-so says he thinks this nationwide attack of hyperpilosity' (swell word, huh? Wish I could remember the name of the doc who invented it) 'is due to this, that, or the other thing.'

"Our usual February dance had to be called off because almost none of the students could get their girls to go. Attendance at the movie houses had fallen off pretty badly for much the same reason. It was a cinch to get a good seat, even if you arrived around 8:00 P.M. I noticed one funny little item in the paper to the effect that the filming of 'Tarzan and the Octopus Men' had been called off because the actors were supposed to go running around in G-strings, and the company found they had to clip and shave the whole cast all over every few days if they didn't want their fur to show.

"It was fun to ride on a bus about ten o'clock and watch the people, who were pretty well bundled up. Most of them scratched, and those who were too well-bred to scratch just squirmed and looked unhappy.

"Next I read that applications for marriage licenses had fallen off so that three clerks were able to handle the entire business for Greater New York, including Yonkers, which had just been incorporated into the Bronx.

"I was gratified to see that my cosmetic stock were going up nicely. I tried to get my roommate, Bert Kafket, to get in on them too. But he just smiled mysteriously, and said he had other plans. Bert was a kind of professional pessimist. 'Pat,' he said. 'Maybe you and Oliveira will lick this business, and maybe not. I'm betting that you won't. If I win, the stocks that I've bought will be doing famously long after your depilatories are forgotten.'

"As you know, people were pretty excited about the plague. But when the weather began to get warm the fun really started. First the four big underwear companies ceased operations, one after another. Two of them were placed in receivership, another liquidated completely, and the fourth was able to pull through by switching to the manufacture of tablecloths and American flags. The bottom dropped entirely out of the cotton market, as this alleged hair-growing flu had spread all over the world by now. Congress had been planning to go home early, and was, as usual, being urged to do so by the conservative newspapers. But now Washington was jammed with cotton planters demanding that the Government *do something,* and they didn't dare. The Government was willing enough to Do Something, but unfortunately didn't have the foggiest idea of how to go about it.

"All this time Oliveira, more or less assisted by me, was working night and day on the problem, but we didn't seem to have any better luck than the Government.

"You couldn't hear anything on the radio in the building where I lived, because of the interference from the big, powerful electric clippers that everybody had installed and kept going all the time.

"It's an ill wind, as the prophet saith, and Bert Kafket got some good out of it. His girl, whom he had been pursuing for some years, had been making a good salary as a model at Josephine Lyon's exclusive dress establishment on Fifth Avenue, and she had been leading Bert a dance. But now all of a sudden the Lyon place folded up, as nobody seemed to be buying any clothes, and the girl was only too glad to take Bert as her lawful wedded husband. Not much hair was grown on the women's faces, fortunately for them, or God knows what would have become of the race. Bert and I flipped a coin to see which of us should move, and I won.

"Congress finally passed a bill setting up a reward of a million dollars for whoever should find a permanent cure for hyperpilosity, and then adjourned, having, as usual, left a flock of important bills not acted upon.

"When the weather became really hot in June, all the men quit wearing shirts, as their pelts covered them quite as effectively. The police force kicked so about having to wear their regular uniforms, that they were allowed to go around in dark blue polo shirts and shorts. But pretty soon they were rolling up their shirts and sticking them in the pockets of their shorts. It wasn't long before the rest of the male population of the United States was doing likewise. In growing hair the human race hadn't lost any of its capacity to sweat, and you'd pass out with the heat if you tried to walk anywhere on a hot day with any amount of clothes on. I can still remember holding on to a hydrant at Third Avenue and 60th Street and trying not to faint, with the sweat pouring out the ankles of my pants and the buildings going round and round. After that I was sensible and stripped down to shorts like everyone else.

"In July Natasha, the gorilla in the Bronx Zoo, escaped from her cage and wandered around the park for hours before anyone noticed her. The zoo visitors all thought she was merely an unusually ugly member of their own species.

"If the hair played hob with the textile and clothing businesses generally, the market for silk simply disappeared. Stockings were just quaint things that our ancestors had worn, like cocked hats and periwigs.

"Neither Oliveira nor I took any vacation that summer, as we were working like fury on the hair problem. Roman promised me a cut of the reward when and if he won it.

"But we didn't get anywhere at all during the summer. When classes started we had to slow down a bit on the research, as I was in my last year, and Oliveira had to teach. But we kept at it as best we could.

"It was funny to read the editorials in the papers. The *Chicago Tribune* even suspected a Red plot. You can imagine the time that the cartoonists for the *New Yorker* and *Esquire* had.

"With the drop in the price of cotton, the South was really flat on its back this time. I remember when the Harwick bill was introduced in Congress, to require every citizen over the age of five to be clipped at least once a week. A bunch of Southerners were back of it, of course. When that was defeated, largely on the argument of unconstitutionality, the you-alls put forward one requiring every person to be clipped before he'd be allowed to cross a state line. The theory was that human hair is a commodity, which it is sometimes, and that crossing a state line with a coat of the stuff, whether your own or someone else's, constituted interstate commerce, and brought you under control of the Federal Government. It looked for a while as though it would pass, but the Southerners finally accepted a substitute bill requiring all Federal employees, and cadets at the military and naval academies to be clipped.

"About this time—in the autumn of 1971—the cotton and textile interest got out a big advertising campaign to promote clipping. They had slogans, such as 'Don't be a Hairy Ape!' and pictures of a couple of male swimmers, one with hair and the other without, and a pretty girl turning in disgust from the hirsute swimmer and fairly pouncing on the clipped one.

"I don't know how much good their campaign would have done, but they overplayed their hand. They, and all the clothing outfits, tried to insist on boiled shirts, not only for evening wear, but for daytime as well. I never thought a long-suffering people would really revolt against the tyrant Style, but we did. The thing that really tore it was the inauguration of President Passavant. There was an unusually warm January thaw that year, and the President, the V. P., and all the Justices of the Supreme Court appeared without a stitch on above the waist and damn little below.

"We became a nation of confirmed near-nudists, just as did everybody else sooner or later. The one drawback to real nudism was the fact that, unlike the marsupials, man hasn't any natural pockets. So we compromised between the hair, and the need for something to hold fountain pens, money, and so forth, and our traditional ideas of modesty by adopting an up-to-date version of the Scottish sporran.

"The winter was a bad one for flu, and everybody who hadn't caught it the preceding winter got it now, so soon a hairless person became such a rarity that one wondered if the poor fellow had the mange.

"In May of 1972 we finally began to get somewhere. Oliveira had the bright idea—which both of us ought to have thought of sooner—of examining ectogenic babies. Up to now nobody had noticed that they began to develop hair a little later than babies born the normal way. You remember that human ectogenesis was just beginning to be worked about then; test-tube babies aren't yet practical for large-scale production by a long shot, but we'll get there some day.

"Well, Oliveira found that if the ectogens were subjected to a really rigid quarantine, they never developed hair at all, at least not in more than the normal quantities. By really rigid quarantine, I mean that the air they breathed was heated to 800 degrees C, and then liquefied, and run through a battery of cyclones, and washed with a dozen disinfectants. Their food was treated in a comparable manner. I don't quite see how the poor little fellows survived such unholy sanitation, but they did, and didn't grow hair—until they were brought in contact with other human beings, or were injected with sera from the blood of hairy babies.

"Oliveira figured out that the cause of the hyperpilosity was what he'd suspected all along: another of these damned self-perpetuating protein molecules. As you know, you can't see a protein molecule, and you can't do much with it chemically because, if you do, it forthwith ceases to be a protein molecule. We have their structure worked out pretty well now, but it's been a slow process with lots of inferences from inadequate data; sometimes the inferences were right and sometimes they weren't.

"But to do much in the way of detailed analysis of the things you need a respectable quantity of them, and these that we were after didn't exist in even a disrespectable amount. Then Oliveira worked out his method of counting them. The reputation he made from that method is about the only permanent thing he got out of all this work.

"When we applied the method, we found something decidedly screwy—an ectogen's virus count after catching hyperpil was the same as it had been before. That didn't seem right: we knew that he had been injected with hyperpil molecules, and had come out with a fine mattress as a result.

"Then one morning I found Oliveira at his desk looking like a medieval monk who had just seen a vision after a forty-days' fast. (Incidentally, you try fasting that long and you'll see visions too, lots of 'em.) He said, 'Pat, don't buy a yacht with your share of that meelion. They cost too much to upkeep.'

" 'Huh?' was the brightest remark I could think of.

" 'Look here,' he said, going up to the blackboard. It was covered with chalk diagrams of protein molecules. 'We have three proteins, alpha, beta, and gamma. No alphas have exeested for thousands of years. Now, you will note that the only deefference between the alpha and the beta is that these nitrogens—' he pointed '—are hooked onto *thees* chain instead of that one. You will also observe, from the energy relations wreeten down here, that, if one beta is eentroduced eento a set of alphas, all the alphas will presently turn into betas.

" 'Now, we know now that all sorts of protein molecules are being assembled inside us all the time; most of them are unstable and break up again, or are inert and harmless, or lack the power of self-reproduction—anyway, nothing happens because of them. But, because they are so beeg and complicated, the possible forms they take are very many, and it is possible that once in a long time some new kind of protein appears with self-reproducing qualities; in other words, a virus. Probably that's how the various disease viruses got started, all because something choggled an ordinary protein molecule that was chust being feenished and got the nitrogens hooked on the wrong chains.

" 'My idea is thees: The alpha protein, which I have reconstructed from what we know about its descendants beta and gamma, once exeested as a harmless and inert protein molecule in the human body. Then one day somebody heecupped as one of them was being formed, and presto! We have a beta. But the beta is not harmless: It reproduces itself fast, and it inheebits the growth of hair on most of our bodies. So presently all our species, wheech at the time was pretty apish, catch this virus, and lose their hair. Moreover, it is one of the viruses that is transmeeted to the embryo, so the new babies don't have hair, either.

" 'Well, our ancestors sheever a while, and then learn to cover themselves with animal skeens to keep warm, and also to keep fire. And so, the march of ceevilizations it is commence! Chust theenk—except for that one original beta protein molecule, we should probably today all be merely a kind of goreela or cheempanzee—anyway, an ordinary anthropoid ape.

" 'Now, I feegure that what has happened is that another change in the form of the molecule has taken place, changing it from beta to gamma—and gamma is a harmless and inert leetle fellow, like alpha. So we are back where we started.

" 'Our problem, yours and mine, is to find how to turn the gammas with wheech we are all swarming back into betas. In other words, now that we have become all of a sudden cured of the disease that was endemic in the whole race for thousands of years, we want our disease back again. And I theenk I see how it can be done.' "

"I couldn't get much more out of him; he went to work harder than ever. After several weeks he announced that he was ready to experiment on himself; his method consisted of a combination of a number of drugs—one of them was the standard cure for glanders in horses, as I recall—and a high-frequency electromagnetic fever.

"I wasn't very keen about it, because I'd gotten to like the fellow, and that awful dose he was going to give himself looked enough to kill a regiment. But he went right ahead.

"Well, it nearly did kill him. But after three days he was more or less back to normal, and was whooping at the discovery that the hair on his limbs and body was rapidly falling out. In a couple of weeks he had no more hair than you'd expect a Mexican professor of virology to have.

"But then our real surprise came, and it wasn't a pleasant one!

"We expected to be more or less swamped by publicity, and had made our preparations accordingly. I remember staring into Oliveira's face for a full minute and then reassuring him that he had trimmed his mustache to exact symmetry, and getting him to straighten my new necktie.

"Our epoch-making announcement dug up two personal calls from bored reporters, a couple of phone interviews from science editors, and not one photographer! We did make the science section of the *New York Times,* but with only about twelve lines of type—the paper merely stated that Professor Oliveira and his assistant—not named—had found the cause and cure of hyperpilosity; not a word about the possible effects of the discovery.

"Our contracts with the Medical Center prohibited us from exploiting our discovery commercially, but we expected that plenty of other people would be quick to do so as soon as the method was made public. But it didn't happen. In fact, we might have discovered a correlation between temperature and the pitch of the bullfrog's croak for all the splash we made.

"A week later Oliveira and I talked to the department head, Wheelock, about the discovery. Oliveira wanted him to use his influence to get a dehairing clinic set up. But Wheelock couldn't see it.

" 'We've had a couple of inquiries,' he admitted, 'but nothing to get excited about. Remember the rush there was when Zimmerman's cancer treatment came out? Well, there's been nothing like that. In fact, I—ah—doubt whether I personally should care to undergo your treatment, surefire though it may be, Doctor Oliveira. I'm not in the least disparaging the remarkable piece of work you've done. But—ah'—here he ran his fingers through the hair on his chest, which was over six inches long, thick, and a beautiful silky white—'you know, I've gotten rather fond of the old pelt, and I'd feel slightly indecent back in my bare skin. Also, it's a lot more economical than a suit of clothes. And—ah—if I may say so with due modesty—I don't think it's bad-looking. My family has always ridden me about my sloppy clothes, but now the laugh's on them; not one of them can show a coat of fur like mine!'

"Oliveira and I left sagging in the breeches a bit. We inquired of people we knew, and wrote letters to a number of them, asking what they thought of the idea of undergoing the Oliveira treatment. A few said they might if enough others did, but most of them responded in much the same vein that Doc Wheelock had; they'd gotten used to their hair, and saw no good reason for going back to their former glabrous state.

" 'So, Pat,' said Oliviera to me, 'it lukes as though we don't get much fame out of our discovery. But we may steel salvage a leetle fortune. You remember that meelion-dollar reward? I sent in my application as soon as I recovered from my treatment and we should hear from the government any day."

"We did. I was up at his apartment, and we were talking about nothing in particular, when Mrs. O. rushed in with the letter, squeaking, '*Abre la!* Open eet, Roman!'

"He opened it without hurry, spread the sheet of paper out, and read it. Then he frowned and read it again. Then he laid it down, very carefully took out and lit the wrong end of a cork-tipped cigarette, and said in his levellest voice, 'I have been stupid again, Pat. I never thought that there might be a time-leemit on that reward offer. Now it seems that some crafty *sanamabiche* in Congress poot one een, so that the offer expired on May first. You remember, I mailed the claim on the nineteenth, and they got it on the twenty-first, three weeks too late!'

"I looked at Oliveira, and he looked at me and then at his wife, and she looked at him and then went without a word to the cabinet and got out two large bottles of *tequilla* and three tumblers.

"Oliveira pulled up three chairs around a little table, and settled with a sigh in one of them. 'Pat,' he said, 'I may not have a meelion dollars, but I have something more valuable by far—a woman who knows what is needed at a time like thees!'

"And that's the inside story of the Great Change, or at least of one aspect thereof. That's how it happens that, when we today speak of a platinum-blonde movie star, we aren't referring to her scalp hair alone, but the beautiful silvery pelt that covers her from crown to ankle.

"There was just one more incident. Bert Kafket had me up to his place to dinner a few nights later. After I had told him and his wife about Oliveira's and my troubles, he asked how I had made out on that depilatory-manufacturer stock I'd bought. 'I notice those stocks are back about where they started from before the Change,' he added.

" 'Didn't make anything to speak of,' I told him. 'About the time they started to slide down from their peak, I was too busy working for Roman to pay much attention to them. When I finally did look them up I was just able to unload with a few cents' profit per share. How did you do on those stocks you were so mysterious about last year?'

" 'Maybe you noticed my new car as you came in?' asked Bert with a grin. 'That's them. Or rather, it; there was only one, Jones and Galloway Company.'

" 'What do Jones and Galloway make? I never heard of them.'

" 'They make'—here Bert's grin looked as if it were going to run around his head and meet behind—'curry-combs!'

"And that was that. Here's Carl with the beer now. It's your deal, isn't it, Hannibal?"

Language for Time Travelers

GRADUALLY, THE RAINBOW flicker of light died away, and Morgan Jones felt the tingle leave his body. The dial read 2438. Five hundred years! He opened the door of the compartment and climbed out.

"At first, he saw nothing but fields and woods. He was evidently in a farming country. Nobody was in sight—No, here came a rustic along the road, trudging through the dust with his eyes on the ground in front of him.

" 'Hey there!' Jones called. 'Could you give me some information?'

"The man looked up; his eyes widened with astonishment at the sight of the machine. 'Wozza ya seh?' he asked.

"Jones repeated his question.

" 'Sy; daw geh,' said the man, shaking his head.

"Now Jones looked puzzled. 'I don't seem to understand you. What language are you speaking?'

" 'Wah lenksh? Inksh lenksh, coss. Wah *you* speak? Said, sah-y, daw geh-ih. Daw, neitha. You fresh? Jumm?'

"Jones had an impulse to shake his head violently, the same feeling he always had when the last word of a crossword puzzle eluded him. The man had understood him, partly, and the noises he made were somehow vaguely like English, but no English such as Jones had ever heard. 'Inksh lenksh' must be 'English language'; 'sah-y daw geh-ih' was evidently 'sorry, don't get it.'

" 'What,' he asked, 'is a fresh jumm?'

" 'Nevva huddum?' said the rustic, scorn in his tone. 'Fresh people, go *Oui, oui, parlez-vous français, va t'en, sale bête!*' He did this with gestures. Then he stiffened. 'Jumms go'—he clicked his heels together—'*Achtung! Vorwärts, marsch! Guten Tag, meine Herren! Verstehen Sie Deutsch?* Fresh from Fress; Jumms from Jummy. Geh ih?'

" 'Yes, I suppose so,' said Jones. His mind was reeling slightly—"

Thus might almost any novel on the time-travel theme or the Rip Van Winkle theme begin. The author, having landed his hero in the far future, may either ascribe telepathy to the people of the time, or remark on how the English language will have changed. The foregoing selection shows—in somewhat more detail than do most of the stories—a few of the actual changes that might take place. To be strictly consistent, I should have changed the French and German selection also, but, in the first place, I don't know enough about French and German to predict their future evolution, and, in the second, it would have made the rustic's explanation utterly unintelligible. It might be interesting to consider in detail just what change may occur. To do this thing right we shall have to first take a brief look at the language's present state and its past history.

English is a Teutonic language, like German, Dutch, and Swedish, with a large infusion—perhaps a majority—of French words. Its parent tongue, Anglo-Saxon, was more highly inflected than its descendant—less so than Latin, but about as much so as modern German*

* For instance, the noun *end* in Anglo-Saxon had these forms:

	Singular	*Plural*
Nominative	ende	endas
Genitive	endes	enda
Dative	ende	endum
Accusative	ende	endas

Anglo-Saxon would sound to a modern hearer as much like a foreign language as German; English didn't become what would be intelligible to us until about the 16th Century. English of the 1500s would sound to us like some sort of Scotch dialect, because it had the rolled "r" and the fricative consonants heard in German: *ich, ach* (that's what all those silent *gh*'s in modern English spelling mean—or rather, used to mean) which have been retained in Scottish English, but lost or transformed in most other kinds of English. We have a fair idea of the pronunciation of Shakespeare's time because about then people began writing books on the subject. It's amusing to reflect that if Shakespeare returned to Earth, he'd get along passably in Edinburgh; he could manage, with some difficulty, in Chicago—but he'd be hopelessly lost in London, whose dialect would differ most radically from his! So much for the "language of Shakespeare"!

Authors are fairly safe in having the people of the future speak English—which is very convenient for the authors. Aside from the fact that nobody can prove them wrong, English is, today, well on the way to becoming the world's international language. It is probably taught in the schools of more countries than any other. In number of speakers it is exceeded only by Cantonese and Mandarin, the chief languages of China, each of which is divided into a myriad of mutually unintelligible dialects; its nearest rivals, Spanish and German, are far behind it in number of speakers. It's a concise language,* and the simplicity of its grammar makes it easy

[I once complained to the late Willy Ley about German's damnable inflected articles and adjectives, which have defeated my half-century of effort to learn to speak the language correctly. In his deep, heavily accented voice, Willy said: "It is very simple. You only have to be born there!" L.S. de C., 1977.]

* The same passage translated into various modern languages has the following numbers of syllables:

Cantonese	89	Ukrainian	189
Annamese	100	Hungarian	196
English	146	Greek	234
Spanish	157	Japanese	242

to learn, though its fearsome spelling is an obstacle to the student. It's a safe bet that another century will see it as the second language of every passably educated person on Earth, and in another millennium it may well be the only living language.

Like all living languages, English is changing slowly but constantly in pronunciation, vocabulary, and syntax. The first would probably cause our hero the most trouble. It changes pretty rapidly, and is responsible for the fantastic irregularity of English spelling, the spelling usually being a few centuries behind the pronunciation. The spelling of *caught* was reasonable when the word was pronounced "kowcht," with the "ch" as in German *ach*. But consider the number of sounds a single letter may represent today, as in *odd, off, come, worry, old, wolf, do, women, lemon*. Shades of sound can't be represented exactly by ordinary spelling, because all readers won't interpret the letters the same way; and some sounds simply can't be spelled: for instance, the *ir* part of *first* as often pronounced in New York City and parts of the South—a sound halfway between "oi" and "ay."

Speech sounds can be analyzed into fundamental units called *phonemes;* these move around like protozoa in a drop of water, and, like protozoa, join together and split up. For instance, a few centuries ago *person* and *parson* were one word, spelled *person* and pronounced "pairson." But the "air" group of words split, some like *jerk* joining the words like *turn,* and some like *heart* joining the words like *march*. In this process *person* acquired two pronunciations with different meanings.

Much commoner is *leveling,* wherein two phonemes merge. For instance, *vain, vein,* and *vane* were once all pronounced differently; so were *right:wright:rite:write*. We can see the process at work in the leveling, by many Americans, of *due:do* and *Mary:merry:marry*. The British, with their loss of "r" except when a vowel follows, do worse, leveling *over:ova, sort:sought,* and *paw:pour:poor*.

If the process goes far enough—as it has in those concise Chinese languages—language becomes a guessing game between speaker and hearer, and speech is one long pun. In some forms of Chinese a single spoken word may have as many as 69 distinct meanings. French is worse than English in this respect, but neither is anything like as terrible as Chinese. In English a hearer can usually tell, upon hearing such an ambiguous sound, which meaning is meant from the context. If, as some people do, you pronounce *whale* like *wail,* nobody will think, hearing you speak of harpooning a *whale,* that you really meant harpooning a *wail.* But if, as some do, you pronounce *oral* like *aural,* you're very likely to confuse your hearer if he doesn't know in advance what is coming.

If we add together all the leveling tendencies of modern English, we can synthesize a dialect in which *cud, card, cowed, coward* are all pronounced like *cod; tarred, torrid, tied, tired, towered* are all pronounced like *Todd; show, shore, sure* are pronounced like *show,* and so forth. This is a reasonable speculation: some Southerners pronounce *shore, sure* like *show;* some Londoners use an "ah" sound in *cud,* etc. I hope it never happens, but it might, and we should probably manage to communicate—though with more misunderstandings, especially over the telephone. Leveling seems to be an inevitable linguistic development, though literacy—a relatively new thing for the masses—may have a countereffect. *Boil* and *bile* were once pronounced alike, but were pried apart by the influence of spelling.

The thing that would most completely bewilder our hero would be another Great Vowel Shift. The last occurred in the years 1400–1800, and resulted in changing *time, teem, team, tame* from "teem," "tame," "tehm," "tahm" to their present pronunciations. All the front vowels except those in *bit, bet* moved up. The top one, "ee," being unable to go higher, became a diphthong.* The back vowels underwent a similar change.

There are signs that another vowel shift, a little different from the last, impends. In London Cockney it has practically taken place: *punt* has become something like *pant, pant* like *pent, pent* like *paint, paint* like *pint,* and *pint* like *point. Call* has become like *coal,* and *coal* something like *cowl.*

Imagine our hero's predicament if this sort of thing becomes general. He crawls out of his time machine in 2438 A.D., as stated at the beginning of the article, and promptly runs afoul of the law.

Hero: Beg pardon, but could you tell me——

Cop: Hanh? Didjue sy samtheng?

Hero: Yes, you see——

Cop: Speak ap; kent mike it aht.

Hero: Well——

Cop: Woss thowse fanny clowse? P'ride?

Hero: I'm sorry, but——

Cop: Downt annersten ja; kentcha speak English?

Hero: Yes, of course——

Cop: Woy downtcha, thane? Luck loik a spicious kerracter; bayter cam 'lohng to the stytion. Jile for you, me led!

Another factor in linguistic evolution is the influence of sounds on those preceding and following them. We tend to take short-cuts in getting from one sound to another. The "k" sounds in *cool* and *cube* differ slightly; the second is nearer "t" than the first, because of the influence of the following "y" sound. If this process goes far enough (as it did in Latin), the "ky" combination may become "ty," and finally "ty" may become "tch," as *statue* has changed from "stat-yue" to "stat-

* If you can watch your tongue in a mirror while saying the vowels of *beet, bit, bait, bet, bat* without the "b" and the "t," you'll see why we say that *beet* has a high vowel and *bat* a low one. *Front* and *back* refer to the part of the tongue that is highest when the vowel is sounded; hence *beet,* etc., have front vowels while *odd, all, go, good, do* have back vowels; those in *above* are intermediate.

chue." Hence our descendants may pronounce *cube* as "chube."

Our weakness for shortcuts—plus plain laziness—results in the complete dropping of sounds. Hence we often hear "prob'ly," "partic'lar," and "comf'table." The contracted forms "int'rest," "gen'ral" have become more or less standard; the others may follow in due course. Most of the "silent" letters in our spelling, as in *askEd, WrotE, KniGHt,* once stood for real sounds. The British outdo us in this respect, with their *Whitehall* "wittle" and *military* "miltry."

The British have slaughtered a large fraction of their r's; some of them have dropped "h" from their speech. The Scotch have dealt similarly with "l" and "v," so that in Broad Scottish *gave* is "gay." The story is told of an Aberdeenian in a dry-goods store who held up a piece of cloth and asked the clerk, "Oo?"

"Ay, oo."

"Ah oo?"

"Ay, ah oo."

"Ah ae oo?"

"Ay, ah ae oo."

Not to keep the reader in suspense any longer, "Ay, ah ae oo" means "Yes, all one wool." (In repeating this story, remember that "Ay" is pronunced like "eye.")

Our chief victim seems to have been "t," whence we often hear *posts, tests, loft, wanted* as "poce," "tess," "loff," "wanned." Sometimes we drop "n," nasalizing the preceding vowel to make up for it, as *don't,* sometimes pronounced "dote" or "doh" with a nasal "o."

Let's suppose that our hero has been hailed before a magistrate. To change the assumptions a little, suppose that the vowels are still recognizable, but that dropping and assimilation have been going full blast.

Magistrate: Wahya, pridna?

Hero: Huh?

Mag: Said, wahya?

Hero: You mean, what's my name?

Mag: Coss ass wah I mee. Ass wah I said, in ih?

Hero: I'm sorry. It's Jones, j-o-n-e-s, Morgan Jones.

Mag: Orrigh. Now, weya from?

Hero: You mean, where am I from?

Mag: Doh like ya attude, pridna. Try to be feh, buh woh tollay dispecfa attude. Iss a majrace coh, ya know.

Hero: You mean, this is a magistrate's court? I don't mean to be disrespectful, but—

Mag: Weh, maybe in yooh faw. Eeah ya fahna, aw nah righ melly. Sodge, lock im up. Gah geh mel zannas dow ih, to zam is satty.

Hero: But look here, I don't need a mental examiner to examine my sanity—I'm all right mentally—

It seems our time-traveling hero may be reduced to the device adopted by a man I once knew who made a trip to Germany. Entering a hotel with a companion, he asked, in what he thought was German, for two rooms and bath. The clerk looked blank, then replied in something that was evidently intended to be English, but which conveyed no sense whatever to the American. After some futile vocalization of this sort, the clerk had an inspiration: he got out a pad and wrote in the plainest of English, "What do you gentlemen want?" The American took the pad and wrote "Two rooms and bath," after which there was no more difficulty.

However, it's unsafe to say that English as a whole will take any particular course, merely because one of its many dialects shows signs of doing so. A phoneme may reverse its direction of change repeatedly: in King Alfred's time the first vowel in *after* was about that of modern *cat;* by 1400 it had moved down and back to the vowel of modern *calm;* by 1600 it had moved back to the *cat* position, where it still is with the great majority of Americans (don't let the dictionaries fool you with their "intermediate 'a' "). Finally in modern Southern British it has moved back down into the *calm* position again. This sort of thing can go on indefinitely.

Sounds that have been dropped can be restored by the influence of spelling. An example is the "t" in *often,* which was dropped long ago with the "t's" in *soften, listen, castle,* but which has been revived by a few speakers, including President Franklin D. Roosevelt.

Such an addition of a sound to a word is called a *spelling pronunciation* and is considered incorrect when first introduced. But sometimes one takes hold and becomes universal, after which it is "correct." Examples are the "h" in *hospital* and the "l" in *fault,* which originally (when the words were taken over from French) weren't sounded at all.

We might here dispose of the illusion that there is an absolute standard of "correctness" to which we can refer. There are no tablets of stone stating once and for all what is and isn't correct, and dictionaries are compiled by fallible human beings and often disagree. The only real standard, aside from individual prejudices, is the actual usage of educated people. The fact is not that we use pronunciations because they're correct, but that they're correct because we—or a large number of us—use them. If a hundred million people pronounce *after* with the vowel of *cat,* that's correct by definition, even though not the only correct form, dictionaries to the contrary notwithstanding.

The rate of change of pronunciation is probably dependent, to some extent, on the state of a civilization, and changes should take place more rapidly in periods when illiteracy is high, and schools and spelling have less braking effect. A collapse of civilization in the English-speaking world would make another vowel shift more likely, and result in more dropping and assimilation of sounds. If our hero knows this, he might be able to make a shrewd guess at the vicissitudes through which the world has passed even before he learns its actual history since his time.

English has numerous dialects, some being beyond the range of mutual intelligibility. A Scotchman I once knew would testify to this: he spent an unhappy afternoon trying to find Myrtle Avenue, Brooklyn. After asking innumerable Brooklynites how to get to "Mair-r-rtle Ahvenü," one of them finally caught on and said, "Oh, you mean Moitle Ehvenya!"

But which dialect most resembles the English of the future? North America has four major dialects: those of

New England, New York City, the South, and General American, which includes everything else. The British Isles have a much bigger variety; that of London and vicinity has, by virtue of London's being the capital and the commercial metropolis of Great Britain, acquired the prestige of a standard. Hence Londoners are wont to say that they speak true English, and anything else is a "bahb'rous dahlect." Often they argue that their form of speech is the "most beautiful," but that merely means that they're accustomed to it and so like it best. One feature of Southern British (the speech of educated Londoners and ruling-class Englishmen generally), the loss of "r" sounds except when a vowel follows, is also heard in New England, New York City and the South: others, such as the use of "ah" in *half, last, dance,* and about 150 similar words, occur in New England but are rare elsewhere in North America.

These dialects tend to evolve in different directions, like species. Unlike species, they also merge into intermediate forms. Right now, the forces tending to merge and homogenize them (radio, etc.) are much stronger than those tending to separate and diversify them. Given our mechanical culture, this is likely to continue until they have all been pretty well leveled. What will the result be?

The prestige of Southern British is high; European schools teach it. Many actors and radio announcers in this country imitate it—though the result is often more funny than impressive. But as a result of economic forces, the commercial and intellectual center of gravity of the English-speaking world seems to be shifting to this side of the Atlantic, which phenomenon should cause a decline in the prestige of Southern British. As this happens, some form of American speech will become a "world standard."

The dialects with the best chance of doing this are probably New York speech and General American. The former has the advantage of being the speech of the country's greatest metropolis and its cultural center. The latter has the advantage of numbers: about as many people speak it (90 or 100 million) as speak all the other kinds of English combined. It conforms more closely to the spelling, so that it is easier for foreigners to learn. My money would go on General American—but then, like most people, I'm probably prejudiced in favor of my native tongue. Very likely the final result will combine features of both dialects.*

Our grammar has been simplified about as much as it can be, so that only limited changes are to be looked for therein. We still have some irregular plurals, such as *child*:*children, mouse*:*mice, deer*:*deer;* these are hangovers from Anglo-Saxon, which had several declensions of nouns forming the plural differently. Given enough time, they will probably be cleaned up: *brethren,* for instance, has been displaced by the regular *brothers.* Our irregular verbs, such as *take*:*took, drink*:*drank, put*:*put* are more numerous and will be harder to get rid of.

Idiomatic word combinations such as *make at, make away with, make bold, make good, make light of, make off, make off with, make out, make sure, make sure of, make up, make up to, make up with* are the despair of foreigners learning English, as their meanings cannot be derived from a consideration of their component words separately. The making of these combinations goes on all the time, and they are likely to cause our hero plenty of headaches.

Another change that may cause him difficulty is the dropping of understood words from sentences, as when we say "the man I saw" for "the man whom I saw," or "Going?" for "Are you going?" That's *ellipsis,* if you want a five-dollar word. We practice it when we write telegrams or newspaper heads. As with leveling and compression of words, we gain in speed at the expense of clarity. I recall once being puzzled by a headline

*[Since this was written, the prestige of General American has risen; the affectation of British English by the theatrical profession has ceased; and the old New Yorkese dialect (pronouncing "oil burner" as "öil böina") shows signs of dying out. L.S. de C., 1977.]

reading "Little British Golf Victor." Did it mean that a horse named "Little British Golf" had won a race? No; it transpired that a man named Little had won a golf tournament in England. Another read "Gold Hunt Started by Skeletons." Alas, a reading of the article dispelled my first cheerful picture of a crew of skeletons slogging off to the gold country with pick, pan, and pack mule. All that had happened was that somebody had dug up some skeletons, quite inanimate, and this discovery had caused local gossip about the possible existence of a buried cache or hoard of gold. Of course, the head writer had meant: "The Starting of a Hunt for Gold Has Been Caused by the Discovery of Skeletons." He simply assumed that the reader would fill in all the missing words.

Again, the Chinese languages are a horrible example: one may say that the Chinese talk in headlines. The table showing the comparative conciseness of languages, in the early part of this article, indicates the extraordinary terseness of Cantonese; Annamese, another Indo-Chinese language, is second on the list. Pitkin's *History of Human Stupidity* cites the Chinese proverb "Shi ju pu ju shi ch'u"—literally "Miss enter not like miss go-out." Even a Chinese would be baffled by this unless he knew that it meant, "It is worse to imprison an innocent man than to release a culprit." As far as the actual words go, it might as well mean the opposite.

Suppose that as a result of a prolonged diet of headlines, English is reduced to a terseness like that of Cantonese. Our hero is being examined by the experts for whom the magistrate has sent. We'll neglect changes in pronunciation—I think you'll have had enough of my quasi-phonetic spelling—and concentrate on changes in syntax.

Hero: Welcome to my cell, gentlemen. Your names please?

1st Expert: I Mack.

2nd Ditto: I Sutton.

Hero: Delighted, you know my name, of course. What do you want me to do?

Mack: From?

Hero: What?

Mack: No what, from.

Hero: Now, let's get this straight. You want to know where I'm from? That's easy; Philadelphia.

Sutton: No hear.

Hero: PHILADELPHIA.

Sutton: No mean no hear you; hear plenty. No hear Philadelphia.

Mack: Such place?

Sutton: Maybe. Ask more. Continent?

Hero: No, it's a city.

Sutton: No mean no. Philadelphia no continent, Philadelphia on continent. Six continent. Which?

Hero: I see—North America.

Mack: No North America Philadelphia.

Sutton: Crazy. Too bad.

Mack: Yes. Word-crazy. Too much word.

Hero: Say what is this? You two sit there like a couple of wooden Indians, and expect me to understand you from one or two words that you drop, and then you say *I've* got a verbal psychosis—

Mack: Proof. Escape. Fingerprint. Check, sanitarium.

Sutton: Right. Interest. Health. Too bad. *(They go out.)*

But actually, I doubt whether headlines will ever bring the language to this sad state. Their influence is probably confined to popularizing a few uncommon words, such as *laud, flay,* which are preferred to *praise* and *denounce* because of their shortness.

Changes in vocabulary are difficult to foresee, though we can classify, if we can't prophesy, them. When we have a new meaning to express, we can do any of several things: we can invent a new word out of whole cloth, like *gas, hooey*. We can combine Latin or Greek roots to make a word, like *Ornithorhynchus, telephone*. We can combine parts of existing English words, as in *brunch* (Hollywood slang for an eleven o'clock meal). We can borrow a word from another modern language, either in something like its original form, as with *knout* (Russian), *khaki* (Hindustani), or corrupted, as with *crawfish* (French écrevisse), *dunk* (German *tunken*). Most often, we pile the new meaning on some unfortunate existing English word, which thereafter does double, triple, etc., duty. Thus *short* has acquired the meanings of a *short* circuit, a *short* story, a *short* movie such as newsreel, a *short* shot in artillery fire, a type of defect in iron castings, etc. Next to pronunciation changes, vocabulary changes will be the most baffling of our hero's troubles with Twenty-Fifth Century English. Perhaps he'd better take a course in sketching before starting his time journey: when words, both spoken and written, fail, he can fall back on pictures!

Words also become obsolete and disappear. Sometimes we adopt another way of saying the same thing, because of convenience, fads, or reasons unknown. Where we once said "I height Brown," we now say "I am called Brown" or "My name is Brown." (Germans still say "Ich heisse Braun.") The old second-person singular pronoun *thou* has become obsolete, the plural *you* being used instead.

Again, words may disappear because the things they refer to disappear. Thus *hacqueton* is obsolete, because nobody has used a hacqueton (a padded shirt worn under armor) for some centuries. *Buggy* and *frigate*, to name a couple, will probably follow *hacqueton* in all vocabularies save those of historians and specialists, unless somebody finds new meanings for them. Thus *clipper* has been saved by a transfer of its meaning to a modern object.

It's not strictly correct to say that today's slang is tomorrow's standard English, if we can judge from history. Of our vast "floating population" of slang terms, only the most useful few (like *mob*, originally a slang word) will be admitted to the company of words used in serious speech and writing. Our hero will find that most of the slang of his time has gone without a trace, and that the people of 2438 have a whole new set of slang terms wherewith to bewilder him. (I'm reminded of a time I had occasion to explain to a South African that by "the grub is fierce" I meant, not "the larva is ferocious," but "the food is unpalatable.")

Let's suppose that our hero has been let out of the psychopathic ward, and has convinced the authorities of his true origin. He's turned over to a local savant who is to act as his guide and interpreter. This time we'll concentrate on changes in vocabulary and idiom.

Savant: Morning, Mr. Jones. I'm Einstein Mobray, who is to symbiose you for a few days until you hoylize yourself.

Hero: I'm sorry—you're going to what me until I what myself?

Mobray: I mean, you're going to reside with me until you adapt yourself. "Symbiose" is from "symbiosis," meaning "living together"; "hoylize" is from "Hoyle," as in the old term "according to Hoyle," "in conformity with the prevailing rules." I'll try to avoid terms like that. I have a surprise for you: another man from the Early Industrial Period—about 1600. Ah, here he is—Come in, Godwin. This is Morgan Jones, who I was telling you of. Mr. Jones, Godwin Hill.

Hill: Verily, 'tis a great pleasure, Sir.

Mobray: Mr. Hill haved a most markworthy accident, whichby he was preserved from his time to ourn. He'll tell you of it, some day.

Hill: Faith, when I awoke I thought I had truly gone mad. And when they told me the date, I said, "Faugh! 'Tis a likely tale!" But they were right, it seems. Pray, how goes your trouble with authority, Einstein?

Mobray: The cachet's still good, but I'll get up with the narrs yet. What happened, Mr. Jones, was that I was gulling my belcher—

Hero: Your what?

Mobray: Oh very well, my aerial vehicle propelled by expanding gasses, like a rocket. I was coasting it, and getted into the wrong layer, and they redded me down. The cachet means an upcough and thirty days' hanging.

Hill: 'Sblood, do they hang you for that?

Mobray: Not me, my silk. I mean, my operating permit will be suspended for thirty days, and I'll have to pay a fine. But I hope to get up with them.

Hero: You'll get up with them? Do you mean you'll arise at the same time they do?

Mobray: No, no, no! I mean I expect to exert influence to have the cachet rubbered.

Hill: You—your???

Mobray: I mean, to have the summons cancelled.

Hero: Oh, *I* see! Just like fixing a ticket!

Hill: What, Mr. Jones? Does that not mean "attaching an admission card"?

Mobray: I'd never neured that he meant, "repairing a public conveyance." What *did* you mean, Mr. Jones?

Hero: Well, in my time, when a cop pinched you—

Mobray: (dials the portable telephone on his wrist) Quick, send up six dictionaries and a box of aspirin!

Hill: Aspirin? You mean "aspen"? There grows a tree by that name—

(CURTAIN)

BIBLIOGRAPHY

Kenyon, *American Pronunciation.* (The best for beginners)

Moore, *Historical Outlines of English Phonology and Morphology.*

Stanley, *The Speech of East Texas.*

Ward, *The Phonetics of English.* (British dialects)

James, *Historical Introduction to French Phonetics.*

Greenough & Kittredge, *Words and Their Ways in English Speech.*

Mencken, *The American Language.*

Bloomfield, *Language.*

Fowler, *Modern English Usage.*

Columbia University Press, *American Speech.* (Periodical)

Columbia University Press, *Phonetic Transcriptions.*

Webster's New International Dictionary, 2nd Edition.

The Command

JOHNNY BLACK TOOK Volume 5 of the *Britannica* off the library shelf and opened it to "Chemistry." He adjusted the elastic that held his spectacles and found the place where he had left off last time. He worried his way through a few sentences, and then thought sadly that it was no use; he'd have to get Professor Methuen to explain some more before he could go on. And he did badly want to know all about chemistry, which had made him what he was—had made it possible for him to read an encyclopedia at all. For Johnny Black was not human.

He was, instead, a fine specimen of black bear, *Euarctos americanus,* into whose brain Methuen had injected a chemical that lowered the resistance of the synapses between his brain cells, making that complicated electrical process called "thought" about as easy for Johnny's little brain as for a man's big one. And Johnny, whose ruling passion was curiosity, was determined to find out all about the process.

He turned the pages carefully with his paw—he'd tried using his tongue once, but had cut it on the paper, and then Methuen had come in and given him hell for wetting the pages—the more so, since Johnny was at that moment indulging in his secret vice, and the Professor had visions of Johnny's drooling tobacco juice over his expensive books.

Johnny read the articles on "Chess" and "Chicago." His thirst for knowledge satisfied for the nonce, he put the book away, stowed his spectacles in the case attached to his collar, and ambled out.

Outside, the island of St. Croix sweltered under a Caribbean sun. The blueness of the sky and the greenness of the hills were lost on Johnny, who, like all bears, was color-blind. But he wished that his bear's eyesight were keen enough to make out the boats in Frederiksted harbor. Professor Methuen could see them easily from the Biological Station, even without his glasses. His eyesight, together with his lack of fingers to manipulate, and articulatable vocal organs to speak, were Johnny's chief grievances against things in general. He sometimes wished that, if he had to be an animal with a hominoid brain, he were at least an ape—like McGinty, the chimpanzee, over there in the cages.

Johnny wondered about McGinty—he hadn't heard a peep out of him all morning, whereas it was usually the old ape's habit to shriek and throw things at everybody who went by. Curious, the bear shuffled across to the cages. The monkeys chattered at him, as usual, but no sound came from McGinty's cage. Standing up, Johnny saw that the chimp was sitting with his back to the wall and staring blankly. Johnny wondered whether he was dead, until he noticed that McGinty was breathing. Johnny tried growling a little; the ape's eyes swung at the sound, and his limbs stirred, but he did not get up. He must be pretty sick, thought Johnny, who wondered whether he should try to drag one of the scientists over. But then his rather self-centered little soul comforted itself with the thought that Pablo would be around shortly with the ape's dinner, and would report McGinty's behavior.

Thinking of dinner reminded Johnny that it was high time he heard Honoria's bell to summon the biologists of the Station to lunch. But no bell came. The place seemed unnaturally quiet. The only sounds were those from the bird and monkey cages, and the *put-put-put* of a stationary engine from Bemis' place, over on the edge of the Station grounds. Johnny wondered what the eccentric botanist was up to. He knew that the other biologists didn't like Bemis; he'd heard Methuen make remarks about men—especially little plump men—who swaggered around in riding boots when there wasn't a horse near the Station. Bemis really didn't belong to the Station, but his financial inducements had led the treasurer to let him put up his house and laboratory there. With Johnny, to wonder was to investigate and he almost started for the place, but remembered the fuss Bemis had made last time.

Well, he could still investigate the reason for Honoria's delinquency. He trotted over to the kitchen and put his yellowish muzzle in the door. He didn't go farther, remembering the cook's unreasonable attitude toward bears in her kitchen. There was a smell of burning food, and on a chair by the window sat Honoria, black and mountainous as ever, looking at nothing. A slight "woof!" from Johnny brought no more reaction than he had gotten from McGinty.

This was definitely alarming. Johnny set out to find Methuen. The Professor wasn't in the social room, but others were. Dr. Breuker, world-famous authority on the psychology of speech, sat in one easy chair, a newspaper across his lap. He didn't move when Johnny sniffed at his leg, and when the bear nipped his ankle he merely pulled the leg back a little. He had dropped a lighted cigarette on the rug, where it had burned a large hole before going out. Doctors Markush and Ryerson, and Ryerson's wife, were there too—all sitting like so many statues. Mrs. Ryerson held a phonograph record—probably one of those dance tunes she liked.

Johnny hunted some more for his lord, and eventually found the lanky Methuen, clad in underwear, lying on his bed and staring at the ceiling. He didn't look sick—his breathing was regular—but he didn't move unless prodded or nipped. Johnny's efforts to arouse him finally caused him to get off the bed and wander dreamily across the room, where he sat down and gazed into space.

An hour later Johnny gave up trying to get sensible action out of the assorted scientists of the Biological Station, and went outside to think. He ordinarily enjoyed thinking, but this time there didn't seem to be enough facts to go on. What ought he to do? He could take the telephone off its stand, but he couldn't talk into it to call a physician. If he went down to Frederiksted to drag one up by main force, he'd probably get shot for his pains.

Happening to glance toward Bemis's, he was surprised to see something round rise into the sky, slowly dwindle, and vanish in the sky. From his reading he guessed that this was a small balloon; he'd heard that Bemis was doing some sort of botanical experiment that involved the use of balloons. Another sphere followed the first, and then another, until they made a continuous procession dwindling into nothingness.

That was too much for Johnny; he *had* to find out why anyone should want to fill the heavens with balloons a yard in diameter. Besides, he might be able to get Bemis to come over to the Station and see about the entranced staff.

To one side of the Bemis house he found a truck, a lot of machinery, and two strange men. There was a huge pile of unfilled balloons, and the men were taking them one at a time, inflating them from a nozzle projecting from the machinery, and releasing them. To the bottom of each balloon a small box was attached.

One man saw Johnny, said "Cheez!" and felt for his pistol holster. Johnny stood up and gravely extended his right paw. He'd found that this was a good gesture to reassure people who were alarmed by his sudden appearance—not because Johnny cared whether they were alarmed, but because they sometimes carried guns and were dangerous if cornered or surprised.

The man shouted, "Get otta deh, youse!"

Johnny, puzzled, opened his mouth and said, "Wok?" His friends knew that this meant "What did you say?"

or "What's going on here?" But the man, instead of sensibly explaining things, jerked out his pistol and fired.

Johnny felt a stunning blow and saw sparks as the .38 slug glanced off his thick skull. The next instant, the gravel of the driveway flew as he streaked for the gate. He could make 35 m.p.h. in a sprint and 30 for miles at a time, and now he was going all out.

Back at the station, he found a bathroom mirror and inspected the two-inch gash in his forehead. It wasn't a serious wound, though the impact had given him a slight headache. He couldn't bandage it. But he could and did turn on the faucet and hold his head under it, mop the wound with a towel, take down the iodine bottle, extract the stopper with his teeth, and, holding the bottle between his paws, pour a few drops on the wound. The sting made him wince and spill some of the solution on the floor, where, he reflected, Methuen would find it and give him hell.

Then he went out, keeping a watchful eye for the tough individuals at Bemis's, and thought some more. Somehow, he suspected, these men, the balloons, and the trancelike state of the people at the Station were all connected. Had Bemis gone into a trance too? Or was he the real author of these developments? Johnny would have liked to investigate some more, but he had the strongest aversion to being shot at.

It occurred to him that if he wanted to take advantage of the scientists' malady he'd better do so while the doing was good, and he made for the kitchen. There he had a glorious time, for he had five effective natural can openers on each foot. He was pouring the contents of a can of peaches down his throat, when a noise outside brought him to the window. He saw the truck that had been at Bemis's back up and the two tough individuals get out. Johnny slipped noiselessly into the dining room and listened through the door, tensing himself to bolt if the intruders came his way.

He heard the outside kitchen door slam and the voice of the man who had shot him: "What's ya name, huh?"

The inert Honoria, still sitting in her chair, answered tonelessly, "Honoria Velez."

"Okay, Honoria, you help us carry some of dis food out to the truck, see? Cheez, Smoke, lookit de mess. Dat beh's been around here. If you see him, plug him. Beh steaks is good eating, I hoid."

The other man mumbled something and Johnny could hear the slapping of Honoria's slippers as she moved about and presently the opening of the outside kitchen door. Still shuddering at the idea of becoming a steak, he pushed his door open a crack. Through the screen of the outside door he could see Honoria, arms full of provisions, docilely obeying commands and piling the cans and bags in the truck. The men sat on their running board and smoked while Honoria, like one hypnotized, made several trips back to the kitchen. When they said "Dat's all," she sat down on the kitchen steps and relapsed into her former state. The truck drove off.

Johnny hurried out and made for the clump of trees on the end of the Station's property opposite Bemis's house. The clump crowned a little hill, making it both a good hiding place and a vantage point. He thought, evidently the Station wasn't big enough for him and the strange men both, if they were going to corner the food supply and kill him on sight. Then he considered Honoria's actions. The Negress, normally a strong-minded person of granite stubbornness, had carried out every order without a peep. Evidently the disease or whatever it was didn't affect a person mentally or physically, except that it deprived the victim of all initiative and will power. Honoria had remembered her own name and understood orders well enough. Johnny wondered why he hadn't been affected also; then, remembering the chimpanzee, concluded that it was probably specific to the higher anthropoids.

He watched more balloons rise and saw two men come out of the bungalow and talk to the inflators. One stocky figure Johnny was sure was Bemis. If that was so, the botanist must be the mastermind of the gang, and Johnny had at least four enemies to deal with. How? He didn't know. Well, he could at least dispose of the remaining food in the Station kitchen before the plug-uglies got it.

He went down and made a quart of coffee, which he could do easily enough because the pilot light of the gas stove had been left on. He poured it into a frying pan to cool, and lapped it up, simultaneously polishing off a whole loaf of bread.

Back in his hideaway he had difficulty sleeping; the coffee stimulated his mind, and plans for attacking the bungalow swarmed into it in clouds, until he almost felt like raiding it right then. But he didn't, knowing that his eyesight was especially poor at night, and suspecting that all four of the enemy would be in.

He awoke at sunrise and watched the house until he saw the two tough ones come out and go to work on the balloons, and heard the little engine start its *put-put-put*. Making a long detour, he sneaked up from the opposite side and crawled under the house, which, like most Virgin Island bungalows, had no cellar. He crept around until the scrape of feet on the thin floor overhead told him he was under the men within. He heard Bemis's voice: ". . . Al and Shorty, and now those fools are caught in Havana with no way of getting down here, because transportation will be tied up all over the Caribbean by now."

Another voice, British, answered: "I suppose that in time it'll occur to them to go up to the owner of a boat or plane, and simply tell the chap to bring them here. That's the only thing for them to do, with everybody in Cuba under the influence of the molds by now, what? How many more balloons should we send up?"

"All we have," replied Bemis.

"But I say, don't you think we ought to keep some in reserve? It wouldn't do to have to spend the rest of our lives sending spores up into the stratosphere, in the hope that the cosmics will give us another mutation like this one—"

"I said all the balloons, not all the spores, Forney. I have plenty of those in reserve, and I'm growing more from my molds all the time. Anyway, suppose we did run out before the whole world was affected—which it will be in a few weeks? There wasn't a chance in a million of that first mutation—yet it happened. That's how I know it was a sign from above, that I was chosen to lead the world out of its errors and confusions, which I shall do! God gave me this power over the world, and He will not fail me!"

So, thought Johnny, his mind working furiously, that was it! He knew that Bemis was an expert on molds. The botanist must have sent a load up into the stratosphere where the cosmic rays could work on them, and one of the mutations thereby produced had the property of attacking the human brain, when the spores were inhaled and got at the olfactory nerve endings, in such a way as to destroy all will power. And now Bemis was broadcasting these spores all over the world, after which he would take charge of the Earth, ordering the inhabitants thereof to do whatever he wished. Since he and his assistants had not been affected, there must be an antidote or preventative of some sort. Probably Bemis kept a supply handy. If there were some way of forcing Bemis to tell where it was—if, for instance, he could tie him up and write out a message demanding the information. . . . But that wouldn't be practical. He'd have to settle with the gang first, and trust to luck to find the antidote.

One of the men working on the balloons spoke: "Ten o'clock, Bert. Time to go for the mail."

"Won't be no mail, you dope. Everybody in Frederiksted's sitting around like he was hopped."

"Yeah, that's so. But we ought to start organizing 'em, before they all croak of starvation. We gotta have somebody to work for us."

"All right, smart guy, you go ahead and organize; I'll take a minute off for a smoke. S'pose you try to get the phone soivice woiking again."

Johnny watched one pair of booted legs disappear

into the truck, which presently rolled out of the driveway. The other pair of legs came over to the front steps and sat down. Johnny remembered a tree on the other side of the house, whose trunk passed close to the eaves.

Four minutes later he paddled silently across the roof and looked down on the smoker. Bert threw away his cigarette butt and stood up. Instantly Johnny's 500 steel-muscled pounds landed on his back and flung him prone. Before he could fill his lungs to shout, the bear's paw landed with a *pop* on the side of his head. Bert quivered and subsided, his skull having acquired a peculiarly lopsided appearance.

Johnny listened. The house was quiet. But the man called Smoke would be coming back in the truck. . . . Johnny quickly dragged the corpse under the house. Then he cautiously opened the front screen door with his paws and stole in, holding his claws up so they wouldn't click against the floor. He located the room from which Bemis's voice had come. He could hear that voice, with its exaggerated oratorical resonance, wafting through the door now.

He pushed the door open slowly. The room was the botanist's laboratory and was full of flowerpots, glass cases of plants, and chemical apparatus. Bemis and a young man, evidently the Englishman, were sitting at the far end talking animatedly.

Johnny was halfway across the room before they saw him. They jumped up; Forney cried, "Good Gad!" Bemis gave one awful shriek as Johnny's right paw, with a swift scooping motion, operated on his abdomen in much the way that a patent ice-cream scoop works in its normal medium. Bemis, now quite a horrible sight, tried to walk, then to crawl, then slowly sank into a pool of his own blood.

Forney, staring at Bemis's trailing guts, snatched up a chair to fend off Johnny, as he had seen circus chappies do with lions. Johnny, however, was not a lion. Johnny rose on his hind legs and batted the chair across the room, where it came to rest with a crash of glass. Forney broke for the door, but Johnny was on his back before he had gone three steps. . . .

Johnny wondered how to dispose of Smoke when he returned. Perhaps if he hid behind the door and pounced on him as he came in, he could finish him before the man could get his gun out. Johnny had a healthy dread of stopping another bullet. Then he noticed four automatic rifles in the umbrella stand in the hall. Johnny was a good shot with a rifle—or at least as good as his eyesight permitted. He partly opened the breech of one gun to assure himself that it was loaded, and found a window that commanded the driveway. When Smoke returned and got out of the truck, he never knew what hit him.

Johnny set out to find the antidote. Bemis should have kept some around, perhaps in his desk. The desk was locked, but, although made of sheet steel, it wasn't designed to keep out a determined and resourceful bear. Johnny hooked his claws under the lowest drawer, braced himself and heaved. The steel bent, and the drawer came out with a rending sound. The others responded in turn. In the last one he found a biggish squat bottle whose label he made out, with his spectacles, to read "Potassium iodide." There were also two hypodermic syringes.

Probably this was the antidote, and worked by injection. But how was he to work it? He carefully extracted the bottle-cork with his teeth, and tried to fill one of the hypodermics. By holding the barrel of the device between his paws and working the plunger with his mouth, he at last succeeded.

Taking the syringe in his mouth, he trotted back to the Station. He found the underwear-clad Methuen in the kitchen, dreamily eating such scraps as had been left by his and the plug-uglies' raids. Breuker, the psychologist, and Dr. Bouvet, the black Haitian bacteriologist, were engaged likewise. Evidently the pangs of hunger caused them to wander around until they found something edible, and their feeble instincts enabled them to eat it without having to be told to do so. Beyond that they were utterly helpless without orders and would sit like vegetables until they starved.

Johnny tried to inject the solution into Methuen's calf, holding the syringe crosswise in his teeth and pushing the plunger with one paw. But at the prick of the needle the man instinctively jerked away. Johnny tried again and again. He finally grabbed Methuen and held him down while he applied the needle, but the man squirmed so that the syringe broke.

A discouraged black bear cleaned up the broken glass. Except possibly for the missing Al and Shorty, he would soon be the only thinking being left on Earth with any initiative at all. He fervently hoped that Al and Shorty were still in Cuba—preferably six feet underground. He didn't care so much what happened to the human race, which contained so many vicious specimens. But he did have a certain affection for his cadaverous and whimsical boss, Methuen. And, more important from his point of view, he didn't like the idea of spending the rest of his life rustling his own food like a wild bear. Such an existence would be much too stupid for a bear of his intelligence. He would, of course, have access to the Station library, but there wouldn't be anybody to explain the hard parts of chemistry and the other sciences to him when he got stuck.

He returned to Bemis's and brought back both the bottle and the remaining hypodermic, which he filled as he had the previous one. He tried inserting the needle very gently into Professor Methuen, but the biologist still jerked away. Johnny didn't dare try any rough stuff for fear of breaking his only remaining syringe. He tried the same tactics with Breuker and Bouvet, with no better results. He tried it on Honoria, dozing on the kitchen steps. But she awoke instantly and pulled away, rubbing the spot where she had been pricked.

Johnny wondered what to try next. He considered knocking one of the men unconscious and injecting him; but, no, he didn't know how hard to hit to stun without killing. He knew that if he really swung on one of them he could crack his skull like an eggshell.

He waddled out to the garage and got a coil of rope, with which he attempted to tie up the again-sleeping Honoria. Having only paws and teeth to work with, he got himself more tangled in the rope than the cook, who awoke and rid herself of the coils without difficulty.

He sat down to think. There didn't seem to be any way that he could inject the solution. But in their present state the human beings would do anything they were told. If somebody ordered one to pick up the hypodermic and inject himself, he'd do it.

Johnny laid the syringe in front of Methuen, and tried to tell him what to do. But he couldn't talk—his attempts to say "Pick up the syringe" came out as "fee-feek opp feef—feef." The Professor stared blankly and looked away. Sign language was no more successful.

Johnny gave up and put the bottle and syringe on a high shelf where the men couldn't get at them. He wandered around, hoping that something would give him an idea. In Ryerson's room he saw a typewriter, and thought he had it. He couldn't handle a pencil, but he could operate one of these machines after a fashion. The chair creaked alarmingly under his weight, but held together. He took a piece of typewriter paper between his lips, dangled it over the machine, and turned the platen with both paws until he caught the paper in it. The paper was in crooked, but that couldn't be helped. He'd have preferred to write in Spanish because it was easy to spell, but Spanish wasn't the native tongue of any of the men at the Station, and he didn't want to strain their faculties, so English it would have to be. Using one claw at a time, he slowly tapped out: "PICK UP SIRINGE AND INJECT SOLUTION INTO YOUR UPPER ARM." The spelling of "siringe" didn't look right, but he couldn't be bothered with that now.

Taking the paper in his mouth he shuffled back to the kitchen. This time he put the syringe in front of Methuen, squalled to attract his attention, and dangled the paper in front of his eyes. But the biologist glanced only briefly at it and looked away. Growling with vexation, Johnny pushed the syringe out of harm's way and tried to force Methuen to read. But the scientist merely squirmed in his grasp and paid no attention to the paper. The longer he was held the harder he tried to escape. When the bear released him, he walked across the room and settled into his trance again.

Giving up for the time being, Johnny put away the syringe and made himself another quart of coffee. It was weak stuff, as there wasn't much of the raw material left. But maybe it would give him an idea. Then he went out and walked around in the twilight, thinking furiously. It seemed absurd—even his little bear's sense of humor realized that—that the spell could be broken by a simple command, that he alone in the whole world knew the command, and that he had no way of giving it. He wondered what would happen if he never did find a way out. Would the whole human race simply die off, leaving him the only intelligent creature on Earth? Of course such an event would have its advantages, but he feared that it would be a dull life. He could take a boat from the harbor and head for the mainland, and then hike north to Mexico where he would find others of his species. But he wasn't sure that they'd be congenial company; they might, resenting his strangeness, even kill him. No, that idea wouldn't do, yet.

The Station's animals, unfed for two days, were noisy in their cages. Johnny slept badly and awoke well before dawn. He thought he'd had an idea, but couldn't remember. . . .

Wait. It had something to do with Breuker. He was a specialist on the psychology of speech, wasn't he? He did things with a portable phonograph recording apparatus; Johnny had seen him catching McGinty's yells. He went up to Breuker's room. Sure enough, there was the machine. Johnny opened it up and spent the next two hours figuring out how it worked. He could crank the motor easily enough, and with some patience learned to operate the switches. He finally adjusted the thing for recording, started the motor, and bawled "Wa-a-a-a-a-ah!" into it. He stopped the machine, threw the playback switch, set the needle in the outer groove of the aluminum disk, and started it. For a few seconds it scraped quietly, then yelled "Wa-a-a-a-a-ah!" at him. Johnny squealed with pleasure.

He was on the track of something, but he didn't quite know what. A phonograph record of his cry would be no more effective in commanding the men than the original of that cry. Well, Breuker must have a collection of records. After some hunting, Johnny found them in a set of cases that looked like letter files. He leafed through them and read the labels. "Bird Cries: Red-and-Green Macaw, Cockatoo, Mayana." That was no help. "Infant Babble: 6–9 Months." Also out. "Lancashire Dialect." He tried this disk and listened to a monologue about a little boy who was swallowed by a lion. From his experience with little boys Johnny thought that a good idea, but there was nothing in the record that would be of use.

The next was labeled "American Speech Series, No. 72-B, Lincoln County, Missouri." It started off: "Once there was a young rat who couldn't make up his mind. Whenever the other rats asked him if he'd like to come out with them, he'd answer, 'I don't know.' And when they said, 'Wouldn't you like to stop at home?' he wouldn't say yes or no either; he'd always shirk making a choice. One day his aunt said to him, 'Now look here! No one will ever care for you if you carry on like this. . . ."

The record ground on, but Johnny's mind was made up. If he could get it to say "Now look here!" to Methuen, his problem ought to be solved. It wouldn't do any good to play the whole record, as those three words didn't stand out from the rest of the discourse. If he could make a separate record of just those words. . . .

But how could he, when there was only one machine? He needed two—one to play the record and one to record the desired words. He squalled with exasperation. To be licked after he'd gotten this far! He felt like heaving the machine out the window. At least it would make a beautiful crash.

Like a flash the solution came to him. He closed the recorder and carried it down to the social room, where there was a small phonograph used by the scientists for their amusement. He put the American Speech disk on this machine, put a blank disk on the recorder, and started the phonograph, with a claw on the switch of the recorder to start it at the right instant.

Two hours and several ruined disks later, he had what he wanted. He took the recorder to the kitchen, set it up, laid the syringe in front of Methuen, and started the machine. It purred and scraped for ten seconds, and then said sharply, "Now look here! Now look here! Now look here!" and resumed its scraping. Methuen's eyes snapped back into focus and he looked intently in front of him—at the sheet of paper with a single line of typing across it that Johnny dangled before his eyes. He read the words, and without a flicker of emotion picked up the syringe and jabbed the needle into his biceps.

Johnny shut off the machine. He'd have to wait now to see whether the solution took effect. As the minutes passed, he had an awful feeling that maybe it wasn't the antidote after all. A half-hour later, Methuen passed a hand across his forehead. His first words were barely audible, but grew louder like a radio set warming up: "What in Heaven's name happened to us, Johnny? I remember everything that's taken place in the last three days, but during that time I didn't seem to have any desires—not enough will of my own to speak, even."

Johnny beckoned, and headed for Ryerson's room and the typewriter. Methuen, who knew his Johnny, inserted a sheet of paper for him. Time passed, and Methuen said, "I see now. What a sweet setup for a would-be dictator! The whole world obeys his orders implicitly; all he has to do is select subordinates and tell them what to order the others to do. Of course the antidote was potassium iodide; that's the standard fungicide, and it cleared the mold out of my head in a hurry.

Come on, old-timer, we've got work to do. The first thing is to get the other men around here to inject themselves. Think of it, Johnny, a bear saving the world! After this you can chew all the tobacco you want. I'll even try to get a female bear for you and inject her brain the way I did yours, so that you can have some company worthy of you."

A week later everyone on St. Croix had been treated, and men had been sent off to the mainland and the other Caribbean islands to carry on the work.

Johnny Black, finding little to arouse his curiosity around the nearly deserted Biological Station, shuffled into the library. He took Volume 5 of the *Britannica,* opened it to "Chemistry," and set to work again. He hoped that Methuen would get back in a month or so and would find time to explain the hard parts to him, but meanwhile he'd have to wade through it as best he could.

The Merman

A JOVE NODS occasionally, so Vernon Brock forgot to wind his alarm clock, and as a result arrived at his office with the slightly giddy feeling that comes of having had no breakfast but a hasty cup of coffee.

He glanced at the apparatus that filled half the scant space in the room, thought, you'll be famous yet if this works, my lad, and sat down at his desk. He thought, being an assistant aquarist isn't such a bad job. Of course there's never enough money or enough room or enough time, but that's probably the case in most lines of work. And the office was really quiet. The chatter and shuffle of the visitors to the New York City Aquarium never penetrated; the only sounds were those of running water, the hum of the pump motors, and the faint ticking of typewriters. And he did love the work. The only thing that he possibly loved better than his fish was Miss Engholm, and for strategic reasons he wasn't telling anybody—least of all the lady—yet.

Then, nothing could have been sweeter than his interview with the boss yesterday. Clyde Sugden had said he was going to retire soon and that he was using his influence to have Brock advanced to his place. Brock had protested without much conviction that, after all, Hempl had been there longer than he, and so ought to have the job.

"No," the head aquarist had said. "The feeling does you credit, Vernon, but Hempl wouldn't do. He's a good subordinate, but has no more initiative than a lamellibranch. And he'd never sit up all night nursing a sick octopus the way you would." And so forth. Well, Brock hoped he really was that good, and that he wouldn't get a swelled head. But, knowing the rarity of direct praise from superiors, he was determined to enjoy that experience to the utmost.

He glanced at his calendar pad. "Labeling": that meant that the labels on the tanks were out of date again. With the constant death of specimens ad acquisition of new ones that characterizes aquaria, this condition was chronic. He'd do some label-shifting this evening. "Alligator": a man had phoned and said that he was coming in to present one to the institution. Brock knew what that meant. Some fatheaded tourist had bought a baby 'gator in Florida without the faintest notion of how to keep it properly, and now he would be dumping the skinny little wretch on the Aquarium before it died of starvation and the effects of well-meant ignorance. It happened all the time. "Legislature": what the Devil? Oh, yes, he was going to write to the Florida state legislature in support of a bill to prohibit the export of live alligators by more fatheaded tourists, while there were still some of the unfortunate reptiles left alive in the state.

Then the mail. Somebody wanted to know why her guppies developed white spots and died. Somebody wanted to know what kind of water plants to keep in a home aquarium, and the name of a reliable seller of such plants in Pocatello, Idaho. Somebody wanted to know how to tell a male from a female lobster. Somebody—this was in nearly illegible longhand, at which Brock cursed with mild irritation—"Dear Mr. Brock: I heard your lecture last June 18th inst., on how we are dissended from fish. Now you made a pretty good speech but I think if you will excuse my frankness that you are all wrong. I got a theory that the fish is really dissended from us . . ."

He picked up the telephone and said, "Please send in Miss Engholm." She came in; they said "Good morning" formally, and he dictated letters for an hour. Then he said without changing his tone, "How about dinner tonight?" (Somebody might come in, and he had a mild phobia about letting the office force in on his private affairs.)

"Fine," said the girl. "The usual place?"

"Okay. Only I'll be late; labeling, you know . . . " He thought, foolish man, how surprised she'd be when he asked her to marry him. That would be after his promotion.

He decided to put in a couple of hours on his research before lunch. He tied on his old rubber apron and soon had the bunsen burners going merrily. Motions were perforce acrobatic in the confined space. But he had to put up with that until the famous extension was finished. Then in a couple of years they'd be as cramped as ever again.

Sugden stuck his white thatch in the door. "May we come in?" He introduced a man as Dr. Dumville of the Cornell Medical Center. Brock knew the physiologist by reputation and was only too glad to explain his work.

"You're of course familiar, Doctor," he said, "with the difference between lung tissue and gill tissue. For one thing, gill tissue has no mucus-secreting cells to keep the surfaces moist out of water. Hence the gills dry and harden, and no longer pass oxygen one way and carbon dioxide the other as they should. But the gills of many aquatic organisms can be made to function out of water by keeping them moist artificially. Some of these forms regularly come out of water for considerable periods, like the fiddler crab and the mud skipper, for instance. They're all right as long as they can go back and moisten their gills occasionally.

"But in no case can a lung be used as a gill, to extract oxygen dissolved in water, instead of absorbing it from the air. I've been studying the reasons for this for some years; they're partly mechanical—the difficulty of getting anything as dense as water in and out of the spongy lung structure fast enough—and partly a matter of the different osmotic properties of the breather cells which are each adapted to operate on oxygen of a given concentration dispersed in a medium of given density.

"I've found, however, that the breather cells of lung tissue can be made to react to certain stimuli so as to assume the osmotic properties of gill tissue. It consists mainly of a mixture of halogen-bearing organic compounds. A good dose of the vapor of that stuff in the lungs of one of the young alligators in this tank should enable him to breathe under water, if my theory is correct."

"I'd suggest one thing," said Dumville, who had been giving polite but interested "uh-huh's," "which is that when you hold your alligator under water, his glottal muscles will automatically contract, sealing off his lungs to keep out the water, and he'll suffocate."

"I've thought of that, and I'll paralyze the nerves controlling those muscles first, so he'll have to breathe water whether he wants to or not."

"That's the idea. Say, I want to be in on this. When are you going to try out your first alligator?"

They talked until Sugden began clearing his throat meaningfully. He said, "There's a lot more to see, Dr. Dumville. You've got to take a look at our new extension. We certainly sweat blood getting the city to put up the money for it." He got Dumville out, and Brock could hear his voice dying away: ". . . it'll be mostly for new pumping and filtering machinery; we haven't half the space we need now. There'll be two tanks big enough for the smaller cetaeca, and we'll finally have some direct sunlight. You can't keep most of the amphibia without it. We had to take half the damned old building apart to do it . . ." Brock smiled. The extension was Sugden's monument, and the old boy would never retire until it was officially opened.

Brock turned back to his apparatus. He had just begun to concentrate on it when Sam Baritz stuck his gargoyle's face in. "Say, Vuinon, where ya gonna put the bichir? It gets in tomorrow."

"Mmm—clear the filefish out of 43, and we'll make up a batch of Nile water this afternoon for it. It's too valuable to risk with other species until we know more about it. And—oh, hell, put the filefish in a reserve tank for the present."

That means another new label, he thought as he turned back to his chemicals. What would be a good wording? "Esteemed as food . . ." Yes. "Closely related to fossil forms"? Too indefinite. "Related to fossil forms from which most modern fish and all the higher vertebrates are descended." More like it. Maybe he could work in the words "living fossil" somehow. . . .

In his abstraction he hadn't noticed that the flask into which the oily liquid was dripping had been nudged too close to the edge of the table. The slam of a dropped plank from the extension where construction was still going on made him start nervously, and the flask came loose and smashed on the floor. Brock yelped with dismay and anger. Three weeks' work was spread over the floor. He took his morning paper apart and swept up glass and solution. As he knelt over the wreckage, the fumes made his eyes water. In his annoyance it never occurred to him that a man's lungs aren't so different from an alligator's.

He answered the telephone. It was Halperin, the goldfish man. "I'm making a little trip down south; do you guys want me to pick up some bowfin or gar?" Brock said he'd have to ask Sugden and would call back. "Well, don't take too long, Vuinon, I'm leaving this afternoon. Be seein' ya."

Brock set out on the long semicircular catwalk over the ground-floor tanks that led around to the rear of the building and the entrance to the extension. As an old aquarium man he walked without faltering; he could imagine Dumville's cautious progress, clutching pipes and the edges of reserve tanks while glancing fearfully into the waters below.

Brock's lungs ached queerly. Must have gotten a whiff of that gunk of mine, he thought; that was a fool thing to do. But there couldn't have been enough to do any real harm. He kept on. The ache got worse; there was a strange suffocating sensation. This is serious, he thought. I'd better see a doctor after I deliver Halperin's message to Sugden. He kept on.

His lungs seemed to be on fire. Hurry—hurry—Dumville's an M.D.; maybe he could fix me up. Brock couldn't breathe. He wanted water—not, oddly, in his throat, but in his lungs. The cool depths of the big tank and the end of the semicircle were below him. This tank held the sharks; the other big tank, for groupers and other giants of the bass tribe, was across from it.

His lungs burned agonizingly. He tried to call out, but only made a faint croaking noise. The tangle of pipes seemed to whirl around him. The sound of running water became a roar. He swayed, missed a snatch at the nearest reserve tank, and pitched into the shark tank.

There was water in his eyes, in his ears, everywhere. The burning in his lungs was lessening, and in place of it came a cold feeling throughout his chest. The bottom came up and bumped him softly. He righted himself. That was wrong; he should have floated. Then the reason came to him; his lungs were full of water, so that his specific gravity was one point something. He wondered for a confused minute if he was already drowned. He didn't feel drowned, only very wet and very cold inside. In any event he'd better get out of here quickly. He kicked himself to the surface, reached up and grabbed the catwalk, and tried to blow the water out of his lungs. It came, slowly, squirting out of his mouth and nostrils. He tried inhaling some air. He thought he was getting somewhere when the burning sensation returned. In spite of himself he ducked and inhaled water. Then he felt all right.

Everything seemed topsy-turvy. Then he remembered the liquid he'd prepared for the alligator; it must have worked on him! His lungs were functioning as gills. He couldn't quite believe it yet. Experimenting on an alligator is one thing; turning yourself into a fish is another—comic-section stuff. But there it was. If he'd been going to drown he'd have done so by now. He tried a few experimental breaths under water. It was amazingly hard work. You put on the pressure, and your lungs slowly contracted, like a pneumatic tire with a leak. In half a minute or so you were ready to inhale again. The reason was the density of water compared with that of air, of course. But it seemed to work. He released the catwalk and sank to the bottom again. He looked around him. The tank seemed smaller than it should be; that was the effect of the index of refraction of water, no doubt. He walked toward one side, which seemed to recede as he approached it. A fat nurse shark lying on the bottom waved its tail and slid forward out of his way.

The other two nurse sharks were lying indifferently on the bottom across the tank. These brutes were sluggish and utterly harmless. The two sand sharks, the four-footer and the five-footer, had ceased their interminable cruising and had backed into far corners. Their mouths opened and closed slowly, showing their formidable teeth. Their little yellow eyes seemed to say to Brock, "Don't start anything you can't finish, buddy." Brock had no intention of starting anything. He'd had a healthy respect for the species since one of them had bitten him in the gluteus maximus while he was hauling it into a boat.

He looked up. It was like looking up at a wrinkled mirror, with a large circular hole in it directly over his head. Through the hole he could see the reserve tanks, the pipes—everything that he could have seen by sticking his head out of water. But the view was distorted and compressed around the edges, like a photograph taken with a wide-angle lens. One of the aquarium's cats peered down inscrutably at him from the catwalk. Beyond the circle on all sides the water surface was a mirror that rippled and shivered. Over the two sand sharks were their reflections upside down.

He turned his attention to the glass front of the tank. That reflected things too, as the lamps suspended over the water made the inside brighter than the outside. By putting his head close to the glass he could see the Aquarium's interior concourse. Only he couldn't see much of it for the crowd in front of the tank. They were staring at him; in the dim light they seemed all eyeballs. Now and then their heads moved and their mouths moved, but Brock got only a faint buzz.

This was all very interesting, Brock thought, but what was he to *do?* He couldn't stay in the tank indefinitely. For one thing, the coldness in his chest was uncomfortable. And God only knew what terrible physiological effect the gas might have had on him. And this breathing water was hard work, complicated by the fact that unless watched carefully his glottis would snap shut, stopping his breath altogether. It was like learning to keep your eyes open under water. He was fortunate in having fallen into a tank of salt water; fresh water is definitely injurious to lung tissue, and so it might have been even to the modified tissue in his lungs.

He sat down crosslegged on the bottom. Behind him the larger sand shark had resumed its shuttling, keeping well away from him and halting suspiciously ever time he moved. Two remoras, attached to the shark by the sucking disks on top of their heads, trailed limply from it. There were six of these original hitchhikers in the tank. He peered at the glass front. He took off his glasses experimentally and found that he could see better without them—a consequence of the different optical properties of water and air. Most of the Aquarium's visitors were now crowded in front of that tank, to watch a youngish man in a black rubber apron, a striped shirt, and the pants of a gray flannel suit sit on the bottom of a tank full of sharks and wonder how in hell he was going to get out of this predicament.

Overhead, there was no sign of anybody. Evidently nobody had heard him fall in. But soon one of the small staff would notice the crowd in front of the tank and investigate. Meanwhile he'd better see just what he could do in this bizarre environment. He tried to speak. But his vocal cords, tuned to operate in a negligibly dense medium, refused to flutter fast enough to emit an audible sound. Well, maybe he could come to the surface long enough to speak and duck under again. He rose to the top and tried it. But he had trouble getting his water-soaked breathing and speaking apparatus dry enough to use for this purpose. All he produced were gurgling noises. And while the air no longer burned his lungs on immediate contact, keeping his head out soon gave him a dizzy, suffocating feeling. He finally gave up and sank to the bottom again.

He shivered with the cold, although the water was at 65° Fahrenheit. He'd better move around to warm up. The apron hampered him, and he tried to untie the knot in back. But the water had swollen the cords so that the knot wouldn't budge. He finally wriggled out of it, rolled it up, stuck his arm out of water, and tossed the apron onto the catwalk. He thought of removing his shoes too, but remembered the sand shark's teeth.

Then he did a bit of leisurely swimming, round and round like the sand sharks. They also went round and round, trying to keep the width of the tank between him and them. The motion warmed him, but he tired surprisingly soon. Evidently the rapid metabolism of a mammal took about all the oxygen that his improvised gills could supply, and they wouldn't carry much overload. He reduced his swimming to an imitation of a seal's, legs trailing and hands flapping at his sides. The crowd, as he passed the front of the tank, was thicker than ever. A little man with a nose that swerved to starboard watched him with peculiar intentness.

A jarring sound came through the water, and presently figures, grotesquely shortened, appeared at the edge of the circle of transparency overhead. They grew rapidly taller, and he recognized Sugden, Dumville, Sam Baritz, and a couple of other members of the staff. They clustered on the catwalk, and their excited voices came to him muffled but intelligible. They knew what had happened to him, all right. He tried by sign language to explain his predicament. They evidently thought he was in a convulsion, for Sugden barked, "Get him out!" Baritz's thick forearm shot down into the water to seize his wrist. But he wrenched loose before they had him clear of the surface, and dove for the bottom.

"Acts like he don't *wanna* come out," said Baritz, rubbing a kicked shin.

Sugden leaned over. "Can you hear me?" he shouted.

Brock nodded vigorously.

"Can you speak to us?"

Brock shook his head.

"Did you do this to yourself on purpose?"

A violent shake.

"Accident?"

Brock nodded.

"Do you want to get out?"

Brock nodded and shook his head alternately.

Sugden frowned in perplexity. Then he said, "Do you mean you'd like to but can't because of your condition?"

Brock nodded.

Sugden continued his questions. Brock, growing impatient at this feeble method of communication, made writing motions. Sugden handed down a pencil and a pocket notebook. But the water immediately softened the paper so that the pencil, instead of making marks, tore holes in it. Brock handed them back.

Sugden said: "What he needs is a wax tablet and stylus. Could you get us one, Sam?"

Baritz looked uncomfortable. "Cheez, boss, what place in N'yawk sells those things?"

"That's right; I suppose we'll have to make it ourselves. If we could melt a candle onto a piece of plywood—"

"It'll take all day fa me to get the candle and stuff and do that, and we gotta do something about poor Vuinon. . . ."

Brock noticed that the entire staff was now lined up on the catwalk. His beloved was well down the line, almost out of sight around the curve. At that angle the refraction made her look as broad as she was tall. He wondered if she'd look like that naturally after they'd been married a while. He'd known it to happen. No, he meant *if* they got married. You couldn't expect a girl to marry a man who lived under water.

While Sugden and Baritz still bickered, he had an idea. But how to communicate it? Then he saw a remora lying below him. He splashed to attract the attention of those above and sank down slowly. He grabbed the fish in both hands and kicked himself over to the glass. The remora's nose—or, to be exact, its undershot lower jaw—made a visible streak on the pane. He rolled over on his back and saw that he was understood; Sugden was calling for someone to go down to the floor and read his message.

His attempt at writing was hampered by the fish's vigorous efforts to escape. But he finally got scrawled on the glass in large wobbly capitals: "2 WEIGHTED STEPLADDERS—1 WEIGHTED PLANK—1 DRY TOWEL."

While they were getting these, he was reminded by his stomach that he'd had no solid food for eighteen hours or thereabouts. He glanced at his wristwatch, which, not being waterproof, had stopped. He handed it up, hoping that somebody would have the sense to dry it out and take it to a jeweler.

The stepladders were lowered into the tank. Brock set them a few feet apart and placed the plank across their tops. Then he lay on his back on the plank, his face a few inches below the surface. He dried his hands on the towel, and by cocking one leg up he could hold a pad out of water against his knee and write on it.

He explained tersely about the accident and his subsequent seizure and told what had happened chemically to his lung tissues. Then he wrote: "As this is first experiment on living organism, don't know when effect will pass if ever. Want lunch."

Baritz called to him: "Don't you want us to take the shoks out fuist?" Brock shook his head. The claims of his stomach were imperious, and he had a vague hope of solving his problem without disturbing the fish. Then too, though he'd have hated to admit it, he knew that everybody knew that the sharks weren't man-eaters, and he didn't want to seem afraid of them. Even a sensible man like Vernon Brock will succumb to a touch of bravado in the presence of his woman, actual or potential.

He relaxed, thinking. Sugden was ordering the staff back to its work. Dumville had to leave, but promised to be back. By and by the faithful Baritz appeared with what Brock hoped was food. Brock's position struck him as an uncomfortable one for eating, so he rolled off the plank and stood on the bottom of the tank. Then he couldn't reach the surface with his hand. Baritz thrust a lamb chop on the end of a stick down to him. He reached for it—and was knocked aside by a glancing blow from something heavy and sandpapery. The lamb chop was gone—or not quite gone; the larger shark had it over in a corner. The shark's jaws worked, and the bone sank slowly to the bottom, minus its meat.

Baritz looked helpless at Sugden. "We betta not try meat again—those shoks can smell it, and they might get dangerous if we got them wuiked up."

"Guess we'll have to get the net and haul them out," said Sugden. "I don't see how he could eat mashed potatoes under water."

Brock swam up and went through the motions of peeling and eating a banana. After Baritz had made a trip for bananas Brock satisfied his hunger, though he found that swallowing food without getting a stomachful of salt water required a bit of practice.

The crowd in front of the tank was larger, if anything. The little man with the wry nose was still there. His scrutiny made Brock vaguely uneasy. He'd always wondered what a fish on exhibit felt like, and now, by George, he knew.

If he could get out and do a few months' research, he might be able to find how to counteract the effect of the lung gas. But how could he perform experiments from where he was? Maybe he could give directions and have somebody else carry them out. That would be awkward, but he didn't want to spend the rest of his life as an exhibit, loyal as he was to the Aquarium. A better idea might be to rig up some sort of diver's helmet to wear out of water with the water inside—if he could find a way of oxygenating the water.

Baritz appeared again and put his head down close to the water. "Hey, Vuinon!" he said, "God's coming down here!"

Brock was interested, though not by the theological aspects of the statement. God, better known as J. Roosevelt Whitney, was the president of the New York Zoölogical Society, and the boss of Minnegerode, the director of the Aquarium (in Bermuda at the moment). Minnegerode was Sugden's boss. God, the head of this hierarchy, owned among other things a bank and a half, 51% of a railroad, and the finest walrus mustache in Greater New York.

Baritz put on his child-frightening grin. "Say, Vuinon, I just thought. We can advatise you as the only muimaid in captivity!"

Brock throttled an impulse to pull his helper into the tank, and motioned for his pad. He wrote: "The male of 'mermaid' is 'merman,' you ape!"

"Okay, a muiman, unless the gas changed more than ya lungs. Oh, good aftanoon, Mista Whitney. Here he is in this tank. Anything I can do, Mista Whitney?"

The famous mustache floated above the water like a diving seagull. "How ah you, my deah boy? Ah you making out all right? Don't you think we'd bettah get the sharks out right away? They're perfectly harmless, of course, of course, but you might accidentally jostle one and get nipped, ha-ha."

Brock, who at thirty-two was pleased rather than irked at being called "my boy," nodded. J. R. started to get to his feet not noticing that one foot was planted on Brock's rolled-up apron, while the toe of the other was caught in it. Brock received a tremendous impact of sound and current and through the sudden cloud of bubbles saw J. R.'s massive rear descending on him. He caught the man and shoved him up. As the shiny pink head cleared the surface, he heard a terrified scream of "Glugg—blubb—Oh God, get me out! The sharks!

Get me out, I say!" Brock boosted and Baritz and Sugden heaved. The dripping deity receded down the catwalk, to Brock's distorted vision broadening to something like a *Daily Worker* cartoon of Capital. He wished he knew whether J. R. would be angry or whether he'd be grateful for the boost. If he inquired about the apron it might be embarrassing.

The cold was biting Brock's innards, and the bananas seemed to have turned into billiard balls in his stomach. The little man with the nose was still there, although it was nearly closing time. Brock climbed onto his plank and wrote directions: "Raise temperature of feed water slowly. Get me thermometer. Will signal when temperature is right. Should be about 90 F. Run more air lines into tank to make up for lowering oxygen saturation point. Put sharks in reserve tank for present; warmth might harm them, and I need all oxygen in tank."

By 9 P.M. all was done. The tearful Miss Engholm had been shooed away. Baritz volunteered to spend the night, which proved the most uncomfortable of Brock's experience. He couldn't sleep because of the constant muscular effort required to work his lungs. He tried to think his way out of the mess, but his thoughts became more and more confused. He began to imagine things: that the little man with the nose had been there for no good, for instance. Just what, he couldn't think, but he was sure it was something. Again and again he wondered what time it was. At first he aroused Baritz to tell him at intervals, but toward 2 o'clock Sam went to sleep on the catwalk, and Brock hadn't the heart to awaken him.

God, would the night never end? Well, what if it did? Would he be any better off? He doubted it. He looked at his hands, at the skin of his fingers swollen and wrinkled by soaking. A crazy idea grew on him with the force of an obsession. His hands would turn into fins. He'd grow scales. . . .

It was getting light. Then all these people would come back to torment him. Yes, and the little man with the nose. The little man would put a worm on a hook and catch him and eat him for supper. . . .

Under sufficiently strange circumstances the human mind is often thrown out of gear and spins ineffectually without definite relationship to external things. Perhaps that is because of a weakness in the structure of the mind, or perhaps it is a provision by nature to disconnect it to avoid stripped gears when the load is too heavy.

People were coming in; it must be after 9 o'clock. People on the catwalk overhead were talking, but he couldn't understand them. His lungs weren't working right. Or rather his gill. But that was wrong. He was a fish, wasn't he? Then what could be wrong with them? All these people who had it in for him must have turned off the oxygen. No, the air lines were still shooting their streams of tiny bubbles into the tank. Then why this suffocating feeling? He knew; that wasn't air in the air lines; it was pure nitrogen or helium or something. They were trying to fool him. Oh, God, if he could only breathe! Maybe he had the fish's equivalent of asthma. Fish came to the surface and gulped sometimes; he'd try that. But he couldn't; his experiences of the preceding day had given him a conditioned reflex against sticking his head out, which his shattered reason was unable to overcome.

Was he going to die? Too bad, when he had been going to marry Miss Engholm and all. But he couldn't have married her anyway. He was a fish. The female fish lays her eggs, and then the male fish comes along and . . . His face twisted in an insane grin at the grotesque thought that struck him.

He was dying. He had to get oxygen. Why not go through the glass? But no, any intelligent fish knew better than to try to make holes in the glass. Then he saw the little man with the nose, standing and staring as he had yesterday. He thought, you'll never catch me on a hook and eat me for supper; you piscicide; I'm going to get you first. He fished out his jackknife and attacked the pane. A long scratch appeared on it, then another, and another. The glass sang softly. The people behind the little man were moving back nervously, but the little man still stood there. The song of the glass rose up—up—up. . . .

The glass, with a final *ping,* gave and several tons of green water flung themselves into the concourse. For a fleeting second Brock, knife in hand, seemed to be flying toward the little man. Then the iron railing in front of the tank came up and hit his head.

He had a vague sense of lying on a wet floor, while a foot from his ringing head a stranded remora flopped helplessly. . . .

He was lying in bed, and Sugden was sitting beside him smoking. The old man said: "Lucky you didn't get a fractured skull. But maybe it was a good thing. It put you out during the critical period when your lungs were changing back to normal. They'd have had to dope you anyway, out of your head as you were."

"I'll say I was out of my head! Wait till I see your friend Dumville; I'll be able to describe a brand-new psychosis to him."

"He's a physiologist," replied Sugden, "not a psychologist. But he'll want to see you just the same.

"The doctor tells me you'll be out tomorrow, so I guess you're well enough to talk business. J. R. didn't mind the ducking, even after the exhibition he made of himself. But there's something more serious. Perhaps you noticed a small man with a crooked nose in front of the tank while you were there?"

"*Did* I *notice* him!"

"Well, you nearly drowned him when you let the water out of the tank. And he's going to sue us for damages—way up in five or six figures. You know what *that* means."

Brock nodded glumly. "I'll say I do. It means that I don't get your job when you retire next winter. And then I can't get ma— Never mind. Who is this little guy? A professional accident faker?"

"No; we investigated him. He was a trapeze artist in a circus until recently; he says he was getting too old for that work, but he didn't know any other. Then he hurt his back in a fall, and he's been on relief since. He just came in to watch you because he had nothing else to do."

"I see." Brock thought. "Say, I have an idea. Nurse! Hey, NURSE! My clothes! I'm going out!"

"No, you're not," said Sugden firmly. "Not till the doc says you can. That'll only be tomorrow, and then you can try out your idea. And I hope," he added grimly, "that it's better than the last one."

Two days later Brock knocked on Sugden's door. He knew that Sugden and J. R. were in there, and he could guess what they were talking about. But he had no fears.

"Morning, Mr. Whitney," he said.

"Oh—ah—yes, my deah boy. We were just talking about this most unfortunate—ah—"

"If you mean the suit, that's off."

"What?"

"Sure, I fixed it. Mr. Oscar Daly, the plaintiff, and I are going into a kind of partnership."

"Partners?"

"Yes, to exploit my discovery of lung conversion. I supply the technique so that he can exhibit himself in circuses as Oscar the Merman. He dopes himself with my gas and parks in a tank. Our only problem is the period when the effect of the gas wears off and the lungs return to normal. That, I think, can be licked by the use of any of several anesthetic drugs that slow down the metabolism. So, when the human fish begins to feel funny, he injects himself and passes out peacefully, while his assistants fish him out and wring the water out of his lungs. There are a few technical details to work out on my alligators yet, but that'll be all right. I'll wear a gas mask. Of course," he added virtuously, "any monetary returns from the use of the process will go the Zoölogical Society. Oscar says to send your lawyer over any time and he'll sign a release."

"Why, that's fine," said Whitney, "that's splendid,

my boy. It makes a big difference." He looked significantly at Sugden.

"Thanks," said Brock. "And now, if you'll excuse me, Sam and I have some fish to shift. So long, cheerio, and I hope you drop in often, Mr. Whitney." He went out, whistling.

"Oh, Vernon!" the head aquarist called after him. "Tomorrow's Sunday, and I'm driving my family out to Jones Beach. Like to come along for a swim?"

Brock stuck his grinning head back in. "Thanks a lot, Clyde, but I'm afraid I might carelessly take a deep breath under water. To be honest, the mere idea gives me the horrors. I've had enough swimming to last me the rest of my natural life!"

Employment

R.F.D. No. 1
Carriesville, Indiana
August 28, 1960

Dear George:

Thanks for your information on the State Geological Survey, and for those civil service blanks. I've already sent them in.

If I land the job you'll probably be my boss, so you're entitled to an explanation of why I want to leave a well-paying private job and go to work for the state.

As you know, I was working for Lucifer Oil in 1957 when the depression hit, and pretty quick I was out of a job, and with a family to support. Through one of the journals I got in touch with Gil Platt, my present employer, who was looking for an experienced geologist. You've probably heard of him—he started out in paleontology, but never worked up very high in that field because he was temperamentally unable to work under anybody. Then he took to inventing prospecting devices, and for twenty years he's been as busy as a cat on fly paper, developing and patenting his gadgets and pursuing his paleo on the side. All the money he made in prospector royal-

ties went into paleo expeditions and into litigation. In time he accumulated outstanding collections of patents, lawsuits pertaining thereto, and fossils.

About 1956 the Linvald Fund decided he'd done such good work as to deserve a little financial elbow room, and put him on their list. He'd designed a new prospector that looked quite wonderful, but that would take time and money to reduce to practice. So those monthly checks from Oslo were welcome.

Mrs. Staples and I were sorry to leave California for Indiana, both of us being natives of San Francisco, but in our business you can't be finicky about where you work.

I worked with Platt for about six months before we were ready to try it out. I'm not revealing any secrets by saying that it works by supersonic wave charting, like the old McCann prospector. The distinctive feature is that, by using two intersecting beams, Platt gets a stereoscopic effect and can chart the major discontinuities at any distance underground that he wants.

We tried it first mounted on a truck. We would set it for, say, two yards below the surface and buzz down the road to Fort Wayne—

The truck purred down the outside lane of the concrete at a steady fifteen miles an hour. Car after car swung to the inside lane and buzzed past, honking. Kenneth Staples, at the wheel, leaned back and shouted through the opening in the back of the cab: "Hey, Gil! Haven't we about reached the end of that strip?"

Something in the way of an affirmative floated back into the cab. Staples ran the truck off the concrete, stopped it, and went around to the rear. He was a big, hard-looking, rather ugly man, on whom the elements had stamped a look of more than his thirty-five years. Under his stiff-brimmed engineer's hat he was very bald. He wore a hat whenever decency permitted. Men who go prematurely bald have, perhaps, a slightly greater tendency than others to select outdoor careers, or to join the army, where hats are kept on heads.

Inside the truck, a smaller, gray-haired man was bending over a machine. The top part of the machine included a long strip of graph paper carried over spools. Above the paper was poised a rank of little vertical pens. While the truck moved, these pens dropped down at intervals to make dots on the paper as it was reeled under them. The dots made irregular outlines and patterns.

Gilmore Platt said: "C'mere, Ken, and see what you think of this. I know what it is but I can't think."

Staples stared at the dots. "Looks to me like the outline of a piece out of a jigsaw puzzle."

"No. No. It isn't— I know what it is! It's a section of a skull! One of the Felidæ, probably *Felis atrox,* from the size. We'll have to dig it up!"

"That squiggle? Well, maybe. You're the paleo man. But you can't go digging holes in a State highway just because there's a fossil lion buried under it."

"But, Ken, a beautiful thing like that—"

"Take it easy, Gil. This little Pleistocene overlay runs back to your place. If we run the truck around your grounds for a few hours we ought to be able to find some fossils."

"It's a rodent. I thought it was a bear at first from the size of the skull, but now I see those front teeth."

"Right so far. But what rodent?"

Staples frowned at the little heap of bones beside the pit. "Seems to me the only North American rodent that size was the giant beaver, *Castoroides.*"

"Fine! Fine! I'll make a paleontologist out of you yet. What's this bone?"

"Scapula."

"Right. That's easy though. This one?"

"Uh . . . humerus."

"No, ulna. But you're doing pretty well. Too bad there isn't more of this one. I think we've about cleaned it out. Do you realize what this means? Hitherto we've been confined to surface indications in barren country.

Now we can ignore the surface and locate all the fossils in a given area within fifteen or twenty feet of it! Only that truck won't do. We need something to carry the prospector cross country. An airplane would fly too high and too fast. I have it, a blimp!"

"Yeah?" Staples looked a trifle startled. "Seems to me like a lot to spend on applying a new device. But it's the Fund's money, not mine."

In due course Platt took delivery on the Goodyear Company's good ship Darwin. *After we learned how to fly it, we covered most of Indiana in a couple of months, and had located more fossils than we could dig up in fifty years. We made out a checklist of their locations and sent copies to all the museums and universities in the country. For the rest of the summer Indiana was one big bone hunters' convention. If you took a drive into the country, the chances were that you'd pass a field in which a couple of tough-looking parties were arguing with a farmer, and you'd know that they were probably paleontologists from the Field Museum or the University of California dickering with the owner of the field for permission to dig. Though Indiana isn't a very rich state as far as fossil vertebrates go. It's mostly Paleozoic with a little Pleistocene scattered around on top.*

A friend of Platt's, a Dr. Wilhelmi of Zürich, arrived for a weekend. He was an archaeologist and a dignified man. Staples felt a certain sympathy for him because he had even less hair than the geologist.

This Wilhelmi had been working in Anatolia, where he had found a carload of relics dating back to Tiridates the Great.

"You see, my fwiends," he explained, "they were mostly vessels and such of bwonze. Here is a picture of one as we found it. It is so corroded that it is nothing but a lump of oxide. Now, here is a picture of that one after we westored it by the anode pwocess."

"Say," said Staples, "are you sure that's the same

one? The thing in the second picture looks like it was just fresh out of the shop."

"Ha-ha, that is witty. Yes, it is the same. We place it in an electwolytic bath, connected to one of the poles, and wun a current thwough. So all the copper and tin atoms in the oxide cwawl back to their pwoper places. It is quite wonderful to see."

After the Swiss gentleman had left, Platt went to Chicago for a consultation with his patent attorney. He returned looking thoughtful.

"Ken," he said, "let's play hooky for a few days."

Staples looked at him with a wary eye. "I suppose you mean to drop the prospector and work on your fossils for a while?"

"That's it exactly."

Thus it happened that the following day found them in the shop breaking a young *Hyracodon*—small hornless rhinoceros—out of its matrix. Staples remarked on what a dull piece the work was from a zoölogical point of view, compared to what it had been in times past.

"To some extent, yes," replied Platt. "Hand me the shellac, please. Though there may be a few whales left that haven't been turned into margarine and gun oil. We're living at the close of one of the many periodic extinctions of the larger forms. The only places you can find a fauna comparable with those of the Pleistocene is on a few preserves in Africa. And with our own bloodthirsty species infesting the earth, it's getting worse all the time. Hm-m-m. The left clavicle and left radius seem to be missing." He carefully chipped slivers of sandstone away with his needle. Being much more of a talker than his assistant, he continued: "I have an idea which, if it works, may do much to relieve the drabness of our present faunæ. You heard Wilhelmi tell about restoring oxidized metal by the anode process. Well, why couldn't we work something like that on fossils?"

"You mean to grow a complete animal, hair and all, from a skeleton?"

"Why not? You know what extraordinary things they

do in medicine nowadays—growing arms and legs on people who have lost their own."

"With all due respect, my dear employer, I think you're screwbox."

"We'll see about that. I'm going to try some experiments, anyway. We'll keep them to ourselves, of course. If they didn't work, a lot of our colleagues might agree with your opinion."

Platt began his work with rabbits—modern rabbits, that is. He would kill a rabbit, remove various parts, and hook it up in a Ringer's solution bath to a current source. To build up the missing parts he used bio-charged amino acids, which will combine to form proteins and, in the presence of other cells, form whole new cells.

After many failures, he one day observed that the tissues of one of the rabbits were building up. He pointed the phenomenon out to Staples.

The geologist protested: "But it can't be that one. I turned the juice off in that tank."

"Yes?" replied Platt. "Let's see. Ah! You *thought* you turned it off, but look at this switch!"

Staples saw that he had accidentally struck the open knife switch so that the bars barely touched the contacts.

Platt said: "Now I know; we've been using too much voltage. It wants something like point oh one volts." And the little man was off like a chipmunk with a bunch of nuts, changing the rheostats to one calibrated for higher resistance.

They perfected their methods of reifying recent animals, which later proved of great value in surgery. Their results were not, however, so incredible when you consider that every cell in an animal's body contains a complete set of chromosomes with all the genes that determine the animal's form. It is as if in each cell there was a complete blueprint of the entire animal.

Their first attempt with fossils—the fragmentary remains of the *Castoroides*—failed. Staples wasn't sorry.

He was worrying about the effect of the news of this bizarre experiment on his professional reputation.

Then at dinner one night Platt jumped up and began orating. He waved his knife and fork so that he almost speared his daughter's boy friend, who slid below the edge of the table until the storm had passed. "Ken!" cried the paleontologist. "I know what to do now! You've got to have a lot of the original organic matter of which the organism was composed, in the solution along with the bones. The current makes the original atoms resume their former places, and they serve as a framework for the amino acid molecules in their building-up work. We need a fairly complete skeleton, with considerable organic matter in the surrounding rock—if possible, with impressions of the soft parts. We'll have to analyze the rock, because if the fossil's at all old the original atoms will be scattered through the surrounding rock as to show no visible traces."

The next day they spent in the storehouse, unwrapping the burlap from fossils and testing their matrices for organic material. They picked a specimen of *Canis dirus* embedded in a big block of sandstone, strung the block up with a chain hoist, and dumped it into one of the tanks.

Nothing happened for a long time. Then the sandstone decomposed into mud, and in its place was a blob of jelly through which they could see the skeleton. The jelly became more and more opaque, and you could see the organs forming as the original atoms took their places, and the others, from the amino acids, polypeptides, and other substances that were introduced into the tank, lined up alongside them. It was uncannily as though the atoms had definite memories of where they belonged in the animal's body back in the Pleistocene.

When the mass in the tank stopped changing, it had the form of a huge wolf, about the size of a great Dane, but twice as muscular and ten times as mean-looking.

They fished the brute out of the tank, emptied the solution out of him, and applied an electric starter to his heart. After three hours of this, the wolf shuddered and began coughing the remainder of the Ringer's solution out of his lungs. It occurred to the experimenters that they had no place to keep the wolf, who would make a rather formidable house pet. They tethered him to a tree while they prepared a pen. But for a few days the wolf hardly moved at all. When he did, he was like a man who has been a year in the hospital, and is having to learn to walk all over again.

But at the end of two weeks he was eating of his own accord. His hair, which had been a mere fuzz at first—the process being effective in recreating the hair roots, but not the hairs, which are dead structures—rapidly grew to normal length. At the end of three weeks he was enough his old self to snarl at Staples when the geologist entered his cage. It was a most impressive snarl, sounding rather like tearing a piece of sheet iron in two.

After that I was careful about getting too near him or turning my back on him. But he didn't give us much trouble, though he never became what you'd call friendly. I always liked him for one reason: Platt's daughter had a fluffy dog that liked to bite people's ankles—no provocation necessary. After one of my kids had been nipped, the girl and I had a real row about the excrescence. Before we could have another, the dog went out one day and yapped at the dire wolf. Mr. Wolf sprang against his bars and growled—once. That was the last we saw of that accursed pooch.

Six months later, Platt and Staples hoisted out of its tank a specimen of *Arctotherium,* the immense bear from the California Pleistocene. Staples had had the busiest six months of his life, between helping the preparation of patent applications and getting the reification of more fossils started. There had been several failures—important parts of the skeletons missing, or insufficient organic matter in the surrounding rocks, or reasons unknown. This proved to be one of the last: the bear looked normal enough, but refused to come to life.

Staples confessed that, looking at the thing's bulk, he had been more afraid of success than of failure. It was later mounted in the American Museum of Natural History, New York.

They had made things as easy as possible by starting with the *Canis,* a moderate-sized species of recent date. They worked in two directions from there: backward in time, and upward in size. Platt had a number of fossils from the Miocene of Nebraska. They were successful in reifying a *Stenomylus hitchcocki,* a small guanacolike ancestral camel. Seeking a more exciting specimen, they went to work on Platt's pride and joy, a new species of *Trilophodon,* the smallest and oldest proboscidean found in America. It was probably the first member of the elephant group to arrive from Asia. The animal turned out to be a female, rather like a large shaggy tapir, with long tapering jaws and four tusks.

After their partial failure with the *Arctotherium,* they succeeded with a bear-dog, *Dinocyon gidleyi.* When Staples looked at the result his throat felt a little dry. The thing was built on the general lines of a polar bear, only bigger than even the Kodiak grizzly. Its large ears gave its head a wolfish appearance, and it had a long bushy tail. It weighed 1,978 pounds, and it didn't like anybody. Platt was delighted. "Now if I could only get an *Andrewsarchus!*" he beamed. "That's a still bigger carnivore, an Asiatic Oligocene creodont. One skull measured thirty-four inches."

"Yeah?" said Staples, still looking at the bear-dog. "You can have him. I haven't lost him. This thing we have here is quite big enough for me."

They had hired an old circus man named Elias to help them with their growing zoo. They had built a concrete barn for the animals with a row of cages down one side. It looked strong enough, until one afternoon Staples went out to investigate a racket from the cages. He found the bars of the bear-dog's cage bowed out—the lower ends had come out of the green concrete easily—and no *Dinocyon.* Staples had a horrible vision of the bear-dog wandering over Kosciusko County and eating everything he could catch.

The beast was not, however, far away. He was, in fact, just around the corner looking for a way to get into the *Stenomylus* cage. In a few seconds he reappeared. He looked at Staples. The geologist could have sworn that the expression in his big yellow eyes said: "Ah, dinner!" The bear-dog growled like a distant thunderstorm and started for Staples.

Staples knew that the animal could run circles around him on level ground, and moreover that if he caught him he wouldn't be satisfied to run circles around him. Staples' best idea was to swarm up the bars around the *Trilophodon*'s enclosure. He couldn't have climbed those bars ordinarily, but he did this time.

Arrived at the top, he couldn't stay there unless he wanted the bear-dog to rear up and scoop him off his perch. On the other hand, the inside of the cage didn't look inviting. The "little" mastodon—standing five feet at the shoulder and weighing slightly over a ton—was half crazed with fear. She was gallumping around the enclosure making noises like a pig under a gate. An elephant's fear of dogs is not unreasonable when the elephant and the dog are about the same size.

Just before the bear-dog arrived, Staples jumped off and landed astride the *Trilophodon*'s neck. He didn't feel like a movie hero who jumps off a balcony onto his horse. He was scared stiff. He got a good grip on his mount's scalp hair and hung on desperately, knowing that he'd be trampled to jelly in no time if she bucked him off.

Staples heard a rifle go off, several times, and got a glimpse of Gil Platt shooting out of the workshop doorway. The *Dinocyon* gave a coughing roar and went over to see about it. Staples was too busy to watch closely, but got a few glimpses of the bear-dog running around the shop, trying to climb in the windows—which were too small. He finally settled down to dig under the house. All this time Platt was popping out of doors and windows to fire and popping back again. Staples had time to reflect that the bear-dog's insides must be taking a terrible beating from the soft-nosed bullets, but that such was his vitality that you could shoot holes in him all day before he'd give up.

He made wonderful progress with his digging; he took the earth out like a bucket chain. Staples remembered that the shop had a thin wooden floor, which wouldn't offer much resistance if the animal got under the house. They needed a .50-caliber machine gun, which they didn't have.

Before it came to that, Elias climbed out on the roof and dropped a stick of dynamite alongside the bear-dog. That did the trick. The effect was rather like hitting a cantaloupe with a mallet. Staples had just gotten his animated calliope calmed down, and the explosion started her off again. It was a question of which would collapse from exhaustion first. The geologist won by a hair.

When he examined the remains of the *Dinocyon,* he asked Platt: "Why didn't you shoot him in the head?"

"But if I'd done that I'd have smashed the skull, and we mightn't have been able to reify him!"

"You mean . . . you're going to—" But Staples didn't finish. He already knew the answer. They gathered up the bear-dog, put him back together more or less the way he had been, and hoisted him into the biggest tank again. Some days later Staples was sorry to observe that the animal was making a record recovery. But Platt had a new cage built that not even this monster could break out of.

But with his size and enormous appetite, Platt decided that he was too expensive and dangerous to keep. He sold him to the Philadelphia Zoo. After the zoo people became acquainted with him they probably regretted their bargain.

The sale attracted some attention, and the Philadelphia Zoo for a while had a capacity audience. Platt inquired about the market for more of his reified animals.

A couple of weeks after the sale, a sunburned man called at Platt's. He said his name was Nively, and that he represented the Marco Polo Co. This, he explained, included all the wild-animal importers and dealers in the country. It was a membership corporation instead of a stock corporation, to get around the antitrust laws.

Feeling that they could now afford some publicity, Platt and Staples showed him the place. He was duly impressed, especially with their new *Dinohyus,* a lower Miocene elothere. It was a piglike animal the size of a buffalo, with a mouth full of teeth like those of a bear. It ate practically anything.

Elias was assembling their biggest tank. Platt explained: "That's for Proboscidea. We haven't one big enough for them now. And out in the storehouse I've got a magnificent *Parelephas jeffersonii.* You know, the Jeffersonian mammoth. That's much bigger than the ordinary or woolly mammoth that the cavemen made such pretty pictures of. The woolly mammoth was a rather small animal, not over nine feet high."

"That so?" said Nively. They were on their way back to the office. "My word! I thought all mammoths were huge things. I say, Dr. Platt, I have a little matter I'd like to discuss in private."

"You can go right ahead, Mr. Nively. I haven't any secrets from Staples."

"Very well. To begin, is this process of yours protected?"

"Sure it is. At least, as far as you can protect any invention by patent applications. What are you getting at, Mr. Nively?"

"I think the Marco Polo might have a proposal that would interest you, Dr. Platt."

"Well?"

"We'd like to buy up your patent applications and all rights pertaining thereto."

"What do you want them for?"

'You see, our business requires considerable capital and involves a lot of risk. You load six giraffes on at Jibouti, and by the time you get to New York one of 'em is alive—if you're lucky. With your process we could put the animals in cold storage at the point of shipment, as it were, and—what's the word you use?—reify them in this country."

"That sounds interesting. Would you be interested in a nonexclusive license?"

"No, we want complete control. To . . . ah . . . keep up the ethical standards of the business."

"Sorry, but I'm not selling."

"Oh, come now, Dr. Platt—"

They argued some more, but Nively left without getting anywhere. A week later, just after the rock containing the mammoth had been hoisted into its tank, he was back.

"Dr. Platt," he began, "we're businessmen, and we're willing to pay a fair price—" So they went at it again—again without result.

After Nively had gone, Platt said to Staples: "He must think I'm pretty obtuse! The reason they're after my process is that they're afraid it'll break their monopoly. There isn't a circus or zoo in the country that wouldn't like one or two prehistoric animals."

The taciturn Staples opined: "I have an idea they'll get really riled when we get a couple of the same species and breed 'em."

"By Jove, I never thought of that! Nobody buys wild lions nowadays. It's too easy to raise your own. That gives me another idea. Suppose we start a race of, say, elotheres, like our big piggy friend over there. And suppose civilization collapses, so that the record of our work here is lost. Won't the paleontologists of a few thousand years hence have a time figuring how the elotheres disappeared completely in the Miocene, and then reappeared again twenty million years later, warts and all?"

"That's easy," retorted Staples. "They'll invent a sunken continent in the Pacific Ocean, where the Elotheridæ hung out during the Pliocene and Pleistocene. And then a land bridge was formed, enabling them to spread over North— Hey, don't throw that! I'll be good!"

Nively's third visit was sometime later, when the mammoth was almost ready to be hoisted out of his tank. The sunburned man came to the point right away.

"Dr. Platt," he said, "we have a big business, built up with a great deal of effort, and we shan't sit around and watch it destroyed just because some scientist gets a bright idea. We'll make you a perfectly fair offer: We buy your patent application, under an agreement whereby you can practice your process, provided you name us exclusive agent for the sale of your animals. In that way you can continue your scientific work; we retain control of the commercial field; everyone's happy. What do you say, old chap?"

"I'm sorry, Mr. Nively, but I'm not in the market for such an arrangement. If you want to talk nonexclusive licenses, I might be willing to listen."

"Now look here, Dr. Platt, you'd better think twice before you turn us down. We're a powerful organization, you know, and we can make things very unpleasant for you."

"I'll take a chance on that."

"A wild-animal collection's a vulnerable piece of property, you know. Accidents—"

"Mr. Nively"—here Platt's color wandered down the spectrum toward the red end—"will you please get to hell out of here?"

Nively got.

Platt, looking after him, mused: "There goes my temper again. Perhaps I should have stalled."

"Maybe," agreed Staples. "He wasn't actually muttering threats when he went out, but he looked as if he were thinking them."

"It's probably bluff," said Platt. "But I think I'll take on another man. We need somebody up and around all the time."

In due season they hoisted the mammoth out of his bath and started his heart. They were nervous, as he was by far the largest animal they had tried the process on. Platt whooped and threw his hat in the air when *Parelaphas* showed signs of life. Staples whooped, too, but he didn't throw his hat in the air.

They named the mammoth Tecumtha, after the famous Shawnee chief. He stood eleven feet six inches, which is about as big as the biggest modern African elephant. He had helically twisted tusks that almost crossed at the tips. When he became fully conscious he made some rumpus, but after a while calmed down like a modern elephant. During his recovery period he grew a thick coat of short, coarse brown hair.

Platt had, as he had said he would, taken on another man to help Elias. Early one morning Tecumtha had a slight stomach ache. This new man, Jake, went out to see what he was squealing about. Jake dissolved his medicine in an elephant highball—one bucketful, equal parts of gin and ginger extract—and took it in to him. Tecumtha was sucking it up his trunk and gurgling happily, and Jake had stepped out of sight, when Nively materialized. He walked up to the enclosure and shot Tecumtha through the upper part of his head with a Birmingham .303.

That was a mistake. The Birmingham .303 is much too light a rifle for shooting elephants. And the upper part of an elephant's head is merely a cellular bone structure to anchor its huge neck muscles. Its brain is much lower down. Nively had done all his field work in South America and didn't know that about an elephant's construction. The bullet went through Tecumtha's head, but it merely made him very, very angry. He trumpeted. That is a most startling sound the first time you hear it; like twenty men blowing bugles full of spit.

Jake heard the commotion and ran out. He took one look at Tecumtha and made for the gate. In his hurry he left it open. Nively took one more shot, which went wild. Then he ran, too, with Tecumtha after him. He had no chance to reach his car. The mammoth would have caught him right there if he hadn't spotted Elias' bicycle leaning against a tree.

The noise brought Kenneth Staples out of bed. He got to the window in time to see Nively and the bicycle whirl down the driveway with Tecumtha close behind, and disappear on the highway headed for Carriesville.

Staples did not wait to dress, but ran downstairs and out to the garage. He did pause long enough to snatch a hat from the rack in the hall. He took the truck Platt had bought for moving large animals, and started after Nively and Tecumtha.

He had not gone a mile when he was stopped by Popenoe, the local state highway cop.

"Oh," said Popenoe, "it's you, Mr. Staples. Well, what the hell do you mean by—"

"I'm looking for my mammoth," Staples told him.

"Your *what?*"

"My mammoth—you know, a big elephant with hair."

"Well, I've sure heard funny excuses in my time, but this beats anything. And in your pajamas, too. I give up. Go ahead and chase your elephant. But I'll follow you, and he better turn out to be real. You sure he wasn't pink, with green spots?"

The geologist said he was sure, and drove on to Carriesville. He found a good part of the town turned out around the public square, although nobody seemed anxious to get close.

Towns like Carriesville almost always have a grassy spot in their middle, and on the grassy spot either a statue or a gun and a pile of cannonballs. A typical combination is that of a Krupp 15-centimeter howitzer, Model 1916, and a pile of four-inch iron roundshot of the vintage of 1845. Carriesville had an equestrian statue of General Philip Sheridan on a tall granite pedestal in front of the courthouse. The sun was just rising, and its pink rays shone on Mr. Nively, who was perched on General Sheridan's hat. Tecumtha was shuffling around the base of the statue and trying to reach Nively with his trunk.

Staples learned later that one local citizen had emptied a pistol at Tecumtha, but the mammoth hadn't even noticed it. Then somebody shot him with a deer rifle, which annoyed him. He took after the shooter, who went away. Nobody tried any more shooting. While Tecumtha's attention was distracted, Nively started to climb down, but the mammoth returned before he had a chance to do so.

Staples drove the truck up near the courthouse and got out. Tecumtha took a few steps toward him. Staples prepared to retreat, but the mammoth recognized him and went back to Nively. He paid no attention to Staples' calls. He figured how to get his head against the pedestal without his tusks being in the way, and with one good heave, over went little Phil Sheridan. As the statue toppled, Nively caught a branch of a big oak nearby and dangled like an oriole's nest. Tecumtha waltzed around underneath and made hostile noises.

Staples drove the truck up alongside the mammoth. He let down the tailboard and called to Nively to swing over so he'd land on the roof of the cab, and stay there. Nively did so. Tecumtha tried to reach him there, but couldn't quite make it. He strolled around the truck. Seeing the tailboard, he ran up it into the body to get closer to Nively. Staples hoisted the tail into place and barred it. Then he went around to the front end and climbed up on the hood.

Nively was sitting on the roof of the cab, looking remarkably pale for such a sunburned man. Staples foresaw difficulties in getting back to Platt's, and he couldn't go around as he was. He thought, it's a shame to take advantage of a man who's so all in, but he has it coming to him. Aloud he said: "Lend me your pants and your money."

Nively protested. Staples was not given to lengthy arguments. He climbed up beside Nively and grabbed his arm. "Want to go over on top of your playmate?" he growled.

Nively was a hard man physically, but he winced under the geologist's grip. "You . . . you extortioner!" he sputtered. "I could have you arrested!"

"Yeah? So could I have you arrested for trespass and vandalism, not to mention stealing a bicycle. Come on, hand 'em over. I'll see that you get them back, and your car, too."

Nively looked at Tecumtha's trunk, which had crawled up over the front wall of the truck body and was feeling around hopefully, and gave in. Staples left him enough money to get back to Chicago, and he departed.

About this time Popenoe, the state policeman, and two of the town's three local cops had gotten up their courage to approach the truck. One of the latter carried a submachine gun.

"Better get out of the way, Mr. Staples," he said. "That there's a dangerous wild animal, and we're gonna kill him."

"Oh, no, you're not," answered Staples. "He's also a valuable piece of property and a scientifically important specimen."

"Don't make no difference. Municipal Ordinance No. 486—" He was peering under the edge of the canvas cover on the side of the truck body. He got the mammoth's location, stepped back, and raised his gun.

Staples did not see that sitting in the cab while his charge was filled with lead would serve any useful purpose. He backed the truck off the courthouse lawn and drove away. All three cops yelled. Staples couldn't go back the way he had come, because the road was blocked by cars and people. He took the opposite direction, toward Warsaw and Chicago. After two blocks he turned off and into a garage where he was known. Half a minute later he had the satisfaction of seeing two police cars shoot past the intersection with sirens going. In a few minutes they came scooting back, evidently thinking that Staples had sneaked around and made for home.

He telephoned Platt and told him what had happened. Platt said: "For God's sake, don't come back now, Ken. There's a state trooper out front waiting for you—or rather, for Tecumtha."

"Well, what'll I do? I've got to take care of him somehow. He'll be getting hungry, and he has a couple of gunshot wounds that need looking at."

Platt paused. "I'll tell you: Drive him up to Chicago and sell him to the zoo. The director's name is Traphagen. The cops won't be expecting you to go that way, and if you bring Tecumtha back here it'll just make more trouble."

As Staples hung up, the garage man asked: "Who's that Tecumtha you was talking about, Mr. Staples?" He was leaning against the truck. At that instant the mammoth gave one of his spine-chilling toots. Kennedy, the garage man, jumped a foot straight up.

"*That's* Tecumtha," said Staples pleasantly. He got into the truck and drove off.

He reached Chicago about ten, and at eleven asked to see Dr. Traphagen. The director's secretary looked at Staples queerly, but then, he was a queer-looking sight, with his pajama coat, Nively's pants—six inches too short—and his bedroom slippers.

The girl asked Staples if he had a card. He got out his wallet and gave her one. When she had disappeared into the inner office, Staples remembered that it was Nively's wallet and cards that he had.

Presently she came out and ushered him in. He said: "Good morning, Dr. Traphagen."

"Mr. Staples . . . ah . . . Nively . . . ah . . . just take it easy; everything's going to be all right."

"It's all right about the card; I can explain. But my name's really Staples, and I—"

"Just what is it you want, Mr. . . . ah . . . Staples?"

"Would you be interested in buying a mammoth?"

"Well, my dear sir, we're only interested in live animals. If you have a fossil, I think the Field Museum is the place to go."

"I didn't say it was a fossil. It's very much alive; a fine adult male of *Parelephas jeffersonii*. Wouldn't you like to take a look at it?"

"Certainly, certainly, my dear sir, I shall be glad to." Traphagen started out. As Staples walked through the door two keepers seized him. Traphagen barked at the girl: "Quick now, call the asylum, or hospital, or whatever it is!"

Staples wriggled, but the keepers had handled tougher game than a mere human being. "Listen, Dr. Traphagen," he said, "you can decide I'm a nut if you like. But I wish you'd take a look at the mammoth first. Did you ever hear of Dr. Gilmore Platt?"

"*Tsk, tsk,* my dear sir, first you say your name is Staples, then you produce a card with 'Nively' on it, and now you say you're Dr. Platt. Now just keep quiet. You're going to a nice place where you can play with all the mammoths you want."

Staples protested some more, but it got him nowhere. He was not a very articulate man, especially with his hat off, and he could make no headway against Traphagen's repeated injunctions to keep calm.

The ambulance arrived, and the men in white coats marched Staples out of the Administration Building and down the walk. Traphagen waddled behind. The truck was standing just in front of the ambulance. Staples yelled: *"Tecumtha!"* The mammoth hoisted his trunk and trumpeted. The horrible brassy sound so startled the internes that they let go of Staples, but to their credit they grabbed their patient again before he could take action.

Traphagen ran over and looked under the canvas. He came back crying: "Oh, dear me! Oh, dear me! I'm so sorry! I'm so sorry! Come to think of it, I do know about Platt and his process. But I never thought you were really him—I mean from him. It's all a mistake, boys, it's all a mistake. He isn't crazy, after all."

The internes released Staples. In a tone of injured dignity, he said: "I've been trying for fifteen minutes to explain who I am, Dr. Traphagen, but you wouldn't let me."

Traphagen apologized some more, and said: "Now, I don't know if you still want to discuss the sale of that animal, my dear sir, but I'd be glad to. I'll have to look at our budget first, to see what our unexpended balance for the quarter is—"

I was really more amused than angry, though I didn't let Traphagen see that until we'd agreed on the price. He was so embarrassed that he gave me a good one. A few dollars of it had to go to the Benefit Fund of the Carriesville police department, to square me with them.

Platt has hired some guards and had the place fenced properly. I don't think the Marco Polo outfit will try anything again. After all that publicity any accidents would look suspicious. Platt also hired another assistant, an enthusiastic young paleontologist named Roubideaux. They're in Wyoming now digging dinosaurs out of the Laramie Cretaceous beds.

We have some fine specimens in the cages, and more coming along in the tanks. One of the latter is a Mastodon americanus, *already promised to the Bronx Zoölogical Park in New York.*

But I started out to tell you why I wanted to leave Platt. In the first place, I'm a geologist, not a wild-animal keeper. The above gives you some idea of what working for Platt is like. In the second, I have, as I said, a family to support, and I want to keep my health. Last week I got a wire from Platt saying they'd found a complete Tyrannosaurus rex *skeleton, fifty feet long and with a mouth full of six-inch teeth. I know what that means, and I'd better clear out while I'm still in one piece.*

Best personal regards to you and Georgia. See you soon, I hope. Ken.

The Gnarly Man

DR. MATILDA SADDLER first saw the gnarly man on the evening of June 14th, 1956, at Coney Island. The spring meeting of the Eastern Section of the American Anthropological Association had broken up, and Dr. Saddler had had dinner with two of her professional colleagues, Blue of Columbia and Jeffcott of Yale. She mentioned that she had never visited Coney and meant to go there that evening. She urged Blue and Jeffcott to come along, but they begged off.

Watching Dr. Saddler's retreating back, Blue of Columbia crackled: "The Wild Woman from Wichita. Wonder if she's hunting another husband?" He was a thin man with a small gray beard and a who-the-Hell-are-you-Sir expression.

"How many has she had?" asked Jeffcott of Yale.

"Three to date. Don't know why anthropologists lead the most disorderly private lives of any scientists. Must be that they study the customs and morals of all these different peoples, and ask themselves, 'If the Eskimos can do it why can't we?' I'm old enough to be safe, thank God."

"I'm not afraid of her," said Jeffcott. He was in his early forties and looked like a farmer uneasy in store-bought clothes. "I'm so very thoroughly married."

"Yeah? Ought to have been at Stanford a few years

ago, when she was there. It wasn't safe to walk across the campus, with Tuthill chasing all the females and Saddler all the males."

Dr. Saddler had to fight her way off the subway train, as the adolescents who infest the platform of the B.M.T.'s Stillwell Avenue Station are probably the worst-mannered people on earth, possibly excepting the Dobu Islanders of the Western Pacific. She didn't much mind. She was a tall, strongly built woman in her late thirties, who had been kept in trim by the outdoor rigors of her profession. Besides, some of the inane remarks in Swift's paper on acculturation among the Arapaho Indians had gotten her fighting blood up.

Walking down Surf Avenue toward Brighton Beach, she looked at the concessions without trying them, preferring to watch the human types that did and the other human types that took their money. She did try a shooting gallery, but found knocking tin owls off their perch with a .22 too easy to be much fun. Long-range work with an army rifle was her idea of shooting.

The concession next to the shooting gallery would have been called a sideshow if there had been a main show for it to be a sideshow to. The usual lurid banner proclaimed the uniqueness of the two-headed calf, the bearded woman, Arachne the spider-girl, and other marvels. The piece de resistance was Ungo-Bungo the ferocious ape-man, captured in the Congo at a cost of twenty-seven lives. The picture showed an enormous Ungo-Bungo squeezing a hapless Negro in each hand, while others sought to throw a net over him.

Although Dr. Saddler knew perfectly well that the ferocious ape-man would turn out to be an ordinary Caucasian with false hair on his chest, a streak of whimsicality impelled her to go in. Perhaps, she thought, she could have some fun with her colleagues about it.

The spieler went through his leather-lunged harangue. Dr. Saddler guessed from his expression that his feet hurt. The tattooed lady didn't interest her, as her decorations obviously had no cultural significance, as they have among the Polynesians. As for the ancient Mayan, Dr. Saddler thought it in questionable taste to exhibit a poor microcephalic idiot that way. Professor Yogi's legerdemain and fire-eating weren't bad.

A curtain hung in front of Ungo-Bungo's cage. At the appropriate moment there were growls and the sound of a length of chain being slapped against a metal plate. The spieler wound up on a high note: ". . . ladies and gentlemen, the one and only Ungo-Bungo!" The curtain dropped.

The ape-man was squatting at the back of his cage. He dropped his chain, got up, and shuffled forward. He grasped two of the bars and shook them. They were appropriately loose and rattled alarmingly. Ungo-Bungo snarled at the patrons, showing his even yellow teeth.

Dr. Saddler stared hard. This was something new in the ape-man line. Ungo-Bungo was about five feet three, but very massive, with enormous hunched shoulders. Above and below his blue swimming trunks, thick grizzled hair covered him from crown to ankle. His short stout-muscled arms ended in big hands with thick gnarled fingers. His neck projected slightly foward, so that from the front he seemed to have but little neck at all.

His face— Well, thought Dr. Saddler, she knew all the living races of men, and all the types of freaks brought about by glandular maladjustment, and none of them had a face like *that*. It was deeply lined. The forehead between the short scalp hair and the brows on the huge supraorbital ridges receded sharply. The nose, though wide, was not apelike; it was a shortened version of the thick hooked Armenoid or "Jewish" nose. The face ended in a long upper lip and a retreating chin. And the yellowish skin apparently belonged to Ungo-Bungo.

The curtain was whisked up again.

Dr. Saddler went out with the others, but paid another dime, and soon was back inside. She paid no attention to the spieler, but got a good position in front of

Ungo-Bungo's cage before the rest of the crowd arrived.

Ungo-Bungo repeated his performance with mechanical precision. Dr. Saddler noticed that he limped a little as he came forward to rattle the bars, and that the skin under his mat of hair bore several big whitish scars. The last joint of his left ring finger was missing. She noted certain things about the proportions of his shin and thigh, of his forearm and upper arm, and his big splay feet.

Dr. Saddler paid a third dime. An idea was knocking at her mind somewhere, trying to get in; either she was crazy or physical anthropology was haywire or—something. But she knew that if she did the sensible thing, which was to go home, the idea would plague her from now on.

After the third performance she spoke to the spieler. "I think your Mr. Ungo-Bungo used to be a friend of mine. Could you arrange for me to see him after he finishes?"

The spieler checked his sarcasm. His questioner was so obviously not a—not the sort of dame who asks to see guys after they finish.

"Oh, him," he said. "Calls himself Gaffney—Clarence Aloysius Gaffney. That the guy you want?"

"Why, yes."

"Guess you can." He looked at his watch. "He's got four more turns to do before we close. I'll have to ask the boss." He popped through a curtain and called, "Hey, Morrie!" Then he was back. "It's okay. Morrie says you can wait in his office. Foist door to the right."

Morrie was stout, bald, and hospitable. "Sure, sure," he said, waving his cigar. "Glad to be of soivice, Miss Saddler. Chust a min while I talk to Gaffney's manager." He stuck his head out. "Hey, Pappas! Lady wants to talk to your ape-man later. I meant *lady*. Okay." He returned to orate on the difficulties besetting the freak business. "You take this Gaffney, now. He's the best damn ape-man in the business; all that hair really grows outa him. And the poor guy really has a face like that. But do people believe it? No! I hear 'em going out, saying about how the hair is pasted on, and the whole thing is a fake. It's mortifying." He cocked his head, listening. "That rumble wasn't no rolly-coaster; it's gonna rain. Hope it's over by tomorrow. You wouldn't believe the way a rain can knock ya receipts off. If you drew a coive, it would be like this." He drew his finger horizontally through space, jerking it down sharply to indicate the effect of rain. "But as I said, people don't appreciate what you try to do for 'em. It's not just the money; I think of myself as an ottist. A creative ottist. A show like this got to have balance and proportion, like any other ott . . ."

It must have been an hour later when a slow, deep voice at the door said, "Did somebody want to see me?"

The gnarly man was in the doorway. In street clothes, with the collar of his raincoat turned up and his hat brim pulled down, he looked more or less human, though the coat fitted his great sloping shoulders badly. He had a thick knobby walking stick with a leather loop near the top end. A small dark man fidgeted behind him.

"Yeah," said Morrie, interrupting his lecture. "Clarence, this is Miss Saddler, Miss Saddler, this is our Mister Gaffney, one of our outstanding creative ottists."

"Pleased to meetcha," said the gnarly man. "This is my manager, Mr. Pappas."

Dr. Saddler explained, and said she'd like to talk to Mr. Gaffney if she might. She was tactful; you had to be to pry into the private affairs of Naga headhunters, for instance. The gnarly man said he'd be glad to have a cup of coffee with Miss Saddler; there was a place around the corner that they could reach without getting wet.

As they started out, Pappas followed, fidgeting more and more. The gnarly man said, "Oh, go home to bed, John. Don't worry about me." He grinned at Dr. Saddler. The effect would have been unnerving to anyone but an anthropologist. "Every time he sees me talking to anybody, he thinks it's some other manager trying to steal me." He spoke General American, with a suggestion of Irish brogue in the lowering of the vowels in words like "man" and "talk." "I made the lawyer who drew up our contract fix it so it can be ended on short notice."

Pappas departed, still looking suspicious. The rain had practically ceased. The gnarly man stepped along smartly despite his limp. A woman passed with a fox terrier on a leash. The dog sniffed in the direction of the gnarly man, and then to all appearances went crazy, yelping and slavering. The gnarly man shifted his grip on the massive stick and said quietly, "Better hang on to him, ma'am." The woman departed hastily. "They just don't like me," commented Gaffney. "Dogs, that is."

They found a table and ordered their coffee. When the gnarly man took off his raincoat, Dr. Saddler became aware of a strong smell of cheap perfume. He got out a pipe with a big knobbly bowl. It suited him, just as the walking stick did. Dr. Saddler noticed that the deep-sunk cycs under the beetling arches were light hazel.

"Well?" he said in his rumbling drawl.

She began her questions.

"My parents were Irish," he answered. "But I was born in South Boston—let's see—forty-six years ago. I can get you a copy of my birth certificate. Clarence Aloysius Gaffney, May 2, 1910." He seemed to get some secret amusement out of that statement.

"Were either of your parents of your somewhat unusual physical type?"

He paused before answering. He always did, it seemed. "Uh-huh. Both of 'em. Glands, I suppose."

"Were they both born in Ireland?"

"Yep. County Sligo." Again that mysterious twinkle.

She paused. "Mr. Gaffney, you wouldn't mind having some photographs and measurements made, would you? You could use the photographs in your business."

"Maybe." He took a sip. "Ouch! Gazooks, that's hot!"

"What?"

"I said the coffee's hot."

"I mean, before that."

The gnarly man looked a little embarrassed. "Oh, you mean the 'gazooks'? Well, I—uh—once knew a man who used to say that."

"Mr. Gaffney, I'm a scientist, and I'm not trying to get anything out of you for my own sake. You can be frank with me."

There was something remote and impersonal in his stare that gave her a slight spinal chill. "Meaning that I haven't been so far?"

"Yes. When I saw you I decided that there was something extraordinary in your background. I still think there is. Now, if you think I'm crazy, say so and we'll drop the subject. But I want to get to the bottom of this."

He took his time about answering. "That would depend." There was another pause. Then he said, "With your connections, do you know any really first-class surgeons?"

"But—yes, I know Dunbar."

"The guy who wears a purple gown when he operates? The guy who wrote a book on *God, Man, and the Universe*?"

"Yes. He's a good man, in spite of his theatrical mannerisms. Why? What would you want of him?"

"Not what you're thinking. I'm satisfied with my—uh—unusual physical type. But I have some old injuries—broken bones that didn't knit properly—that I want fixed up. He'd have to be a good man, though. I have a couple of thousand in the savings bank, but I know the sort of fees those guys charge. If you could make the necessary arrangements—"

"Why, yes, I'm sure I could. In fact I could guarantee it. Then I *was* right? And you'll—" She hesitated.

"Come clean? Uh-huh. But remember, I can still prove I'm Clarence Aloysius if I have to."

"Who *are* you, then?"

Again there was a long pause. Then the gnarly man said, "Might as well tell you. As soon as you repeat any of it, you'll have put your professional reputation in my hands, remember.

"First off, I wasn't born in Massachusetts. I was born on the upper Rhine, near Mommenheim, and as nearly as I can figure out, about the year 50,000 B.C."

Dr. Saddler wondered whether she'd stumbled on the biggest thing in anthropology or whether this bizarre man was making Baron Munchausen look like a piker.

He seemed to guess her thoughts. "I can't prove that, of course. But so long as you arrange about that operation, I don't care whether you believe me or not."

"But—but—*how?*"

"I think the lightning did it. We were out trying to drive some bison into a pit. Well, this big thunderstorm came up, and the bison bolted in the wrong direction. So we gave up and tried to find shelter. And the next thing I knew I was lying on the ground with the rain running over me, and the rest of the clan standing around wailing about what had they done to get the storm-god sore at them, so he made a bull's-eye on one of their best hunters. They'd never said *that* about me before. It's funny how you're never appreciated while you're alive.

"But I was alive, all right. My nerves were pretty well shot for a few weeks, but otherwise I was all right except for some burns on the soles of my feet. I don't know just what happened, except I was reading a couple of years ago that scientists had located the machinery that controls the replacement of tissue in the medulla oblongata. I think maybe the lightning did something to my medulla to speed it up. Anyway I never got any older after that. Physically, that is. And except for those broken bones I told you about. I was thirty-three at the time, more or less. We didn't keep track of ages. I look older now, because the lines in your face are bound to get sort of set after a few thousand years, and because our hair was always gray at the ends. But I can still tie an ordinary *Homo sapiens* in a knot if I want to."

"Then you're—you mean to say you're—you're trying to tell me you're—"

"A Neanderthal man? *Homo neanderthalensis?* That's right."

Matilda Saddler's hotel room was a bit crowded, with the gnarly man, the frosty Blue, the rustic Jeffcott, Dr. Saddler herself, and Harold McGannon the historian. This McGannon was a small man, very neat and pink-skinned. He looked more like a New York Central director than a professor. Just now his expression was one of fascination. Dr. Saddler looked full of pride; Professor Jeffcott looked interested but puzzled; Dr. Blue looked bored. (He hadn't wanted to come in the first place.) The gnarly man, stretched out in the most comfortable chair and puffing his overgrown pipe, seemed to be enjoying himself.

McGannon was asking a question. "Well, Mr.—Gaffney? I suppose that's your name as much as any."

"You might say so," said the gnarly man. "My original name was something like Shining Hawk. But I've gone under hundreds of names since then. If you register in a hotel as 'Shining Hawk' it's apt to attract attention. And I try to avoid that."

"Why?" asked McGannon.

The gnarly man looked at his audience as one might look at willfully stupid children. "I don't like trouble. The best way to keep out of trouble is not to attract attention. That's why I have to pull up stakes and move every ten or fifteen years. People might get curious as to why I never got any older."

"Pathological liar," murmured Blue. The words were barely audible, but the gnarly man heard them.

"You're entitled to your opinion, Dr. Blue," he said affably. "Dr. Saddler's doing me a favor, so in return I'm letting you all shoot questions at me. And I'm answering. I don't give a damn whether you believe me or not."

McGannon hastily threw in another question. "How is it that you have a birth certificate, as you say you have?"

"Oh, I knew a man named Clarence Gaffney once. He got killed by an automobile, and I took his name."

"Was there any reason for picking this Irish background?"

"Are you Irish, Dr. McGannon?"

"Not enough to matter."

"Okay. I didn't want to hurt any feelings. It's my best bet. There are real Irishmen with upper lips like mine."

Dr. Saddler broke in. "I meant to ask you, Clarence." She put a lot of warmth into his name. "There's an argument as to whether your people interbred with mine, when mine overran Europe at the end of the Mousterian. It's been thought that the 'old black breed' of the west coast of Ireland might have a little Neanderthal blood."

He grinned slightly. "Well—yes and no. There never was any back in the Stone Age, as far as I know. But these long-lipped Irish are my fault."

"How?"

"Believe it or not, but in the last fifty centuries there have been some women of your species that didn't find me too repulsive. Usually there were no offspring. But in the sixteenth century I went to Ireland to live. They were burning too many people for witchcraft in the rest of Europe to suit me at that time. And there was a woman. The result this time was a flock of hybrids—cute little devils they were. So the 'old black breed' are my descendants."

"What did happen to your people?" asked McGannon. "Were they killed off?"

The gnarly man shrugged. "Some of them. We weren't at all warlike. But then the tall ones, as we called them, weren't either. Some of the tribes of the tall ones looked on us as legitimate prey, but most of them let us severely alone. I guess they were almost as scared of us as we were of them. Savages as primitive as that are really pretty peaceable people. You have to work so hard, and there are so few of you, that there's no object in fighting wars. That comes later, when you get agriculture and livestock, so you have something worth stealing.

"I remember that a hundred years after the tall ones had come, there were still Neanderthalers living in my part of the country. But they died out. I think it was that they lost their ambition. The tall ones were pretty crude, but they were so far ahead of us that our things and our customs seemed silly. Finally we just sat around and lived on what scraps we could beg from the tall ones' camps. You might say we died of an inferiority complex."

"What happened to you?" asked McGannon.

"Oh, I was a god among my own people by then, and naturally I represented them in dealings with the tall ones. I got to know the tall ones pretty well, and they were willing to put up with me after all my own clan were dead. Then in a couple of hundred years they'd forgotten all about my people, and took me for a hunchback or something. I got to be pretty good at flint-working, so I could earn my keep. When metal came in I went into that, and finally into blacksmithing. If you put all the horseshoes I've made in a pile, they'd—well, you'd have a damn big pile of horseshoes anyway."

"Did you limp at that time?" asked McGannon.

"Uh-huh. I busted my leg back in the Neolithic. Fell out of a tree, and had to set it myself, because there wasn't anybody around. Why?"

"Vulcan," said McGannon softly.

"Vulcan?" repeated the gnarly man. "Wasn't he a Greek god or something?"

"Yes. He was the lame blacksmith of the gods."

"You mean you think that maybe somebody got the idea from me? That's an interesting idea. Little late to check up on it, though."

Blue leaned forward, and said crisply, "Mr. Gaffney, no real Neanderthal man could talk as entertainingly as you do. That's shown by the poor development of the frontal lobes of the brain and the attachments of the tongue muscles."

The gnarly man shrugged again. "You can believe

what you like. My own clan considered me pretty smart, and then you're bound to learn something in fifty thousand years."

Dr. Saddler said, "Tell them about your teeth, Clarence."

The gnarly man grinned. "They're false, of course. My own lasted a long time, but they still wore out somewhere back in the Paleolithic. I grew a third set, and they wore out too. So I had to invent soup."

"You *what?*" It was the usually taciturn Jeffcott.

"I had to invent soup, to keep alive. You know, the bark-dish-and-hot-stones method. My gums got pretty tough after a while, but they still weren't much good for chewing hard stuff. So after a few thousand years I got pretty sick of soup, and mushy foods generally. And when metal came in I began experimenting with false teeth. I finally made some pretty good ones. Amber teeth in copper plates. You might say I invented them too. I tried often to sell them, but they never really caught on until around 1750 A.D. I was living in Paris then, and I built up quite a little business before I moved on." He pulled the handkerchief out of his breast pocket to wipe his forehead; Blue made a face as the wave of perfume reached him.

"Well, Mr. Caveman," snapped Blue sarcastically, "how do you like our machine age?"

The gnarly man ignored the tone of the question. "It's not bad. Lots of interesting things happen. The main trouble is the shirts."

"Shirts?"

"Uh-huh. Just try to buy a shirt with a 20 neck and a 29 sleeve. I have to order 'em special. It's almost as bad with hats and shoes. I wear an 8-1/2 hat and a 13 shoe." He looked at his watch. "I've got to get back to Coney to work."

McGannon jumped up. "Where can I get in touch with you again, Mr. Gaffney? There's lots of things I'd like to ask you."

The gnarly man told him. "I'm free mornings. My working hours are two to midnight on weekdays, with a couple of hours off for dinner. Union rules, you know."

"You mean there's a union for you show people?"

"Sure. Only they call it a guild. They think they're artists, you know."

Blue and Jeffcott watched the gnarly man and the historian walking slowly toward the subway together. Blue said, "Poor old Mac! I always thought he had sense. Looks like he's swallowed this Gaffney's ravings hook, line, and sinker."

"I'm not so sure," said Jeffcott, frowning. "There's something funny about the business."

"What?" barked Blue. "Don't tell me that *you* believe this story of being alive fifty thousand years? A caveman who uses perfume? Good God!"

"N-no," said Jeffcott. "Not the fifty thousand part. But I don't think it's a simple case of paranoia or plain lying either. And the perfume's quite logical, if he were telling the truth."

"Huh?"

"Body odor. Saddler told us how dogs hate him. He'd have a smell different from ours. We're so used to ours that we don't even know we have one, unless somebody goes without a bath for a couple of months. But we might notice his if he didn't disguise it."

Blue snorted. "You'll be believing him yourself in a minute. It's an obvious glandular case, and he's made up this story to fit. All that talk about not caring whether we believe him or not is just bluff. Come on, let's get some lunch. Say, did you see the way Saddler looked at him every time she said 'Clarence'? Wonder what she thinks she's going to do with him?"

Jeffcott thought. "I can guess. And if he *is* telling the truth, I think there's something in Deuteronomy against it."

The great surgeon made a point of looking like a great surgeon, to pince-nez and Vandyke. He waved the X-ray negatives at the gnarly man, pointing out this and that.

"We'd better take the leg first," he said. "Suppose we do that next Tuesday. When you've recovered from that we can tackle the shoulder."

The gnarly man agreed, and shuffled out of the little private hospital to where McGannon awaited him in his car. The gnarly man described the tentative schedule of operations, and mentioned that he had made arrangements to quit his job at the last minute. "Those two are the main things," he said. "I'd like to try professional wrestling again some day, and I can't unless I get this shoulder fixed so I can raise my left arm over my head."

"What happened to it?" asked McGannon.

The gnarly man closed his eyes, thinking. "Let me see. I get things mixed up sometimes. People do when they're only fifty years old, so you can imagine what it's like for me.

"In 42 B.C. I was living with the Bituriges in Gaul. You remember that Caesar shut up Werkinghetorich—Vercingetorix to you—in Alesia, and the confederacy raised an army of relief under Caswallon."

"Caswallon?"

The gnarly man laughed shortly. "I meant Wercaswallon. Caswallon was a Briton, wasn't he? I'm always getting those two mixed up.

"Anyhow, I got drafted. That's all you can call it; I didn't want to go. It wasn't exactly *my* war. But they wanted me because I could pull twice as heavy a bow as anybody else.

"When the final attack on Caesar's ring of fortifications came, they sent me forward with some other archers to provide a covering fire for their infantry. At least that was the plan. Actually I never saw such a hopeless muddle in my life. And before I even got within bowshot, I fell into one of the Romans' covered pits. I didn't land on the point of the stake, but I fetched up against the side of it and busted my shoulder. There wasn't any help, because the Gauls were too busy running away from Caesar's German cavalry to bother about wounded men."

The author of *God, Man, and the Universe* gazed after his departing patient. He spoke to his head assistant. "What do you think of him?"

"I think it's so," said the assistant. "I looked over those X-rays pretty closely. That skeleton never belonged to a human being."

"Hmm. Hmm," said Dunbar. "That's right, he wouldn't be human, would he? Hmm. You know, if anything happened to him—"

The assistant grinned understandingly. "Of course there's the S.P.C.A."

"We needn't worry about *them*. Hmm." He thought, you've been slipping: nothing big in the papers for a year. But if you published a complete anatomical description of a Neanderthal man—or if you found out why his medulla functions the way it does—hmm—of course it would have to be managed properly—

"Let's have lunch at the Natural History Museum," said McGannon. "Some of the people there ought to know you."

"Okay," drawled the gnarly man. "Only I've still got to get back to Coney afterward. This is my last day. Tomorrow Pappas and I are going up to see our lawyer about ending our contract. It's a dirty trick on poor old John, but I warned him at the start that this might happen."

"I suppose we can come up to interview you while you're—ah—convalescing? Fine. Have you ever been to the Museum, by the way?"

"Sure," said the gnarly man. "I get around."

"What did you—ah—think of their stuff in the Hall of the Age of Man?"

"Pretty good. There's a little mistake in one of those big wall paintings. The second horn on the wooly rhinoceros ought to slant forward more. I thought about writing them a letter. But you know how it is. They say 'Were you there?' and I say 'Uh-huh' and they say 'Another nut.' "

"How about the pictures and busts of Paleolithic men?"

"Pretty good. But they have some funny ideas. They always show us with skins wrapped around our middles. In summer we didn't wear skins, and in winter we hung them around our shoulders where they'd do some good.

"And then they show those tall ones that you call Cro-Magnon men clean shaven. As I remember they all had whiskers. What would they shave with?"

"I think," said McGannon, "that they leave the beards off the busts to—ah—show the shape of the chins. With the beards they'd all look too much alike."

"Is that the reason? They might say so on the labels." The gnarly man rubbed his own chin, such as it was. "I wish beards would come back into style. I look much more human with a beard. I got along fine in the sixteenth century when everybody had whiskers.

"That's one of the ways I remember when things happened, by the haircuts and whiskers that people had. I remember when a wagon I was driving in Milan lost a wheel and spilled flour bags from hell to breakfast. That must have been in the sixteenth century, before I went to Ireland, because I remember that most of the men in the crowd that collected had beards. Now—wait a minute—maybe that was the fourteenth. There were a lot of beards then too."

"Why, why didn't you keep a diary?" asked McGannon with a groan of exasperation.

The gnarly man shrugged characteristically. "And pack around six trunks full of paper every time I moved? No, thanks."

"I—ah—don't suppose you could give me the real story of Richard III and the princes in the Tower?"

"Why should I? I was just a poor blacksmith or farmer or something most of the time. I didn't go around with the big shots. I gave up all my ideas of ambition a long time before that. I had to, being so different from other people. As far as I can remember, the only real king I ever got a good look at was Charlemagne, when he made a speech in Paris one day. He was just a big tall man with a walrus mustache and a squeaky voice."

Next morning McGannon and the gnarly man had a session with Svedberg at the Museum, after which McGannon drove Gaffney around to the lawyer's office, on the third floor of a seedy old office building in the West Fifties. James Robinette looked something like a movie actor and something like a chipmunk. He glanced at his watch and said to McGannon: "This won't take long. If you'd like to stick around I'd be glad to have lunch with you." The fact was that he was feeling just a trifle queasy about being left with this damn queer client, this circus freak or whatever he was, with his barrel body and his funny slow drawl.

When the business had been completed, and the gnarly man had gone off with his manager to wind up his affairs at Coney, Robinette said, "Whew! I thought he was a halfwit, from his looks. But there was nothing halfwitted about the way he went over those clauses. You'd have thought the damn contract was for building a subway system. What is he, anyhow?"

McGannon told him what he knew.

The lawyer's eyebrows went up. "Do you *believe* his yarn?"

"I do. So does Saddler. So does Svedberg up at the Museum. They're both topnotchers in their respective fields. Saddler and I have interviewed him, and Svedberg's examined him physically. But it's just opinion. Fred Blue still swears it's a hoax or a case of some sort of dementia. Neither of us can prove anything."

"Why not?"

"Well—ah—how are you going to prove that he was or was not alive a hundred years ago? Take one case: Clarence says he ran a sawmill in Fairbanks, Alaska, in 1906 and '07, under the name of Michael Shawn. How are you going to find out whether there was a sawmill operator in Fairbanks at that time? And if you did stumble on a record of a Michael Shawn, how would you know whether he and Clarence were the same? There's not a chance in a thousand that there'd be a photograph or a detailed description you could check with. And you'd have an awful time trying to find anybody who remembered him at this late date.

"Then, Svedberg poked around Clarence's face, and said that no human being ever had a pair of zygomatic arches like that. But when I told Blue that, he offered to produce photographs of a human skull that did. I know what'll happen: Blue will say that the arches are practically the same, and Svedberg will say that they're obviously different. So there we'll be."

Robinette mused, "He does seem damned intelligent for an ape-man."

"He's not an ape-man really. The Neanderthal race was a separate branch of the human stock; they were more primitive in some ways and more advanced in others than we are. Clarence may be slow, but he usually grinds out the right answer. I imagine that he was—ah—brilliant, for one of his kind, to begin with. And he's had the benefit of so much experience. He knows us; he sees through us and our motives." The little pink man puckered up his forehead. "I do hope nothing happens to him. He's carrying around a lot of priceless information in that big head of his. Simply priceless. Not much about war and politics; he kept clear of those as a matter of self-preservation. But little things, about how people lived and how they thought thousands of years ago. He gets his periods mixed up sometimes, but he gets them straightened out if you give him time.

"I'll have to get hold of Pell, the linguist. Clarence knows dozens of ancient languages, such as Gothic and Gaulish. I was able to check him on some of them, like vulgar Latin; that was one of the things that convinced me. And there are archaeologists and psychologists. . . .

"If only something doesn't happen to scare him off. We'd never find him. I don't know. Between a man-crazy female scientist and a publicity-mad surgeon—I wonder how it'll work out."

The gnarly man innocently entered the waiting room of Dunbar's hospital. He as usual spotted the most comfortable chair and settled luxuriously into it.

Dunbar stood before him. His keen eyes gleamed with anticipation behind their pince-nez. "There'll be a wait of about half an hour, Mr. Gaffney," he said. "We're all tied up now, you know. I'll send Mahler in; he'll see that you have anything you want." Dunbar's eyes ran lovingly over the gnarly man's stumpy frame. What fascinating secrets mightn't he discover once he got inside it?

Mahler appeared, a healthy-looking youngster. Was there anything Mr. Gaffney would like? The gnarly man paused as usual to let his massive mental machinery grind. A vagrant impulse moved him to ask to see the instruments that were to be used on him.

Mahler had his orders, but this seemed a harmless enough request. He went and returned with a tray full of gleaming steel. "You see," he said, "these are called scalpels."

Presently the gnarly man asked, "What's this?" He picked up a peculiar-looking instrument.

"Oh, that's the boss's own invention. For getting at the midbrain."

"Midbrain? What's that doing here?"

"Why, that's for getting at your—that must be there by mistake—"

Little lines tightened around the queer hazel eyes. "Yeah?" He remembered the look Dunbar had given him, and Dunbar's general reputation. "Say, could I use your phone a minute?"

"Why—I suppose—what do you want to phone for?"

"I want to call my lawyer. Any objections?"

"No, of course not. But there isn't any phone here."

"What do you call that?" The gnarly man rose and walked toward the instrument in plain sight on a table. But Mahler was there before him, standing in front of it.

"This one doesn't work. It's being fixed."

"Can't I try it?"

"No, not till it's fixed. It doesn't work, I tell you."

The gnarly man studied the young physician for a few seconds. "Okay, then I'll find one that does." He started for the door.

"Hey, you can't go out now!" cried Mahler.

"Can't I? Just watch me!"

"Hey!" It was a full-throated yell. Like magic more men in white coats appeared. Behind them was the great surgeon. "Be reasonable, Mr. Gaffney," he said. "There's no reason why you should go out now, you know. We'll be ready for you in a little while."

"Any reason why I shouldn't?" The gnarly man's big face swung on his thick neck, and his hazel eyes swiveled. All the exits were blocked. "I'm going."

"Grab him!" said Dunbar.

The white coats moved. The gnarly man got his hands on the back of a chair. The chair whirled, and became a dissolving blur as the men closed on him. Pieces of chair flew about the room, to fall with the dry sharp *pink* of short lengths of wood. When the gnarly man stopped swinging, having only a short piece of the chair back left in each fist, one assistant was out cold. Another leaned whitely against the wall and nursed a broken arm.

"Go on!" shouted Dunbar when he could make himself heard. The white wave closed over the gnarly man, then broke. The gnarly man was on his feet, and held young Mahler by the ankles. He spread his feet and swung the shrieking Mahler like a club, clearing the way to the door. He turned, whirled Mahler around his head like a hammer thrower, and let the now mercifully unconscious body fly. His assailants went down in a yammering tangle.

One was still up. Under Dunbar's urging he sprang after the gnarly man. The latter had gotten his stick out of the umbrella stand in the vestibule. The knobby upper end went *whoowh* past the assistant's nose. The assistant jumped back and fell over one of the casualties.

The front door slammed, and there was a deep roar of "Taxi!"

"Come on!" shrieked Dunbar. "Get the ambulance out!"

James Robinette sat in his office on the third floor of a seedy old office building in the West Fifties, thinking the thoughts that lawyers do in moments of relaxation.

He wondered about that damn queer client, that circus freak or whatever he was, who had been in a couple of days before with his manager. A barrel-bodied man who looked like a halfwit and talked in a funny slow drawl. Though there had been nothing halfwitted about the acute way he had gone over those clauses.

There was a pounding of large feet in the corridor, a startled protest from Miss Spevak in the outer office, and the strange customer was before Robinette's desk, breathing hard.

"I'm Gaffney," he growled between gasps. "Remember me? I think they followed me down here. They'll be up any minutc. I want your help."

"They? Who's they?" Robinette winced at the impact of that damned perfume.

The gnarly man launched into his misfortunes. He was going well when there were more protests from Miss Spevak, and Dr. Dunbar and four assistants burst into the office.

"He's ours," said Dunbar, his glasses agleam.

"He's an ape-man," said the assistant with the black eye.

"He's a dangerous lunatic," said the assistant with the cut lip.

"We've come to take him away," said the assistant with the torn pants.

The gnarly man spread his feet and gripped his stick like a baseball bat, by the small end.

Robinette opened a desk drawer and got out a large pistol. "One move toward him and I'll use this. The use of extreme violence is justified to prevent commission of a felony, to wit, kidnapping."

The five men backed up a little. Dunbar said, "This isn't kidnapping. You can only kidnap a person, you know. He isn't a human being, and I can prove it."

The assistant with the black eye snickered. "If he wants protection, he better see a game warden instead of a lawyer."

"Maybe that's what *you* think," said Robinette. "You aren't a lawyer. According to the law he's human. Even corporations, idiots, and unborn children are legally persons, and he's a damn sight more human than they are."

"Then he's a dangerous lunatic," said Dunbar.

"Yeah? Where's your commitment order? The only persons who can apply for one are (a) close relatives and (b) public officials charged with the maintenance of order. You're neither."

Dunbar continued stubbornly. "He ran amuck in my hospital and nearly killed a couple of my men, you know. I guess that gives us some rights."

"Sure," said Robinette. "You can step down to the nearest station and swear out a warrant." He turned to the gnarly man. "Shall we slap a civil suit on 'em, Gaffney?"

"I'm all right," said the individual, his speech returning to its normal slowness. "I just want to make sure these guys don't pester me anymore."

"Okay. Now listen, Dunbar. One hostile move out of you and we'll have a warrant out for you for false arrest, assault and battery, attempted kidnapping, criminal conspiracy, and disorderly conduct. We'll throw the book at you. *And* there'll be a suit for damages for sundry torts, to wit, assault, deprivation of civil rights, placing in jeopardy of life and limb, menace, and a few more I may think of later."

"You'll never make that stick," snarled Dunbar. "We have all the witnesses."

"Yeah? And wouldn't the great Evan Dunbar look sweet defending such actions? Some of the ladies who gush over your books might suspect that maybe you weren't such a damn knight in shining armor. We can make a prize monkey of you, and you know it."

"You're destroying the possibility of a great scientific discovery, you know, Robinette."

"To hell with that. My duty is to protect my client. Now beat it, all of you, before I call a cop." His left hand moved suggestively to the telephone.

Dunbar grasped at a last straw. "Hmm. Have you got a permit for that gun?"

"Damn right. Want to see it?"

Dunbar sighed. "Never mind. You *would* have." His greatest opportunity for fame was slipping out of his fingers. He drooped toward the door.

The gnarly man spoke up. "If you don't mind, Dr. Dunbar. I left my hat at your place. I wish you'd send it to Mr. Robinette here. I have a hard time getting hats to fit me."

Dunbar looked at him silently and left with his cohorts.

The gnarly man was giving the lawyer further details when the telephone rang. Robinette answered: "Yes . . . Saddler? Yes, he's here . . . Your Dr. Dunbar was going to murder him so he could dissect him . . . Okay." He turned to the gnarly man. "Your friend Dr. Saddler is looking for you. She's on her way up here."

"Herakles!" said Gaffney. "I'm going."

"Don't you want to see her? She was phoning from around the corner. If you go out now you'll run into her. How did she know where to call?"

"I gave her your number. I suppose she called the hospital and my boarding house, and tried you as a last resort. This door goes into the hall, doesn't it? Well, when she comes in the regular door I'm going out this one. And I don't want you saying where I've gone. Nice to have known you, Mr. Robinette."

"Why? What's the matter? You're not going to run out now, are you? Dunbar's harmless, and you've got friends. I'm your friend."

"You're durn tootin' I'm gonna run out. There's too much trouble. I've kept alive all these centuries by staying away from trouble. I let down my guard with Dr. Saddler, and went to the surgeon she recommended. First he plots to take me apart to see what makes me tick. If that brain instrument hadn't made me suspicious I'd have been on my way to the alcohol jars by now. Then there's a fight, and it's just pure luck I didn't kill a couple of those internes or whatever they are and get sent up for manslaughter. Now Matilda's after me with a more than friendly interest. I know what it means when a woman looks at you that way and calls you 'dear.' I wouldn't mind if she weren't a prominent person of the kind that's always in some sort of garboil. That would mean more trouble sooner or later. You don't suppose I *like* trouble, do you?"

"But look here, Gaffney, you're getting steamed up over a lot of damn—"

"Ssst!" The gnarly man took his stick and tiptoed over to the private entrance. As Dr. Saddler's clear voice sounded in the outer office, he sneaked out. He was closing the door behind him when the scientist entered the inner office.

Matilda Saddler was a quick thinker. Robinette hardly had time to open his mouth when she flung herself at and through the private door with a cry of "Clarence!"

Robinette heard the clatter of feet on the stairs. Neither the pursued nor the pursuer had waited for the creaky elevator. Looking out the window he saw Gaffney leap into a taxi. Matilda Saddler sprinted after the cab, calling, "Clarence! Come back!" But the traffic was light and the chase correspondingly hopeless.

They did hear from the gnarly man once more. Three months later Robinette got a letter whose envelope contained, to his vast astonishment, ten ten-dollar bills. The single sheet was typed even to the signature.

Dear Mr. Robinette:

I do not know what your regular fees are, but I

hope that the enclosed will cover your services to me of last July.

Since leaving New York I have had several jobs. I pushed a hack (as we say) in Chicago, and I tried out as pitcher on a bush-league baseball team. Once I made my living by knocking over rabbits and things with stones, and I can still throw fairly well. Nor am I bad at swinging a club like a baseball bat. But my lameness makes me too slow for a baseball career.

I now have a job whose nature I cannot disclose because I do not wish to be traced. You need pay no attention to the postmark; I am not living in Kansas City, but had a friend post this letter there.

Ambition would be foolish for one in my peculiar position. I am satisfied with a job that furnishes me with the essentials and allows me to go to an occasional movie, and a few friends with whom I can drink beer and talk.

I was sorry to leave New York wthout saying good-bye to Dr. Harold McGannon, who treated me very nicely. I wish you would explain to him why I had to leave as I did. You can get in touch with him through Columbia University.

If Dunbar sent you my hat as I requested, please mail it to me, General Delivery, Kansas City, Mo. My friend will pick it up. There is not a hat store in this town where I live that can fit me.

With best wishes, I remain,

Yours sincerely,
Shining Hawk
alias Clarence Aloysius Gaffney

Reward of Virtue

Sir Gilbert de Vere was a virtuous knight;
He succored the weak and he fought for the right
But cherished a goal that he never could sight:
        He wanted a dragon to fight.

He prayed all the night and he prayed all the day
That God would provide him a dragon to slay;
And God heard his prayer and considered a way
        To furnish Sir Gilbert his prey.

And so, to comply with Sir Gilbert's demand
But having no genuine dragons to hand,
God whisked him away to an earlier land,
        With destrier, armor, and brand.

And in the Cretaceous, Sir Gilbert de Vere
Discovered a fifty-foot carnosaur near.
He dug in his spurs and he leveled his spear
        And charged without flicker of fear.

The point struck a rib, and the lance broke in twain;
The knight clapped a hand to his hilt, but in vain:
The dinosaur swallowed that valorous thane,
        And gallant Sir Gilbert was slain.

The iron apparel he wore for his ride,
However, was rough on the reptile's inside.
That dinosaur presently lay down and died,
    And honor was thus satisfied.

But Gilbert no longer was present to care;
So pester not God with your wishes. Beware!
What happens when Heaven has answered your prayer
    Is your, and no other's, affair!

Nothing in the Rules

NOT MANY SPECTATORS turn out for a meet between two minor women's swimming clubs, and this one was no exception. Louis Connaught, looking up at the balcony, thought casually that the single row of seats around it was about half full, mostly with the usual bored-looking assortment of husbands and boy friends, and some of the Hotel Creston's guests who had wandered in for want of anything better to do. One of the bellboys was asking an evening-gowned female not to smoke, and she was showing irritation. Mr. Santalucia and the little Santalucias were there as usual to see mamma perform. They waved down at Connaught.

Connaught—a dark devilish-looking little man—glanced over to the other side of the pool. The girls were coming out of the shower rooms, and their shrill conversation was blurred by the acoustics of the pool room into a continuous buzz. The air was faintly steamy. The stout party in white duck pants was Laird, coach of the Knickerbockers and Connaught's arch rival. He saw Connaught and boomed: "Hi, Louie!" The words rattled from wall to wall with a sound like a stick being drawn swiftly along a picket fence. Wambach of the A. A. U. Committee, who was refereeing, came in with his overcoat still on and greeted Laird, but the booming reverberations drowned his words before they got over to Connaught.

Then somebody else came through the door; or rather, a knot of people crowded through it all at once, facing inward, some in bathing suits and some in street clothes. It was a few seconds before Coach Connaught saw what they were looking at. He blinked and looked more closely, standing with his mouth half open.

But not for long. *"Hey!"* he yelled in a voice that made the pool room sound like the inside of a snare drum in use. "Protest! PROTEST! *You can't do that!"*

It had been the preceding evening when Herbert Laird opened his front door and shouted, "H'lo, Mark, come on in." The chill March wind was making a good deal of racket but not so much as all that. Laird was given to shouting on general principle. He was stocky and bald.

Mark Vining came in and deposited his briefcase. He was younger than Laird—just thirty, in fact—with octagonal glasses and rather thin, severe features, which made him look more serious than he was.

"Glad you could come, Mark," said Laird. "Listen, can you make our meet with the Crestons tomorrow night?"

Vining pursed his lips thoughtfully. "I guess so. Loomis decided not to appeal, so I don't have to work nights for a few days anyhow. Is something special up?"

Laird looked sly. "Maybe. Listen, you know that Mrs. Santalucia that Louie Connaught has been cleaning up with for the past couple of years? I think I've got that fixed. But I want you along to think up legal reasons why my scheme's okay."

"Why," said Vining cautiously, "what's your scheme?"

"Can't tell you now. I promised not to. But if Louie can win by entering a freak—a woman with webbed fingers—"

"Oh, look here, Herb, you know those webs don't really help her—"

"Yes, yes, I know all the arguments. You've already got more water resistance to your arms than you've got muscle to overcome it with, and so forth. But I know Mrs. Santalucia has webbed fingers, and I know she's the best damned woman swimmer in New York. And I don't like it. It's bad for my prestige as a coach." He turned and shouted into the gloom: "Iantha!"

"Yes?"

"Come here, will you please? I want you to meet my friend Mr. Vining. Here, we need some light."

The light showed the living room as usual buried under disorderly piles of boxes of bathing suits and other swimming equipment, the sale of which furnished Herbert Laird with most of his income. It also showed a young women coming in in a wheelchair.

One look gave Vining a feeling that, he knew, boded no good for him. He was unfortunate in being a push-over for any reasonably attractive girl and at the same time being cursed with an almost pathological shyness where women were concerned. The fact that both he and Laird were bachelors and took their swimming seriously was the main tie between them.

This girl was more than reasonably attractive. She was, thought the dazzled Vining, a wow, a ten-strike, a direct sixteen-inch hit. Her smooth, rather flat features and high cheekbones had a hint of Asian or American Indian and went oddly with her light-gold hair, which, Vining could have sworn, had a faint greenish tinge. A blanket was wrapped around her legs.

He came out of his trance as Laird introduced the exquisite creature as "Miss Delfoiros."

Miss Delfoiros did not seem exactly overcome. As she extended her hand, she said with a noticeable accent: "You are not from the newspapers, Mr. Vining?"

"No," said Vining. "Just a lawyer. I specialize in wills and probates and things. Not thinking of drawing up yours, are you?"

She relaxed visibly and laughed. "No. I 'ope I shall not need one for a long, long time."

"Still," said Vining seriously, "you never know—"

Laird bellowed: "Wonder what's keeping that sister of mine. Dinner ought to be ready. *Martha!*" He marched out, and Vining heard Miss Laird's voice, something about "—but Herb, I had to let those things cool down—"

Vining wondered with a great wonder what he should say to Miss Delfoiros. Finally he said, "Smoke?"

"Oh, no, thank you very much. I do not do it."

"Mind if I do?"

"No, not at all."

"Whereabouts do you hail from?" Vining thought the question sounded both brusque and silly. He never did get the hang of talking easily under these circumstances.

"Oh, I am from Kip—Cyprus, I mean. You know, the island."

"Will you be at this swimming meet?"

"Yes, I think so."

"You don't"—he lowered his voice—"know what scheme Herb's got up his sleeve to beat La Santalucia?"

"Yes . . . no . . . I do not . . . what I mean is, I must not tell."

More mystery, thought Vining. What he really wanted to know was why she was confined to a wheelchair; whether the cause was temporary or permanent. But you couldn't ask a person right out, and he was still trying to concoct a leading question when Laird's bellow wafted in: "All right, folks, soup's on!" Vining would have pushed the wheelchair in, but before he had a chance, the girl had spun the chair around and was halfway to the dining room.

Vining said: "Hello, Martha, how's the schoolteaching business?" But he was not really paying much attention to Laird's capable spinster sister. He was gaping at Miss Delfoiros, who was quite calmly emptying a teaspoonful of salt into her water glass and stirring.

"What . . . what?" he gulped.

"I 'ave to," she said. "Fresh water makes me—like what you call drunk."

"Listen, Mark!" roared his friend. "Are you sure you can be there on time tomorrow night? There are some questions of eligibility to be cleared up, and I'm likely to need you badly."

"Will Miss Delfoiros be there?" Vining grinned, feeling very foolish inside.

"Oh, sure. Iantha's our . . . say, listen, you know that little eighteen-year-old Clara Havranek? She did the hundred in one-oh-five yesterday. She's championship material. We'll clean the Creston Club yet—" He went on, loud and fast, about what he was going to do to Louie Connaught's girls. The while, Mark Vining tried to concentrate on his own food, which was good, and on Iantha Delfoiros, who was charming but evasive.

There seemed to be something special about Miss Delfoiros' food, to judge by the way Martha Laird had served it. Vining looked closely and saw that it had the peculiarly dead and clammy look that a dinner once hot but now cold has. He asked about it.

"Yes," she said, "I like it cold."

"You mean you don't eat *anything* hot?"

She made a face. " 'Ot food? No, I do not like it. To us it is—"

"Listen, Mark! I hear the W. S. A. is going to throw a postseason meet in April for novices only—"

Vining's dessert lay before him a full minute before he noticed it. He was too busy thinking how delightful Miss Delfoiros' accent was.

When dinner was over, Laird said, "Listen, Mark, you know something about these laws against owning gold? Well, look here—" He led the way to a candy box on a table in the living room. The box contained, not candy, but gold and silver coins. Laird handed the lawyer several of them. The first one he examined was a silver crown, bearing the inscription "Carolus II Dei Gra" encircling the head of England's Merry Monarch with a wreath in his hair—or, more probably, in his wig. The second was an eighteenth-century Spanish dollar. The third was a Louis d'Or.

"I didn't know you went in for coin collecting, Herb," said Vining. "I suppose these are all genuine?"

"They're genuine all right. But I'm not collecting 'em. You might say I'm taking 'em in trade. I have a chance to sell ten thousand bathing caps, if I can take payment in those things."

"I shouldn't think the U. S. Rubber Company would like the idea much."

"That's just the point. What'll I do with 'em after I get 'em? Will the government put me in jail for having 'em?"

"You needn't worry about that. I don't think the law covers old coins, though I'll look it up to make sure. Better call up the American Numismatic Society—they're in the phone book—and they can tell you how to dispose of them. But look here, what the devil is this? Ten thousand bathing caps to be paid for in pieces-of-eight? I never heard of such a thing."

"That's it exactly. Just ask the little lady here." Laird turned to Iantha, who was nervously trying to signal him to keep quiet. "The deal's her doing."

"I did . . . did—" She looked as if she were going to cry. " 'Erbert, you should not have said that. You see," she said to Vining, "we do not like to 'ave a lot to do with people. Always it causes us troubles."

"Who," asked Vining, "do you mean by 'we'?"

She shut her mouth obstinately. Vining almost melted, but his legal instincts came to the surface. If you don't get a grip on yourself, he thought, you'll be in love with her in another five minutes, and that might be a disaster. He said firmly:

"Herb, the more I see of this business, the crazier it looks. Whatever's going on, you seem to be trying to get me into it. But I'm damned if I'll let you unless I know what it's all about."

"Might as well tell him, Iantha," said Laird. "He'll know when he sees you swim tomorrow, anyhow."

She said: "You will not tell the newspaper men, Mr. Vining?"

"No, I won't say anything to anybody."

"You promise?"

"Of course. You can depend on a lawyer to keep things under his hat."

"Under his— I suppose you mean, not to tell. So, look." She reached down and pulled up the lower end of the blanket.

Vining looked. Where he expected to see feet, there was a pair of horizontal flukes, like those of a porpoise.

Louis Connaught's having kittens, when he saw what his rival coach had sprung on him, can thus be easily explained. First he doubted his own senses; then he doubted whether there was any justice in the world.

Meanwhile, Mark Vining proudly pushed Iantha's wheelchair in among the cluster of judges and timekeepers at the starting end of the pool. Iantha herself, in a bright green bathing cap, held her blanket around her shoulders, but the slate-gray tail with its flukes was plain for all to see. The skin of the tail was smooth and the flukes were horizontal; artists who show mermaids with scales and a vertical tail fin, like a fish's, simply do not know their zoölogy.

"All right, all right," bellowed Laird. "Don't crowd around. Everybody get back to where they belong. Everybody, please."

One of the spectators, leaning over the rail of the balcony to see, dropped a fountain pen into the pool. One of Connaught's girls, a Miss Black, dove in after it.

Ogden Wambach, the referee, poked a finger at the skin of the tail. He was a well-groomed, gray-haired man.

"Laird," he said, "is this a joke?"

"Not at all. She's entered in the back stroke and all the free styles, just like any other club member. She's even registered with the A. A. U."

"But . . . but . . . I mean, is it alive? Is it real?"

Iantha spoke up. "Why do you not ask me those

questions, Mr. . . . Mr. . . . I do not know you—"

"Good grief," said Wambach. "It talks! I'm the referee, Miss—"

"Delfoiros. Iantha Delfoiros."

"My word. Upon my word. That means—let's see—Violet Porpoise-tail, doesn't it? *Delphis* plus *oura*—"

"You know Greek? Oh, 'ow nice!" She broke into a string of *dimotiki*.

Wambach gulped a little. "Too fast for me, I'm afraid. And that's *modern* Greek, isn't it?"

"Why, yes. I am modern, am I not?"

"Dear me. I suppose so. But is that tail really real? I mean, it's not just a piece of costumery?"

"Oh, but yes." Iantha threw off the blanket and waved her flukes. Everyone in the pool seemed to have turned into a pair of eyeballs to which a body and a pair of legs were vaguely attached.

"Dear me," said Ogden Wambach. "Where are my glasses? You understand, I just want to make sure there's nothing spurious about this."

Mrs. Santalucia, a muscular-looking lady with a visible mustache and fingers webbed down to the first joint, said, "You mean I gotta swim against *her?*"

Louis Connaught had been sizzling like a dynamite fuse. "You can't do it!" he shrilled. "This is a woman's meet! I protest!"

"So what?" said Laird.

"But you can't enter a fish in a woman's swimming meet! Can you, Mr. Wambach?"

Mark Vining spoke up. He had just taken a bunch of papers clipped together out of his pocket and was running through them.

"Miss Delfoiros," he asserted, "is not a fish. She's a mammal."

"How do you figure that?" yelled Connaught.

"*Look* at her."

"Um-m-m," said Ogden Wambach. "I see what you mean."

"But," howled Connaught, "she still ain't human!"

"There is a question about that, Mr. Vining," said Wambach.

"No question at all. There's nothing in the rules against entering a mermaid, and there's nothing that says the competitors have to be human."

Connaught was hopping about like an overwrought cricket. He was now waving a copy of the current A. A. U. swimming, diving, and water polo rules. "I still protest! Look here! All through here it only talks about two kinds of meets, men's and women's. She ain't a woman, and she certainly ain't a man. If the Union had wanted to have meets for mermaids they'd have said so."

"Not a woman?" asked Vining in a manner that juries learned meant a rapier thrust at an opponent. "I beg your pardon, Mr. Connaught. I looked the question up." He frowned at his sheaf of papers. "Webster's International Dictionary, Second Edition, defines a woman as 'any female person.' And it further defines 'person' as 'a being characterized by conscious apprehension, rationality, and a moral sense.' " He turned to Wambach. "Sir, I think you'll agree that Miss Delfoiros has exhibited conscious apprehension and rationality during her conversation with you, won't you?"

"My word . . . I really don't know what to say, Mr. Vining . . . I suppose she has, but I couldn't say—"

Horwitz, the scorekeeper, spoke up. "You might ask her to give the multiplication table." Nobody paid him any attention.

Connaught exhibited symptoms of apoplexy. "But you can't— What the hell you talking about—conscious ap-ap—"

"Please, Mr. Connaught!" said Wambach. "When you shout that way I can't understand you because of the echoes."

Connaught mastered himself with a visible effort. Then he looked crafty. "How do I know she's got a moral sense?"

Vining turned to Iantha. "Have you ever been in jail, Iantha?"

Iantha laughed. "What a funny question, Mark! But of course, I have not."

"That's what *she* says," sneered Connaught. "How you gonna prove it?"

"We don't have to," said Vining loftily. "The burden of proof is on the accuser, and the accused is legally innocent until proved guilty. That principle was well established by the time of King Edward the First."

"Oh, damn King Edward the First," cried Connaught. "That wasn't the kind of moral sense I meant anyway. How about what they call moral turp-turp— You know what I mean."

"Hey," growled Laird, "what's the idea? Are you trying to cast— What's the word, Mark?"

"Aspersions?"

"—cast aspersions on one of my swimmers? You watch out, Louie. If I hear you be— What's the word, Mark?"

"Besmirching her fair name?"

"—besmirching her fair name, I'll drown you in your own tank."

"And after that," said Vining, "we'll slap a suit on you for slander."

"Gentlemen! Gentlemen!" said Wambach. "Let's not have any more personalities, please. This is a swimming meet, not a lawsuit. Let's get to the point."

"We've made ours," said Vining with dignity. "We've shown that Iantha Delfoiros is a woman, and Mr. Connaught has stated, himself, that this is a woman's meet. Therefore, Miss Delfoiros is eligible. Q. E. D."

"Ahem," said Wambach. "I don't quite know—I never had a case like this to decide before."

Louis Connaught almost had tears in his eyes; at least he sounded as if he did. "Mr. Wambach, you can't let Herb Laird do this to me. I'll be a laughingstock."

Laird snorted. "How about your beating me with your Mrs. Santalucia? I didn't get any sympathy from you when people laughed at me on account of that. And how much good did it do me to protest against her fingers?"

"But," wailed Connaught, "if he can enter this Miss Delfoiros, what's to stop somebody from entering a trained sea lion or something? Do you want to make competitive swimming into a circus?"

Laird grinned. "Go ahead, Louie. Nobody's stopping you from entering anything you like. How about it, Ogden? Is she a woman?"

"Well . . . really . . . oh, dear—"

"Please!" Iantha Delfoiros rolled her violet-blue eyes at the bewildered referee. "I should so like to swim in this nice pool with all these nice people!"

Wambach sighed. "All right, my dear, you shall!"

"Whoopee!" cried Laird, the cry being taken up by Vining, the members of the Knickerbocker Swimming Club, the other officials, and lastly the spectators. The noise in the enclosed space made sensitive eardrums wince.

"Wait a minute," yelped Connaught when the echoes had died. "Look here, page 19 of the rules. 'Regulation Costume, Women: Suits must be of dark color, with skirt attached. Leg is to reach—' and so forth. Right here it says it. She can't swim the way she is, not in a sanctioned meet."

"That's true," said Wambach. "Let's see—"

Horwitz looked up from his little score-sheet-littered table. "Maybe one of the girls has a halter she could borrow," he suggested. "That would be something."

"Halter, phooey!" snapped Connaught. "This means a regular suit with legs and a skirt, and everybody knows it."

"But she hasn't got any legs!" cried Laird. "How could she get into—"

"That's just the point! If she can't wear a suit with legs, and the rules say you gotta have legs, she can't wear the regulation suit, and she can't compete; I gotcha that time! Ha-ha, I'm sneering!"

"I'm afraid not, Louie," said Vining, thumbing his own copy of the rulebook. He held it up to the light and read: " 'Note.—These rules are approximate, the idea being to bar costumes which are immodest, or will attract undue attention and comment. The referee shall have the power'—et cetera, et cetera. If we cut the legs out of a regular suit, and she pulled the rest of it on over her head, that would be modest enough for all practical purposes. Wouldn't it, Mr. Wambach?"

"Dear me—I don't know—I suppose it would."

Laird hissed to one of his pupils, "Hey, listen, Miss Havranek! You know where my suitcase is? Well, you get one of the extra suits out of it, and there's a pair of scissors in with the first-aid things. You fix that suit up so Iantha can wear it."

Connaught subsided. "I see now," he said bitterly, "why you guys wanted to finish with a 300-yard free style instead of a relay. If I'da' known what you were planning—and, you, Mark Vining, if I ever get in a jam, I'll go to jail before I hire you for a lawyer, so help me!"

Mrs. Santalucia had been glowering at Iantha Delfoiros. Suddenly she turned to Connaught. "Thissa no fair. I swim against people. I no-gotta swim against mermaids."

"Please, Maria, don't *you* desert me," wailed Connaught.

"I no swim tonight."

Connaught looked up appealingly to the balcony. Mr. Santalucia and the little Santalucias, guessing what was happening, burst into a chorus of: "Go on, mamma! You show them, mamma!"

"Aw right. I swim one, maybe two races. If I see I no got a chance, I no swim no more."

"That's better, Maria. It wouldn't really count if she beat you anyway." Connaught headed for the door, saying something about "telephone" on the way.

Despite the delays in starting the meet, nobody left the pool room through boredom. In fact, the empty seats in the balcony were full by this time and people were standing up behind them. Word had gotten around the Hotel Creston that something was up.

By the time Louis Connaught returned, Laird and Vining were pulling the altered bathing suit on over

Iantha's head. It did not reach quite so far as they expected, having been designed for a slightly slimmer swimmer. Not that Iantha was fat. But her human part, if not exactly plump, was at least comfortably upholstered, so that no bones showed. Iantha squirmed around in the suit a good deal and threw a laughing remark in Greek to Wambach, whose expression showed that he hoped it did not mean what he suspected it did.

Laird said, "Now listen, Iantha, remember not to move till the gun goes off. And remember that you swim directly over the black line on the bottom, not between two lines."

"Are they going to shoot a gun? Oh, I am afraid of shooting!"

"It's nothing to be afraid of; just blank cartridges. They don't hurt anybody. And it won't be so loud inside that cap."

"Herb," said Vining, "won't she lose time getting off, not being able to make a flat dive like the others?"

"She will. But it won't matter. She can swim a mile in *four* minutes, without really trying."

Ritchey, the starter, announced the fifty-yard free style. He called: "All right, everybody, line up."

Iantha slithered off her chair and crawled over to the starting platform. The other girls were all standing with feet together, bodies bent forward at the hips and arms pointing backward. Iantha got into a curious position of her own, with her tail bent under her and her weight resting on her hand and flukes.

"Hey! Protest!" shouted Connaught. "The rules say that all races, except back strokes, are started with dives. What kind of a dive do you call that?"

"Oh, dear," said Wambach. "What—"

"That," said Vining urbanely, "is a mermaid dive. You couldn't expect her to stand upright on her tail."

"But that's just it!" cried Connaught. "First you enter a nonregulation swimmer. Then you put a nonregulation suit on her. Then you start her off with a nonregulation dive. Ain't there anything you guys do like other people?"

"But," said Vining, looking through the rule book, "it doesn't say—here it is. 'The start in all races shall be made with a dive.' But there's nothing in the rules about what kind of dive shall be used. And the dictionary defines a dive simply as 'a plunge into water.' So if you jump in feet first holding your nose, that's a dive for the purpose of the discussion. And in my years of watching swimming meets, I've seen some funnier starting dives than Miss Delfoiros'."

"I suppose he's right," said Wambach.

"Okay, okay," snarled Connaught. "But the next time I have a meet with you and Herb, I bring a lawyer along too, see?"

Ritchey's gun went off. Vining noticed that Iantha flinched a little at the report and was perhaps slowed down a trifle in getting off by it. The other girls' bodies shot out horizontally to smack the water loudly, but Iantha slipped in with the smooth, unhurried motion of a diving seal. Lacking the advantage of feet to push off with, she was several yards behind the other swimmers before she really got started. Mrs. Santalucia had taken her usual lead, foaming along with the slow strokes of her webbed hands.

Iantha did not bother to come to the surface except at the turn, where she had been specifically ordered to come up so that the judge of the turns would not raise arguments as to whether she had touched the end, and at the finish. She hardly used her arms at all, except for an occasional flip of her trailing hands to steer her. The swift up-and-down flutter of the powerful tail flukes sent her through the water like a torpedo, her wake appearing on the surface six or eight feet behind her. As she shot through the as yet unruffled waters at the far end of the pool on the first leg, Vining, who had gone around to the side to watch, noticed that she had the power of closing her nostrils tightly underwater, like a seal or a hippopotamus.

Mrs. Santalucia finished the race in the very creditable time of 29.8 seconds. But Iantha Delfoiros arrived, not merely first, but in the time of 8.0 seconds. At the finish she did not reach up to touch the starting platform and then hoist herself out by her arms the way human swimmers do. She simply angled up sharply, left the water like a leaping trout, and came down with a moist smack on the concrete, almost bowling over a timekeeper. By the time the other contestants had completed the turn she was sitting on the platform with her tail curled under her. As the girls foamed laboriously down the final leg, she smiled dazzlingly at Vining, who had had to run to be in at the finish.

"That," she said, "was much fun, Mark. I am so glad you and 'Erbert put me in these races."

Mrs. Santalucia climbed out and walked over to Horwitz's table. That young man was staring in disbelief at the figures he had just written.

"Yes," he said, "that's what it says. Miss Iantha Delfoiros, 8.0; Mrs. Maria Santalucia, 29.8. Please don't drip on my score sheets, lady. Say, Wambach, isn't this a world's record or something?"

"My word!" said Wambach. "It's less than half the existing short-course record. Less than a third, maybe; I'd have to check it. Dear me! I'll have to take it up with the Committee. I don't know whether they'd allow it; I don't think they will, even though there isn't any specific rule against mermaids."

Vining spoke up. "I think we've complied with all the requirements to have records recognized, Mr. Wambach. Miss Delfoiros was entered in advance like all the others."

"Yes, yes, Mr. Vining, but don't you see, a record's a serious matter? No ordinary human being could ever come near a time like that."

"Unless he used an outboard motor," said Connaught. "If you allow contestants to use tail fins like Miss Delfoiros, you oughta let 'em use propellers. I don't see why these guys should be the only ones to be let bust rules all over the place, and then think up lawyer arguments why it's okay. I'm gonna get me a lawyer, too."

"That's all right, Ogden," said Laird. "You take it up with the Committee, but we don't really care much about the records anyway, so long as we can lick Louie here." He smiled indulgently at Connaught, who sputtered with fury.

"I no swim," announced Mrs. Santalucia. "This is all crazy business. I no got a chance."

"Now, Maria," said Connaught, taking her aside, "just once more, won't you please? My reputation—" The rest of his words were drowned in the general reverberation of the pool room. But at the end of them the redoubtable female appeared to have given in to his entreaties.

The hundred-yard free style started in much the same manner as the fifty-yard. Iantha did not flinch at the gun this time and got off to a good start. She skimmed along just below the surface, raising a wake like a tuna clipper. These waves confused the swimmer in the adjacent lane, who happened to be Miss Breitenfeld of the Creston Club. As a result, on her first return leg, Iantha met Miss Breitenfeld swimming athwart her—Iantha's—lane, and rammed the unfortunate girl amidships. Miss Breitenfeld went down without even a gurgle, spewing bubbles.

Connaught shrieked: "Foul! Foul!" although in the general uproar it sounded like "Wow! Wow!" Several swimmers who were not racing dove in to the rescue, and the race came to a stop in general confusion and pandemonium. When Miss Breitenfeld was hauled out, it was found that she had merely had the wind knocked out of her and had swallowed considerable water.

Mark Vining, looking around for Iantha, found her holding on to the edge of the pool and shaking her head. Presently she crawled out, crying:

"Is she 'urt? Is she 'urt? Oh, I am so sorree! I did not think there would be anybody in my lane, so I did not look ahead."

"See?" yelled Connaught. "See, Wambach? See what

happens? They ain't satisfied to walk away with the races with their fish-woman. No, they gotta try to cripple my swimmers by butting their slats in. Herb," he went on nastily, "why dontcha get a pet swordfish? Then when you rammed one of my poor girls she'd be out of competition for good!"

"Oh," said Iantha, "I did not mean—it was an accident!"

"Accident my foot!"

"But it was. Mr. Referee, I do not want to bump people. My 'ead 'urts, and my neck also. You think I try to break my neck on purpose?" Iantha's altered suit had crawled up under her armpits, but nobody noticed particularly.

"Sure it was an accident," bellowed Laird. "Anybody could see that. And listen, if anybody was fouled it was Miss Delfoiros."

"Certainly," chimed in Vining. "She was in her own lane, and the other girl wasn't."

"Oh dear me," said Wambach. "I suppose they're right again. This'll have to be re-swum anyway. Does Miss Breitenfeld want to compete?"

Miss Breitenfeld did not, but the others lined up again. This time the race went off without untoward incident. Iantha again made a spectacular leaping finish, just as the other three swimmers were halfway down the second of their four legs.

When Mrs. Santalucia emerged this time, she said to Connaught: "I no swim no more. That is final."

"Oh, but Maria—" It got him nowhere. Finally he said, "Will you swim in the races that she don't enter?"

"Is there any?"

"I think so. Hey, Horwitz, Miss Delfoiros ain't entered in the breast stroke, is she?"

Horwitz looked. "No, she isn't," he said.

"That's something. Say, Herb, how come you didn't put your fish-woman in the breast stroke?"

Vining answered for Laird. "Look at your rules, Louie. 'The feet shall be drawn up simultaneously, the knees bent and open,' et cetera. The rulcs for back stroke and free style don't say anything about how the legs shall be used, but those for breast stroke do. So no legs, no breast stroke. We aren't giving you a chance to make any legitimate protests."

"Legitimate protests!" Connaught turned away, sputtering.

While the dives were being run off, Vining, watching, became aware of an ethereal melody. First he thought it was in his head. Then he was sure it was coming from one of the spectators. He finally located the source; it was Iantha Delfoiros, sitting in her wheelchair and singing softly. By leaning nearer he could make out the words:

"Die schoenste Jungfrau sitzet
Dort ober wunderbar;
Ihr goldnes Geschmeide blitzet;
Sie kaemmt ihr goldenes Haar."

Vining went over quietly. "Iantha," he said. "Pull your bathing suit down, and don't sing."

She complied, looking up at him with a giggle. "But that is a nice song! I learn it from a wrecked German sailor. It is about one of my people."

"I know, but it'll distract the judges. They have to watch the dives closely, and the place is too noisy as it is."

"Such a nice man you are, Mark, but so serious!" She giggled again.

Vining wondered at the subtle change in the mermaid's manner. Then a horrible thought struck him.

"Herb!" he whispered. "Didn't she say something last night about getting drunk on fresh water?"

Laird looked up. "Yes. She— My God, the water in the pool's fresh! I never thought of that. Is she showing signs?"

"I think she is."

"Listen, Mark, what'll we do?"

"I don't know. She's entered in two more events, isn't she? Back stroke and 300-yard free style?"

"Yes."

"Well, why not withdraw her from the back stroke, and give her a chance to sober up before the final event?"

"Can't. Even with all her firsts, we aren't going to win by any big margin. Louie has the edge on us in the dives, and Mrs. Santalucia'll win the breast stroke. In the events Iantha's in, if she takes first and Louie's girls take second and third, that means five points for us but four for him, so we have an advantage of only one point. And her world's record time don't give us any more points."

"Guess we'll have to keep her in and take a chance," said Vining glumly.

Iantha's demeanor was sober enough in lining up for the back stroke. Again she lost a fraction of a second in getting started by not having feet to push off with. But once she got started, the contest was even more one-sided than the free-style races had been. The human part of her body was practically out of water, skimming the surface like the front half of a speedboat. She made paddling motions with her arms, but that was merely for technical reasons; the power was all furnished by the flukes. She did not jump out on to the starting platform this time; for a flash Vining's heart almost stopped as the emerald-green bathing cap seemed about to crash into the tiles at the end of the pool. But Iantha had judged the distance to a fraction of an inch, and braked to a stop with her flukes just before striking.

The breast stroke was won easily by Mrs. Santalucia, although her slow, plodding stroke was less spectacular than the butterfly of her competitors. The shrill cheers of the little Santalucias could be heard over the general hubbub. When the winner climbed out, she glowered at Iantha and said to Connaught:

"Louie, if you ever put me in a meet wit' mermaids again, I no swim for you again, never. Now I go home." With which she marched off to the shower room.

Ritchey was just about to announce the final event, the 300-yard free style, when Connaught plucked his sleeve. "Jack," he said, "wait a second. One of my swimmers is gonna be delayed a coupla minutes." He went out a door.

Laird said to Vining: "Wonder what Louie's grinning about. He's got something nasty, I bet. He was phoning earlier, you remember."

"We'll soon see— What's that?" A hoarse bark wafted in from somewhere and rebounded from the walls.

Connaught reappeared carrying two buckets. Behind him was a little round man in three sweaters. Behind the little round man gallumped a glossy California sea lion. At the sight of the gently rippling, jade-green pool, the animal barked joyously and skidded into the water, swam swiftly about, and popped out on the landing platform, barking. The bark had a peculiarly nerve-racking effect in the echoing pool room.

Ogden Wambach seized two handfuls of his sleek gray hair and tugged. "Connaught!" he shouted. "What is that?"

"Oh, that's just one of my swimmers, Mr. Wambach."

"Hey, listen!" rumbled Laird. "We're going to protest this time. Miss Delfoiros is at least a woman, even if she's a kind of peculiar one. But you can't call *that* a woman."

Connaught grinned like Satan looking over a new shipment of sinners. "Didn't you just say to go ahead and enter a sea lion if I wanted to?"

"I don't remember saying—"

"Yes, Herbert," said Wambach, looking haggard. "You did say it. There didn't used to be any trouble in deciding whether a swimmer was a woman or not. But now that you've brought in Miss Delfoiros, there doesn't seem to be any place we can draw a line."

"But look here, Ogden, there is such a thing as going too far—"

"That's just what I said about you!" shrilled Connaught.

Wambach took a deep breath. "Let's not shout,

please. Herbert, technically you may have an argument. But after we allowed Miss Delfoiros to enter, I think it would be only sporting to let Louie have his seal. Especially after you told him to get one if he could."

Vining spoke up. "Oh, we're always glad to do the sporting thing. But I'm afraid the sea lion wasn't entered at the beginning of the meet as is required by the rules. We don't want to catch hell from the Committee—"

"Oh, yes, she was," said Connaught. "See!" He pointed to one of Horwitz's sheets. "Her name's Alice Black, and there it is."

"But," protested Vining, "I thought *that* was Alice Black." He pointed to a slim dark girl in a bathing suit who was sitting on a window ledge.

"It is," grinned Connaught. "It's just a coincidence that they both got the same name."

"You don't expect us to believe *that?*"

"I don't care whether you believe it or not. It's so. Ain't the sea lion's name Alice Black?" He turned to the little fat man, who nodded.

"Let it pass," moaned Wambach. "We can't take time off to get this animal's birth certificate."

"Well, then," said Vining, "how about the regulation suit? Maybe you'd like to try to put a suit on your sea lion?"

"Don't have to. She's got one already. It grows on her. Yah, yah, yah, gotcha that time."

"I suppose," said Wambach, "that you *could* consider a natural sealskin pelt as equivalent to a bathing suit."

"Sure you could. That's the point. Anyway, the idea of suits is to be modest, and nobody gives a damn about a sea lion's modesty."

Vining made a final point. "You refer to the animal as 'her,' but how do we know it's a female? Even Mr. Wambach wouldn't let you enter a male sea lion in a women's meet."

Wambach spoke: "How do you tell on a sea lion?"

Connaught looked at the little fat man. "Well, maybe

we had better not go into that here. How would it be if I put up a ten-dollar bond that Alice is a female, and you checked on her sex later?"

"That seems fair," said Wambach.

Vining and Laird looked at each other. "Shall we let 'em get away with that, Mark?" asked the latter.

Vining rocked on his heels for a few seconds. Then he said, "I think we might as well. Can I see you outside a minute, Herb? You people don't mind holding up the race a couple of minutes more, do you? We'll be right back."

Connaught started to protest about further delay but thought better of it. Laird presently reappeared, looking unwontedly cheerful.

" 'Erbert!" said Iantha.

"Yes?" He put his head down.

"I'm afraid—"

"You're afraid Alice might bite you in the water? Well, I wouldn't want that—"

"Oh, no, not afraid that way. Alice, poof! If she gets nasty I give her one with the tail. But I am afraid she can swim faster than me."

"Listen, Iantha, you just go ahead and swim the best you can. Twelve legs, remember. And don't be surprised, no matter what happens."

"What you two saying?" asked Connaught suspiciously.

"None of your business, Louie. Whatcha got in that pail? *Fish?* I see how you're going to work this. Wanta give up and concede the meet now?"

Connaught merely snorted.

The only competitors in the 300-yard free-style race were Iantha Delfoiros and the sea lion, allegedly named Alice. The normal members of both clubs declared that nothing would induce them to get into the pool with the animal. Not even the importance of collecting a third-place point would move them.

Iantha got into her usual starting position. Beside her, the little round man maneuvered Alice, holding her by an improvised leash made of a length of rope. At the far end, Connaught had placed himself and one of the buckets.

Ritchey fired his gun; the little man slipped the leash and said: "Go get 'em, Alice!" Connaught took a fish out of his bucket and waved it. But Alice, frightened by the shot, set up a furious barking and stayed where she was. Not till Iantha had almost reached the far end of the pool did Alice sight the fish at the other end. Then she slid off and shot down the water like a streak. Those who have seen sea lions merely loafing about a pool in a zoo or aquarium have no conception of how fast they can go when they try. Fast as the mermaid was, the sea lion was faster. She made two bucking jumps out of water before she arrived and oozed out onto the concrete. One gulp and the fish had vanished.

Alice spotted the bucket and tried to get her head into it. Connaught fended her off as best he could with his feet. At the starting end, the little round man had taken a fish out of the other bucket and was waving it, calling: "Here Alice!"

Alice did not get the idea until Iantha had finished her second leg. Then she made up for lost time.

The same trouble occurred at the starting end of the pool; Alice failed to see why she should swim twenty-five yards for a fish when there were plenty of them a few feet away. The result was that, at the halfway-mark, Iantha was two legs ahead. But then Alice caught on. She caught up with and passed Iantha in the middle of her eighth leg, droozling out of the water at each end long enough to gulp a fish and then speeding down to the other end. In the middle of the tenth leg, she was ten yards ahead of the mermaid.

At that point, Mark Vining appeared through the door, running. In each hand he held a bowl of goldfish by the edge. Behind him came Miss Havranek and Miss Tufts, also of the Knickerbockers, both similarly burdened. The guests of the Hotel Creston had been mildly curious when a dark, severe-looking young man and two girls in bathing suits had dashed into the lobby and made off with the six bowls. But they had been too well-bred to inquire directly about the rape of the goldfish.

Vining ran down the side of the pool to a point near the far end. There he extended his arms and inverted the bowls. Water and fish cascaded into the pool. Miss Havranek and Miss Tufts did likewise at other points along the edge of he pool.

Results were immediate. The bowls had been large, and each had contained about six or eight fair-sized goldfish. The forty-odd bright-colored fish, terrified by their rough handling, darted hither and thither about the pool, or at least went as fast as their inefficient build would permit them.

Alice, in the middle of her ninth leg, angled off sharply. Nobody saw her snatch the fish; one second it was there, and the next it was not. Alice doubled with a swirl of flippers and shot diagonally across the pool. Another fish vanished. Forgotten were her master and Louis Connaught and their buckets. This was much more fun. Meanwhile, Iantha finished her race, narrowly avoiding a collision with the sea lion on her last leg.

Connaught hurled the fish he was holding as far as he could. Alice snapped it up and went on hunting. Connaught ran toward the starting platform, yelling: "Foul! Foul! Protest! Protest! Foul! Foul!"

He arrived to find the timekeepers comparing watches on Iantha's swim, Laird and Vining doing a kind of war dance, and Ogden Wambach looking like the March Hare on the twenty-eighth of February.

"Stop!" cried the referee. "Stop, Louie! If you shout like that you'll drive me mad! I'm almost mad now! I know what you're going to say."

"Well . . . well . . . why don't you do something, then? Why don't you tell these crooks where to head in? Why don't you have 'em expelled from the Union? Why don't you—"

"Relax, Louie," said Vining. "We haven't done anything illegal."

"*What?* Why, you dirty—"

"Easy, easy." Vining looked speculatively at his fist. The little man followed his glance and quieted somewhat. "There's nothing in the rules about putting fish into a pool. Intelligent swimmers, like Miss Delfoiros, know enough to ignore them when they're swimming a race."

"But—what—why you—"

Vining walked off, leaving the two coaches and the referee to fight it out. He looked for Iantha. She was sitting on the edge of the pool, paddling in the water with her flukes. Beside her were four feebly flopping goldfish laid out in a row on the tiles. As he approached, she picked one up and put the front end of it in her mouth. There was a flash of pearly teeth and a spasmodic flutter of the fish's tail, and the front half of the fish was gone. The other half followed immediately.

At that instant Alice spotted the three remaining fish. The sea lion had cleaned out the pool and was now slithering around on the concrete, barking and looking for more prey. She gallumped past Vining toward the mermaid.

Iantha saw her coming. The mermaid hoisted her tail out of the water, pivoted where she sat, swung the tail up in a curve, and brought the flukes down on the sea lion's head with a loud *spat*. Vining, who was twenty feet off, could have sworn he felt the wind of the blow.

Alice gave a squawk of pain and astonishment and slithered away, shaking her head. She darted past Vining again, and for reasons best known to herself hobbled over to the center of argument and bit Ogden Wambach in the leg. The referee screeched and climbed up on Horwitz's table.

"Hey," said the scorekeeper. "You're scattering my papers!"

"I still say they're publicity-hunting crooks!" yelled Connaught, waving his copy of the rule book at Wambach.

"Bunk!" bellowed Laird. "He's just sore because we

can think up more stunts than he can. He started it, with his web-fingered woman."

"Damn your complaints!" screamed Wambach. "Damn your sea lions! Damn your papers! Damn your mermaids! Damn your web-fingered women! Damn your swimming clubs! Damn all of you! I'm going mad! You hear? Mad, mad, mad! One more word out of either of you and I'll have you suspended from the Union!"

"Ow, ow, ow!" barked Alice.

Iantha had finished her fish. She started to pull the bathing suit down again; changed her mind, pulled it off over her head, rolled it up, and threw it across the pool. Halfway across it unfolded and floated down onto the water. The mermaid then cleared her throat, took a deep breath, and, in a clear ringing soprano, launched into the heart-wrenching strains of:

"Rheingold!
Reines Gold,
Wie lauter und hell
Leuchtest hold du uns!
Um dich, du klares—"

"Iantha!"

"What is it, Markee?" she giggled.

"I said, it's getting time to go home!"

"Oh, but I do not want to go home. I am having much fun.

"Nun wir klagen!
Gebt uns das Gold—"

"No, really, Iantha, we've got to go." He laid a hand on her shoulder. The touch made his blood tingle. At the same time, it was plain that the remains of Iantha's carefully husbanded sobriety had gone. That last race in fresh water had been like three oversized Manhattans. Through Vining's head ran a paraphrase of an old song:

"What shall we do with a drunken mermaid
At three o'clock in the morning?"

"Oh, Markee, always you are so serious when people are 'aving fun. But if you say please I will come."

"Very well, please come. Here, put your arm around my neck, and I'll carry you to your chair."

Such, indeed was Mark Vining's intention. He got one hand around her waist and another under her tail. Then he tried to straighten up. He had forgotten that Iantha's tail was a good deal heavier than it looked. In fact, that long and powerful structure of bone, muscle, and cartilage ran the mermaid's total weight up to the surprising figure of over two hundred and fifty pounds. The result of his attempt was to send himself and his burden headlong into the pool. To the spectators it looked as though he had picked Iantha up and then deliberately dived in with her.

He came up and shook the water out of his head. Iantha popped up in front of him.

"So!" she gurgled. "You are 'aving fun with Iantha! I think you are serious, but you want to play games! All right, I show you!" She brought her palm down smartly, filling Vining's mouth and nose with water. He struck out blindly for the edge of the pool. He was a powerful swimmer, but his street clothes hampered him. Another splash cascaded over his luckless head. He got his eyes clear in time to see Iantha's head go down and her flukes up.

"Markeeee!" The voice was behind him. He turned, and saw Iantha holding a large black block of soft rubber. This object was a plaything for users of the Hotel Creston's pool, and it had been left lying on the bottom during the meet.

"Catch!" cried Iantha gaily, and let drive. The block took Vining neatly between the eyes.

The next thing he knew, he was lying on the wet concrete. He sat up and sneezed. His head seemed to be full of ammonia. Louis Connaught put away the smelling-salts bottle, and Laird shoved a glass containing a snort of whiskey at him. Beside him was Iantha, sitting on her curled tail. She was actually crying.

"Oh, Markee, you are not dead? You are all right? Oh, I am so sorry! I did not mean to 'it you."

"I'm all right, I guess," he said thickly. "Just an accident. Don't worry."

"Oh, I am so glad!" She grabbed his neck and gave it a hug that made its vertebrae creak alarmingly.

"Now," he said, "if I could dry out my clothes. Louie, could you—uh—"

"Sure," said Connaught, helping him up. "We'll put your clothes on the radiator in the men's shower room, and I can lend you a pair of pants and a sweatshirt while they're drying."

When Vining came out in his borrowed garments, he had to push his way through the throng that crowded the starting end of the pool room. He was relieved to note that Alice had disappeared. In the crowd, Iantha was holding court in her wheel chair. In front of her stood a large man in a dinner jacket and a black cloak, with his back to the pool.

"Permit me," he was saying. "I am Joseph Clement. Under my management, nothing you wished in the way of a dramatic or musical career would be beyond you. I heard you sing, and I know that with but little training, even the doors of the Metropolitan would fly open at your approach."

"No, Mr. Clement. It would be nice, but tomorrow I 'ave to leave for 'ome." She giggled.

"But my dear Miss Delfoiros—where is your home, if I may presume to ask?"

"Cyprus."

"Cyprus? Hm-m-m—let's see, where's that?"

"You do not know where Cyprus is? You are not a nice man. I do not like you. Go away."

"Oh, but my dear, dear Miss Del—"

"Go away, I said. Scram."

"But—"

Iantha's tail came up and lashed out, catching the cloaked man in the solar plexus.

Little Miss Havranek looked at her teammate Miss Tufts, as she prepared to make her third rescue of the evening. "Poisonally," she said, "I am getting damn sick of pulling dopes out of this pool."

The sky was just turning gray the next morning when Laird drove his huge old limousine out into the driveway of his house in the Bronx. The wind was driving a heavy rain almost horizontally.

He got out and helped Vining carry Iantha into the car. Vining got in the back with the mermaid. He spoke into the voice tube: "Jones Beach, Chauncey."

"Aye, aye, sir," came the reply. "Listen, Mark, you sure we remembered everything?"

"I made a list and checked it." He yawned. "I could have done with some more sleep last night. Are you sure you won't fall asleep at the wheel?"

"Listen, Mark, with all the coffee I got sloshing around in me, I won't get to sleep for a week."

"We certainly picked a nice time to leave."

"I know we did. In a coupla hours, the place'll be covered six deep with reporters. If it weren't for the weather, they might be arriving now. When they do, they'll find the horse has stolen the stable door—that isn't what I mean, but you get the idea. Listen, you better pull down some of those curtains until we get out on Long Island."

"Righto, Herb."

Iantha spoke up in a small voice. "Was I very bad last night when I was drunk, Mark?"

"Not very. At least, not worse than I'd be if I went swimming in a tank of sherry."

"I am so sorry—always I try to be nice, but the fresh water gets me out of my head. And that poor Mr. Clement, that I pushed in the water—"

"Oh, he's used to temperamental people. That's his business. But I don't know that it was such a good idea on the way home to stick your tail out of the car and biff that cop under the chin with it."

She giggled. "But he looked so surprised!"

"I'll say he did! But a surprised cop is sometimes a tough customer."

"Will that make trouble for you?"

"I don't think so. If he's a wise cop, he won't report it at all. You know how the report would read: 'Attacked by mermaid at corner Broadway and Ninety-eighth Street, 11:45 P.M.' And *where* did you learn the unexpurgated version of 'Barnacle Bill the Sailor'?"

"A Greek sponge diver I met in Florida told me. 'E is a friend of us mer-folk, and he taught me my first English. 'E used to joke me about my Cypriot accent when we talked Greek. It is a pretty song, is it not?"

"I don't think 'pretty' is exactly the word I'd use."

" 'Oo won the meet? I never did 'ear."

"Oh, Louie and Herb talked it over, and decided they'd both get so much publicity out of it that it didn't much matter. They're leaving it up to the A. A. U., who will get a first-class headache. For instance, we'll claim we didn't foul Alice, because Louie had already disqualified her by his calling and fish-waving. You see that's coaching, and coaching a competitor during an event is illegal.

"But look here, Iantha, why do you have to leave so abruptly?"

She shrugged. "My business with 'Erbert is over, and I promised to be back to Cyprus for my sister's baby being born."

"You don't lay eggs? But of course you don't. Didn't I just prove last night you were mammals?"

"Markee, what an idea! Anyway, I do not want to stay around. I like you and I like 'Erbert, but I do not like living on land. You just imagine living in water for yourself, and you get an idea. And if I stay, the newspapers come, and soon all New York knows about me. We mer-folk do not believe in letting the land men know about us."

"Why?"

"We used to be friends with them sometimes, and always it made trouble. And now they 'ave guns and go around shooting things a mile away, to collect them. My great-uncle was shot in the tail last year by some aviator man who thought he was a porpoise or something. We don't like being collected. So when we see a boat or an airplane coming, we duck down and swim away quick."

"I suppose," said Vining slowly, "that that's why there were plenty of reports of mer-folk up to a few centuries ago, and then they stopped, so that now people don't believe they exist."

"Yes. We are smart, and we can see as far as the land men can. So you do not catch us very often. That is why this business with 'Erbert, to buy ten thousand bathing caps for the mer-folk, 'as to be secret. Not even his company will know about it. But they will not care if they get their money. And we shall not 'ave to sit on rocks drying our 'air so much. Maybe later we can arrange to buy some good knives and spears the same way. They would be better than the shell things we use now."

"I suppose you get all these old coins out of wrecks?"

"Yes. I know of one just off—no, I must not tell you. If the land men know about a wreck, they come with divers. Of course, the very deep ones we do not care about, because we cannot dive down that far. We 'ave to come up for air, like a whale."

"How did Herb happen to suck you in on that swimming meet?"

"Oh, I promised him when he asked—when I did not know 'ow much what-you-call-it fuss there would be. When I found out, he would not let me go back on my promise. I think he 'as a conscience about that, and that is why he gave me that nice fish spear."

"Do you ever expect to get back this way?"

"No, I do not think so. We 'ad a committee to see about the caps, and they chose me to represent them. But now that is arranged, and there is no more reason for me going out on land again."

He was silent for a while. Then he burst out: "Damn it all, Iantha, I just can't believe that you're starting off this morning to swim the Atlantic, and I'll never see you again."

She patted his hand. "Maybe you cannot, but that is so. Remember, friendships between my folk and yours always make people un'appy. I shall remember you a long time, but that is all there will ever be to it."

He growled something in his throat, looking straight in front of him.

She said: "Mark, you know I like you, and I think you like me. 'Erbert 'as a moving-picture machine in his house, and he showed me some pictures of 'ow the land folk live.

"These pictures showed a custom of the people in this country, when they like each other. It is called—kissing, I think. I should like to learn that custom."

"Huh? You mean *me?*" To a man of Vining's temperament, the shock was almost physically painful. But her arms were already sliding around his neck. Presently twenty firecrackers, six Roman candles, and a skyrocket seemed to go off inside him.

"Here we are, folks," called Laird. Getting no response, he repeated the statement more loudly. A faint and unenthusiastic "Yeah" came through the voice tube.

Jones Beach was bleak under the lowering March clouds. The wind drove the rain against the car windows.

They drove down the beach road a way, till the tall tower was lost in the rain. Nobody was in sight.

The men carried Iantha down on the beach and brought the things she was taking. These consisted of a boxful of cans of sardines, with a strap to go over the shoulders; a similar but smaller container with her personal belongings, and the fish spear, with which she might be able to pick up lunch on the way.

Iantha peeled off her land-woman's clothes and pulled on the emerald bathing cap. Vining, watching her with the skirt of his overcoat whipping about his legs, felt as if his heart was running out of his damp shoes onto the sand.

They shook hands, and Iantha kissed them both. She squirmed down the sand and into the water. Then she was gone. Vining thought he saw her wave back from the crest of a wave, but in that visibility he couldn't be sure.

They walked back to the car, squinting against the drops. Laird said: "Listen, Mark, you look as if you'd just taken a right to the button."

Vining merely grunted. He had gotten in front with Laird and was drying his glasses with his handkerchief, as if that were an important and delicate operation.

"Don't tell me you're hooked?"

"So what?"

"Well, I suppose you know there's absolutely nothing you can do about it."

"Herb!" Vining snapped angrily. "Do you have to point out the obvious?"

Laird, sympathizing with his friend's feelings, did not take offense. After they had driven a while, Vining spoke on his own initiative. "That," he said, "is the only woman I've ever known that made me feel at ease. I could talk to her."

Later, he said, "I never felt so damn mixed up in my life. I doubt whether anybody else ever did, either. Maybe I ought to feel relieved it's over. But I don't."

Pause. Then: "You'll drop me in Manhattan on your way back, won't you?"

"Sure, anywhere you say. Your apartment?"

"Anywhere near Times Square will do. There's a bar there I like."

So, thought Laird, at least the normal male's instincts were functioning correctly in the crisis.

The Hardwood Pile

THIS IS A world wherein virtue often goes unrewarded. If R. B. Wilcox had not been such a moral man, he might have gotten the true story of the haunted woodpile for his book on the lore and legends of upstate New York. Mr. Wilcox's morals, alone, were not responsible for his failure to get the inside dope. There was also the fact that carroty-red hair did not appeal to him.

The hair belonged to Miss Aceria Jones, the hostess at The Pines. This was a self-styled tea room in the village of Gahato, county of Herkimer, State of New York. The Pines, despite the misleading sobriquet of "tea room," served liquor of all degrees of hardness and had a passable dance orchestra. Not the least of its attractions was Miss Aceria Jones. She was an uncommonly pretty girl, looking rather like a plane hostess.

R. B. Wilcox had landed at The Pines in the course of his prowl around the country after lore and legends. After dinner he tried to collect some material. The restaurateur, a Mr. Earl Delacroix, was out; so the writer tackled Miss Jones. She gave him a little lore on the theory and practice of hostessing in an Adirondack sawmill town, but nothing that could be called a legend. To his questions about the haunted woodpile, she replied that she paid no attention to such silly stories.

In the hope of squeezing a little usable copy out of

his charming questionee, Wilcox tried praise: "I'm surprised that you live up here in the sticks. I should think with your looks you could get a job in the city."

"You mean Utica?"

"New York."

"No, I would not like that. No trees."

"You're crazy about trees?"

"Well, some trees. If there was a job in a place with a Norway maple in front of it, I would take it at once."

"A what in front of the place?"

"A Norway maple—*Acer platanoides*. Do you know of a place that has one such?"

"Why . . . uh . . . no. But I don't know much about trees. Is that a native species?"

"No, a European."

"Wouldn't another species do?"

"No; it must be that. I cannot explain. But, Mr. Wilcox, it would mean much to me." She rolled her large eyes meltingly at him.

Wilcox's morals began to assert themselves. He said stiffly: "I'm afraid I don't know what *I* could do for you."

"You could find a nice, clean place that has a job open, and a Norway maple growing in front of it. If you did, I would like you very, *very* much." Another roll of the optics.

At the second "very," Wilcox could fairly feel his morals tugging him toward the door. He, or rather his morals, may have been doing Miss Jones an injustice. But he did not stay to investigate this melancholy redhead's passion for Norway maples, or her definition of "very." He paused only long enough to assure Miss Jones that he would let her know if he heard of anything. Then he passed out of the restaurant and out of this tale.

To get a proper perspective, we must go back to 1824. In that year there landed in New York a dark, paunchy, dignified man who said he was August Rudli of Zürich, Switzerland. He was, he said, a member of an old Swiss banking family, and also related to the Wittelsbachs, so that he was about forty-third in line for the Bavarian throne. He had been a colonel under Napoleon—he had a medal to prove it—and, finding the banking business too stuffy, had taken his share of the family fortune and come to America.

But it must be recorded that Herr Rudli's story contained one or two inexactitudes. He was related neither to the Wittelsbachs nor to any family of bankers. He had seen no military service; the medal was a phony. He had been in the banking business, but not in the way he had said. He had risen by sheer merit to the post of cashier. Thereupon, on a dark and stormy night, he had walked off with all the assets not securely nailed down.

As people were seldom if ever extradited across the Atlantic in those days, at least for embezzlement, Herr Rudli might have enjoyed the fruits of his enterprise for years, if he had not fallen in with an even slicker article. This article, one John A. Spooner, separated Rudli from most of his cash for a "country estate" consisting of several thousand acres of granite ridges, bog holes, and black flies in the Adirondacks. Rudli spent most of the rest in having a road run in, a biggish house built, and gewgaws imported from Europe to furnish the house. Among the more puzzling importations were two young Norway maples, which were planted in front of the house. Rudli's tract was already covered by a dense mixed forest consisting partly of sugar maple, red maple, and silver maple, the first of which grow at least as large and as fast as any European maple. But Rudli had his own ideas about being a country gentleman, and the planting of imported trees evidently formed part of them.

Rudli never learned how thoroughly he had been roodled. He died of pneumonia in the middle of the first winter he attempted to spend in his new house.

After Rudli's death, the tract went through various hands. Some of it ended up as the property of the International Paper Co.; some went to the State of New York; the piece on which Rudli's house had stood went to a man named Delahanty. After a century of neglect, all that could be seen of the house was a broad, low mound covered with leaf mold, from which one stone chimney stuck up. The clearing in which the house had stood and most of the road leading to it were completely grown up. Of the two Norway maples, one had died in infancy. The other was now a fine, big tree.

Delahanty the elder sold his pulpwood stumpage in 1903. Thirty-five years later, Delahanty the younger sold the hardwood on the tract. In went the lumberjacks through the snow, and down came the beeches, birches, and hard maples. Down, too, came Rudli's surviving Norway maple, mistaken for a sugar maple, the "hard" maple of the lumberman.

In due course, the two logs that had been cut from this tree arrived in the hot pond of Dan Pringle's sawmill at Gahato. The name of the village is Mohawk for "log-in-the-water"; very appropriate for a sawmill town. In the spring, they were hauled up the jacker chain and sawn into about nine hundred feet of one-inch boards. These were put in Pile No. 1027, which consisted of one-inch FAS hard maple. FAS—Firsts and Seconds—is the highest hardwood classification.

The following summer, Pringle got a hardwood order from Hoyt, his wholesaler, that included twenty thousand feet of one-inch FAS hard maple. The yard crew loaded the top halves of Piles No. 1027 and 1040 into a box car. The foreman, Joe Larochelle, ordered them to transfer the remaining half of Pile 1027 to Pile 1040. So Henri Michod lowered himself from the hardwood tramway to the top of Pile No. 1027. He picked up a board and handed it to Olaf Bergen, who turned and plunked it on a lumber truck, which stood on the tramway with its wheels chocked. Bergen took his pipe out long enough to spit—aiming between the tramway and the pile—steered the pipe back through the mossy curtain of yellow hair that hung from his upper lip, grabbed the next board, and so forth. When Michod had finished the topmost course of boards, he gathered up the stickers—the one-by-two's that keep the courses apart—piled them on the tramway, and went on to the next course.

That was all very well. But when Michod started on the fourth course, the pile began to sway. First it swayed east and west, then north and south, then with a circular motion. It also set up a dismal moaning and squeaking as board and stickers rubbed together.

Olaf Bergen stared in childish wonder at the phenomenon. "Hey, Henri, what the Holy Jumping Judas you doing with that pile?"

"Me?" cried the harassed Michod. "I don't do nothing. It does it. Earthquake, maybe. I think I get the hell off." He jumped off the pile on a lower one with a clatter.

"Can't be no earthquake," Bergen called down to him. "You don't see the other piles actin' up, do you?"

"No."

"Well, if it was an earthquake, the other piles would have swayed, too, wouldn't they? So there wasn't no earthquake. Stands to reason, don't it?"

"Yeah? Then what makes the pile sway?"

"Nothin'. An earthquake's the only thing that could, and there wasn't no earthquake. So the pile didn't sway. Now get back up and gimme some more boards."

"So the pile didn't sway, huh? *Les nuts,* Mr. Bergen. I know better. And, by damn, I don't get back up there."

"Aw, come on, Henri. Stands to reason it must have been your imagination."

"All right, you stand on the pile then. I take the tramway." Michod swarmed up onto the trestle. Bergen, looking confident, jumped down onto No. 1027.

But No. 1027 had its own ideas, if lumber piles can be said to have ideas. The pile began to sway again. Bergen, staggering to keep his balance, perforce had to sway, too. And with each sway his china-blue eyes got bigger.

The motion was not a very unpleasant or difficult one; in fact, it was rather like that of the deck of a ship in a stiff breeze. But that did not calm Olaf Bergen. The trouble was that this lumber pile was not the deck of a ship. Lumber piles do not, normally, act that way. A pile that does so is unnatural, perhaps unholy. Olaf Bergen wanted no part of such a pile; not even a splinter.

So he shrieked: "The damn thing's haunted!" and tumbled off even more quickly than Michod had done. There was a brief swishing of his work shoes through the weeds, and the lumber yards knew him no more, at least not that day.

Henri Michod sat down on the tramway and took out a pack of cigarettes. He would have to report this singular occurrence to Joe Larochelle, but that was no reason for not relaxing a little first.

Then he heard Larochelle's quick footsteps coming down the tramway and put away his cigarettes. Nobody walked quite so fast as Larochelle. He always arrived places slightly out of breath, and when he talked his sentences fell over one another. By these means he created an illusion of being an intensely busy man, passionately devoted to his employer's interests. Medium-sized, baldish, and snaggle-toothed, he trotted up and gasped: "Wh-where . . . where's Ole?"

"Ole?" replied Michod. "He's gone home."

"You mean to say that lousy guy went home without saying anything to me and here I've got three cars of grain-door board to get loaded in time for the noon freight?"

"That's it, Joe."

"Was he sick?"

"Maybe. He got kind of upset when this pile began to sway under him."

"Well, of all the lousy tricks! You wait here; I'll send Jean Camaret over from the pine tram. What the hell kind of a place does he think this is, anyhow?"—and Larochelle was off again.

Presently Jean Camaret appeared. He was older and even beefier than Henri Michod, who was pretty beefy himself. Between themselves they spoke Canuck French, which is not quite the same as French French.

More than one Frenchman has indignantly denied that it is French at all.

Camaret got on Pile No. 1027. Before he had time to do more, the pile began to sway again. Camaret looked up. "Is it that I am dizzy, or is it that this sacred pile shakes herself?"

"The pile shakes herself, I think. It is a thing most extraordinary. It is not the wind, and it is not the earthquake. But it makes nothing. Give me a board just the same."

Camaret was, through no desire of his own, giving a first-rate imitation of a reed in a gale, but anyone could see that his heart was not in the part. He was not suited to it. There was nothing reedlike about him. He spread his feet to brace himself, made a fumbling effort to pick up a board, then turned a large, red, joyless face up to Michod.

"I cannot move," he said. "This unhappy pile gives me the sickness of the sea. Aid me to mount, my old."

His old helped him on the tramway. He sat down, put his head in his hands, and groaned like a soul in purgatory.

Michod grinned unsympathetically. At this rate, he would get a day's pay for doing no work at all. He started to take out his cigarettes again, but Joe Larochelle bustled down the tramway. "Wh-what . . . what's the matter with Jean? Is he sick or something?"

Camaret groaned again, more horribly. "I have the sick to the stomach. The pile goes *comme ci—comme ça.*"

"Whaddya mean the pile goes this way and that way? What the hell's the matter with you? Scared because a pile sways a little?"

"This pile is different. You get on and see."

"Huh! Never thought I'd see a grown man like you scared of a little pile. What the hell, I'm not scared—" And Larochelle hopped off the tramway. The pile began its rocking-chair act. Larochelle yelped and scrambled back on the trestle.

"Anybody can see that pile ain't safe!" he bawled.

"Must be the foundation beams are gone all to hell. Why the hell didn't you tell me sooner, Henri? Want us to break our necks?"

Henri Michod knew better than to argue. He grinned cynically and shrugged.

Larochelle concluded: "Well, anyway, you guys go over and help on the pine tram. Come back here at one."

When Camaret and Michod returned to Pile No. 1027 after the noon hour, they saw that Larochelle had tied it to the neighboring piles with a half-inch rope. He explained: "The foundation beams are okay; I don't see what the hell's wrong unless the supports are high in the middle so she's—whatcha call it?—unstable. But she ought to hold still with all this guying."

Neither yard worker showed any enthusiasm for getting back on the pile. Finally Larochelle shouted: "Damn it, Henri, you get on that pile or I'll put you on the soda tank!"

So Michod got, albeit sullenly. Larochelle referred to the tank of preserving solution in which freshly sawn pine planks were dunked. In pulling boards out of this tank, one had to move quickly to keep the next board from hitting one, and the solution made one's hands crack after a day. Larochelle's favorite method of settling arguments was to threaten to put a man on the disagreeable tank job out of his regular turn.

They loaded the truck, pushed it down to Pile No. 1040, and unloaded it. When this had been done twice, Larochelle put another man on the job, to stand on the edge of the pile and pass boards up. No. 1027 groaned and creaked a good deal, but the guying kept it from doing its hula.

The new man, Edward Gallivan, picked up a board and handed it to Michod, who passed it up to Camaret. Gallivan had picked up another board, when the first board twisted itself out of Camaret's hands. It flew back down, landing on Gallivan's board. Thus Camaret found himself boardless, while Gallivan had two boards.

Now Edward Gallivan liked mill-yard work well

enough, but not to the point of collecting hard-maple planks for the fun of it. He cried:

"Hey, Frenchy, watch what you're doin'! You damn near took the head off me with that thing."

Camaret muttered something apologetic and looked puzzled. Michod passed the errant board up again. Again it twisted itself away from Camaret and returned to the pile with a clatter.

Camaret looked down with an expression of perplexity, suspicion, reproach, and growing alarm. That is, he would have looked that way if the human face were capable of expressing so many emotions at once. "Henri," he said, "did you grab that board away from me?"

"Why would I go grabbing boards away from you? I got enough boards already."

"I don't ask that. Did you snatch her?"

"No, by damn, I didn't. I ain't no board-snatcher."

"Now, boys," said Gallivan, "we ain't getting nowheres arguin' like this. You do it over and I'll watch."

So Michod passed the board up a third time. When Camaret took it, it swung wildly and twisted like a live thing. Camaret released it to keep from being pulled off the tramway, and it floated gently back to the place from which Gallivan had picked it. "Saints preserve us!" cried Gallivan. "I don't like that."

Michod folded his arms triumphantly. "You satisfied, Jean? I didn't have nothing to do with that."

Camaret replied hollowly: "Me, I am satisfied. I am satisfied too much. I get the sick to the stomach when I think of that. You tell Joe I go. I go home, get drunk, beat my wife, forget all about these damn boards."

Joe Larochelle blew up when the state of affairs was explained to him. Ned Gallivan smiled paternally, and Henri Michod shrugged. Larochelle had recently turned in a certain credit slip for eight hundred feet of No. 1 Common Birch, of which the local customer had not returned all the allegedly unused lumber. Maybe it was a bona fide mistake; maybe Larochelle had not split the proceeds of the discrepancy with the customer. But Gallivan and Michod knew about the slip and were pretty sure of their own positions in consequence.

Finally Larochelle yelled: "All right, all right! I'll show you how to handle these jumping boards. You wait here—" When he returned he carried a double-bitted ax. "Now," he said, "Henri, you hand a board to Ned."

When Gallivan took the board, it apparently tried to pull him off the trestle. Larochelle, standing beside him, smacked the board with the flat of the ax. It quivered a bit and subsided.

"Ouch!" said Gallivan. "You're making my hands sting."

"Never mind that, it's the way to handle 'em. I'm the guy who has to figure everything out—" Larochelle's expedient seemed to have cowed the boards, temporarily at least. They went up without protest.

Michod thought, that was just like the stupid, pretending that nothing was wrong. Anybody could see that here was something of the most extraordinary. That was the way of the world. The stupids like Larochelle had the authority, while the intelligents like himself . . .

This reverie was interrupted by another singular occurrence. Michod carelessly shot a board up to Gallivan when the latter was busy fishing his eating tobacco out of his pants pocket. Gallivan made a one-handed grab and missed. It did not much matter, for the board kept right on going. It described a graceful arc and settled cozily into its appointed place on the truck.

"Hey!" yelled Larochelle. "Don't go throwing those boards; you're liable to hit somebody."

Michod kept silent, not wanting to disillusion the others about his strength and adroitness. Gallivan caught the next board; it hoisted him a foot into the air before he stopped it.

"What the hell are you trying to do, Henri?" cried the surprised Gallivan.

It was all very well to get credit for the mill yard equivalent of tossing the caber, but to be blamed for all the vagaries of these athletic boards was something else. So Michod spoke up:

"I'm not trying to do nothing, by damn. I—" He was interrupted by finding his hands unexpectedly full of board. But the board did not stay there. It ripped his mittens in its eagerness to get up into Gallivan's hands, and thence on the truck.

Larochelle shrieked: "Stop it! Stop them!" As well try to stop a nestful of hornets by reading Jean Jacques Rousseau to them. All over the pile, boards were bouncing into Michod's uneager grasp, then flinging themselves up to Gallivan and on the truck. The load grew by leaps and even a bound or two. When they stopped, the truck was piled dangerously high. The last board took time out to thwack Joe Larochelle in passing. The foreman toppled from the tramway. As he did so he grabbed Gallivan for support. Both landed on the unfortunate Michod with a great clatter.

They picked themselves up to see the truck moving down the track of its own accord. Larochelle, who among his very modest list of virtues certainly counted energy, scrambled back onto the tramway in pursuit. The truck stopped in front of No. 1040, and its load cascaded crashingly off.

"Hey, look down!" said Michod.

The three men got down on their knees and peered over the edge of the trestle. A board had fallen off the truck during its trip and gone down between the tramway and the piles. It was now crawling after the fashion of an inchworm through the weeds. Arriving at No. 1040, it began to hump itself up the pile's side. Now and then it would be jerked upward without visible effort on its part. Its motions were like those of a rather obtuse puppy whose owner is trying to teach it tricks and putting it through them by *force majeure* when it fails to get the idea. Finally, it left the stepboards on the side of the pile and swooped up on the disorderly tangle on top of No. 1040.

Joe Larochelle did not acknowledge defeat easily. No matter how red-handed one caught him in a bit of grafting, he was as firm as an early Christian martyr and as plausible as a street map in his denials. But now he said:

"It's too much for me. You boys can go home; I gotta see the boss."

Joe Larochelle repaired to Pringle's office, which was downstairs in his home. He told his story.

Dan Pringle was a small, plump man with a large watch chain decorated with an incisor tooth of *Cervus canadensis*—the wapiti. He asked: "You been drinking lately, Joe?"

"No, Mr. Pringle. I ain't touched a thing."

Pringle got up and sniffed. "Well, I guess maybe not. Do you suppose a union organizer was back of this?"

"No, there ain't been any around. I been watching for them."

"Did you look between the piles and under the tramways?"

"Sure, I looked everywhere."

"Well, maybe. They're apt to sneak in no matter how careful you are, you know. Suppose you come back after supper and we'll take a look at these fancy boards. And bring a flashlight. We'll look around for union organizers, just in case."

Pringle and Larochelle arrived at the lumber yard as the sun was sliding down behind Gahato Mountain. Pringle insisted on creeping around the piles with his flashlight as if he were playing gangsters and G-men. He was, he explained, hoping to surprise a lurking union organizer. At Pile No. 1040 Larochelle said:

"That's her. See them boards lying in a heap on top?"

Pringle saw the boards. He also saw a young woman sitting on the edge of the pile, swinging her sandaled feet. Her green dress had obviously seen better days. About her hair, the kindest comment would be that it looked "nonchalant" or "carefree." It had apparently been red, but it had been singed off. It had grown out again but was still black at the ends and presented a distressing aspect.

"Good evening," said the young woman. "You are Mr. Pringle, the owner of the sawmill, are you not?"

"Why—uh—maybe," said Pringle suspiciously. "Who—I mean, what can I do for you?"

"Huh?" said a puzzled voice at his side. "What do you mean, Mr. Pringle?" Joe Larochelle was looking at him, ignoring the girl, whose feet were a few feet away on a level with his face.

"Why—I was talking—"

"You *are* the owner, Mr. Pringle? I have heard the men talking about you," said the girl.

"Just thinking out loud?" said Larochelle.

"Yes— I mean maybe," said the confused Pringle. "She just asked me—"

"Who's 'she'?" asked Larochelle.

"That young lady."

"What young lady?"

Pringle decided that his foreman was simply dithering and asked the girl: "You're not a union organizer, are you?"

The girl and Larochelle answered simultaneously: "I don't know what that is. I don't think so." "Who, *me?* Aw, come on, Mr. Pringle, you oughta know I hate 'em as much as you—"

"Not you, Joe!" cried Pringle. "Not you! I was just asking her—"

Larochelle's patience began to wear thin. "And I been asking you who 'her' is?"

"How should I know? I've been trying to find out myself."

"I think we're kinda mixed up. Here you talk about some skirt and I ask who and you say you don't know. That don't make sense, does it?"

Pringle wiped his forehead.

The girl said: "I would like to see you, Mr. Pringle, only without this M'sieu' Larochelle."

"We'll see, miss," said Pringle.

Larochelle spoke: "Say, Mr. Pringle, are you feeling

well? Damned if you don't sound like you was talking to somebody who ain't there."

Pringle began to feel like a rat in the hands of an experimental psychologist who is, with the best of motives, trying to drive it crazy. "Don't be ridiculous, Joe. I sound as though I were talking to somebody who *is* there."

"I know; that's just the trouble."

"What's the trouble?"

"There *ain't* anybody there, of course!"

This statement, despite its alarming implications, gave Pringle a feeling of relief. Theretofore, this maddening dispute had been like fighting blindfolded with broadswords at sixty paces. Now he had a solid point of disagreement. He said sharply: "Are you sure *you're* feeling well, Joe?"

"Sure, of course, I'm well."

"Do you, or don't you, see a girl in a green dress sitting on the edge of the pile?"

"No. I just said there ain't anybody there."

"Didn't ask you whether anybody *was* there, but whether you *saw* anybody there."

"Well, if there was anybody there I'd see 'em, wouldn't I? Makes sense, don't it?"

"We'll waive that."

"Wave what? This green dress I'm supposed to see that ain't there?"

Pringle danced distractedly on his short legs. "Never mind, never mind! Have you heard a woman's voice coming from that pile?"

"No, of course not. What gives you the idea—"

"All right, all right, that's what I wanted to know. You can run along home now. I'll do the rest of the investigating myself. No"—as Larochelle started to protest—"I mean that."

"Oh, all right. But look out the union organizers don't get you."

Larochelle grinned maliciously and trotted off. Pringle winced visibly at the last words but bravely faced the pile.

"Now, young lady," he said grimly, "are you *sure* you're not a union organizer?"

"Would I know if I was, Mr. Pringle?"

"You bet you would! I guess you aren't one, maybe. More likely an hallucination."

"Mr. Pringle! I did not ask to see you so you could call me bad names."

"No offense meant. But something's very funny around here. Either Joe or I are seeing things."

"If you have good eyes, you always see things. What is wrong with that?"

"Nothing, when the things are there. What I'm trying to find out is, are you real or am I imagining you?"

"You scc mc, no?"

"Sure. But that doesn't prove you're real."

"What do I do to prove I am real?"

"I'm not just sure myself. You could put out your hand," he said doubtfully. The girl reached down, and Pringle touched her hand. "Feels real enough. But maybe I'm imagining the feel. How come Joe didn't see you?"

"I did not want him to."

"Oh, just like that, eh? You don't want him to, so he looks right through you."

"Naturally."

"It may be natural to you. But when I look at somebody I generally see him. Let's forget that question for a while. Let's not even think about it. If I'm not nuts already, I will be soon at this rate. Just what is all this funny business?"

"I don't think it is funny to have my home broken up."

"Huh?"

"You broke up my home."

"I broke up your home. I broke up your home. Young lady— What's your name, by the way?"

"Aceria."

"Miss Aceria, or Aceria something?"

"Just Aceria."

"Oh, well, skip it. I used to consider myself a pretty

intelligent man. Not any parlor-pink intellectual, you understand, but a good, competent American businessman. But I'm not sure anymore. Nothing seems to make sense. What in the name of the great horn spoon do you mean, I've broken up your home? Did I lead your husband astray, maybe?"

"Oh, not like that. Like *that!*" She pointed to the tangle of boards behind her. "That was my home."

"Those boards? Come on, don't try to tell me some man of mine tore your house down and sneaked the boards onto the pile."

"Well, yes and no. Those boards were my tree."

"Your *what?*"

"My tree. I lived in it."

"I suppose you'll say next you were responsible for that commotion today?"

"I am afraid yes."

"Well." Others had testified to the occurrence of the commotion. Or had Pringle imagined that Joe Larochelle had told that story— No, no, no! He wasn't going to think about that anymore. "What was the idea?"

"I wanted to keep my home together. First I tried to keep the men from moving the boards. When I could not, I hurried the last ones up to get them together again."

"What *are* you? Some kind of spook?"

"I am a sphendamniad. That is a kind of wood nymph. Some people would say dryad, but that is not just right. They are oak spirits. I am a maple spirit. A man brought my tree from Austria more than a hundred years ago. Last winter your men cut my tree down. I could not stop them, because I was hibernating, I think you call it, and by the time I woke up it was too late. That is how my hair got burned, when the men burned the branches and tops. It has grown out, but I know it looks terrible. I cannot leave my home on weekdays to go to the hairdresser, for fear the men will move the boards."

"You mean those aren't real hard maple?" snapped

Pringle with sudden alertness. He climbed the side of the pile with an agility remarkable in a man of his age and girth. He looked at the boards with his flashlight. "Yeah, the grain *isn't* quite the same. Let's see; if they fooled the grader . . . I guess maybe they can go out with the rest on Tuesday."

"You mean you are going to sell these boards?"

"Sure. Just got a big order from Hoyt."

"What will happen to them?"

"Dunno. They'll be made into desks and bureau drawers and things, maybe. Depends on who buys them from Hoyt."

"But you must not do that, Mr. Pringle! My home, it will be scattered. I will have no place to live."

"Can't you set up housekeeping in another tree?"

"I can only live in Norway maples, and there are no more around here."

"Well, do you want to buy them? I'll let you have them at eighty dollars a thousand, which is less than I could get in the open market."

"I have no money."

"Well then, they'll have to go out with the rest. Sorry if it inconveniences you, but the sawmill costs alone are over seven dollars a thousand, counting insurance and depreciation."

"I do not know about such things, Mr. Pringle. I know you will break up my home so I can never get it together again. You would not do that, yes? I would like you *so* much if you did not."

She looked appealingly at him, a tear trickling down one cheek. If she had done this earlier, while it was still light, it might have worked. But all Pringle could see of her face was a dim, pale oval in the darkness; so he snapped:

"You bet I'd do that! This is business, young lady. If I let sentiment interfere with business, I'd have gone broke long ago. Anyway, I'm not convinced that you exist. So why should I give away lumber I paid good money for to somebody who's a mere hallucination, maybe?"

"You are a bad, wicked man. I will never let you send these boards away."

"Oh," he grinned through the dark. "It's to be a fight, huh? Nobody ever accused Dan Pringle of running away from a good, honest business fight. We'll see. Good night, Miss Aceria."

Pringle was as good as his word. Monday morning, he called in Larochelle and told him to load the lumber in Pile No. 1040 that day, instead of Tuesday as planned.

Michod, Camaret, Gallivan, and Bergen all looked solemn when they saw they were to work on No. 1040. But Larochelle forestalled any objections by mention of the soda tank.

So they set up the rollers. These were objects that looked like iron ladders, except that on what would be the rungs were mounted steel sleeves rotating on ball bearings. The rollers were mounted end to end on sawhorses so that they could carry boards across the tramway and across the tops of the two low piles between the tramway and the railroad spur.

Fassler, the inspector, turned the first board over with the sharpened T-piece on the end of his flexible lumber rule and made a note on his tally sheet. Gallivan, wondering if he hadn't been several kinds of fool for taking the job on Pile No. 1040, picked up the board and gave it to Michod. Michod put it on the nearest roller and shoved. *Zing!* went the rolls and away went the board.

In the normal course of events, the board should have continued its way to the box car, where Camaret and Bergen awaited it. Their mittens were outstretched to seize it, when it slowed down, stopped, and reversed its motion. *Zing!* went the rolls, but this time in reverse. Michod stared at it dumbly as it shot past under his nose, left the end of the line of rollers, and slammed down on the top of the pile.

Aceria had not been caught napping.

But Fassler knew nothing about Aceria, except for some vague talk, which he had discounted, about jumping boards. Sincc the tramway was between him and the box car, he could not see what had happened and assumed that somebody had pushed the board back up the rollers. He said so, with embellishments. He was a very profane man, though a slight, stoop-shouldered, harmless-looking one. People liked to play jokes on him so that they could stand around and admire his profanity.

Gallivan grinned at him. "Hey, Archie, will you say some more? Sure, it's as good as an education for a man to listen to you."

But the others were not so amused. Camaret and Bergen came up from the car. Camaret said: "I begin to get the sick to the stomach again."

Bergen said: "I'm damned if I'll work in a yard that's full of spooks."

Michod cocked a skeptical eyebrow. "You don't belive in those things, Ole?"

"Well, not exactly. But there's a powerful lot of queer things you don't know about."

"All right. You argue. I take a rest." And Michod sat down to enjoy a smoke.

The others explained to the incredulous Fassler. Finally, not knowing what else to do, they went back to work. Michod undertook to conduct the next board personally down to the box car. It went along reluctantly; just before they arrived, it shot forward, in one door of the car and out the other into the weeds before Camaret and Bergen could stop it.

So Joe Larochelle presently found his workers sitting on the tramway and settling the affairs of the universe. He yelled:

"You get back there and load that stuff or, by jeepers, you can start looking for another job!"

Gallivan grinned. "Sure, now, wouldn't that be a terrible thing?" He lowered his voice. "And wouldn't it be terrible, Joe, if the boss found out about that credit slip you turned in for Jack Smeed?"

"I dunno what you're talking about," said Larochelle. "But, anyway, I guess there's some other stuff you can pile."

So nothing more was done to Pile No. 1040 that day. Larochelle, if he had a soul, wrestled with it mightily. He had definite orders from Pringle, but he could not adopt the usual method of enforcing them because of the delicate credit-slip situation. By Tuesday night he worked up enough courage to report to Pringle.

Pringle snapped: "Sounds like they're getting pretty damned independent. Maybe a union organizer got next to them, after all. Let's see. I'll think of something by tomorrow, maybe."

Neither was altogether candid. Larochelle obviously could not explain why he could not get tougher with the yard crew, and Pringle could not explain about Aceria for fear of having people tap their foreheads. He was not too sure about his sanity himself. He thought of going down the line to Utica to be looked over, but he was afraid to do that for fear the doctor *would* find something wrong with his clockwork.

Wednesday morning, Pringle wandered down to the sawmill. There he saw something that filled him with dismay and apprehension. It was nothing more than an elderly, dried-up man looking at a box car standing on the end of the spur. That seems like a harmless enough combination. But the elderly man was the New York Central freight agent, and the car was one that had arrived with a carload of lime some months before. Pringle had not had any place to store the lime, had not wanted to build a shed, and had not wanted to pay demurrage on the car. So he had had the car jacked down to the end of the spur and hidden with brush. There it had stood, serving as free storage space, while Pringle unloaded at his leisure and the Central wondered vaguely what had become of their car. Now the camouflage had been removed.

"We been wondering where that car was," accused Adams, the agent.

"I guess maybe it just slipped my mind," replied Pringle lamely.

"Mebbe. Looks like you owe us about three months'

demurrage. I'll get the bill out first thing tomorra." And Adams walked off uncompromisingly.

Later, Pringle grated to Larochelle: "If I find who took that brush away, I'll kill the—"

When Larochelle departed, a woman's voice said: "I took the branches away from the car, Mr. Pringle." There she was, standing between a couple of piles.

"You—" sputtered Pringle. He got a grip on himself. "I suppose maybe you think you're smart, young lady?"

"Oh, but I *know* I am smart," she replied innocently. "I thought out that you wanted the car hidden all by myself."

"Well, if you think it's going to make any difference about those boards, you can change your idea. They're going in spite of hell or high water."

"Yes? We will see, as you said that night." And she vanished.

Pringle yelled after Larochelle: "Hey, Joe! Spot a car for No. 1040 right away. If the hardwood gang don't want to work on it, get some men from the pine gang." Hc muttered to himself: "I'll show this wood spook! Thinks she can scare me—"

But the men from the pine gang fared no better than the hardwood gang. They fared rather worse, in fact. The boards slewed crosswise on the rollers, jumped off the pile, paddled the men, and finally hit one man, Dennis Ahearn, over the head. He required two stitches in his scalp, and there were no more attempts to load the car that day.

As Ahearn himself explained: "It may be the spooks, or it may be the wood, or it may be the sap runnin', but the divil himself won't get me to touch another of them damn live boards. What you need, Mr. Pringle, is a crew of lion tamers."

Pringle was angry enough over his failure to get the car loaded. But he was a shrewd man; he would not have lasted so long as he had in the precarious Adirondack lumber business otherwise. He suspected that Aceria would try some devilment or other in retaliation for his latest attempt to load the car. Maybe there would be an accident in the mill—so he ordered extra guard rails installed around the saws. Or, he thought, he might find some morning that all the lumber trucks were at the bottom of the Moose River. True, they weighed over three hundred pounds apiece, but he was not taking any chances with Aceria's supernatural powers, whatever they were. So he hired some of the workers overtime as night watchmen.

But Aceria was not exactly stupid either. Uninformed, perhaps, as a result of living in the woods for so many centuries, but she learned quickly. So her next attack was in a quarter that Pringle had not thought of.

Mrs. Pringle, a waspish woman, was due back at Pringle's home from a visit to some relatives. There was not much pleasurable anticipation of the reunion on either side. The corrosive effect of Helen Pringle's disposition, applied over a period of thirty years, had seen to that. But whatever Helen Pringle expected, she did not expect to find a comely young woman sitting at *her* dressing table, in *her* bedroom, calmly drying a head of freshly shampooed carroty-red hair.

Aceria looked up with a quick smile at Mrs. Pringle's gasp. "Yes?" she said politely.

Mrs. Pringle's mouth moved soundlessly. Then she said: "Gug."

"I'm sorry."

"You . . . you . . . what . . . what are you doing in my room?"

It was the first time since she had been five years old that words had failed—or almost failed—Mrs. Pringle. But then, the fact that Aceria was not wearing her green dress might have had something to do with it.

Aceria, still polite, remarked: "Your room? Oh, *I* see, you are Mrs. Pringle! This is embarrassing. It was stupid of Danny not to send me away before you came back, no? But if you will leave me for a minute, I will be gone like a flash."

Thus it came to pass that Pringle found the reunion more exciting, if no more pleasant, than he had expected. Helen descended on him and demanded to know, in a voice like a band saw going through a twenty-four-inch pine log—with knots in it—who that creature was, and didn't he have sense enough to know that nobody would want an old fool like him for anything but his money, and if he had to make a fool of himself couldn't he have the decency to keep his follies out of his wife's sight, and it was a good thing she hadn't unpacked because she was leaving forthwith. Which she did.

Through this tirade, Pringle was merely bewildered until the end. As Helen slammed the door behind her he saw the light and dashed upstairs. There was nobody there, of course.

Dan Pringle started for the mill, intending to denounce Aceria up one side and down the other. But he cooled off on the way. He began to grin and arrived feeling like a triumphal procession.

He looked around to see that nobody was within hearing, and called softly: "Aceria!"

There she was, between two piles. Pringle accused: "I suppose it was you who appeared to my wife just now?"

"I am afraid yes. I do not like to interfere in the affairs of mortals. But I had to teach you not to try to move my boards."

Pringle grinned. "That's okay, little lady. Don't give it a thought. You did me a favor. If I can count on my wife staying away awhile, maybe I can really enjoy life. So better not try any more stunts, or they're liable to backfire."

"You are still determined to break up my home?"

"Yep. Might have gotten soft-hearted if you hadn't pulled all these stunts. But now that lumber's going out if it's the last thing I do."

"I warn you, Mr. Pringle. I have some more stunts, as you call them."

"Such as?"

"You will see."

Pringle's pride—at least, the quality that his competitors called his orneriness—prevented him from giving in. He could not let things go on as they were; the turmoil at the mill was costing him money every day, and he operated on a slim margin of profit. So next day he called all his mill workers together. They assembled in a silence made obtrusive by the lack of the band saw's shriek. Pringle called for volunteers for a risky job.

Those who had not experienced the athletic boards had heard about them and were not too anxious to learn more firsthand. But Pringle offered time and a half, and they had to eat. Twenty-one responded. Pringle had decided against the use of rollers. Most of the gang would simply sit on Pile No. 1040 to hold the boards down, and four men would carry each board across the intervening piles to the box car.

The boards tugged and wiggled a bit first, but Larochelle hit them with his ax and they went along. All went well until the car had been partly filled. Then there was an outbreak of yells from the car. Seconds later Michod and a man named Chisholm popped out of it, scrambled up the nearest pile to the tramway, and raced along the trestle. After them flew a short length of board. It swung this way and that, exactly as if somebody were chasing the two men and trying to hit them with it.

Pringle knew very well who was on the rear end of that piece of board, but he could not think of anything to do. While he watched, the board dropped lifeless to the tramway. Then there was a mighty clatter from the car, and most of the load of one-inch FAS maple spilled out the open car door on the side away from the piles. The boards, instead of being nice and rigid, like respectable maple planks, were writhing like a nestful of loathsome larvae. As they flopped out onto the cinders, they bent into semicircles like bows, then straightened out with a snap, and soared off toward the woods.

"After 'em!" yelled Pringle. "You, Joe! Two bits a board for every one that's brought back!"

He scrambled down and set out after his lumber as fast as his short legs would carry him. Larochelle followed. The crew's nerves, already shaken by the sight of the unnatural pursuit of Michod and Chisholm, were now completely demoralized. But a few men followed Pringle and Larochelle.

They ran and they ran, tripping over logs and falling into brooks. Eventually Aceria ran out of ectoplasm, or something, and the boards ceased their bounding flight. They were gathered up in armfuls and brought back. They were piled on No. 1040 again. The men flatly refused to enter the box car with them, where there would be no room to dodge. It took all Pringle's authority and gifts of leadership to get them to go back to work at all; the scream of the saw did not ring out over hill and pond again until after the noon hour.

After lunch, Pringle hopped about the mill yard nervously, awaiting the counterattack, which he was sure was coming. It came soon enough. A mill like Pringle's, which is not equipped for turning out little things like chessmen, accumulates a vast amount of waste. Some of the slabs and edgings can be used as boiler fuel; some can be sold locally as firewood. But there is a surplus and also a lot of useless sawdust. On the edge of the mill yard stood a pile of sawdust twenty feet high, waiting to be fed into the waste burner, a huge sheet-iron incinerator.

Presently this pile of sawdust did a curious thing. It swirled up into a whirling, top-shaped cloud, as if a whirlwind had settled on its apex. The cloud grew until there was no more sawdust on the ground, and the cloud was as big as a house. Then it swooped hither and thither about the yard. It hid the workers from each other and stung their faces. They were not encouraged when one of them pointed out that, while the cloud itself seemed to be borne on a miniature tornado, the far-off trees stood stiff in still air. They stampeded, yelling, into the sawmill. The engineer, hearing the tumult, prudently shut down the engine, and again the band saw and the edging, trimming, and slashing saws fell silent. Nobody else was silent. Pringle, rubbing sawdust out of his bloodshot eyes, could not make himself heard at all.

The cloud made a couple of tentative rushes at the mill. But Aceria's powers were apparently not equal to getting it in a lot of separate doors and windows and re-forming it inside. It hovered, teetering and swooshing menacingly, about the yard.

Many people did not love Dan Pringle, but they admitted that he had what it takes. He got the sneezing and blaspheming Larochelle and Fassler aside and sent them on an errand. They went out and ran to Fassler's car. The cloud swooped after them, but they jumped in and cranked up the windows, and off they went.

When they came back, they had two boxes full of colored sunglasses with little metal shields that made passable goggles out of them. Fassler said: "That's all there are of these things around here. We went clear up to Old Forge and cleaned out the stores. And my car stopped just before we got back. Sawdust in the carburetor."

Pringle yelled for attention. He put on a pair of the goggles, tied a handkerchief over the lower part of his face, turned up his shirt collar, pulled his hat down over his ears, and said:

"Now, if you guys have got any guts, you'll do like me and go out there and get back to work. The sawdust can't hurt you. I'm going out if I have to load the damn cars myself. Who's with me? Time and a half as long as that cloud's around."

Nobody said anything for a minute. Then Edward Gallivan mumbled something and put on a pair of goggles. Most of the others did likewise. They were, after all, a strong, tough lot, and the sight of their fat and aging boss preparing to face the cloud alone may have shamed them.

So, masked and goggled, they went back down the tramways, clutching at the piles for support as the whirlwind buffeted them and the sawdust stung every exposed inch of skin. Pringle grinned behind his handkerchief as he watched them get slowly on with their work, while Aceria's top shrieked about their ears. So, the wood spook still thought she could lick him? If this was her last stunt, he'd won, by jeepers. Or at least it was still a draw.

But it was not Aceria's last stunt. The cloud rose up and up until it looked no bigger than a marble. Everybody thought it was leaving for good, although they continued to glance up nervously at it.

Then it started down again. As it came near, they saw that it was a lot smaller and more opaque than when it had gone up. As it approached, it resolved itself into something that might be imagined by a paleontologist with the d.t.'s It looked somewhat like a pterodactyl, somewhat like an octopus, and somewhat like Fafner in "Siegfried." It had huge batlike wings and six long tentacular limbs with hands on their ends.

The shouts that had sounded on previous occasions about the yard were but as the chirp of canaries compared with the yells that now arose. As the thing glided over the yard, workers, foreman, inspectors, everybody went away. They went in straight radial lines, like droplets of mercury when a gob falls on a table top, only much faster. They jumped fences and waded neck-deep across the Moose River. Those inside the mill looked out to see what was up. They saw, and they went, too.

Pringle danced on the tramway. "Come back!" he screamed. "It can't hurt you. It's only sawdust! Look!" The monster was bobbing up and down in front of him, moving its horrid yellow jaws. He strode up to it and punched it. His fist went right through the sawdust, which swirled out in little puffs around his wrist. The hole made by his fist closed up as soon as he drew his arm back. For it was, as he surmised, merely the same cloud of animated sawdust, somewhat condensed and molded into this horrifying form.

"Look here! It's not a real thing at all! Come on back!" He passed his hand right through one of its groping limbs, which joined together again immediately.

But there was nobody to appreciate this display of nerve. Across the river, Pringle could see the rear elevation of a couple of small figures in drab work clothes, getting smaller every minute. As he watched, they disappeared into the forest. The form floated low over the site of the sawdust pile and collapsed. The pile was back where it had been, and Pringle was alone.

The thing that perhaps annoyed Pringle the most was that this time the engineer had run off without shutting down the engines, so that all the saws were whirling merrily in the empty mill. Pringle had to go down and turn the valve himself.

It was almost dark when Pringle and Larochelle appeared at the sawmill. They looked odd. Pringle was wearing, among other things, a catcher's mask and chest protector. Larochelle wore an old football helmet, several sweaters, and a lumber yard worker's heavy leather apron. Pringle carried a flashlight; Larochelle, a five-gallon can of kerosene and a gasoline blowtorch.

"What are you going to do, Mr. Pringle?" asked Aceria. She was sitting on No. 1040. Larochelle had gone off to start the water pump and uncoil the fire hose.

"Going to have a little fire."

"You are going to burn my home?"

"Maybe."

"Won't you burn up the whole yard?"

"Not if we can help it. We're going to wet down the neighboring piles first. It's taking a chance, but what the hell?"

"Why are you so determined to destroy my home?"

"Because, damn it," Pringle's voice rose, "I've had all I can stand of this business! It's cost me a hundred times the value of those boards. But I won't give in to you, see? You won't let me load the boards. Okay, they're no good to me. So I might as well burn 'em up and end this nonsense for good. And you can't stop me. Your boards are tied down so you can't crawl inside 'em and animate 'em. Joe and I are protected, so it won't do you any good to get rough with us. And your sawdust monsters won't have a chance against this blowtorch."

Aceria was silent for a while. The only sounds were the hum of insects, the slap of Pringle's hand as he hit a punkie on his cheek, the whir of an automobile on the state highway, and Joe Larochelle's distant footsteps.

Then she said: "I do not think you will burn my home, Mr. Pringle."

"Who's going to stop me?"

"I am. You were very clever and very brave about facing my magics, no? And now you say, 'Ho-ho, I have beaten all Aceria's tricks.' "

"Yep." Pringle had been making a heap of edgings and bark, well away from the pile. A loud swish in the dark showed that Joe had begun his wetting down. "Now, Joe," Pringle called, "you catch the other end of this rope. We want to tighten up on the pile as soon as we pull a couple of boards out, so the rest can't get loose."

"Okay, Mr. Pringle. Here goes." There were sounds in the semidark as the two men moved around the pile, making sure that their enterprise would suffer neither from spreading of the flames nor unwonted activity on the part of the boards.

"Very clever," continued Aceria, "but I should have remembered sooner that it is not always the most complicated magic that is most effective."

"Uh," said Pringle. He splashed kerosene over his pile of kindling and lighted it. It flared up at once into a big, cheerful flame. "No wind," said Pringle, "so I guess she's safe enough. All right, Joe, let's haul the first board out."

Aceria seemed not to mind being ignored so pointedly. As Pringle and Larochelle laid hands on the board, she said:

"You were only so-so afraid of the boards when I went into them and made them alive, no? And you stood up to my monster. But there is something you are more afraid of than the boards or the monsters."

Pringle just grinned. "Is there? All right, Joe, heave! Don't pay any attention if I seem to be talking to myself."

"Yes. Union organizers," said Aceria.

"Huh?" Pringle stopped pulling on the board.

"Yes. You would like it, no, if *I* organized your men."

Pringle's mouth dropped open.

"I could do it. I have been listening to them talk, and I know something about unions. And you know me. I appear, I disappear. You could not keep me away, like you do those men from the A.F.L. and the C.I.O. Oh, I would have a nice revenge for the burning of my home."

For the space of thirty seconds there was no sound but the breathing of the two men and the crackle of the flames. When Pringle made a noise, it was a ghastly strangling sound, like the death rattle of a man dying of thirst in the desert.

"You—" he said. And again, "You—"

"You sick, Mr. Pringle?" asked Larochelle.

"No," said Pringle, "I'm dying."

"Well?" spoke Aceria.

Pringle sat down heavily in the muck, took off his wire mask, and buried his face in his hands. "Go away, Joe," he said, and would listen to no remonstrances from the alarmed Larochelle.

Pringle said: "You win. What do you want me to do with the damn boards? We can't just leave 'em sit here until they rot."

"I would like them put in some nice dry place. I do not mind having them sold, if they are kept together until I can find another tree of the right kind."

"Let's see," said Pringle. "Earl Delacroix needs a new dance floor in his joint. But Earl's so tight he'll wait till somebody falls through the old one. Maybe if I offered him the boards at half price—or even a quarter—"

So it came to pass that, three weeks later, Earl Delacroix surprised those who knew his penurious habits by installing a new dance floor in The Pines. He surprised them somewhat less by hiring a luscious, red-haired girl as hostess. He himself was not too pleased over that innovation. But Pringle had brought the girl in personally and given her the strongest recommendation. Delacroix's mental eyebrows had gone up a bit. Hadn't Pringle's wife left him a while before? Oh, well, it was none of his business. If Pringle, who owned most of the town, wanted a—friend—employed, it was a good idea to employ the friend, without asking too many questions.

Delacroix had been particularly intrigued when the girl gave her name as Aceria; then, when he asked her full name, a whispered consultation between the girl and Pringle produced the surname of Jones. Jones, eh? Heh, heh.

Since then, Aceria has worked at The Pines. For appearance's sake, she has a room in the boarding house next door. But its bed is never slept in. Her landlady does not know that, every night, Aceria returns to the restaurant. It is dark then, and nobody is there to see her do whatever she does to merge herself with the floorboards. Probably she just fades out of sight. On these nocturnal trips, she always wears her old green dress. Or rather, it was green, but with the coming of fall it gradually turned a rich orange-yellow.

She dances divinely, and the local boys like her but find her a little odd. For instance, sooner or later she asks every acquaintance whether he knows of a place where a Norway maple grows. She is still asking, and if you know of one I am sure she would be grateful if you would inform her. . . .

The Reluctant Shaman

ONE FINE JULY day, a tourist took his small boy into a shop in Gahato, New York. The sign over the shop read:

CHIEF SOARING TURTLE
Indian Bead-Work—Pottery

Inside, a stocky, copper-colored man stood amidst a litter of burnt-leather cushions, Navajo blankets made in Connecticut, and similar truck.

"Have you got a small bow-and-arrow outfit?" the tourist asked.

"Ugh," said the Indian. He rummaged and produced a small bow and six arrows with rubber knobs for heads.

"Are you a real Indian?" the boy asked.

"*Ugh*. Sure. Heap big chief."

"Where are your feathers?"

"Put away. Only wear um for war dance."

The tourist paid and started out. At that instant, a copper-colored boy of fifteen years entered from the back.

"Hey, Pop, one of the kittens just et the other!" he called loudly.

The Indian lost his barbaric impassiveness. "What? Jeepers Cripus, what kind of mink farmer do you call yourself? I told you to shift 'em to separate cages yesterday, before they began to fight!"

"I'm sorry, Pop. I guess I forgot."

"You'd better be sorry. That be good money throwed down the sewer."

The tourist's car door slammed, and as the car moved off, the thin voice of the tourist's little boy was wafted back:

"He talks just like anybody else. He don't sound like a real Indian to me."

But Virgil Hathaway, alias Chief Soaring Turtle, was a real Indian. He was a Penobscot from Maine, forty-six years old, a high-school graduate, and—except that he did not bathe as often as some people thought he should—a model citizen.

Shortly after the departure of the tourist, another man came in. This visitor had Hathaway's distinctive muddy coloring and Mongoloid features, though he was fatter, shorter, and older than Hathaway.

"Morning," he said. "You're Virgil Hathaway, ain't-cha?"

"That's who I be, mister."

The man smiled so that his eyes disappeared in fat. "Pleased to know you, Mr. Hathaway. I'm Charlie Catfish, of the Senecas."

"That so? Glad to know you, Mr. Catfish. How about stopping over for some grub?"

"Thanks, but the folks want to make Blue Mountain Lake for lunch. Tell you what you can do. I got eight stone throwers with me. They was let come up here providing they behaved. I got enough to do without dragging them all over, so if you don't mind I'll leave 'em in your charge."

"Stone throwers?" repeated Hathaway blankly.

"You know, *Gahunga*. You can handle 'em even though you're Algonquin, being as you're a descendant of Dekanawida."

"I be what?"

"A descendant of Hiawatha's partner. We keep track—" A horn blast interrupted him. "Sorry, Mr.

Hathaway, gotta go. You won't have no trouble." And the fat Indian was gone.

Hathaway was left puzzled and uneasy. It was nice to be descended from Dekanawida, the great Huron chief and cofounder of the Iroquois League. But what were *Gahunga?* His smattering of the Iroquoian dialects included no such term.

Then there was another customer, and after her Harvey Pringle lounged in, wearing a sport shirt that showed off his strength and beauty.

"Hi, Virgil," he drawled. "How's every little thing?"

"Pretty good, considering." Hathaway felt a sudden urge to bring his accounts up to date. Young Pringle could waste more time in one hour than most men could in three.

"I finished my ragweed pulling for today."

"Huh?" said Hathaway.

"Yeah. The old man got shirty again about my not doing anything. I said, why take a job away from some poor guy that needs it? So I appointed myself the county's one-man ragweed committee. I pull the stuff up for one hour a day, heh-heh! Babs been in?"

"No," replied Hathaway.

"Oh, well, she knows where to find me." Harvey Pringle yawned and sauntered out. Hathaway wondered what Barbara Scott could see in that useless hulk. Then he listened to the noise.

It was like a quick, faint drumming, queerly muffled, as though the drum were half full of water. Hathaway looked out the screen door; no parade. Timothy weeds nodded peacefully in the breeze, and from the Moose River came the faint scream of old man Pringle's sawmill.

The noise seemed to be behind Hathaway, in the shop, like the sound of a small Delco plant in the cellar. The noise increased. It waxed, and eight figures materialized on the rug. They looked like Iroquois warriors two feet tall, complete with moccasins, buckskin leggings, and scalps shaven except for stiff crests on the crown. One squatted and tapped a three-inch drum.

The other seven circled around him, occasionally giving the loon cry by slapping the hand against the mouth while uttering a long, shrill yell.

"Hey!" barked Hathaway. The drumming stopped. "Who the devil be you?"

The drummer spoke:

"Adenlozlakstengen agoiyo—"

"Whoa! Don't you speak English?"

"Ayuh, mister. I thought if you was a medicine man, you'd talk Iroquois—"

"If I was what?"

"Medicine man. Charlie said he was gonna leave us with one while he went to Canada."

"Be you the stone throwers?"

"Ayuh. I'm chief, name of Gaga, from Cattaraugus County. Anything you want us to do?"

"Yeah. Just disappear for a while." The *Gahunga* disappeared. Hathaway thought that Charlie Catfish had played a dirty trick on him to spring these aboriginal spooks without explanation.

He brightened when Barbara Scott entered, trim, dark, and energetic. Hathaway approved of energy in other people.

"Have you seen Harvey, Virgil?" she asked. "I had a lunch date with him."

"Uh-huh," said Hathaway. "Prob'ly sleeping on somebody's lawn."

Miss Scott stiffened. "You're as bad as the rest, Virgil. Nobody's fair to poor Harvey."

"Forget it," said Hathaway with a helpless motion of his hands. When a girl toward whom you felt a fatherly affection seemed bent on marrying the worthless son of the town's leading businessman, who was also your landlord, there wasn't much a moderate man could do. "You still be having that séance tomorrow night?"

"Yep. Dan Pringle's coming."

"*What?* He swears you're a fake."

"I know, but maybe I can win him over."

"Look here, Babs, why does a nice girl like you do all this phony spook business?"

"Money, that's why. Being a secretary and notary won't get me through my last year of college. As for being phony, how about that *ug-wug* dialect you use on the tourists?"

"That be different."

"Oh, that be different, be it? Here's Harvey now; so long."

The eight *Gahunga* reappeared.

"What you want us to do for you, mister?" asked Gaga. "Charlie told us to be helpful, and by *Iuskeha,* we're gonna be."

"Don't exactly know," Hathaway cautiously replied.

"Is there anything you want?"

"Well," said Hathaway, "I got a good breeding female mink I wish somebody'd offer me five hundred bucks for."

The *Gahunga* muttered together.

"I'm afraid we can't do anything about that," Gaga said finally. "Anything else?"

"Well, I wish more customers would come in to buy my Indian junk."

"Whoopee! U-u-u-u!" shrilled Gaga, drumming. "Come on!"

The seven pranced and stamped for a few seconds, then vanished. Hathaway uneasily waited on a customer, wondering what the *Gahunga* were up to.

Earl Delacroix, owner of The Pines Tea-Shoppe, was passing on the other side of the street, when he leaped and yelled. He came down rubbing his shoulder and looking about resentfully. As soon as he started to walk, there was a flat *spat* of a high-speed pebble striking his clothes, and he jumped again. *Spat! Spat!* The bombardment continued until he hurled himself into Chief Soaring Turtle's shop.

"Somebody's shooting me with an air rifle!" he gasped.

"Bad business," agreed Hathaway.

There was another yell, and Hathaway looked out. Leon Buttolf was being driven inexorably down the street to the shop. As soon as he was inside, the bombardment overtook Mrs. Camaret, wife of a worker in Pringle's mill.

By the time she had been herded in, the streets were deserted.

"Somebody ought to go to jail for this," Buttolf said.

"That's right," said Delacroix. He looked keenly at Hathaway. "Wonder how everybody gets chased in here?"

"If I sink you have somesing to do wiz zis, Virgil, I tell my Jean," Mrs. Camaret said. "He come, beat you up, stomp you into a leetle jelly!"

"Jeepers Cripus!" protested Hathaway. "How should I make a BB shot fly out in a circle to hit a man on the far side? And my boy Calvin's out back with the mink. You can go look."

"Aw, we ain't suspecting you," said Buttolf.

"I'll walk with you wherever you be going, and take my chance of getting hit," Hathaway said.

"Fair enough," said Delacroix. So the four went out and walked down the street a way. Delacroix turned into his restaurant, and the others went about their business. Hathaway hurried back to his shop just as a pebble hit Wallace Downey in the seat of the pants.

"Gaga!" Hathaway yelled in desperation. "Stop it, blast your hide!"

The bombardment ceased. Downey walked off with a look of deep suspicion. When Hathaway entered his shop, the *Gahunga* were sitting on the counter.

Gaga grinned infuriatingly.

"We help you, huh, mister?" he said. "Want some more customers?"

"No!" shouted Hathaway. "I don't want your help. I hope I shan't ever see you again!"

The imps exchanged startled glances. Gaga stood up.

"You don't want to be our boss no more?"

"No! I only want you to leave me alone!"

Gaga drew himself to his full twenty-five inches and folded his arms.

"Okay. We help somebody who appreciates us. Don't

like Algonquins anyway." He drummed, and the other seven *Gahunga* did a solemn dance down the counter, disappearing as they came to the pile of miniature birchbark canoes.

In a few minutes Hathaway's relief was replaced by a faint unease. Perhaps he had been hasty in dismissing the creatures; they had dangerous potentialities.

"Gaga!"

Nothing happened. Calvin Hathaway put in his head.

"Did you call me, Pop?"

"No. Yes, I did. Ask your maw when dinner's gonna be ready."

It *had* been a mistake; what would he tell Catfish?

After dinner, Hathaway left his wife in charge of the shop while he went for a walk, to think. In front of Tate's hardware store he found a noisy group consisting of old man Tate, Wallace Downey, and a state trooper. Tate's window was broken, and he was accusing Downey of breaking it and stealing a fishing rod. Downey accused Tate of throwing the rod at him through the window. Each produced witnesses.

"I was buying some film for my camera in the store when bingo! away goes the winda," a witness said. "Mr. Tate and me, we look around, and we see Wally making off with the rod."

"Did you see Downey inside the window?" asked the trooper.

"No, but it stands to reason—"

"What's your story?" the trooper interrupted him, as he turned inquiringly at Downey.

"I was sitting on the steps of the bank havin' a chaw, when Wally comes along carrying that reel, and *zowie!* out comes the rod through the winda, with busted glass all over the place. If old man Tate didn't throw it at him somebody musta."

Puzzled, the trooper scratched his head. Finally, since Tate had his rod back and the window was insured, he persuaded the two angry men to drop the matter.

"Hello, Virgil," said Downey. "Why does everything screwy have to happen in this town? Say, do you know anything about those BB shot? You yelled something, and they quit."

"I don't know nahthing," said Hathaway innocently. "Some kid with an air rifle, I suppose. What was all this run-in with Tate?"

"I went down to the river to fish," explained Downey. "I had a new tackle, and I no sooner dropped it off the bridge than I got a strike that busted the rod right off short. Musta been the biggest bass in the river. Well, I saved the reel, and I was bringin' it back home when old man Tate shies a new rod at me, right through his window."

Hathaway could see how the *Gahunga* were responsible for these events; they were being "helpful." He left Downey and sauntered down Main Street, passing the Adirondack Association office. Barbara Scott made a face at him through the glass. Hathaway thought she needed to be spanked, either on account of the séances, or her infatuation with Harvcy Pringle, or both.

Returning to his shop, the middle-aged Indian noted that the Gahato Garage seemed to have an unusually brisk trade in the repair of tires. The cars included the trooper's Ford with all four tires flat. Bill Bugby and his mechanics were working on tires like maniacs.

The trooper who had handled the Tate-Downey incident was walking about the street, now and then stooping to pick up something. Presently he came back.

"Hey, Bill!" he shouted, and conferred in low tones with Bugby, who presently raised his voice. "You're crazy, Mark!" he cried. "I ain't never done a thing like that in all the years I been here!"

"Maybe so," said the trooper. "But you got to admit that somebody scattered bright new nails all over this street. And if you didn't, who did?"

Hathaway prudently withdrew. He knew who had scattered the nails.

Newcomb, the game warden, lounged into Chief Soaring Turtle's shop and spread his elbows along a counter. Hathaway asked him what he was looking so sad about.

The warden explained.

"I was walking by the bank this afternoon, when a big car drives up and a young man gets out and goes in the bank," he said. "There was a canvas bundle on the back of the car. I didn't think anything of it, only just as I get past it the canvas comes tearing off the bundle, like somebody is pulling it, and there on the bumper is tied a fresh-killed fawn."

"You don't say so?"

"Three months out of season, and no more horns than a pussycat. Well, you know and I know there's some of that all the time. I run 'em in when I catch 'em, and if it makes me unpopular that's part of my job. But when this young man comes out and I ask him about it, he admits it—and then it turns out he's Judge Dusenberry's son. Half the village is looking on, so I got to run young Dusenberry in."

"Will that get you into trouble?"

"Don't know; depends on who wins the election next fall. Now, Virgil, I'm not superstitious myself. But some of these people are, especially the Canucks. There's talk of your putting a hoodoo on the town. Some have had rocks thrown at 'em, or something, and Wallace Downey is saying you stopped them. If you can stop it, why can't you start it?"

"I don't know a thing about it," said Hathaway.

"Of course, you don't—I realize that's all nonsense. But I thought you ought to know what folks are saying." And Newcomb slouched out, leaving behind him a much worried Indian.

The next day, Hathaway left his wife in charge of the shop and drove towards Utica. As he was turning on to the state highway, Barbara Scott walked past and called good morning. He leaned out.

"Hi, Barbara! Be you still going to have your spook hunt?"

"You bet, Chief Wart-on-the-Nose."

"What'll you do if old man Pringle gets up and denounces you as a fake?"

"I don't tell my victims I'm not a fake. I say they can watch and judge for themselves. You don't believe in spirits, do you?"

"Never did. Until a little while ago, that is."

"What the devil do you mean by that crack, Virgil?"

"Oh, just some funny things that happened."

Barbara tactfully refrained from pressing for details. "I never did either, but lately I've had a feeling I was being followed," she said. "And this morning I found *this* on my dresser." She held out a slip of paper on which was scrawled:

"Don't you worry none about Daniel Pringle that old sower-puss. We will help you against him—G."

"I got an idea who sent this, but it won't do no good to explain now," Hathaway mused. "Only I'd like to see you before your séance. G'by."

Three hours later, Hathaway gave up his search through the stacks of the Utica Public Library, having gone through every volume on anthropology, folklore, and allied subjects. He had learned that the stone throwers belonged to the genus of sprite known to the Iroquois as *Dzhungeun*. They all lived in the southwest part of the state and comprised the stone-throwing *Gahunga,* the fertility-prouducing *Gendayah,* and the hunting and burrowing *Ohdowa*. But, although it was intimated in several places that the Iroquois shamans had known how to control these spirits, nowhere did it tell how.

Hathaway thought a while. Then he left the library and walked along Genesee Street to a pay telephone. He grunted with pain when he learned the cost of a call to the vicinity of Buffalo, but it couldn't be helped. He resolved, if he ever caught up with Charlie Catfish, to take the money either out of the Seneca's pocket or out of his hide.

"Give me the Tonawanda Reservation," he said.

When he got the reservation, he asked for Charlie Catfish. After a long wait, during which he had to feed the coin box, he was told that Catfish would not be back for weeks.

"Then give me Chief Cornplanter."

Another pause. Then: "He's gone to Buffalo for the day."

"Listen," said Hathaway. "Have you got any medicine men, hexers, spook mediums, or such people among you?"

"Who wants to know?"

"I be Virgil Hathaway, of the Penobscots, member of the Turtle clan and descendant of Dekanawida."

He explained his difficulties. The voice said to wait. Presently an aged voice, speaking badly broken English, came from the receiver.

"Wait, please," said Hathaway. "I got to get me a pencil. My Seneca ain't so hot. . . ."

When Hathaway was driving back to Gahato, he attempted to pass a truck on one of the narrow bridges over the Moose River at McClintock. The truck driver misjudged his clearance, and Hathaway's car stopped with a rending crunch, wedged between the truck and the bridge girders. When the garage people got the vehicles untangled and towed to the garage, Hathaway learned that he faced a four-hour, fifty-dollar repair job before he could start moving again, let alone have his fenders straightened. And the afternoon train north had just left McClintock.

That evening, Barbara Scott had collected the elite of Gahato for her séance: Doc Lenoir and his wife; Levi Macdonald, the bank cashier, and his better half; the Pringles, father and son; and a couple of other persons. Dan Pringle greeted Barbara with a polite but cynical smile. He was plump and wheezed and had seldom been worsted in a deal.

Barbara sat her guests in a circle in semidarkness to

await the arrival of her "influences." When Harvey Pringle had fallen asleep, she got out her paraphernalia. She sat on a chair in the cabinet, a thing like a curtained telephone booth, and directed the men to tie her securely to the chair. Then she told them to drop the curtain and put out the lights. She warned them not to risk her health by turning on the lights without authorization. It was not an absolutely necessary warning, as she could control the lights herself by a switch inside the cabinet.

On the table between the cabinet and the sitters were a dinner bell, a trumpet, and a slate. The chair on which Barbara sat came apart easily. Concealed in the cabinet was a quantity of absorbent cotton for ectoplasm. There was also a long-handled grasping device, painted black. Her own contribution to the techniques of this venerable racket was a system of small lights which would warn her if any of the sitters left his chair.

Soon, Barbara gave the right kind of squirm, and the trick chair came apart. The loose bonds could now be removed. Barbara moaned to cover the sounds of her preparations and chanted a few lines from the *Iliad* in Greek. She intended to have Socrates as one of her controls this time.

She was still peeling rope when she was astonished to hear the dinner bell ring. It wasn't a little *ting* such as would be made by someone's accidentally touching it, but a belligerent clangor, such as would be made by a cook calling mile-away farmhands. The little signal lights showed all the sitters to be in their seats. The bell rang this way and that, and the trumpet began to toot.

Barbara Scott had been séancing for several years and had come to look upon darkness as a friend, but now childish fears swarmed out of her. The cabinet began to rock. She screamed. The cabinet rocked more violently. The door of the false side flew open; the cotton and the grasper were snatched out. The curtain billowed. The table began to rock too. From the darkness came an angry roar as the grasper tweaked Doc Lenoir's nose.

From somewhere came the muffled beat of a drum and a long, ululating loon-cry:

"U-u-u-u-u-u-u-u!"

The cabinet tipped over against the table. Barbara fought herself out of the wreckage She remembered that her private light switch was in series with the room's main switch, so that the lights could not be turned on until the secret switch had been thrown. She felt for it, pushed it, and struggled out of the remains of the cabinet.

The terrified sitters were blinded by the lights and dumb at the spectacle of the medium swathed in loose coils of rope with her hand on the switch, her dress torn, and the beginnings of a black eye. Next they observed that the bell, slate, grasper, and other objects were swooping about the room under their own power.

When the lights came on, there was a yell and a command in an unknown language. The slate smashed down on Dan Pringle's head. While he stood blinking, glasses dangling from one ear and the frame of the slate around his neck, other articles went sailing at him. He stumbled over his overturned chair and bolted for the door. The articles followed.

When Pringle reached the street, pebbles began picking themselves up and throwing themselves after the mill owner. It took about three tries to get his range. Then a pebble no bigger than the end of one's thumb, traveling with air-rifle speed, hit the back of his thigh with a flat *spat*. Pringle yelled, staggered, and kept running. Another glanced off his scalp, drawing blood and making him see stars.

The inhabitants of Gahato were entertained by the unprecedented sight of their leading businessman panting down the main street and turning purple with effort. Every now and then there would be the sound of a pebble striking. Pringle would make a bucking jump and come down running harder than ever.

His eye caught a glimpse of Virgil Hathaway letting himself into his shop, and a faint memory of silly talk about the Indian's supernatural powers stirred his mind. He banked and galloped up the porch steps of Soaring Turtle's establishment just as Hathaway closed the screen door behind him. Pringle went through the door without bothering to reopen it.

"Jeepers Cripus!" exclaimed Hathaway mildly. "What be the matter, Dan?"

"L-l-isten, Virgil! Are you a medicine man?"

"Aw, don't pay no attention to superstitious talk like that—"

"But I gotta have help! They're after me!" And he told all.

"Well!" said Hathaway doubtfully. "I'll see what I can do. But they're Iroquois spooks, and don't think much of us Algonquins. Got some tobacco? All right, pull down the shades."

Hathaway took Pringle's tobacco pouch and opened his shattered screen door. He threw a pinch of tobacco into the dark and chanted in bad Seneca:

I give you tobacco, Dzhungeun,
Wanderers of the mountains.
You hear me and will come.
I give you tobacco.
I have done my duty towards you.
Now you must do yours.
I have finished speaking.

All eight *Gahunga* imps materialized on the lawn. Hathaway sternly ordered them to come inside. When they were in, he questioned them:

"What have you little twerps been up to now?"

Gaga squirmed. "We was only trying to do Miss Scott a favor," he said. "She wants to put on a good spook show. So we help. She don't like this old punkin Pringle. All right, we throw a scare into him. We wasn't going to hurt him none."

"You know you was let come up here for your vacations only if you don't use your stone-throwing powers," Hathaway said. "And you know what Eitsinoha does to little imps who don't behave."

"Eitsinoha?" cried Gaga. "You wouldn't tell *her!*"

"Dunno, yet. You deserve it."

"Please, mister, don't say nothing! We won't throw even a sand grain! I swear by *Iuskeha!* Let us go, and we'll head right back to Cattaraugus!"

Hathaway turned to the quivering Pringle. "Changed your mind about raising my rent, Dan?"

"I'll lower it! Five dollars!"

"Ten?"

"Seven and a half!"

"Okay. Gaga, you and your boys can disappear. But stick around. And don't do *anything*—understand?—unless I tell you to." The *Gahunga* vanished.

Pringle recovered some of his usual self-assurance and said:

"Thanks, Virgil! Don't know what I'd have done without you."

"That's all right, Dan. You better not say anything about this, though. Remember, being a medicine man is a kind of joke among us Indians, like being the High Exalted Potentate of one of those there lodges."

"I understand. So they were doing her a favor, huh? It would be bad enough to have my son marry a phony medium, but I can see where a real one would be worse. No sale, and you can tell her I said so. And Harvey'll do what I say, because he has to in order to eat."

"But—" said Hathaway. He wanted to defend Barbara Scott; to tell Pringle that even if she was a crooked medium in a mild way, she was still better than that no-count son of his.

"What?" said Pringle.

"Nahthing." Hathaway reconsidered; everything was working out fine. Barbara would get over her crush on that big loafer, finish her college, and be able to drop the medium racket. Why stir things up? "Good night, Dan."

He hadn't done badly, thought Hathaway as he locked up, considering that he had only been in the medicine-man business a couple of days. He must take a trip out to Tonawanda in the fall and look up Charlie Catfish. Maybe the thing had commercial possibilities.

The Inspector's Teeth

A.D. 2054-2088

WORLD MANAGER CHAGAS sat waiting for the Osirian ambassador, mentally practicing the brisk handshake and the glassy smile. Across the conference table the First Assistant to the Manager, Wu, chain-smoked, while the Minister of External Affairs, Evans, filed his nails. Although the faint rasp annoyed Chagas, he gave no sign, imperturbability being one of the qualities for which he was paid. The indirect lighting threw soft highlights from the silver skullcaps covering the shaven crania of the three.

Chagas said: "I shall be glad when I can let my hair grow again like a civilized man."

"My dear Chagas," said Wu, "with the hair you have, I don't see what difference it makes."

Evans put away his nail file and said: "Gentlemen, when I was a kid a century ago, I wondered what it would be like to be on the inside of a great historical moment. Now I'm in on one, I find it queer I'm the same old Jefferson Evans, and not Napoleon or Caesar." He looked at his nails. "Wish we knew more Osirian psychology . . ."

Wu said: "Don't start that Neo-Paretan nonsense again about Osirians being guided by sentiments, so we need only know which one to play on, like pressing a button. Osirians are rational people; would have to be to invent space travel independently of us. Therefore will be guided by their economic interests alone."

"Neo-Marxist tapioca!" snapped Evans. "Sure, they're rational, but also sentimental and capricious like us. There's no contradiction—"

"But there is!" said Wu excitedly. "Environment makes the man, and not the contrary."

"Do not start that, I beg," said Chagas. "This is too important to get your systems full of adrenalin over theory. Thank God I am a plain man who tries to do his duty and does not worry about sociological theories. If he takes our terms, the Althing will ratify the treaty and we shall have an Interplanetary Council to keep peace. If he insists on the terms we privately think he is entitled to, the Althing will not ratify. Then we shall have separate sovereignties, and it will be the history of our poor Earth all over again."

"You borrow trouble, chief," said Wu. "There are no serious disputes between our system and the Procyonic. Even if there were, there is no economic advantage to a war at such distance, even though Osirians have capitalistic economy like Evans's country . . ."

"Who said wars are always fought for economic advantage?" said Evans. "Ever hear of the Crusades? Or the war that was fought over one pig?"

Wu said: "You mean the war some sentimental historian without grasp of social and economic factors *thought* was fought for pig—"

"Stop it!" said Chagas.

"Okay," said Evans. "But I'll bet you a drink, Wu, that the Osirian takes our offer as it stands."

"You are on," said Wu.

A bell chimed, bringing the men to their feet.

As the Osirian came in, they advanced with outstretched hands, uttering polite platitudes. The Osirian set down his bulging briefcase and shook their hands. He looked like a small dinosaur, a head taller than a man—one of the little ones that ran about on its hind legs with its tail stuck out behind to balance. A complex pattern of red-and-gold paint decorated his scales.

The Osirian took the backless chair that had been provided for him. "A kreat pleashure, chentlemen," he said slowly in an accent they could barely understand. This was natural, considering the difference between his vocal organs and theirs. "I haff stuttiet the offer of the Worlt Fetteration and reached my tecishion."

Chagas gave him a meaningless diplomatic smile. "Well, sir?"

The ambassador, whose face was not built for smiles, flicked his forked tongue out and back. With irritating deliberation he began ticking off points on his claws:

"On one hant, I know political conditions in the Solar System and on Earth in particular. Hence I know why you hat to ask me the things you dit. On the other, my people will not like some of these things. They will consitter many of your demants unchust. I could go ofer the grounts of opchection one py one. Howeffer, since you alretty know these opchections, I can make my point better py tellink you a little story."

Wu and Evans exchanged a quick glance of impatience.

The forked tongue flicked out again. "This is a true story, of the old tays when the mesonic drive had first enapled you to fly to other stars and put your system in touch with ours. Pefore there was talk apout galactic government, and pefore you learnt to guart akainst our little hypnotic powers with those pretty silfer hats. When a younk Sha'akhfa, or as you say an Osirian, hat come to your Earth to seek wistom . . ."

When Herbert Lengyel, a junior, proposed that they bid Hithafea, the Osirian freshman, the Iota Gamma Omicron's council was thrown into turmoil. Herb persisted, glasses flashing:

"He's got everything! He's got money, and he's smart and good-natured, and good company, and full of college spirit. Look how he got elected yell-leader when he'd been here only a few weeks! Of course it would be easier if he looked less like a fugitive from the reptile house in the zoo, but we're civilized people and should judge by the personality inside—"

"Just a minute!" John Fitzgerald, being a three-letter man and a senior, threw much weight in the council. "We got too many queer types in this fraternity already."

He looked hard at Lengyel, though Herb, who would like to have punched his handsome face, was merely a sober and serious student instead of a rah-rah boy. Fitzgerald went on:

"Who wants the Iotas to be a haven for all the campus freaks? Next thing you'll find a thing like a bug, a praying mantis a couple of meters high sitting in your chair, and you'll be told that's the new pledge from Mars—"

"Another thing," said Lengyel. "We have an antidiscrimination clause in our charter. So we can't bar this man—this student, I should say—"

"Oh yes we can," said Fitzgerald, stifling a yawn. "That refers only to the races of mankind; it don't apply to nonhuman beings. We're still a club of gentlemen—get that, gentle-*men*—and Hithafea sure ain't no man."

"Principle's the same," said Lengyel. "Why d'you think Atlantic's one of the few universities left with fraternities? Because the frats here have upheld the democratic tradition and avoided snobbery and discrimination. Now—"

"Nuts!" said Fitzgerald. "It isn't discriminatory to pick folks you think will be congenial. It wouldn't be so bad if Herb had merely proposed some guy from Krishna, where they look more or less human—"

"There aren't any Krishnans at Atlantic this year," muttered Lengyel.

"—but no, he has to foist a shuddery scaly reptile—"

"John's got a phobia against snakes," said Lengyel.

"So does every normal person—"

"Nuts to you, Brother Fitzgerald. It's merely a neurosis, implanted by—"

"You're both getting away from the subject," said Brother Brown, president of the chapter.

They went on like that for some time until a vote was called for. Since Fitzgerald blackballed Hithafea, Lengyel blackballed Fitzgerald's young brother.

"Hey!" cried Fitzgerald. "You can't do that!"

"Says who?" said Lengyel. "I just don't like the young lout."

After further wrangling, each withdrew his veto against the other's protegé.

On his way out, Fitzgerald punched Lengyel in the solar plexus with a thumb the size of a broomstick end and said: "You're taking Alice to the game tomorrow for me, see? And be sure you give her back in the same condition as you got her!"

"Okay, Stinker," said Lengyel, and went to his room to study. Although they did not like each other, they managed to get along. Lengyel secretly admired Fitzgerald for being the perfect movie idea of Joe College, while Fitzgerald secretly envied Lengyel's brains. It amused Fitzgerald to turn over his coed to Lengyel because he regarded Herb as a harmless gloop who wouldn't dare try to make time with her himself.

Next day, the last Saturday of the 2054 football season, Atlantic played Yale on the home field. Herb Lengyel led Alice Holm into the stands. As usual, when he got near her his tongue got glued to the roof of his mouth. So he studied the pink card he found thumbtacked to the back of the bleacher seat in front of him. On this were listed, by number, the things he was supposed to do with a big square of cardboard, orange on one side and black on the other, when the cheerleader gave the command, in order to present a letter, number, or picture to the opposite side of the stadium.

He finally said: "D'I tell you we decided to bid Hithafea? Speak it not in Gath, though; it's confidential."

"I won't," said Alice, looking very blonde and lovely. "Does that mean that when John takes me to your dances Hithafea will ask to dance with me?"

"Not if you don't want him to. I don't know if he dances."

"I'll try not to shudder. Are you sure he didn't use

his mysterious hypnotic powers to make you propose him?"

"Fooey! Professor Kantor in psych says all this talk about the hypnotic powers of the Osirians is bunk. If a man's a naturally good hypnotic subject he'll be hypnotizable, otherwise not. There aren't any mysterious rays the Osirians shoot from their eyes."

"Well," said Alice, "Professor Peterson doesn't agree. He thinks there's something to it, even though nobody has been able to figure out how it works— Oh, here they come. Hithafea makes a divine yell-leader, doesn't he?"

Although the adjective was perhaps not well chosen, the sight of Hithafea, flanked by three pretty coeds on each side, and prancing and waving his megaphone, was certainly unforgettable. It was made even more so by the fact that he was wearing an orange sweater with a big black A on the chest and a freshman beanie on his head. His locomotive-whistle voice rose above the general uproar:

"Atlantic! A-T-L-A-N . . ."

At the end of each yell Hithafea flung out his arms with talons spread and leaped three meters into the air on his birdlike legs. He got much more kick out of the rooters' reaction to his yell-leading than the players did, since they were busy playing football. Hithafea himself had had hopes of going out for intercollegiate athletics, preferably track, until the coach had broken it to him as gently as possible that nobody would compete against a being who could broad jump twelve meters without drawing a deep breath.

As both teams were strong that year, the score at the end of the first quarter still stood 0-0. Yale completed a pass and it looked as if the receiver were in the clear until John Fitzgerald, the biggest of the fourteen right tackles of the Atlantic varsity, nailed him. Hithafea screamed:

"Fitzcheralt! Rah, rah, rah, Fitzcheralt!"

A drunken Yale senior, returning to his seat after visiting the gentleman's room under the stands, got turned around and showed up on the grass strip in front of the Atlantic side of the stadium. There he tramped up and down and bumped into people and fell over the chairs of the Atlantic band and made a general nuisance of himself.

At last Hithafea, observing that everybody else was too much interested in the game to abate this nuisance, caught the man by the shoulder and turned him around. The man looked up at Hithafea and shrieked: "I got 'em! I got 'em!" and tried to break away.

He might as well have saved his trouble. The Sha'akhfi freshman held him firmly by both shoulders and hissed something at him. Then he let him go.

Instead of running away, the man threw off his hat with its little blue feather, his furry overcoat, his coat and vest and shirt and pants. Despite the cold he ran out onto the field in his underwear, hugging his bottle under one arm and pretending it was a football.

Before he was finally taken away, the man had caused Yale to be penalized for having twelve men on the field during a play. Luckily the Yale rooters were too far away on the other side of the stadium to understand what was happening, or there might have been a riot. As it was, they were pretty indignant when they found out later, feeling that somebody had pulled a fast one on them. Especially as the game ended 21-20 favor of Atlantic.

After the game Hithafea went to his mailbox in the Administration Building. All the other frosh were eagerly pushing around the pigeonholes to get theirs, for this was the day when fraternity bids were distributed. When Hithafea softly hissed: "Excuse me, please," they made plenty of room for him.

He took three little white envelopes from his box and scooted for his room in the freshman dorm. He burst in to find his roommate, Frank Hodiak, studying his one bid. Hithafea sat down on his bed with his tail curling up against the wall and opened his envelopes, slitting them neatly along the edge with his claws.

"Frank!" he cried. "They want me!"

"Hey," said Hodiak, "what's the matter with you? You're drooling on the rug! Are you sick?"

"No, I am cryink."

"What?"

"Sure. That is the way we Sha'akhfi cry."

"And why are you crying?"

"Pecause I am so happy! I am ofercome with emotion!"

"Well for goodness' sake," said Hodiak unfeelingly, "go cry in the sink, then. I see you got three. Which you gonna take?"

"I think the Iota Gamma Omicrons."

"Why? Some of the others got more prestige."

"I do not care. I am takink them anyway, for sentimental reasons."

"Don't tell me a cold-blooded reptile like you is sentimental!"

"Sure. All we Sha'akhfi are. You think we are not pecause we do not show our feelinks in our faces."

"Well," persisted Hodiak, "what are these sentimental reasons, huh?"

"First," (Hithafea counted on his claws) "pecause Herp Lengyel iss one. He was the first man on the campus to treat me like a fellow beink. Second, pecause the kreat de Câmara was an Iota when he attendet Atlantic many years ako."

"Who's this guy de Câmara?"

"Dit you neffer know? My, some of you echucated Earthmen are iknorant of your own history! He was one of the great space pioneers, the founter of the Viagens Interplanetarias, and the first Earthman to set foot on Osiris."

"Oh. Another Brazzy, eh?"

"Yes. It wass de Câmara who prought the false teeth of our Chief Inspector Ficèsaqha back to Earth from Osiris, and gafe them to Atlantic when they presented him with an honorary degree. Pefore I leat yells at a game, I go up to the museum and gaze upon those teeth. Their sentimental associations inspire me. I am fery sentimental apout Senhor de Câmara, although some of our people claim he stole those teeth and other thinks as well when he left our planet."

At the first pledge meeting, Hithafea squatted down humbly among his fellow pledges, who looked at him with traces of distaste or apprehension. When the prospective members' duties had been explained to them, Fitzgerald and a couple of the other brothers undertook to have a little fun of the sadistic sort associated with initiations. They brought out a couple of wooden paddles, like ping-pong racquets but heavier, and fired nonsensical questions at the freshmen. Those who failed to answer glibly were paddled for ignorance, whereas those who answered glibly were paddled for being fresh.

By and by Hithafea said: "Will nopody pattle me?"

"Why, Monster?" said Fitzgerald. "D'you wanna be?"

"Of course! It is part of peink a pletch. It would preak my heart if I were not pattled the same as the others."

The brothers looked at each other with expressions of bafflement. Brother Brown, indicating Hithafea's streamlined stern, asked:

"How the hell can we? I mean, where's his—uh—I mean, where shall we hit him?"

"Oh, anywhere!" said Hithafea.

Brother Brown, looking a bit unhappy about the whole thing, hauled off with his paddle and whacked Hithafea's scaly haunch. He hit again and again, until Hithafea said:

"I do not efen feel it. Are you sure you are not goink easy on me on purpose? It would wound my feelinks if you dit."

Brown shook his head. "Might as well shoot an elephant with a peashooter. You try, John."

Fitzgerald swung his massive arm and dealt Hithafea a swat that broke the paddle. He wrung his hand, looked at the other brothers, and said:

"Guess we'll have to consider you constructively paddled, Hithafea. Let's go on to business."

The other pledges grinned, evidently glad to escape any further beating. As the brothers had been made to feel a little foolish, the fun seemed to have gone out of paddling for the time being. The brothers sternly commanded the pledges to show up at the house the following night for the Thanksgiving dance, to do the serving and messwork. Moreover they were told to bring three cats each to the next pledge meeting the following week.

Hithafea as usual showed up an hour early for his duties at the dance, wearing a black bow tie around his scaly neck in deference to the formality of the occasion. John Fitzgerald, of course, brought Alice Holm, while Herbert Lengyel came stag and hovered uneasily, trying by an air of bored superiority to mask the fact that he would have liked to bring her himself.

When Hithafea stalked in bearing a tray of refreshments, some of the girls, who were not Atlantic coeds and so had never seen him before, shrieked. Alice, mastering her initial revulsion, said:

"Are you dancing, Hithafea?"

Hithafea said: "Alas, Miss Holm, I could not!"

"Oh, I bet you dance divinely!"

"It is not that. At home on Osiris I perform the fertility tance with the pest of them. Put look at my tail! I should neet the whole floor to myself, I fear. You have no idea how much trouple a tail is in a worlt where peinks do not normally have them. Every time I try to go through a swingink door—"

"Let's dance, Alice," said Fitzgerald abruptly. "And you, Monster, get to work!"

Alice said: "Why John, I think you're jealous of poor Hithafea! I found him sweet!"

"Me jealous of a slithery reptile? Ha!" sneered Fitzgerald as they spun away in the gymnastic measures of the Zulu.

At the next pledge meeting a great yowling arose when the pledges showed up with three cats apiece, for which they had raided alleys and their friends' houses and the city pound. Brother Brown said: "Where's Hithafea? The Monster's not usually late—"

The doorbell rang. When one of the pledges opened it he looked out, then leaped back with the alacrity if not the grace of a startled fawn, meanwhile making a froglike noise in his throat. There on the doorstep stood Hithafea with a full-grown lioness on a leash. The cats frantically raced off to other parts of the fraternity house or climbed curtains and mantelpieces. The brothers looked as if they would have done likewise if they had not been afraid of losing face before the pledges.

"Goot evenink," said Hithafea. "This is Tootsie. I rented her. I thought if I prought one cat bik enough it would do for the three I was tolt to pring. You like her, I trust?"

"A character," said Fitzgerald. "Not only a monster, but a character."

"Do I get pattled?" said Hithafea hopefully.

"Paddling you," said Fitzgerald, "is like beating a rhinoceros with a flyswatter." And he set to work with a little extra vim on the fundaments of the other pledges.

When the pledge meeting was over, the brothers went into conference. Brother Broderick said: "I think we'll have to give 'em something more original to do for next time. Specially Hithafea here. S'pose we tell him to bring—ah—how about that set of false teeth belonging to that guy—that emperor or whatever he was of Osiris, in the museum?"

Hithafea said: "You mean the teeth of our great Chief Inspector, Ficèsaqha?"

"Yeah, Inspector Fish—well, you pronounce it, but that's what I mean."

"That will be a kreat honor," said Hithafea. "Pefore we go, Mr. Fitzcherald, may I speak to you alone for a moment?"

Fitzgerald frowned and said: "Okay, Monster, but hurry it up. I got a date." He followed the Sha'akhfa out, and the other brothers heard Hithafea hissing something to him in the corridor.

Then Hithafea stuck his head in the doorway and

said: "Mr. Lengyel, may I speak to you too, now?" And the same thing happened to Lengyel.

The other brothers did not listen to the conversation between Lengyel and Hithafea because they were more interested in what was happening in the parlor. John Fitzgerald came through, all slicked up in his best clothes, and the lioness tackled him and tried to wrestle with him. The more he tried to get away the more vigorously she wrestled. He finally gave up and lay on his back while Tootsie sat on his chest and licked his face. As having your face licked by a lion is something like having it gone over with coarse sandpaper, Fitzgerald was somewhat the worse for wear by the time Hithafea came back into the room and pulled his pet off.

"I am fery sorry," he told them. "She is playful."

The night before the next pledge meeting, shadows moved in the shrubbery around the museum. The front door opened and a shadow came out—unmistakably that of a big, broad-shouldered man. The shadow looked about, then back into the darkness whence it had come. Sounds came from the darkness. The shadow trotted swiftly down the front steps and whispered: "Here!"

Another shadow rose from among the shrubs; not that of a man, but of something out of the Mesozoic. The human shadow tossed a package to the reptilian shadow just as the museum's watchman appeared in the doorway and shouted:

"Hey, you!"

The human shadow ran like the wind, while the reptilian shadow faded into the bushes. The watchman yelled again, blew on a police whistle, and ran after the human shadow, but gave up, puffing, after a while. The quarry had disappeared.

"Be goddamned," muttered the watchman. "Gotta get the cops on this one. Let's see, who came in late this afternoon, just before closing? There was that little Italian-looking girl, and that red-haired professor, and that big football-type guy . . ."

Frank Hodiak found his roommate packing his few simple belongings, and asked:

"Where you going?"

"I am gettink retty to leave for the Christmas vacation," said Hithafea. "I got permission to leafe a few tays aheat of the rest." He shut his small suitcase with a snap and said: "Goot-pye, Frank. It is nice to have known you."

"Good-bye? Are you going right now?"

"Yes."

"You sound as if you weren't coming back!"

"Perhaps. Some tay. *Sahacikhthasèf,* as we say on Osiris."

Hodiak said: "Say, what's that funny-looking package you put in your—"

But before he finished, Hithafea was gone.

When the next pledge meeting was called, Hithafea, hitherto the outstanding eager beaver among the pledges, was absent. They called the dormitory and got in touch with Frank Hodiak, who said that Hithafea had shoved off hours previously.

The other curious fact was that John Fitzgerald had his right wrist bandaged. When the brothers asked him why, he said:

"Damn'f I know! I just found myself in my room with a cut on my wrist, and no idea how it got there."

The meeting was well underway and the paddles were descending, when the doorbell rang. Two men came in: one of the campus cops and a regular municipal policeman.

The former said: "Is John Fitzgerald here?"

"Yeah," said Fitzgerald. "I'm him."

"Get your hat and coat and come with us."

"Whaffor?"

"We wanna ask you a few questions about the disappearance of an exhibit from the museum."

"I don't know anything about it. Run along and peddle your papers."

That was the wrong line to take, because the city cop

brought out a piece of paper with a lot of fancy printing on it and said: "Okay, here's a warrant. You're pinched. Come—" and he took Fitzgerald by the arm.

Fitzgerald cut loose with a swing that ended, splush, on the cop's face, so that the policeman fell down on his back and lay there, moving a little and moaning. The other brothers got excited and seized both cops and threw them out the front door and bumpety-bump down the stone steps of the fraternity house. Then they went back to their pledge meeting.

In five minutes four radio patrol cars stopped in front of the frat house and a dozen cops rushed in.

The brothers, so belligerent a few minutes before, got out of the way at the sight of the clubs and blackjacks. Hands reached out of blue-clad sleeves toward Fitzgerald. He hit another cop and knocked him down, and then the hands fastened onto all his limbs and held him fast. When he persisted in struggling, a cop hit him on the head with a blackjack and he stopped.

When he came to and calmed down, on the way to the police station, he asked: "What the hell is this all about? I tell you, I never stole nothing from a museum in my whole life!"

"Oh yes you did," said a cop. "It was the false teeth of one of them things from another planet. O'Riley, I think they call it. You was seen going into the museum around closing time, and you left your fingerprints all over the glass case when you busted it. Boy, this time we'll sure throw the book at you! Damn college kids, think they're better than other folks. . . ."

Next day Herbert Lengyel got a letter:

Dear Herb:

When you read this I shall be enroute to Osiris with the teeth of Chief Inspector Ficèsaqha, one of our greatest heroes. I managed to get a berth on a ship leaving for Pluto, whence I shall proceed to my own system on an Osirian intersteller liner.

When Fitzgerald suggested I steal the teeth, the temptation to recover this relic, originally stolen by de Câmara, was irresistible. Not being an experienced burglar, I hypnotized Fitzgerald into doing the deed for me. Thus I killed three birds with one stone, as you Earthmen say. I got the teeth; I got even with Fitzgerald for his insults; and I got him in Dutch to give you a clear field with Miss Holm.

I tell you this so you can save him from being expelled, as I do not think he deserves so harsh a penalty. I also gave you the Osirian hypnosis to remove some of your inhibitions, so you shall be able to handle your end of the project.

I regret not having finished my course at Atlantic and not being finally initiated into Iota Gamma Omicron. However, my people will honor me for this deed, as we admire the refined sentiments.

Fraternally,

Hithafea

Lengyel put the letter away and looked at himself in the mirror. He now understood why he had felt so light, daring, and self-confident the last few hours. Not like his old self at all. He grinned, brushed back his hair, and started for the house phone to call Alice.

"So, chentlemen," said Hithafea, "now you unterstant why I have decidet to sign your agreement as it stants. I shall perhaps be criticized for giffink in to you too easily. But you see, I am soft-heartet apout your planet. I have been on many planets, and nowhere have I peen taken in and mate to feel at home as I was py the Iota Gamma Omicron fraternity many years ago."

The ambassador began to gather up his papers. "Have you a memorantum of this meetink for me to initial? Goot." Hithafea signed, using his claw for a pen. "Then we can have a formal signink next week, eh? With cameras and speeches? Some tay if you feel like erecting a monument to the founders of the Interplanetary Council, you might erect it to Mr. Herbert Lengyel."

Evans said: "Sir, I'm told you Osirians like our

Earthly alcoholic drinks. Would you care to step down to the Federation bar. . . ."

"I am so sorry, not this time. Next time, yes. Now I must catch an airplane to Baltimore, U.S.A."

"What are you doing there?" said Chagas.

"Why, Atlantic University is giving me an honorary degree. How I shall balance one of those funny hats with the tassel on my crest I do not yet know. But that was another reason I agreet to your terms. You see, we are a sentimental race. What is the matter with Mr. Wu? He looks sick."

Chagas said: "He has been watching his lifelong philosophy crumble to bits, that is all. Come, we will see you to your aircraft."

As Wu pulled himself together and rose with the rest, Evans grinned wryly at him, saying:

"After we've dropped the ambassador, I think I'll make it a champagne cocktail!"

The Guided Man

"ALL YOU DO," said the salesman for the Telagog Company, "is flip this switch at the beginning of the crisis. That sends out a radio impulse, which is picked up here and routed by the monitor to the proper controller."

Ovid Ross peered past the salesman at the man seated in the booth. Gilbert Falck, he understood the man's name to be, but nobody would know him under that helmet, from which a thick cable passed in a sagging curve to the control board before him.

"So he takes over?" said Ross.

"Exactly. Suppose you've let yourself in for a date where there'll be dancing, and you don't know how?"

"I do, kind of," said Ovid Ross.

"Well, let's suppose you don't. We have in the booth, by prearrangement, our Mr. Jerome Bundy, who's been a ballet dancer and a ballroom dancing teacher—"

"Did somebody call me?" said a man, putting his head out of another control booth into the corridor behind the row of booths.

"No, Jerry," said the salesman, whose name was Nye. "Just using you as an example. Aren't you still on?"

"No, he gave me the over-and-out."

"See?" said the salesman. "Mr. Bundy is controlling a man—needless to say we don't mention our clients' names—who's trying to become a professional ballet dancer. He's only so-so, but with Jerry running him by remote control he puts on the finest *tour-jeté* you ever saw. Or suppose you can't swim—"

"Shucks," said Ovid Ross, staring at his knuckles. He was a long, big-boned young man with hands and feet large even in proportion to the rest of him, and knuckles oversized for even such hands. "I can swim and dance, kind of, and most of those things. Even play a little golf. My trouble is—well, you know."

"Well?"

"Here I am, just a big hick from Rattlesnake, Montana, trying to get on among all these slick operators in New York, where everybody's born with his hand in somebody else's pocket. When I go up against them it scares the behooligers out of me. I get embarrassed and trip over my big feet."

"In such a case," said Nye, "we choose controllers specializing in the rôles of sophisticate, man-of-the-world, and so forth. Our Mr. Falck here is experienced in such parts. So are Mr. Abrams and Mr. Van Etten. Mr. Bundy is what you might call a second-string sophisticate. When he's not controlling a man engaged in dancing or athletic sports, he relieves one of the others I mentioned."

"So, if I sign up with you, and tomorrow I go see this publisher guy who eats horseshoes and spits out the nails, to ask for a job, you can take over?"

"Easiest thing in the world. Our theory is: no man is a superman! So, when faced with a crisis you can't cope with, call us in. Let a specialist take control of your body! You don't fill your own teeth or make your own shoes, do you? Then why not let our experts carry you through such crises as getting a job, proposing to a girl, or making a speech? Why not?" Nye's eyes shone.

"I dunno why not," said Ross. "But that reminds me. I got—I've got girl trouble too. Can you really take care of that?"

"Certainly. One of the controllers is the former actor Barry Wentworth. During his youth, he was the idol of frustrated women throughout the nation, and he succeeded in acquiring nine real-life wives as well as innumerable less formal romances. We'll do the courtship, the proposal, and everything for you."

Ross looked suspiciously at the salesman. "Dunno as I like that 'everything.' "

Nye spread his hands. "Only at your request. We have no thought of controlling a client beyond his desires. What we do is to compel you to do what you really wish to do, but lack the skill or the nerve to do."

"Say, here's another thing."

"Yes?"

"Is there any carry-over effect? In other words, uh, if a controller puts me through some act like swimming, will I learn to do that better from having the controller do an expert job with my carcass?"

"We believe so, though the psychologists are still divided. We think that eventually telagog control will be accepted as a necessary part of all training for forms of physical dexterity or skill, including such things as singing and speech-making. But that's in the future."

"Another thing," said Ross. "This gadget would give a controller a wonderful chance for—uh—practical jokes. Say the controllee was a preacher who hired you to carry him through a tough sermon, and the controller had it in for him, or maybe just had a low sense of humor. What would stop the controller from making the preacher tell stag-party stories from the pulpit?"

The salesman's face took on a look of pious horror. "Nobody in this organization would think of such a thing! If he did, he'd be fired before he could say 'hypospatial transmission.' This is a serious enterprise, with profound future possibilities."

Ross gave the sigh of a man making a fateful decision. "Okay, then. Guess I'll have to go without lunch for a while to pay for it, but if your service does what you say, it'll be worth it. Give me the forms."

When Ross had signed the contract with the Telagog Company, the salesman said: "Now, we'll have to decide which class of telagog receiver to fit you with. For full two-way communication you use this headset with this hypospatial transmitter in your pocket. It's fairly conspicuous . . ."

"Too much so for me," said Ross.

"Then we have this set, which looks like a hearing aid and has a smaller pocket control unit. This doesn't let you communicate by hypospatial broadcast with the controller, but it does incorporate an off-switch so you can cut off the controller. And, if you have to communicate with him, you can write a note and hold it up for him to see with your eyes."

"Still kind of prominent. Got 'ny others?"

"Yes, this last kind is invisible for practical purposes." The salesman held up a lenticular object about the size of an eyeglass lens but thicker, slightly concave on one face and thin around the edge. "This is mounted on top of your head, between your scalp and your skull."

"How about controls?"

"You can't cut off the controller, but you can communicate by clicks with this pocket wireless key. One click means 'take over,' two is 'lay off but stand by,' and three is 'over and out,' or 'that's all until the next schedule.' If you want to arrange a more elaborate code with your controller, that's up to you."

"That looks like me," said Ross. "But have you got to bore holes in my skull for the wires?"

"No. That's the beauty of this Nissen metal. Although the wires are only a few molecules thick, they're so strong that when the receiver is actuated and their coils are released they shoot right through your skull into your brain without making holes you can see except under the strongest microscope."

"Okay," said Ovid Ross.

"First we'll have to fit you and install the receiver. You'll take a local anesthetic, won't you?"

"I guess so. Whatever you say."

"Then you'd better have a practice session with your controllers. They have to get used to your body, you know."

"Rather," said Gilbert Falck, taking off his helmet. He was a smallish blond young man about Ovid Ross's age. "You wouldn't want to knock your coffee cup over because your arm is longer than mine, would you?"

The gold lettering on the frosted-glass part of the door said:

1026

HOOLIHAN PUBLICATIONS

THE GARMENT GAZETTE

Ovid Ross had stood in front of this door for fifteen awful seconds with his hand outstretched but not quite touching the knob, as if he feared an electric shock. God almighty, why did one have to be young and green and embarrassable? And from Rattlesnake, Montana? Then he remembered, reached into his pocket, and pushed the switch-button, once.

He remembered what he had been taught: as the controller took over, relax gradually. Not too suddenly, or you might fall in a heap on the floor. That would not make a good impression on a prospective employer.

The feeling of outside control stole over him with an effect like that of a heavy slug of hard liquor. He relaxed. A power outside his body was seeing with his eyes and sensing with his other senses. This power reached his arm out and briskly opened the door. Without volition on his part, he realized that he had stridden in and said to the girl at the switchboard behind the hole in the glass window, in friendly but firm and confident tones:

"Will you please tell Mr. Sharpe that Mr. Ross is here to see him? I'm expected."

Ross thought that alone he would have stumbled in, goggled wordlessly at the girl, stuttered, and probably ended by slinking out without seeing Sharpe at all. The control was not really complete—semiautomatic acts like breathing and walking were still partly under Ross's control—but Falck had taken over all the higher functions.

Presently he was shaking hands with Addison Sharpe, the managing editor, a small man with steel-rimmed glasses. Ross amazed himself by the glibness with which his tongue threw off the correct pleasantries:

"A very nice plant you have, sir . . . I'm sure I shall enjoy it . . . Yes, the salary mentioned by the agency will be satisfactory, though I hope eventually to convince you I'm really worth more . . . References? Mr. Maurice Vachek of *The Clothing Retailer;* Mr. Joseph McCue of A. S. Glickman Fabrics . . ."

Not a word to indicate that this same McCue had pounded his desk and shouted, when firing Ovid Ross: "And here you are, a college man, who couldn't sell bed warmers to Eskimos! What the hell good's your fancy education if it don't teach you nothing useful?"

Luckily, McCue had promised to give him a good reference—provided the job were anything but selling. Ross was pleased to observe that his body's deportment under Falck's control, while much improved, was not altered out of all recognition. He still spoke his normal General American instead of with Falck's more easterly accents.

Addison Sharpe was saying: "You'll find working conditions here a little unusual."

"So?" said Falck-Ross.

"For one thing, Mr. Hoolihan likes neatness. That means everybody cleans his desk completely before he goes home at night. Everything but the telephone, the calendar, the ashtray, and the blotter pad has to be out of sight."

Ross felt his controller start a little. No wonder! This would be Ovid Ross's third trade journal, and never before had he come across such a ruling. Normally, staff writers and editors were allowed to build mares' nests of paper on their desks to suit themselves, so long as they delivered the goods.

"For another," continued Sharpe, "Mr. Hoolihan disapproves of his employees' fraternizing with each other outside of working hours. He considers it bad for discipline."

At this outrageous ukase, Ross felt Falck jerk again.

"Finally," said Sharpe, "Mr. Hoolihan has a very acute sense of time. He takes it much amiss if his employees show up so much as one minute late, so the rest of us make a habit of arriving fifteen minutes early in the morning to allow for delays. Also, I advise you not to get in the habit of taking your newspaper down to the men's room to read, or ducking out for a midmorning cup of coffee. The staff writer you're replacing thought he couldn't live without his ten-o'clock coffee. That's why you're here and he isn't."

Ross had an urge to ask how you got to be a trusty. However, he had no control over his vocal organs, and Falck was too well-trained for any such breaks.

"Now," said Sharpe, "we'll go in to see Mr. Hoolihan."

The tyrant overflowed his swivel chair: a big stout red-faced man with a fringe of graying hair around his pink dome of a scalp and great bushy eyebrows. Timothy Hoolihan extended a paw and wrung Ross's hand. He made Ross's bones creak, despite the fact that Ross had gotten his start in life by pitching hay and throwing calves around.

"Glad to have you!" barked Hoolihan in a staccato voice like a burst of machine-gun fire. "You do as we tell you, no reason we can't get along. Here! Read this! Part of every new employee's indoctrination. Ever hear of Frederick Winslow Taylor? Should have! Hundred years old and still makes sense."

Falck-Ross glanced down at the brochure: a reprint of an ancient homily by Taylor on the duties of an employee.

"Now, you hang around a couple of days, reading the files, getting oriented, and we'll put you on a definite assignment. Good luck! Take him away, Addison!"

Overawed by this human dynamo, Ross was conscious of Falck's making some glib but respectful rejoinder and directing his body out of the office.

For the first time since he had entered the office suite occupied by *The Garment Gazette,* Ross began to try to regain control. He urged his right hand toward the pocket in which reposed the little clicker key by which he communicated with Falck. Evidently Falck realized what he was up to, for he relaxed control long enough for Ross to get his hand into that pocket and press the knob, twice.

At once Falck's control ceased. Ross, not catching himself quite in time, stumbled and recovered. Sharpe turned his head to give him an owlish stare. The managing editor took him around and introduced him to a half-dozen other people: staff writers (called "editors" on this paper), an advertising manager, and so forth. Then Sharpe showed Ross a cubicle with a desk.

"Yours," he said. "Say, are you feeling all right?"

"Sure. Why?"

"I don't know. When we came out of Mr. Hoolihan's office your manner seemed to change. You're not sick, are you?"

"Never felt better."

"Heart all right? We wouldn't like you to conk out on us before you've worked long enough to pull your weight."

"No, sir. My heart was good enough for me to bc a practicing cowboy, so I guess this won't hurt it."

Ross settled down at his new desk to read the Taylor article, the burden of which seemed to be that to get ahead one should practice abject submission to one's employer's slightest whim. While he was absorbing the eminent engineer's advice, one of the girls came in and placed on his desk a big ring binder containing last year's accumulation of file copies of *The Garment Gazette,* which he read.

What Mr. Hoolihan really needed, he thought, was a multiple telagog set by which he could control all his employees all at once and all the time.

During the lunch hour, Ovid Ross telephoned the Telagog Company and asked for Gilbert Falck. After some delay a voice said:

"Falck speaking."

"This is Ross, Ovid Ross. Say, it worked! I got the job!"

"Oh, I know that. I monitored you for a half-hour after you shut me off, and cut in on you at odd minutes later."

"Oh. But say, I just wanted to tell you how much I appreciated it. Uh. It's wonderful. Could I—could I blow you to a drink this evening after work?"

"Wait till I look at my schedule . . . Okay, five to six is free. Drop by on your way from work, eh?"

Ovid Ross did. He found Falck, in line with his role as professional man-of-the-world, cordial but not unduly impressed by his accomplishment in getting Ross a job. When the first pair of drinks had been drunk, Falck bought a second round. Ross asked:

"What I don't see is, how on earth do you do it? I have a hard enough time managing things like that for myself, let alone for some other guy."

Falck made an airy motion. "Experience, my lad, practice. And balance. A certain mental coordination so you automatically roll with the punch and shoot for every opening. I've got rather a tough case coming up tomorrow. Client wants to put over a merger, and it'll take all my *savoir faire* to see him through it." He sipped. "Then, too, the fact that it's not *my* job or *my* business deal or *my* dame helps. Gives me a certain detachment I mightn't have about my own affairs."

"Like surgeons don't usually operate on their own kinfolk?"

"Exactly."

Ovid Ross did some mental calculations, subtracting the employment agency's fee and the charges of the Telagog Company from his assets, and decided that he could afford to buy one more round. By the time this had been drunk, he was in excellent spirits. He told Falck of Hoolihan's quirks. Falck commented:

"Why, the damned little Napoleon! If he said that to me, I'd tell him where to stick his job." Falck glanced at his watch. "What's next on your agenda?"

"I don't think I'll need any control for the next day or two, but as soon as I get oriented they're liable to send me out on an interview. So you better stand by."

"Okay. Try to call me a little in advance to brief me. I want to cut Bundy in on your sensory circuits in case he has to substitute for me."

When he got to the Y.M.C.A. where he lived, Ovid Ross telephoned a White Plains number and got an answer in a strong Russian accent:

"Who is cullink, pliz?"

"Mr. Ross would like to—uh—speak to Miss La Motte."

"Oh. Vait." Then after a long pause: "Is that you, Ovid?"

"Uh. Sure is. Know what? I got the job!"

"Splendid! Are you working now?"

"Yeah. It's a high-powered place as trade journals go. I only hope I can stick the boss."

"Don't you like him?"

"No, and neither does anybody else. But it's money. Say, Claire!"

"Yes?"

"I met a swell guy. Name of Falck. A real man-of-the-world. Knows his way around."

"Good. I hope you see more of him."

"How are the wild Russians?"

"About the same. I had a terrible row with Peshkova."

"Yeah? How come?"

"I was teaching the boys American history, and she claimed I wasn't putting enough dialectical materialism into it. I should have explained that the American Revolution was a plot by the American bourgeoisie to acquire exclusive exploitation of the masses instead of having to share it with the British aristocracy. And I said a few things about if even the Russians had given up that line, why should I teach it? We were yelling at one another when Peshkov came in and made peace."

"Has he made any more passes?" asked Ross anxiously.

"No, except to stare at me with that hungry expression all the time. It gives me the creeps."

"Well, someday . . ." Ross's voice trailed off. He wanted to say something like: "Someday I'll marry you and then you won't have to tutor an exiled ex-commissar's brats anymore."

But, in the first place, he was too shy; in the second, he did not know Claire La Motte well enough; and, in the third, he was not in a position to take on costly commitments.

"Did you say something?" inquired Claire.

"No—that is—uh—I wondered when we'd get together again."

"I know! Are you busy Sunday?"

"Nope."

"Then come on up here. The Peshkovs will be gone all weekend, and the hired couple are going down to Coney. Bring your friend Mr. Falck, and his girl friend if he has one."

"Uh? Swell idea! I'll ask him."

Claire La Motte gave Ross directions for reaching the estate which the Peshkovs had bought in Westchester County. After they had hung up, Ovid Ross sat staring at the telephone. He had been hoping for such an invitation. Ever since he had met Claire the previous winter, she had promised to have him to the Peshkovs' place in May or June, and now June was almost over. The Peshkovs had never absented themselves long enough.

Then his old fear of embarrassment—erythrophobia, a psychologist had told him—rose up to plague him. Suppose Falck rebuffed his invitation? The thought gave him shivers. If only he could tender the invitation while under telagog control! But since Falck was his regular controller, he could hardly work it that way. And, having promised Claire, he would have to go through with this project.

Through Wednesday and Thursday, orientation continued at *The Garment Gazette*. Ross read proof, helped Sharpe with makeup, and wrote heads: AUS-

TRALIAN WOOL DOWN; FALL FASHIONS FEATURE FUCHSIA; ILGWU ELECTS KATZ. Friday morning Addison Sharpe said:

"We're sending you out this afternoon to interview Marcus Ballin."

"The Outstanding Knitwear man?"

"Yes."

"What about? Anything special?"

"That's what you're to find out. He called up to say he was planning something new in shows. First he talked to Mr. Hoolihan, who got mad and passed the call on to me. Ballin asked if we'd like to run a paragraph or two on this show, so I said I'd send a man. Heffernan's out so you'll have to take care of it."

"I'll do my best," said Ross.

Sharpe said: "It's about time we ran a feature on Marcus anyway. Quite a versatile and picturesque character."

"What's his specialty?"

"Oh, he plays the violin. He once went on an expedition he financed himself to find some bug in South America. Take the portrait Leica along and give him the works. His place is at 135 West Thirty-seventh Street."

Ovid Ross telephoned the Telagog Company and made a luncheon date with Gilbert Falck. During lunch he told what he knew of his impending ordeal. Falck found a spot on his schedule when he could take charge of the interview.

Ross also screwed up his nerve to pass on Claire's proposal for the weekend to Falck, who said:

"Thanks, rather. I shall be glad to. Shall we go in your car or mine?"

"Mine, since I made the invitation."

"Fine. I'll get a girl."

"Hey!" said Ross. "If you come along to Westchester, you can't be in your booth controlling me if I run into an embarrassing situation."

Falck raised his blond eyebrows. "What's embarrassing about a picnic with your best girl?"

"Oh, you know."

"No I don't, unless you tell me."

Ross twisted his fingers. "I don't know her awfully well, but I think she's—she's—uh—well, I suppose you'd say I was nuts about her. And—and I always feel like I'm making a fool of myself."

Falck laughed. "Oh, that. Jerry Bundy's on Sunday, so I'll tell him to monitor you and be ready to take over."

Ross said: "You should call yourselves the John Alden Company."

Falck smiled. "Bring on your Priscilla, and we'll bundle her for you."

They parted, and Ross plunged back into the swarming garment district. He killed time, watching sweating shipping clerks push hand trucks loaded with dresses, until his controller returned to his booth and came on the hypospace. Then Ross sent in the signal.

Marcus Ballin (Outstanding Knitwear: sweaters, T-shirts, bathing suits) was a medium-sized man with sparse gray hair and somewhat the air of one of the more amiable Roman emperors. Ovid Ross soon learned that his trepidations about having the man insult him or clam up had been needless. Marcus Ballin loved to talk, he was a fascinating talker, and best of all he loved talking about himself.

Over the background noise of the knitting machines in the suite of lofts that comprised his empire, Ballin, with eloquent gestures of his cigar, poured into Falck-Ross's ears the story of his many activities. He told of his travels, his fun with his airplane and his violin, his charitable and settlement work, until Ross, a prisoner for the nonce in his own skull, wondered how this man of parts found time to be also one of the most successful garment manufacturers in New York.

Falck-Ross said: "But, sir, how about that special show?"

"Oh, that." Ballin chuckled. "Just a little stunt to help my fall line. I'm putting on a show for the buyers with a contest."

"A contest?"

"Absolutely. To choose the most beautiful bust in America."

"What? But Mr. Ballin, won't the cops interfere?"

Ballin laughed. "I wasn't intending to parade the girls in the nude. Nobody in the garment trade would encourage nudism; he'd be ostracized. They'll all be wearing Outstanding sweaters."

"But how can you be sure some of 'em aren't—ah—boosting their chances by artificial means?"

"Not this time. These sweaters will be so thin the judges can tell."

"Who are the judges?"

"Well, I'm one, and I got the sculptor Joseph Aldi for the second. The third I haven't picked out. I called that stuffed-shirt publisher of yours, but he turned me down. Let me see . . ."

"Mr. Ballin," Ross to his horror heard himself say, "I'm sure I should make a good judge."

Ovid Ross was horrified for three reasons: first, to judge so intimate a matter in public would embarrass him to death; second, he thought it would impair his standing with Claire La Motte if she found out; finally, he would never, never come right out and ask anybody for anything in that crass way. He struggled to get his hand on the switch, but Gilbert Falck kept the bit in his teeth.

"Yeah?" said Ballin. "That's an idea."

"I've got good eyesight," continued Falck, ignoring the mental squirmings of Ross, "and no private axes to grind . . ."

Falck continued his line of sales chatter until Ballin said: "Okay, you're in, Mr. Ross."

"When is it to be?"

"Next Thursday. I've already got over thirty entries, but next year if I repeat it there ought to be a lot more. We'd have to set up some sort of preliminary screening."

Falck wound up the interview and took Ross's body

out of the Outstanding Knitwear offices. Ross heard his body say:

"Well, Ovid old boy, there's an opportunity most men would fight tooth and nail for. Anything to say before I sign off? Write it on your pad."

As Falck released control, Ross wrote a couple of dirty words on the pad, adding: "You got me into this; you'll have to see me through."

Falck, taking over again, laughed. "Rather! I have every intention of doing so, laddie."

Back at the *Gazette,* Addison Sharpe whistled when he heard Ross's story. He said:

"I don't know how the boss will like your getting in on this fool stunt. He turned Ballin down in no uncertain terms."

"I'd think it would be good publicity for the paper," said Ross.

"Well, Mr. Hoolihan has funny ideas; quite a Puritan. You wait while I speak to him."

Ross sat down and wrote notes on his interview until Sharpe said: "This way, Ovid."

The managing editor led him into Hoolihan's office, where the advertising manager was already seated. Hoolihan barked:

"Ross, call up Ballin and tell him it's no go! At once! I won't have my clean sheet mixed up in his burlesque act!"

"But, Mr. Hoolihan!" wailed the advertising manager. "Mr. Ballin has just taken a whole page for the October issue, and if you insult him he'll cancel it! And you know what our advertising account looks like right now."

"Oh?" said Hoolihan. "I don't let advertisers dictate my editorial policies!"

"But that's not all. Mike Ballin, his brother—or rather one of his brothers—is the bigshot at the Pegasus Cutting Machine Company, another advertiser."

"Hm. That's another story."

As the great man pondered his problems, the advertising manager added slyly: "Besides, if you don't let

Ross judge, Ballin will simply get somebody from *The Clothing Retailer* or *Women's Wear* or one of the other sheets, and they'll get whatever benefit—"

"I see," interrupted Hoolihan. "Ross! You go through with this act as planned, but heaven help you if you bring us any unfavorable notoriety! Keep yourself in the background. Play it close to your chest. No stunts! Get me? All right, back to work!"

"Yes, Mr. Hoolihan," said Ovid Ross.

"Yes, Mr. Hoolihan," said Addison Sharpe.

"Yes, Mr. Hoolihan," said the advertising manager.

Ovid Ross spent most of Saturday shining up his small middle-aged convertible and touching up the nicks in the paint. He had to journey up to the Bronx to get to it, because automobile storage fees had become prohibitively high in Manhattan.

Sunday morning, the sky was so overcast that Ross had doubts about his party. The paper, however, said fair, warm, and humid. By the time he went all the way up again by subway, got the car, and drove back to Manhattan to pick up Falck and his girl, the sun was burning its way through the overcast.

Falck directed Ross to drive around to a brownstone front house in the west seventies to get the girl, whom he introduced as a Miss Dorothea Dunkelberg. She was a plump girl, very young-looking, and pretty in a round-faced bovine way. She was the kind whom their elders describe as "sweet" for want of any more positive attribute.

They spun through a hot, humid forenoon up the Westchester parkways to the Peshkov estate near White Plains. As they turned in the driveway between the stone posts, Falck said:

"These Russkys rather did all right by themselves, didn't they?"

"Yeah," said Ross. "When they liquidated all the Commies in the revolution ten years ago, Peshkov was Commissar of the Treasury or something and got away with a couple of trunkloads of foreign securities."

"And he's been allowed to keep them?"

"The new Russian Commonwealth has been trying to get hold of that dough ever since, but Peshkov keeps it hidden away or tied up in legal knots."

"And your Miss La Motte tutors his kids?"

"That's right. She doesn't like 'em much, but it's money."

"Why, what sort of folks are they?"

"Well, to give you an idea, Peskhov's idea of a jolly evening is to sit all alone in his living room with a pistol on the table beside him, drinking vodka and staring into space. Claire tells me he's been getting moodier and moodier ever since those anti-Communist Russians tried to assassinate him last year."

A tremendous barking broke out. Around the corner of the house streaked a half-dozen Russian wolfhounds with long snaky heads thrust forward and long legs pumping like steel springs. The dogs rushed to where the automobile was slowly crunching up the winding gravel driveway and began racing around it like Indians circling a prairie schooner.

"Do we have to fight our way through those?" said Dorothea Dunkelberg. "They scare me."

"Claire will handle 'em," said Ross with more conviction than he felt. "She says they're friendly but dumb."

The sun glinted on red hair as a figure in a playsuit appeared beside the mansion. Claire La Motte's voice came shrilly:

"Ilya! Olga! Come here! Here, Dmitri! Behave yourself, Anastasia!"

The dogs loped off toward the house, where the girl seized a couple by their collars and dragged them out of sight around the corner. The others followed. Presently, Claire appeared again and waved an arm toward the parking space. Ross parked and got out.

As Claire La Motte approached the car, Ovid Ross reached into his pocket and pressed his switch button, once. Now, he hoped, he would show up all right in comparison with his slick friend Falck!

He felt Jerome Bundy take over his body and stride

it toward the approaching Claire. Behind him he heard a faint wolf whistle from Falck. Instead of formally shaking hands with her and mumbling something banal while his ears pinkened and his knuckles seemed to swell to the size of baseballs, Ross heard his body bellow:

"Hi there, beautiful!"

Then it clamped its hands around Claire's small waist and hoisted her to arm's length overhead. He let her slip back into his arms, briefly hugged the breath out of her, and dropped her to the ground. As he did so he thought he caught a smothered murmur:

"Why, Ovid!"

At least, thought Ross, he was glad that Bundy hadn't made him kiss her or spank her behind. It was all very well for his controller to take an attitude of hearty familiarity, but that sort of thing could easily be carried too far. Popular mythology to the contrary notwithstanding, many girls really disliked caveman tactics.

Ross's body then affably introduced Claire La Motte to his new friends. Claire said:

"I thought we'd take a walk around the grounds and then eat a picnic lunch on the edge of the pool. Then later we can take a swim."

"Oh," said Bundy-Ross. "Gil, grab the suits and towels."

Falck brought these objects out of the rear seat of the car and walked after the others.

"Over that way," said Claire, pointing over the trees, "is the Untereiner estate. The Wyckman estate used to be beyond it, but now they're putting up apartment houses on it."

There were the conventional murmurs about the never-ending growth of New York's commutershed, both in size and in population. Claire continued:

"And over that way is the MacFadden estate, only the Mutual Fidelity bought it as a club for their employees. And in that direction is the Heliac Health Club."

"What's that?" said Dorothea Dunkelberg.

"A nudist camp."

"Oh. I thought they weren't allowed in this state?"

"They aren't, but it's become so popular the law's not enforced anymore. On the other hand, it can't be repealed because the legislators are afraid the religious groups would raise a fuss."

They started toward the pool when another outbreak of barking halted them. Claire wailed:

"Oh, goodness, they got out again! Dmitri has learned to work the latch with his paw!"

The borzois boiled around the corner of the mansion as if pursuing the biggest wolf in Siberia. One made a playful fifteen-foot spring with its forepaws against Gilbert Falck, sending the telagog controller rolling on the greensward. Towels and bathing suits flew about, to be snatched up by the dogs and borne off fluttering. Claire screamed:

"Yelena! Igor! Behave yourselves!"

No attention did they pay. A couple raced off having a running tug-of-war with Dorothea Dunkelberg's suit, while another amused itself by throwing one of the bath towels into the air and catching it again.

"Playful little fellows," said Falck, getting up and brushing the grass off his pants.

"Very," said Claire, and started to apologize until Falck stopped her.

"Not your fault, lassie. Don't give it a thought." Falck wiped a drop of sweat from his nose. "I'm going to miss those suits, rather. If you find them in the woods, not too badly tattered, you might send 'em back to us."

"Sticky, isn't it?" said Claire. "Anyway we still have the lunch."

"What's to keep these Hounds of the Baskervilles from raiding our food?" asked Ross's body.

"I don't know, until I can get them shut up again and tie the gate closed."

Dorothea said in her faint squeak: "Maybe we could sit in a row on the springboard. They'd be scared to come out over the water, wouldn't they?"

And so it was done. The smell of food attracted the dogs, who lined up on the edge of the pool and whined until Claire, with the men's help, collared them two at a time and led them back to their kennels.

Gilbert Falck wiped his hands on his paper napkin and said: "Excuse me, people. I just remembered a phone call. May I use the Peshkov phone, Claire?"

He followed Claire into the Peshkovs' palatial living room, where a life-sized portrait of Stalin hung on the wall. As she was pointing out the telephone, Falck casually captured her hand and said:

"I say, Claire, that sofa looks rather comfortable. Why don't we sit down and get better acquainted?"

Claire slipped her hand out of his and said: "You make your call, Gil. I have my other guests to entertain."

Falck sighed and called the Telagog Company. He got Jerome Bundy on the line and said:

"Jerry, your control is laying an egg again. He does all right while you control him, but the minute you let go he just sits staring at the dame with an expression like a hungry wolf."

"Well?"

"I rather thought the next time you take over you'd better give him a more aggressive and uninhibited pattern. The poor jerk will never get anywhere under his own steam."

"I don't know," said Bundy dubiously. "I thought I was giving him an aggressive pattern. I don't want to queer his pitch by—"

"Don't worry about that. His girl just confided to me she wishes he weren't such a stick. Give him the works."

"Okay," said Bundy.

Falck walked out with a knowing grin. When he came in sight of the other three he called:

"Did somebody say something about tennis?"

Ovid Ross immediately switched his control back to Bundy. He had no illusions about his game: a powerful serve and a bulletlike forehand drive, but no control to speak of.

They made it mixed doubles, Ross and Claire against the other two. To his amazement, Ross found his smashes going, not into the net or the wire as usual, but into the corners of the other court where nobody could touch them. Claire was pretty good, Dorothea rather poor, but Gilbert Falck excellent, with a catlike agility that more than made up for his lack of Ross's power. The first set got up to 5–5, then 6–5, then 6–6, then 7–6 . . .

Dorothea Dunkelberg wailed: "I can't anymore, Gil. I'll pass out in this heat."

"Okay," said Falck smoothly. "No law says we have to. Boy, I rather wish we had those bathing suits. Claire, the Commies wouldn't have some spares, would they?"

"I don't think so; they never keep old clothes. They say in Russia nothing was too good for them and they expect to have it that way here."

They trailed down the little hill from the tennis court and stood looking longingly at the clear, pale-green water in the pool. Ross was aware that Bundy was wiping his forehead for him. Thoughtful of him . . . But then Ross was horrified to hear his controller say in that masterful way:

"Who wants bathing suits? Come on, boys and girls, take your clothes off and jump in!"

"What?" squealed Dorothea.

"You heard me. Off with 'em!"

"Well, I have a suit—" began Claire, but Bundy-Ross roared:

"No you don't! Not if the rest of us—"

The next few minutes were, for Ovid Ross's impotent psyche, a time of stark horror. How he got through them without dying of an excess of emotion he never knew. He frantically tried to regain control of his right arm to reach his switch, but Bundy would not let him. Instead Bundy took off Ross's sportshirt and shorts, wadded them into a ball, and threw them under the springboard, meanwhile exhorting the others to do likewise and threatening to throw them in clad if they refused. . . .

They were sitting in a row on the edge of the pool, breathing hard with drops streaming off them and splashing the water with their feet. Ross caught a glimpse of Falck looking at him with a curious expression, between displeasure and curiosity, as if something he had carefully planned had gone awry. The controller was showing a tendency to play up to Claire more than Ross liked, so that poor Dorothea was rather ignored. Ross heard Bundy say with his vocal organs:

"We want to be careful not to get that white strip around our middles burned."

"How about finishing that set now?" said Falck.

They got up and walked up the slope to the court. Bundy-Ross, whose serve it was, was just getting his large knobby toes lined up on the backline for a smash when a fresh outburst of barking made all turn. Claire cried:

"Damn! I'll bet they've gotten loose again."

"Isn't that a car?" said Dorothea.

"Oh, gosh!" said Claire as the sun flashed on a windshield down the driveway. "It's the Peshkovs! They weren't supposed to be here till this evening! What'll we do?"

"Make a dash for our clothes," said Falck.

"Too late," said Claire, as the purr of the car, hidden behind the mansion, grew louder and then stopped. "Run for the woods!"

She ran into the woods, the others trailing. There were ouches and grunts as bushes scratched their shins and their unhardened soles trod on twigs. Dorothea said:

"Isn't that poison ivy?"

Falck looked. "I rather *think* it's Virginia creeper, but we'd better not take chances."

"Oh, dear! I hope we don't find a hornets' nest."

Bundy-Ross said: "It would be more to the point to hope a ncst of hornets doesn't find us."

They came to a wire fence. Ross heard Bundy say: "That's easy to climb over. Hook your toes over the wire, like this."

"Ouch," said Dorothea. "What's on the other side?"

"The Heliac Health Club," said Claire.

"Rather a bit of luck," said Falck, climbing. "The one place in Westchester County where we're dressed for calling."

Ross thought desperately of the switch that would return control of his body to him. The switch was in the right side pocket of his shorts, and his shorts, along with his other clothes and those of his companions, lay in a heap under the springboard at the edge of the pool.

"Have you ever been here, Claire?" asked Dorothea.

"No, but I have an idea of the layout. This way."

They straggled again through the woods. Presently they found a trail. Dorothea shrieked at the sight of a garter snake.

Claire led them along the trail, until they came out of the woods on to a grassy field. On this field stood, in irregular rows, forty-odd canvas-covered platforms about the size and height of beds. On over half these platforms, the guests of the Heliac Club sat or sprawled in the costume of their avocation, reading, talking, card-playing, or dozing.

One scholarly-looking man, unadorned save for a pipe and pince-nez, sat on the edge of his cot with a portable typewriter in his lap. Beyond, some people played volleyball and others tennis. On the right rose the rear of an old ex-mansion; on the left, a row of dilapidated-looking one-room cabins could be seen.

As his eyes, under Bundy's control, took in the scene, Ovid Ross observed several things about the nudists. There were three or four times as many men as women. Most of the people were middle-aged. They were certainly not there to show off their beauty, for many of the men were paunchy and the women pendulous.

After the initial shock had passed off, Ross became conscious of the white equatorial bands of himself and his companions, compared to the uniform brownness of the sun worshippers. A few of the latter, however, though well-browned elsewhere, displayed an angry red on the areas that gleamed white on his own party: the parts normally covered by shorts and halters.

"Good afternoon," said a voice. Ross saw a severe-looking gray-haired woman, deeply and uniformly browned, confronting them. "Have you people registered and paid your grounds fee?"

"No, but . . ." said Falck, then stumbled for words despite his professional suavity.

"Have you references?" said the woman. "We like to know who our guests are."

Ross expected his controller to step into the breach, but even the self-possessed Bundy appeared unable to cope with this situation.

Claire La Motte took the woman aside and explained their predicament. Ross saw the woman's face melt into a smile, then a laugh. Bundy turned Ross's head away to survey the rest of the scene.

Near at hand, on one of the platforms, a well-built middle-aged man with sparse gray hair and the air of an affable Roman emperor smoked a cigar and read a newspaper. Ross was sure that he had seen the man before. The same thought must have occurred to his controller, for Ross's eyes stopped roving with the man right in the center of the field. The man looked up as if conscious of scrutiny. His gaze froze as it rested on Ross as if he, too, thought that he recognized Ross.

Ross heard his voice say: "Why hello, Mr. Ba—"

"Please!" said Marcus Ballin, with so earnest a gesture that Bundy stopped in the middle of the name.

"Everybody goes by first names only here," continued Ballin. "I'm Marcus, you're—uh—what was that first name of yours?"

"Ovid."

"Okay, Ovid. Come a little closer, please." Ballin lowered his voice. "For me it would be particularly bad if this got out. I'd be considered a traitor to my trade. Why, even the garment-trade magazines, yours for instance, run editorials knocking nudism."

"I shouldn't think they'd take it so seriously as that."

"No? Well, you're not old enough to remember when there was a straw hat industry. Where is it now? Gone, because men don't wear hats in summer anymore. And women used to wear stockings in summer too. If everybody . . ." Ballin spread his hands.

"What would happen if the word got around?" asked Bundy-Ross. "Would the cutters and operators and pressers line up in a hollow square while the head buyer at Sachs' cut off your buttons?"

"No, but I'd be ostracized at least. It would even affect my business contacts. And my particular branch of the industry, summer sportswear, feels the most keenly about it of any. So you'll keep it quiet, won't you?"

"Sure, sure," said Bundy-Ross, and turned to his companions. The gray-haired woman was going away. Claire explained:

"She's gone to get a playsuit to lend me so I can go back and pick up our clothes."

Bundy-Ross introduced his companions by given names to Ballin, who said: "You've got nice taste in girls, Ovid. Claire should be a model. Did you ever try that, Claire?"

"I thought of it, but I'm not long and skinny enough for a clothes model and not short and fat enough for an artists' model."

"Anyway, Claire's too well educated," put in Falck.

"To me you look just right," said Ballin. "Say, Ovid, why couldn't she be entered in my contest? The local talent" (he indicated the rest of the club by a motion of an eyebrow) "isn't too promising."

"What contest?" said Claire.

Ballin started to explain, then changed his mind. "Ovid will tell you. I think you'd have an excellent chance, and there's a nice little cash prize. Three prizes, in fact."

"You certainly make me curious," said Claire.

Bundy-Ross said: "If she's a friend of mine, and I'm a judge, wouldn't it look kind of funny?"

"No, no. If Aldi and I thought you were favoring her,

we'd outvote you. Anyway, it's my contest, so I can run it as I please. When you can, take her aside and tell her about it."

The gray-haired woman returned with a playsuit. Claire departed at a trot. A few minutes later, she was back with a bundle of clothes.

Ross, as soon as he got his shorts on, strained to get his right hand into his pocket. Bundy let him do so and he pressed the button twice.

Under his own power, Ross walked back along the trail. He lagged behind Falck and Dorothea so that he could begin an elaborate and groveling apology:

"Uh. Claire."

"Yes?"

"I'm—uh—awfully sorry. I don't—uh—know . . ."

"Sorry about what?"

"All this. This afternoon. I don't know what got into me."

"For heaven's sake don't apologize! I haven't had so much fun in years."

"You haven't?"

"No. I've had the time of my life. I didn't know you had it in you. By the way, what *is* this contest?"

A little confused, Ross told her about the contest to select the most beautiful bust. He expected her to spurn the suggestion with righteous wrath and outraged propriety. Instead, she said:

"Why, that was sweet of him! I'm very much flattered." She glanced down at her exhibits. "Tell him I'll be glad to enter if I can arrange to get off early enough Thursday."

Women, thought Ovid Ross, have no shame. As he climbed the fence, he revised the intention he had held to drop in at the offices of the Telagog Company, knock Mr. Jerome Bundy's block off, and demand that the company remove the receiver from his cranium forthwith. Bizarre though the actions of his controller might seem, they seemed to have added up to a favorable impression on Claire.

Moreover, this infernal contest still loomed ahead of

him. While he could no doubt beg off from Ballin, such a cowardly act would lower him in Claire's eyes. He'd better plan for telagog control during this crisis at least.

Back on the Peshkovs' grounds, as he neared his automobile, he was intercepted by a stocky man with an expressionless moonface. The man wore an old-fashioned dark suit and even a necktie. Claire introduced the man as Commissar Peshkov—Bogdan Ipolitovich Peshkov.

Behind the man hovered another of similar appearance, wearing a derby hat. From what he had heard, Ross took this to be Fadei, the chauffeur-bodyguard. Peshkov extended a limp hand.

"Glad to mit you, Comrade," he said in a mournful voice. "I hup you had a nice time."

Ross shook the hand, collected his party, and drove off.

Early Thursday morning, Gilbert Falck entered the offices of the Telagog Company when nobody else was present. There was not even a single controller carrying a client through an early-morning crisis. Without hesitation, the young man got to work on the mechanism of his control booth and Jerome Bundy's next to it.

With a screwdriver he removed the panel that covered the wiring at the front of the booth. He traced the wiring until he found a place where the return motor leads of his booth and Bundy's ran side by side. With wire cutters he cut both wires and installed a double-pole double-throw knife switch. When the switch was down the controls would operate as usual; when it was up, he would control Bundy's client while Bundy controlled his. However, as the sensory circuits were not affected, each would continue to see, hear, and feel the sensations of his own client.

Falck did not consider himself a heel. But he had fallen heavily in love with Claire La Motte and deemed all fair in love. His effort to have Ross disgrace himself by uninhibited behavior in Westchester had backfired, so that Ross had ended up more solid with Claire than ever.

Ross, while he had not exactly complained to the company about the paces that Bundy had put him through, had asked them to go easy. This request had caused Falck's and Bundy's supervisor to glower suspiciously and to warn the two controllers not to try stunts. Therefore, Falck did not dare to undertake any direct bollixing of his client's actions or to ask Bundy to. He must work by a more subtle method.

He had already tried to date Claire by telephone. She, however, was free only on weekends and had been dated up solidly for the next two by Ross. After this afternoon's contest, some of those dates might no longer be so solid.

Falck measured the panel. With a hand auger, he drilled two tiny holes in it. Then he looped a length of fishline around the crosspiece of the knife switch and pushed both ends back through the upper hole in the panel from the back. He did likewise with another length of line through the lower hole, screwed the panel back into place, and tautened the lines.

Now he had only to pull hard on the upper double length of fishline to pull the switch from the down to the up position. Then, if he released one end of the line and reeled in the other, he would remove the line entirely from the works and could stuff it into his pocket. Similar operations with the lower line would return the switch to its original position.

Later, when the excitement had died down, he would remove the panel again and take out the switch. There was a chance, of course, that the electricians would come upon the switch in checking for trouble, but Gilbert Falck was no man to boggle at risks.

About ten on Thursday morning, Ross's telephone in the *Gazette* offices rang.

"Ovid? This is Claire. You won't have to meet my train after all."

"Why not?"

"Because Peshkov's driving me down."

"That guy! Is he planning to attend the contest?"

"So he says. Would Mr. Ballin mind?"

"Hm. I don't think so, but I'll call him and straighten it out. I got—I've got influence with him. Is Peshkov coming alone?"

"Well, he wouldn't let his family be contaminated by this example of bourgeois frivolity, but he wants to bring Fadei."

"The goon? No sir! Tell him he'll be welcome (I think) but no bodyguards."

Ross called the Outstanding Knitwear Company and persuaded a dubious Marcus Ballin to let Peshkov attend the showing.

The contest took place in Marcus Ballin's showroom, directly underneath his lofts. Despite the swank décor of the showroom, the noise and vibration of the knitting machines came faintly through the ceiling. The showroom had been fixed up something like a nightclub, with a stage a foot high on one side and little round tables spread around in a double horseshoe.

There were over three hundred spectators present, including representatives from *The Clothing Retailer* and other garment-trade magazines. These distributed themselves around the tables, to which a group of hardworking servitors brought trayloads of cocktails and small edible objects on toothpicks.

While Ivory Johnstone's band from Harlem entertained the audience, Ballin and Ross lined up the contestants behind scenes. Each of the lovely ladies wore a lightweight Outstanding sweater.

These sweaters were so sheer that to Ross they seemed practically nonexistent, following every contour of their wearers' bodies with implacable fidelity. Under normal conditions, this spectacle would have reduced Ross to a state of stuttering embarrassment. But as Gilbert Falck was now operating his body, he could give no outward sign of his feelings.

With a worried frown, Ballin said: "Say, Ovid, where's that little redhead of yours?"

"I'll look." Ross put his head around the end of the backdrop to look over the audience.

Claire La Motte and Bogdan Peshkov were just coming in, the latter the only man in the room wearing a coat. Peshkov said something that Ross could not catch over the distance and hubbub, patted Claire's arm, waved her toward the stage, seated himself at one of the tables, and haughtily beckoned a waiter. Claire started uncertainly toward the stage, then sighted Ross and walked quickly to where he stood.

Ballin said: "All right, Miss La Motte, here's your sweater. This is the third judge, Joe Aldi." He indicated a swarthy, muscular young man with a dense glossy-black beard, who stood by with his hands on his hips. "Just step behind that curtain to put it on. Nothing under it, you know."

With these sweaters, thought Ross, it made little difference where she put it on. In looking over the talent, Falck-Ross had already eliminated many of the girls. He had also picked several whom he expected to place high. Among these were (according to the badges pinned to their waist) Miss Loretta Day (née Wieniawski), the noted burlesque queen; and Miss Shirley Archer, a model from the Towers agency. Claire, the unknown amateur, would find stiff competition.

"Line up, girls," said Ballin. "Look at the girls next to you to make sure you're in alphabetical order. The A's are at this end."

A female voice down the line said: "Does M come before or after N?"

Ballin continued: "You introduce them first time around, Ovid. Here's the list. As you call each one I'll send her out. Make it snappy, so one's coming out while the previous one's going."

Ballin strolled out upon the stage, waited for applause to die down, and gave a little speech: "So glad to see you all here this fine summer day . . ." (It was drizzling outside.) ". . . our new line of fall sportswear . . . the preëminent position of the Outstanding

Knitwear Company . . . an assortment of fine, healthy upstanding American beauties . . . will be introduced by one of the judges, Mr. Ovid Ross of *The Garment Gazette*."

Ross came out in his turn. During the first few steps, his spirit quailed within him. After that he found that he did not mind. In fact, if Falck had not been controlling him, he thought that he would be able to manage the act as well as Falck.

As the girls came out he called their names: "Miss Wilma Abbott . . . Miss Miriam Amter . . . Miss Shirley Archer . . ."

The spectators applauded each one—all but the ex-commissar. Bogdan Peshkov sat alone, his potbelly bulging out over his thighs, drinking down cocktails with great gulps, staring somberly at the scene and occasionally glancing nervously over his shoulder.

Ballin stood just out of sight of the spectators with a duplicate list in his hand, checking the girls' names as they filed past him so that there should be no mix-ups.

Then all forty-six girls came out and lined up on the stage in a double rank. Ballin and Aldi came out, too. The three judges paraded back and forth. The plan was that any judge who thought that any girl had a good chance should tap her on the shoulder, the idea being to reduce the contestants to a mere dozen or so. Falck-Ross tapped Claire La Motte, Miss Archer, Miss Day, and a couple of other lovelies.

The contestants filed off again. As soon as they were off the stage, a couple of those who had not been chosen dissolved into tears, causing their eye makeup to run. Claire La Motte paused near Ross to murmur:

"Ovid, I don't like the look on Peshkov's face. He's drinking himself stiff, and he looks the way he did the night he shot all the panes out of the picture window."

"Oh," said Falck-Ross.

"Can't you hurry this thing through before he gets worse?"

"It'll take half or three-quarters of an hour yet, but I'll do my best."

Ross went back on the stage. The thirteen girls remaining in the contest paraded as before while Falck-Ross introduced them: "Miss Shirley Archer . . . Miss Loretta Day . . . Miss Mary Ferguson . . ."

It did, as he had foreseen, take a lot of time, during which Peshkov's pudding-face stared at him with unnerving blankness between cocktails.

After consultation, the judges eliminated all but three contestants: Shirley Archer, Loretta Day, and Claire La Motte. These paraded one by one as before, then lined up on the stage. Falck-Ross began a whispered consultation with Ballin and Aldi. Left to himself, Ross would have had trouble choosing among the three girls. He thought that, aside from personal sentiments, Miss Day had perhaps a slight edge.

Marcus Ballin, whose taste ran to cones, preferred Miss Archer. Joseph Aldi, whose bent lay in the direction of hemispheres, argued as stoutly for Miss Day. Falck-Ross spoke up for Miss La Motte on the ground that, presenting an intermediate or spheroconoidal form, she embodied the golden mean.

Ballin and Aldi would not be budged. At last Ballin whispered:

"Put down your second and third choices. We can't stand here arguing all afternoon."

When the choices for the lesser places were written down, it was found that both Ross and Ballin had named Miss Day for second.

"Okay," said Ballin. "Ovid and I will go along with you, won't you, Ovid? Day it is. Now we'll pick second and third prizes. I'd give La Motte second . . ."

As Claire was chosen second, Miss Archer took third. Ballin stepped to the edge of the stage with his arms up and cried:

"Ladies and gentlemen: By unanimous opinion of the judges, first prize in this great and unique Outstanding Knitwear Company bust-beauty contest is awarded to Miss Loretta Day—"

"Stop!" said a voice.

"What was that?" said Ballin.

"I said stop!" It was Peshkov, erect and weaving. "De best-looking girl is obvious Miss Claire La Motte. To give de first prize to anodder one is obvious capitalistic injostice. I order you to change your decision. Oddervise, to de penal camps of Siberia!"

"What—what—" sputtered Ballin. Then he pulled himself together and assumed an air as regal as that of the ex-commissar. He gestured to a couple of waiters. "Remove this man!"

At that moment, in a control booth of the Telagog Company, Gilbert Falck reached down, felt around until he had located his upper fishline, and pulled. When he had drawn the line as far as it would go, he let go one end and pulled on the other until he had the whole thing in his hands. He stuffed the string into his pants pocket. Now he was controlling Bundy's ballet dancer, while Bundy, unknowing in the next booth, was controlling his trade-journal staff writer.

In a dance studio, where the ballet dancer was performing hopefully under the eyes of a troupe manager in the expectation of being hired, he suddenly fell to the floor. Questions and shaking failed to rouse him. He lay where he had fallen, staring blankly and making odd walking motions with his legs and arms as if he were still erect.

At the same instant, while the waiters designated by Ballin as bouncers were staring apprehensively at their quarry, Ovid Ross took off in a tremendous leap from the stage and began bounding around the showroom, leaping high into the air to kick his heels together and flinging his arms about. Ross, imprisoned in his skull, was as astonished as anyone. He thought Falck must have gone mad.

Ross's astonishment changed to terror as he saw that he was bearing down on Bogdan Peshkov. The ex-commissar took a pistol from under his coat and waved it, shouting in Russian.

Bang! Glass tinkled. Ross took off in another leap that brought him down right on top of Peshkov. His body slammed into that of the ex-commissar. The two crashed into Peshkov's table. They rolled to the floor in a tangle of limbs and broken glass and table legs.

Ross found that his body was still kicking and flapping its arms. A kick accidentally sank into Peshkov's paunch and reduced the Muscovite to a half-comatose condition.

Then the seizure left Ross's body. He rose to his feet, fully under his own control. Everybody was talking at once. Several men gripped Peshkov while another gingerly held his pistol. Spectators crawled out from under tables.

Ross looked around, took a deep breath, and walked to the stage. Ballin was flapping his hands while Miss Archer had hysterics.

Ross faced the disorganized audience and bellowed: "Attention, everybody! All but those holding Mr. Peshkov take your seats. We will now go on with the contest. Waiters, mop up the spilled liquor. See that everybody has what he wants. Mr. Ballin was announcing the final results when he was interrupted. He will continue from there on."

So successful was Ross in restoring order that hardly a ripple of excitement was caused by the arrival of policemen to take Peshkov away.

After it was over, Ballin said: "You sure handled that, Ovid. How did you have nerve to jump on a man with a gun? That was reckless."

Ross made a deprecating movement. "Shucks, just an impulse, I guess. Too bad your show got kind of beat up, though."

"That's all right. We got the publicity."

"The only thing that worries me," said Ross, "is that Mr. Hoolihan's apt to think I got entirely too much publicity and fire me. Maybe you as a big advertiser could bring a little—uh—moral pressure?"

Ballin drew on his cigar and looked sharply at Ross. He said:

"Ovid, I've been thinking. The way things stand, you'll be tempted to try a little gentle blackmail on me because of the Heliac Club."

As Ross started to protest, Ballin held up a hand. "The only way to make sure you don't, as I see it, is to make your interests identical with my own."

"Yes?"

"I've got a little venture capital lying loose, and I've been thinking of starting a new trade journal, something like *The Garment Gazette* but specializing in sportswear."

"You mean a house organ?"

"God forbid! Nothing's duller than house organs. This would be a regular general-circulation journal, run independently of the Outstanding Knitwear Company. The managing editor would have a free hand to call his shots as he saw them. How would you like the job?"

When Ross got his breath back he could only say: "Gosh, Mr. Ballin!"

"However, your first assignment will have nothing to do with the magazine at all."

"Huh? What then?"

"It will be to accompany me to the Heliac Health Club for a weekend of healthful relaxation. After that, we'll be in the same boat!"

The following morning, Ovid Ross turned in his story and pictures on the bust-beauty contest and gave notice. Timothy Hoolihan grumped about Ross's pay's having been wasted, since he had not been on long enough to become useful.

"But Mr. Hoolihan!" said Ross. "Look at the opportunity! If I asked Mr. Ballin to wait a month, he'd find somebody else. And didn't the Taylor article say to try to please your employer in all things? And isn't he my future employer?"

"Huh," snorted Hoolihan. "Suppose so. Damn it, I don't know what's the matter with this firm! We have the highest turnover of any trade journal I know of. No sooner get 'em broken in than off they go!"

Ross could have told Hoolihan that his violent power complex might have something to do with it. But he forebore. It would only lead to an argument, and he might want a reference from Hoolihan some day.

Then Ross walked across town to the Telagog Company and told the receptionist: "Uh—send in that salesman, that Mr. Nye."

The salesman came in full of apologies: ". . . and while of course you waived damages in your contract, we are so anxious to please you that we're offering a one-year free extension of your three-months' trial telagog subscription. Moreover, Mr. Falck is no longer in our employ."

"What happened?"

"Our Mr. Bundy, whose wires were crossed with Mr. Falck's, suspected something and came in early this morning to find Falck taking out that switch he installed behind his panel. Falck, knowing how complicated hypospatial circuits are, had figured the electricians would get down to tracing the crossover this afternoon. Now about that extension—"

"Never mind. Just take this gadget out of my head, will you?"

"You mean you don't want any more telagog control?"

"That's right. I found I can do well enough by myself."

"But you don't know. Your erythrophobia may take you unawares—"

"I'll worry about that when the time comes. Right now I feel that, with all I've been through in the past week, I can never be embarrassed again."

Nye looked dubious. "That's not psychologically sound."

"I don't care. That's the way it is."

"We're pretty busy today. Couldn't you come in again next week?"

"No. I'm getting married tomorrow and leaving on a two weeks' trip, and starting a new job when I get back."

"Congratulations! Is it that Miss La Motte that Bundy and Falck were talking about?"

"Yes."

"They said she was a pip. How did you manage it with your shyness?"

"When I walked her to the train, I just asked her, and she said yes. Simple as that."

"Fine. But after all, you know, a man's wedding day and the night following it constitute a crisis of the first magnitude. With one of our experts at your personal helm you need not fear—"

"No!" shouted Ovid Ross, smiting the chair arm with his fist. "By gosh, there's some things I'm gonna do for myself! Now get that neurosurgeon out of his office and get to work!"

The Ameba

An ameba, grown too portly,
Elongates itself and shortly
Parts itself into amebae twain.
Now, this form of reproduction
Has its points, if your construction
Lets you split yourself without a pain.
It avoids the complications
That beset our copulations,
Which we try to regulate in vain.

Thus a piece of protoplasm
Undergoes bipartite spasm,
As it did in Eozoic clime;
Each ameba, now existing,
Is a unit, yet persisting,
Which has flourished since the dawn of time.
In this neat and sober fashion,
Unbetrayed by human passion,
Multiplies this deathless bit of slime.

Still, there must be something missing
To a life that knows no kissing,
Nor the other games the sexes play.
Surely, Solomon and Sheba
Had more fun than that ameba

E'er will know forever and a day.
    So I'd rather love my lassie
    Than to be a little, glassy,
Protoplasmic speck and live for ay.

Judgment Day

IT TOOK ME a long time to decide whether to let the earth live. Some might think this an easy decision. Well, it was and it wasn't. I wanted one thing, while the mores of my culture said to do the other.

This is a decision that few have to make. Hitler might give orders for the execution of ten million, and Stalin orders that would kill another ten million. But neither could send the world up in a puff of flame by a few marks on a piece of paper.

Only now has physics got to the point where such a decision is possible. Yet, with due modesty, I don't think my discovery was inevitable. Somebody might have come upon it later—say, in a few centuries, when such things might be better organized. My equation was far from obvious. All the last three decades' developments in nuclear physics have pointed away from it.

My chain reaction uses *iron,* the last thing that would normally be employed in such a series. It's at the bottom of the atomic energy curve. Anything else can be made into iron with a release of energy, while it takes energy to make iron into anything else.

Really, the energy doesn't come from the iron, but from the—the other elements in the reaction. But the iron is necessary. It is not exactly a catalyst, as it is transmuted and then turned back into iron again, whereas a true catalyst remains unchanged. But the effect is the same. With iron so common in the crust of the earth, it should be possible to blow the entire crust off with one big *poof*.

I recall how I felt when I first saw these equations here in my office last month. I sat staring at my name on the glass of the door, "Dr. Wade Ormont," only it appears backwards from the inside. I was sure I had made a mistake. I checked and rechecked and calculated and recalculated. I went through my nuclear equations at least thirty times. Each time my heart, my poor old heart, pounded harder and the knot in my stomach grew tighter. I had enough sense not to tell anybody else in the department about my discovery.

I did not even then give up trying to find something wrong with my equations. I fed them through the computer in case there was some glaring, obvious error I had been overlooking. Didn't that sort of thing—a minus for a plus or something—once happen to Einstein? I'm no Einstein, even if I am a pretty good physicist, so it could happen to me.

However, the computer said it hadn't. I was right.

The next question was: what to do with these results? They would not help us toward the laboratory's objectives: more powerful nuclear weapons and more efficient ways of generating nuclear power. The routine procedure would be to write up a report. This would be typed and photostated and stamped "Top Secret." A few copies would be taken around by messenger to those who needed to know about such things. It would go to the AEC and the others. People in this business have learned to be pretty close-mouthed, but the knowledge of my discovery would still spread, even though it might take years.

I don't think the government of the United States would ever try to blow up the world, but others might. Hitler might have, if he had known how, when he saw he faced inevitable defeat. The present Commies are pretty cold-blooded calculators, but one can't tell who'll be running their show in ten or twenty years. Once this knowledge gets around, anybody with a reasonable store of nuclear facilities could set the thing off. Most would not, even in revenge for defeat. But some might threaten to do so as blackmail, and a few would actually touch it off if thwarted. What's the proportion of paranoids and other crackpots in the world's population? It must be high enough, as a good fraction of the world's rulers and leaders have been of this type. No government yet devised—monarchy, aristocracy, theocracy, timocracy, democracy, dictatorship, soviet, or what have you—will absolutely stop such people from coming to the top. So long as these tribes of hairless apes are organized into sovereign nations, the nuclear Ragnarök is not only possible but probable.

For that matter, am I not a crackpot myself, calmly to contemplate blowing up the world?

No. At least the psychiatrist assured me my troubles were not of that sort. A man is not a nut if he goes about gratifying his desires in a rational manner. As to the kind of desires, that's nonrational anyway. I have adequate reasons for wishing to exterminate my species. It's no high-flown, farfetched theory either; no religious mania about the sinfulness of man, but a simple, wholesome lust for revenge. Christians pretend to disapprove of vengeance, but that's only one way of looking at it. Many other cultures have deemed it right and proper, so it can't be a sign of abnormality.

For instance, when I think back over my fifty-three years, what do I remember? Well, take the day I first entered school . . .

I suppose I was a fearful little brute at six: skinny, stubborn, and precociously intellectual. Because my father was a professor, I early picked up a sesquipedalian way of speaking (which has been defined as a tendency to use words like "sesquipedalian"). At six I was sprinkling my conversation with words like "theoretically" and "psychoneurotic." Because of illnesses I was as thin as a famine victim, with just enough muscle to get me from here to there.

While I always seemed to myself a frightfully good little boy whom everyone picked on, my older relatives in their last years assured me I was nothing of the sort, but the most intractable creature they ever saw. Not that I was naughty or destructive. On the contrary, I meticulously obeyed all formal rules and regulations with a zeal that would have gladdened the heart of a Prussian drill sergeant. It was that in those situations that depend, not on formal rules, but on accommodating oneself to the wishes of others, I never considered any wishes but my own. These I pursued with fanatical single-mindedness. As far as I was concerned, other people were simply inanimate things put into the world to minister to my wants. What they thought I neither knew nor cared.

Well, that's my relatives' story. Perhaps they were prejudiced too. Anyway, when I entered the first grade in a public school in New Haven, the fun started the first day. At recess a couple grabbed my cap for a game of "siloochee." That meant that they tossed the cap from one to the other while the owner leaped this way and that like a hooked fish trying to recover his headgear.

After a few minutes I lost my temper and tried to brain one of my tormentors with a rock. Fortunately, six-year-olds are not strong enough to kill each other by such simple means. I raised a lump on the boy's head, and then the others piled on me. Because of my weakness I was no match for any of them. The teacher dug me out from the bottom of the pile.

With the teachers I got on well. I had none of the normal boy's spirit of rebellion against all adults. In my precocious way I reasoned that adults probably knew more than I, and when they told me to do something I assumed they had good reasons and did it. The result was that I became teacher's pet, which made my life that much harder with my peers.

They took to waylaying me on my way home. First they would snatch my cap for a game of siloochee. The game would develop into a full-fledged baiting session, with boys running from me in front, jeering, while others ran up behind to hit or kick me. I must have chased them all over New Haven. When they got tired of being chased they would turn around, beat me (which they could do with absurd ease), and chase me for a while. I screamed, wept, shouted threats and abuse, made growling and hissing noises, and indulged in pseudo-fits like tearing my hair and foaming at the mouth in hope of scaring them off. This was just what they wanted. Hence, during most of my first three years in school, I was let out ten minutes early so as to be well on my way to my home on Chapel Street by the time the other boys got out.

This treatment accentuated my bookishness. I was digging through Millikan's *The Electron* at the age of nine

My father worried vaguely about my troubles but did little about them, being a withdrawn, bookish man himself. His line was medieval English literature, which he taught at Yale, but he still sympathized with a fellow intellectual and let me have my head. Sometimes he made fumbling efforts to engage me in ball-throwing and similar outdoor exercises. This had little effect, since he really hated exercise, sport, and the outdoors as much as I did, and was as clumsy and uncoördinated as I, to boot. Several times I resolved to force myself through a regular course of exercises to make myself into a young Tarzan, but when it came to executing my resolution I found the calisthenics such a frightful bore that I always let them lapse before they had done me any good.

I'm no psychologist. Like most followers of the exact sciences, I have an urge to describe psychology as a "science," in quotes, implying that only the exact sciences like physics are entitled to the name. That may be unfair, but it's how many physicists feel.

For instance, how can the psychologists all these years have treated sadism as something abnormal, brought on by some stupid parent's stopping his child from chopping up the furniture with a hatchet, thereby filling him with frustration and insecurity? On the basis of my own experience I will testify that all boys—well, perhaps ninety-nine percent—are natural-born sadists. Most of them have it beaten out of them. Correct that: most of them have it beaten down into their subconscious, or whatever the headshrinkers call that part of our minds nowadays. It's still there, waiting a chance to pop up. Hence crime, war, persecution, and all the other ills of society. Probably this cruelty was evolved as a useful characteristic back in the Stone Age. An anthropological friend once told me this idea was fifty years out of date, but he could be wrong also.

I suppose I have my share of it. At least I never wanted anything with such passionate intensity as I wanted to kill those little fiends in New Haven by lingering and horrible tortures. Even now, forty-five years after, that wish is still down there at the bottom of my mind, festering away. I still remember them as individuals and can still work myself into a frenzy of hatred and resentment just thinking about them. I don't suppose I have ever forgotten or forgiven an injury or insult in my life. I'm not proud of that quality, but neither am I ashamed of it. It is just the way I am.

Of course I had reasons for wishing to kill the little bastards, while they had no legitimate grudge against me. I had done nothing to them except to offer an inviting target, a butt, a punching bag. I never expected, as I pored over Millikan's book, that this would put me on the track of as complete a revenge as anybody could ask.

So much for boys. Girls I don't know about. I was the middle one of three brothers; my mother was a masterful character lacking the qualities usually thought of as feminine; and I never dated a girl until I was nearly thirty. I married late, for a limited time, and had no children. It would neatly have solved my present problem if I had found how to blow up the male half of the human race while sparing the female. That is not the desire for a superharem, either. I had enough trouble keeping one woman satisfied when I was married. It is just that the female half has never gone out of its way to make life hell for me, day after day for years, even though one or two women, too, have done me dirt. So, in a mild, detached way, I should be sorry to destroy the women along with the men.

By the time I was eleven and in the sixth grade, things had got worse. My mother thought that sending me to a military academy would "make a man of me." I should be forced to exercise and mix with the boys. Drill would teach me to stand up and hold my shoulders back. And I could no longer slouch into my father's study for a quiet session with the encyclopedia.

My father was disturbed by this proposal, thinking that sending me away from home would worsen my lot by depriving me of my only sanctuary. Also he did not think we could afford a private school on his salary and small private income.

As usual, my mother won. I was glad to go at first. Anything seemed better than the torment I was enduring. Perhaps a new crowd of boys would treat me better. If they didn't, our time would be so fully organized that nobody would have an opportunity to bully me.

So in the fall of 1927, with some fears but more hopes, I entered Rogers Military Academy at Waukeegus, New Jersey.

The first day, things looked pretty good. I admired the gray uniforms with the little brass strip around the edge of the visors of the caps.

But it took me only a week to learn two things. One was that the school, for all its uniforms and drills, was loosely run. The boys had plenty of time to think up mischief. The other was that, by the mysterious sense boys have, they immediately picked me as fair game.

On the third day somebody pinned a sign to my back, reading CALL ME SALLY. I went around all day unconscious of the sign and puzzled by being called "Sally." "Sally" I remained all the time I was at Rogers. The reason for calling me by a girl's name was merely that I was small, skinny, and unsocial, as I have never had any tendencies towards sexual abnormality. Had I had, I could easily have indulged them, Rogers being like other boys' boarding schools in this regard.

To this day I wince at the name "Sally." Some years ago, before I married, matchmaking friends introduced me to an attractive girl and could not understand why I dropped her like a hot brick. Her name was Sally.

There was much hazing of new boys at Rogers; the teachers took a fatalistic attitude and looked the other way. I was the favorite hazee, only with me it did not taper off after the first few weeks. They kept it up all through the first year. One morning in March, 1928, I was awakened around five by several boys' seizing my arms and legs and holding me down while one of them forced a cake of soap into my mouth.

"Look out he don't bite you," said one.

"Castor oil would be better."

"We ain't got none. Hold his nose; that'll make him open up."

"We should have shaved the soap up into little pieces. Then he'd have foamed better."

"Let me tickle him; that'll make him throw a fit."

"There, he's foaming fine, like a old geyser."

"Stop hollering, Sally," one of them addressed me, "or we'll put the suds in your eyes."

"Put the soap in 'em anyway. It'll make a red-eyed monster out of him. You know how he glares and shrieks when he gits mad?"

"Let's cut his hair all off. That'll *reely* make him look funny."

My yells brought one of the masters, who sharply ordered the tormenters to cease. They stood up while I rose to a sitting position on my bunk, spitting out soapsuds. The master said:

"What's going on here? Don't you know this is not allowed? It will mean ten rounds for each of you!"

"Rounds" were Rogers' form of discipline. Each round consisted of marching once around the track in uniform with your piece on your shoulder. (The piece was a Springfield 1903 army rifle with the firing pin removed, lest some student get .30 cartridges to fit and blow somebody's head off.) I hoped my tormentors would be at least expelled and was outraged by the lightness of their sentence. They on the other hand were indignant that they had been so hardly treated and protested with the air of outraged virtue:

"But Mr. Wilson, sir, we was only *playing* with him!"

At that age I did not know that private schools do not throw out paying students for any but the most heinous offenses; they can't afford to. The boys walked their ten rounds and hated me for it. They regarded me as a tattletale because my howls had drawn Mr. Wilson's attention and devoted themselves to thinking up new and ingenious ways to make me suffer. Now they were more subtle. There was nothing so crude as forcing soap down my throat. Instead it was hiding parts of my uniform, putting horse manure and other undesirable substances in my bed, and tripping me when I was drilling, so my nine-pound Springfield and I went sprawling in the dirt.

I fought often, always getting licked and usually being caught and given rounds for violating the school's rules. I was proud when I actually bloodied one boy's nose, but it did me no lasting good. He laid for me in the swimming pool and nearly drowned me. By now I was so terrorized that I did not dare to name my attackers, even when the masters revived me by artificial respiration and asked me. Wilson said:

"Ormont, we know what you're going through, but we can't give you a bodyguard to follow you around. Nor can we encourage you to tattle as a regular thing; that'll only make matters worse."

"But what can I *do,* sir? I try to obey the rules . . ."

"That's not it."

"What, then? I don't do anything to these kids; they just pick on me all the time."

"Well, for one thing, you could deprive them of the pleasure of seeing you yelling and making wild swings that never land . . . ." He drummed on his desk with his fingers. "We have this sort of trouble with boys like you, and if there's any way to stop it I don't know about it. You—let's face it; you're *queer.*"

"How?"

"Oh, your language is much too adult—"

"But isn't that what you're trying to teach us in English?"

"Sure, but that's not the point. Don't argue about it; I'm trying to help you. Then another thing. You argue about everything, and most of the time you're right. But you don't suppose people like you for putting them in the wrong, do you?"

"But people *ought—*"

"Precisely, they ought, but they don't. You can't change the world by yourself. If you had muscles like Dempsey you could get away with a good deal, but you haven't. So the best thing is to adopt a protective coloration. Pay no attention to their attacks or insults. Never argue; never complain; never criticize. Flash a glassy smile at everybody, even when you feel like murdering them. Keep your language simple and agree with what's said whether you feel that way or not. I hate to give you a counsel of hypocrisy, but I don't see any alternative. If we could only make some sort of athlete out of you . . ."

This was near the end of the school year. In a couple of weeks I was home. I complained about the school and asked to return to public school in New Haven. My parents objected on the ground that I was getting a better education at Rogers than I should get locally, which was true.

One day some of my old pals from public school caught me in a vacant lot and gave me a real beating, so that my face was swollen and marked. I realized that, terrible though the boys at Rogers were, they did not include the most fearful kind of all: the dimwitted muscular lout who has been left behind several grades in public school and avenges his boredom and envy by tormenting his puny classmates. After that I did not complain about Rogers.

People talk of "School days, school days, dear old golden rule days . . ." and all that rubbish. Psychologists tell me that, while children suffer somewhat, they remember only the pleasant parts of childhood and hence idealize it later.

Both are wrong as far as I am concerned. I had a hideous childhood, and the memory of it is as sharp and painful forty years later as it was then. If I want to spoil my appetite, I have only to reminisce about my dear, dead childhood.

For one thing, I have always hated all kinds of roughhouse and horseplay, and childhood is full of them unless the child is a cripple or other shut-in. I have always had an acute sense of my own dignity and integrity, and any japery or ridicule fills me with murderous resentment. I have always hated practical jokes. When I'm asked "Can't you take a joke?" the truthful answer is no, at least not in that sense. I want to kill the joker, then and for years afterwards. Such humor as I have is expressed in arch, pedantic little witticisms which amuse my academic friends but which mean nothing to most people. I might have got on better in the era of duelling. Not that I should have made much of a duellist, but I believe men were more careful then how they insulted others who might challenge them.

I set out in my second year at Rogers to try out Wilson's advice. Nobody will ever know what I went through learning to curb my hot temper and proud, touchy spirit, and literally to turn the other cheek. All that year I sat on my inner self, a mass of boiling fury and hatred. When I was teased, mocked, ridiculed, poked, pinched, punched, hair-pulled, kicked, tripped, and so on, I pretended that nothing had happened, in the hope that the others would get tired of punching a limp bag.

It didn't always work. Once I came close to killing a teaser by hitting him over the head with one of those long window openers with a bronze head on a wooden pole with which every classroom was equipped in the days before air-conditioned schools. Luckily I hit him with the wooden shaft and broke it, instead of with the bronze part.

As the year passed and the next began, I made myself so colorless that sometimes a whole week went by without my being baited. Of course I heard the hated nickname "Sally" every day, but the boys often used it without malice from habit. I also endured incidents like this: Everybody, my father, the masters, and the one or two older boys who took pity on me had urged me to go in for athletics. Now, at Rogers one didn't have to join a team. One had compulsory drill and calisthenics, but beyond that things were voluntary. (It was, as I said, a loosely run school.)

So I determined to try. One afternoon in the spring of 1929 I wandered out to the athletic field to find a group of my classmates getting up a game of baseball. I quietly joined them.

The two self-appointed captains squared off to choose their teams. One of them looked at me incredulously and asked: "Hey, Sally, are *you* in on this?"

"Yeah."

They began choosing. There were fifteen boys there, counting the captains and me. They chose until there was one boy left: me. The boy whose turn it was to choose said to the other captain:

"You can have him."

"Naw, I don't want him. You take him."

They argued while the subject of their mutual generosity squirmed and the boys already chosen grinned unsympathetically. Finally one captain said:

"Suppose we let him bat for both sides. That way, the guys the side of he's on won't be any worse off than the other."

"Okay. That suit you, Sally?"

"No, thanks," I said. "I guess I don't feel good anyway." I turned away before visible tears disgraced a thirteen-year-old.

Just after I started my third year, in the fall of 1929, the stock market fell flat. Soon my father found that his small private income had vanished as the companies in which he had invested, such as New York Central, stopped paying dividends. As a result, when I went home for Christmas, I learned that I could not go back to Rogers. Instead I should begin again with the February semester at the local high school.

In New Haven my 'possum tactics were put to a harder test. Many boys in my class had known me in former days and were delighted to take up where they had left off. For instance . . .

For decades, boys who found study hall dull have enlivened the proceedings with rubber bands and bits of paper folded into a V shape for missiles. The trick is to keep your missile weapon palmed until the teacher is looking elsewhere, and then to bounce your wad off the neck of some fellow student in front of you. Perhaps this was tame compared to nowadays, when, I understand, the sudents shoot ball bearings and knock the teacher's teeth and eyes out, and carve him with switchblade knives if he objects. All this happened before the followers of Dewey and Watson, with their lunacies about "permissive" training, had made classrooms into a semblance of the traditional cannibal feast with teacher playing the rôle of the edible missionary.

Right behind me sat a small boy named Patrick Hanrahan: a wiry, red-haired young hellion with a South Boston accent. He used to hit me with paper wads from time to time. I paid no attention because I knew he could lick me with ease. I was a head taller than he, but though I had begun to shoot up I was as skinny, weak, and clumsy as ever. If anything I was clumsier, so that I could hardly get through a meal without knocking over a glass.

One day I had been peppered with unusual persistence. My self-control slipped, as it would under a determined enough assault. I got out my own rubber band and paper missiles. I knew Hanrahan had shot at me before, but of course one never saw the boy who shot a given wad at you.

When a particularly hard-driven one stung me behind the ear, I whipped around and let Hanrahan have one in the face. It struck just below his left eye, hard enough to make a red spot. He looked astonished, then furious, and whispered:

"What you do that for?"

"You shot me," I whispered back.

"I did not! I'll git you for this! You meet me after class and I'll beat the ____ out of you!"

"You did too—" I began, when the teacher barked: "Ormont!" I shut up.

Perhaps Hanrahan really had not shot that last missile. One could argue that it was not more than his due for the earlier ones he *had* shot. But that is not how boys' minds work. They reason like the speaker of Voltaire's lines:

Cet animal est très méchant;
Quand on l'attaque, il se défend!

I knew if I met Hanrahan on the way out I should get a fearful beating. When I saw him standing on the marble steps that led up from the floor of study hall to the main exit, I walked quietly out the rear door.

I was on my way to the gym when I got a kick in the behind. There was Paddy Hanrahan, saying: "Come on, you yellow dog, fight!"

"Hello there," I said with a sickly grin.

He slapped my face.

"Having fun?" I said.

He kicked me in the leg.

"Keep right on," I said. "I don't mind."

He slapped and kicked me again, crying: "Yellow dog! Yellow dog!" I walked on toward the gymnasium as if nothing were happening, saying to myself: pay no attention, never criticize or complain, keep quiet, ignore it, pay no attention. . . . At last Paddy had to stop hitting and kicking me to go to his own next class.

I felt as if I had been dipped in manure. Nothing would have given me more pleasure than the sight of the whole school burning up with all the pupils trapped inside, screaming as they were broiled.

Next day I had a few bruises where Hanrahan had struck me—nothing serious. When he passed me he snarled: "Yellow dog!" but did not renew his assault. I have wasted much time in the forty years since then, imagining revenges on Paddy Hanrahan. Hanrahan coming into my office in rags and pleading for a job, and my having him thrown out . . . All that nonsense. I never saw him again after I finished school in New Haven.

There were a few more such incidents during that year and the following one. For instance at the first class meeting in the autumn of 1930, when the student officers of my class were elected for the semester, after several adolescents had been nominated for president, somebody piped up: "I nominate Wade Ormont!"

The whole class burst into a roar of laughter. One of the teachers pounced on the nominator and hustled him out for disturbing an orderly session by making frivolous nominations. Not knowing how to decline a nomination, I could do nothing but stare stonily ahead as if I hadn't heard. I need not have worried; the teachers never even wrote my name on the blackboard with those of the other nominees, nor did they ask for seconds. They just ignored the whole thing, as if the nominator had named Julius Caesar.

Then I graduated. As my marks put me in the top one percentile in scientific subjects and pretty high in the others, I got a scholarship at M.I.T. Without it I don't think my father could have afforded to send me.

When I entered M.I.T. I had developed my protective shell to a good degree of effectiveness, though not so perfectly as later: the automatic, insincere, glassy smile turned on as by a switch; the glad hand; the subdued, modest manner that never takes an initiative or advances an opinion unless it agrees with somebody's else. And I never, *never* showed emotion no matter what. How could I, when the one emotion inside me, overwhelming all others, was a blazing homicidal fury and hatred, stored up from all those years of torment? If I really let myself go I should kill somebody. The incident with the window opener had scared me. Much better never to show what you're thinking. As for feeling, it is better not to feel—to view the world with the detachment of a visitor at the zoo.

M.I.T. was good to me: it gave me a sound scientific education without pulverizing my soul in a mortar every day. For one thing, many other undergraduates were of my own introverted type. For another, we were kept too busy grinding away at heavy schedules to have time or energy for horseplay. For another, athletics did not bulk large in our program, so my own physical inferiority did not show up so glaringly. I reached medium height—about five-eight—but remained thin, weak, and awkward. Except for a slight middle-aged bulge around the middle I am that way yet.

For thousands of years, priests and philosophers have told us to love mankind without giving any sound reason for loving the creatures. The mass of them are a lot of cruel, treacherous, hairless apes. They hate us intellectuals, longhairs, highbrows, eggheads, or doubledomes, despite (or perhaps because) without us they would still be running naked in the wilderness and turning over flat stones for their meals. Love them? Hah!

Oh, I admit I have known a few of my own kind who were friendly. But by the time I had learned to suppress all emotion to avoid baiting, I was no longer the sort of man to whom many feel friendly. A bright enough physicist, well-mannered and seemingly poised, but impersonal and aloof, hardly seeing my fellow men except as creatures whom I had to manipulate in order to live. I have heard my colleagues describe others of my type as a "dry stick" or "cold fish," so no doubt they say the same of me. But who made me that way? I might not have become a fascinating *bon vivant* even if I had not been bullied, but I should probably not have become such an extreme aberrant. I might even have been able to like individuals and to show normal emotions.

The rest of my story is routine. I graduated from M.I.T. in 1936, took my Ph.D. from Chicago in 1939, got an instructorship at Chicago, and next year was scooped up the Manhattan Engineer District. I spent the first part of the war at the Argonne Labs and the last part at Los Alamos. More by good luck than good management, I never came in contact with the Communists during the bright pink era of 1933–45. If I had, I might easily, with my underdog complex and my store of resentment, have been swept into their net. After the war I worked under Lawrence at Berkeley.

I've had a succession of such jobs. They think I'm a sound man, perhaps not a great creative genius like Fermi or Teller, but a bear for spotting errors and judging the likeliest line of research to follow. It's all part of the objective, judicious side of my nature that I have long cultivated. I haven't tried to get into administrative work, which you have to do to rise to the top in bureaucratic setups like this. I hate to deal with people as individuals. I could probably do it—I have forced myself to do many things—but what would be the purpose? I have no desire for power over my fellows. I make enough to live on comfortably, especially since my wife left me. . . .

Oh, yes, my wife. I had got my Ph.D. before I had my first date. I dated girls occasionally for the next decade, but in my usual reserved, formal manner. I didn't even try to kiss them, let alone lay them. Why? Not religion. To me that's merely the sort of puerile superstition one would expect of a tribe of hairless apes. But I knew I should be awkward in making approaches, and perhaps be rebuffed or laughed at. The strongest drive in my life has been to put myself in a position where, and to mold my own personality so that, I shall not be laughed at.

Why did I leave Berkeley to go to Columbia University, for instance? I had a hobby of noting down people's conversation in shorthand when they weren't noticing. I was collecting this conversation for a statistical analysis of speech: the frequency of sounds, of words, combinations of words, parts of speech, topics of conversation, and so on. It was a purely intellectual hobby with no gainful objective, though I might have written up my results for one of the learned periodicals. One day my secretary noticed what I was doing and asked me about it. In an incautious moment I explained. She looked at me blankly, then burst into laughter and said:

"My goodness, Dr. Ormont, you *are* a nut!"

She never knew how close she came to having her skull bashed in with the inkwell. For a few seconds I sat there, gripping my pad and pencil and pressing my lips together. Then I put the paper quietly away and returned to my physics. I never resumed the statistical study, and I hated that secretary. I hated her particularly because I had had my own doubts about my mental health and so could not bear to be called a nut even in fun. I closed my shell more tightly than ever.

But I could not go on working next to that secretary. I could have framed her on some manufactured complaint, or just told the big boss I didn't like her and wanted another. But I refused to do this. I was the objective, impersonal man. I would never let an emotion make me unjust, and even asking to have her transferred would put a little black mark on her record. The only thing was for *me* to go away. So I got in touch with Columbia.

There I found a superior job with a superior secretary, Georgia Ehrenfels, so superior in fact that in 1958 we were married. I was already in my forties. She was twelve years younger and had been married and divorced once. God knows what she saw in me.

I think it took her about six months to realize that she had made an even bigger mistake than the first time. I never realized it at all. My mind was on my physics, and a wife was a nice convenience but nobody to open up one's shell for. Later, when things began to go bad, I tried to open my shell and found that the hinges were stuck.

My wife tried to make me over, but that is not easy with a middle-aged man, even under the most favorable conditions. She pestered me to get a house in the country until I gave in. I had never owned a house and proved an inefficient householder. I hated the tinkering, gardening, and other minutiae of suburban life. Georgia did most of the work. It brought on a miscarriage the only time she ever got pregnant. I was sorry then, but what could I do? A few months later I came home from work to find her gone and a note beginning:

> Dear Wade:
>
> It is no use. It is not your fault. You are as you are, as I should have realized at the beginning. Perhaps I am foolish not to appreciate your many virtues and to insist on that human warmth you do not have. . . .

Well, she got her divorce and married another academic man. I don't know how they have got on, but the last I heard they were still married. Psychologists say people tend to repeat their marital mistakes rather than to learn from them. I resolved not to repeat mine by the simple expedient of having nothing more to do with women. So far I have kept to it.

This breakup did disturb me for a time, more than Iron Man Ormont would care to admit. I drank heavily, which I had never done. I began to make mistakes in my work. Finally I went to a psychiatrist. They might be one-third quackery and one-third unprovable speculation, but to whom else could one turn?

The psychiatrist was a nice little man, stout and square built, with a subdued manner—a rather negative, colorless personality. I was surprised, for I had expected something with a pointed beard, Viennese gestures, and aggressive garrulity. Instead he quietly drew me out. After a few months he told me:

"You're not the least psychotic, Wade. You do have what we call a schizoidal personality. Such people always have a hard time in personal relations. Now, you have found a solution for your problem in your pose of good-natured indifference. The trouble is that the pose has been practiced so long that it's become the real Dr. Ormont, and it has raised up its own difficulties. You practiced so long and so hard suppressing your emotions that now you can't let them go when you want to. . . ."

There was more of the same, much of which I had already figured out for myself. That part was fine; no disagreement. But what to do about it? I learned that the chances of improvement by psychoanalytical or similar treatment go down rapidly after the age of thirty, and over forty it is so small as hardly to be worth bothering with. After a year of spending the psychiatrist's time and my money, we gave up.

I had kept my house all this time. I had in fact adapted myself intelligently to living in a house, and I had accumulated such masses of scientific books, magazines, pamphlets, and other printed matter that I could no longer have got into an ordinary apartment. I had a maid, old and ugly enough so that sex should not raise its head. Otherwise I spent my time away from the office alone in my house. I learned to plant the lot with ground cover that required no mowing and to hire a gardener a few times a year so as not to outrage the neighbors too much.

Then I got a better job here. I sold my house on Long Island and bought another here, which I have run in the same style as the last one. I let the neighbors strictly alone. If they had done likewise I might have had an easier time deciding what to do with my discovery. As it is, many suburbanites seem to think that if a man lives alone and doesn't wish to be bothered, he must be some sort of ogre.

If I write up the chain reaction, the news will probably get out. No amount of security regulations will stop people from talking about the impending end of the world. Once having done so, the knowledge will probably cause the blowing-up of the earth—not right away, but in a decade or two. I shall probably not live to see it, but it wouldn't displease me if it did go off in my lifetime. It would not deprive me of much.

I'm fifty-three and look older. My doctor tells me I'm not in good shape. My heart is not good; my blood pressure is too high; I sleep badly and have headaches. The doctor tells me to cut down on coffee, to stop this and stop that. But even if I do, he can't assure me a full decade more. There is nothing simple wrong with me that an operation would help; just a poor weak body further abused by too intensive mental work over most of my life.

The thought of dying does not much affect me. I have never got much fun out of life, and such pleasures as there are have turned sour in recent years. I find myself getting more and more indifferent to everything but physics, and even that is becoming a bore.

The one genuine emotion I have left is hatred. I hate mankind in general in a mild, moderate way. I hate the male half of mankind more intensely, and the class of boys most bitterly of all. I should love to see the severed heads of all the boys in the world stuck on spikes.

Of course I am objective enough to know why I feel this way. But knowing the reason for the feeling doesn't change the feeling, at least not in a hardened old character like me.

I also know that to wipe out all mankind would not be just. It would kill millions who have never harmed me or, for that matter, harmed anybody else.

But why in hell should I be just? When have these glabrous primates been just to me? The headshrinker tried to tell me to let my emotions go, and then perhaps I could learn to be happy. Well, I have just one real emotion. If I let it go, that's the end of the world.

On the other hand, I should destroy not only all the billions of bullies and sadists, but the few victims like myself. I have sympathized with Negroes and other downtrodden people because I knew how they felt. If there were some way to save them while destroying the rest . . . But my sympathy is probably wasted; most of the downtrodden would persecute others too if they had the power.

I had thought about the matter for several days without a decision. Then came Mischief Night. This is the night before Halloween, when the local kids raise hell. The following night they go out again to beg candy and cookies from the people whose windows they have soaped and whose garbage pails they have upset. If we were allowed to shoot a few of the little bastards, the rest might behave better.

All the boys in my neighborhood hate me. I don't know why. It's one of those things like a dog's sensing the dislike of another dog. Though I don't scream or snarl at them and chase them, they somehow know I hate them even when I have nothing to do with them.

I was so buried in my problem that I forgot about Mischief Night, and as usual stopped in town for dinner at a restaurant before taking the train out to my suburb. When I got home, I found that in the hour of darkness before my arrival, the local boys had given my place the full treatment. The soaped windows and the scattered garbage and the toilet paper spread around were bad but endurable. However, they had also burgled my garage and gone over my little British two-seater. The tires were punctured, the upholstery slashed, and the wiring ripped out of the engine. There were other damages like uprooted shrubbery. . . .

To make sure I knew what they thought, they had lettered a lot of shirt cardboards and left them around, reading: OLD LADY ORMONT IS A NUT! BEWARE THE MAD SCIENTIST! PSYCOPATH (*sic*) ORMONT! ORMONT IS A FAIRY!

That decided me. There is one way I can be happy during my remaining years, and that is by the knowledge that all these bastards will get theirs someday. I hate them. I hate them. I hate everybody. I want to kill mankind. I'd kill them by slow torture if I could. If I can't, blowing up the earth will do. I shall write my report.

A Gun for Dinosaur

No, I'm sorry, Mr. Seligman, but I can't take you hunting Late Mesozoic dinosaur.

Yes, I know what the advertisement says.

Why not? How much d'you weigh? A hundred and thirty? Let's see; that's under ten stone, which is my lower limit.

I could take you to other periods, you know. I'll take you to any period in the Cenozoic. I'll get you a shot at an entelodont or a uintathere. They've got fine heads.

I'll even stretch a point and take you to the Pleistocene, where you can try for one of the mammoths or the mastodon.

I'll take you back to the Triassic where you can shoot one of the smaller ancestral dinosaurs. But I will jolly well not take you to the Jurassic or Cretaceous. You're just too small.

What's your size got to do with it? Look here, old boy, what did you think you were going to shoot your dinosaur with?

Oh, you hadn't thought, eh?

Well, sit there a minute. . . . Here you are: my own private gun for that work, a Continental .600. Does look like a shotgun, dosn't it? But it's rifled, as you can see by looking through the barrels. Shoots a pair of .600 Nitro Express cartridges the size of bananas; weighs fourteen and a half pounds and has a muzzle energy of over seven thousand foot-pounds. Costs fourteen hundred and fifty dollars. Lot of money for a gun, what?

I have some spares I rent to the sahibs. Designed for knocking down elephant. Not just wounding them, knocking them base-over-apex. That's why they don't make guns like this in America, though I suppose they will if hunting parties keep going back in time.

Now, I've been guiding hunting parties for twenty years. Guided 'em in Africa until the game gave out there except on the preserves. And all that time I've never known a man your size who could handle the six-nought-nought. It knocks 'em over, and even when they stay on their feet they get so scared of the bloody cannon after a few shots that they flinch. And they find the gun too heavy to drag around rough Mesozoic country. Wears 'em out.

It's true that lots of people have killed elephant with lighter guns: the .500, .475, and .465 doubles, for instance, or even .375 magnum repeaters. The difference is, with a .375 you have to hit something vital, preferably the heart, and can't depend on simple shock power.

An elephant weighs—let's see—four to six tons. You're proposing to shoot reptiles weighing two or three times as much as an elephant and with much greater tenacity of life. That's why the syndicate decided to take no more people dinosaur hunting unless they could handle the .600. We learned the hard way, as you Americans say. There were some unfortunate incidents. . . .

I'll tell you, Mr. Seligman. It's after seventeen-hundred. Time I closed the office. Why don't we stop at the bar on our way out while I tell you the story?

. . . It was about the Raja's and my fifth safari into time. The Raja? Oh, he's the Aiyar half of Rivers and Aiyar. I call him the Raja because he's the hereditary monarch of Janpur. Means nothing nowadays, of course. Knew him in India and ran into him in New York running the Indian tourist agency. That dark chap in the photograph on my office wall, the one with his foot on the dead sabertooth.

Well, the Raja was fed up with handing out brochures about the Taj Mahal and wanted to do a bit of hunting again. I was at loose ends when we heard of Professor Prochaska's time machine at Washington University.

Where's the Raja now? Out on safari in the Early Oligocene after titanothere while I run the office. We take turn about, but the first few times we went out together.

Anyhow, we caught the next plane to St. Louis. To our mortification, we found we weren't the first. Lord, no! There were other hunting guides and no end of scientists, each with his own idea of the right way to use the machine.

We scraped off the historians and archaeologists right at the start. Seems the ruddy machine won't work for periods more recent than 100,000 years ago. It works from there up to about a billion years.

Why? Oh, I'm no four-dimensional thinker; but, as I understand it, if people could go back to a more recent time, their actions would affect our own history, which would be a paradox or contradiction of facts. Can't have that in a well-run universe, you know.

But, before 100,000 B.C., more or less, the actions of the expeditions are lost in the stream of time before human history begins. At that, once a stretch of past time has been used, say the month of January, one million B.C., you can't use that stretch over again by sending another party into it. Paradoxes again.

The professor isn't worried, though. With a billion years to exploit, he won't soon run out of eras.

Another limitation of the machine is the matter of size. For technical reasons, Prochaska had to build the transition chamber just big enough to hold four men with their personal gear, and the chamber wallah. Larger parties have to be sent through in relays. That means, you see, it's not practical to take jeeps, launches, aircraft, and other powered vehicles.

On the other hand, since you're going to periods without human beings, there's no whistling up a hundred native bearers to trot along with your gear on their heads. So we usually take a train of asses—burros, they call them here. Most periods have enough natural forage so you can get where you want to go.

As I say, everybody had his own idea for using the machine. The scientists looked down their noses at us hunters and said it would be a crime to waste the machine's time pandering to our sadistic amusements.

We brought up another angle. The machine cost a cool thirty million. I understand this came from the Rockefeller Board and such people, but that accounted for the original cost only, not the cost of operation. And the thing uses fantastic amounts of power. Most of the scientists' projects, while worthy enough, were run on a shoestring, financially speaking.

Now, we guides catered to people with money, a species with which America seems well stocked. No offense, old boy. Most of these could afford a substantial fee for passing through the machine into the past. Thus we could help finance the operation of the machine for scientific purposes, provided we got a fair share of its time. In the end, the guides formed a syndicate of eight members, one member being the partnership of Rivers and Aiyar, to apportion the machine's time.

We had rush business from the start. Our wives—the Raja's and mine—raised hell with us for a while. They'd hoped that, when the big game gave out in our own era, they'd never have to share us with lions and things again, but you know how women are. Hunting's not really dangerous if you keep your head and take precautions.

On the fifth expedition, we had two sahibs to wet-nurse; both Americans in their thirties, both physically sound, and both solvent. Otherwise they were as different as different can be.

Courtney James was what you chaps call a playboy: a rich young man from New York who'd always had his own way and didn't see why that agreeable condition shouldn't continue. A big bloke, almost as big as I am; handsome in a florid way, but beginning to run to fat. He was on his fourth wife and, when he showed up at the office with a blond twist with "model" written all over her, I assumed that this was the fourth Mrs. James.

"Miss Bartram," she corrected me, with an embarrassed giggle.

"She's not my wife," James explained. "My wife is in Mexico, I think, getting a divorce. But Bunny here would like to go along—"

"Sorry," I said, "we don't take ladies. At least, not to the Late Mesozoic."

This wasn't strictly true, but I felt we were running enough risks, going after a little-known fauna, without dragging in people's domestic entanglements. Nothing against sex, you understand. Marvelous institution and all that, but not where it interferes with my living.

"Oh, nonsense!" said James. "If she wants to go, she'll go. She skis and flies my airplane, so why shouldn't she—"

"Against the firm's policy," I said.

"She can keep out of the way when we run up against the dangerous ones," he said.

"No, sorry."

"Damn it!" said he, getting red. "After all, I'm paying you a goodly sum, and I'm entitled to take whoever I please."

"You can't hire me to do anything against my best judgment," I said. "If that's how you feel, get another guide."

"All right, I will," he said. "And I'll tell all my friends you're a God-damned—" Well, he said a lot of things I won't repeat, until I told him to get out of the office or I'd throw him out.

I was sitting in the office and thinking sadly of all that lovely money James would have paid me if I hadn't been so stiff-necked, when in came my other lamb, one

August Holtzinger. This was a little slim pale chap with glasses, polite and formal. Holtzinger sat on the edge of his chair and said:

"Uh—Mr. Rivers, I don't want you to think I'm here under false pretenses. I'm really not much of an outdoorsman, and I'll probably be scared to death when I see a real dinosaur. But I'm determined to hang a dinosaur head over my fireplace or die in the attempt."

"Most of us are frightened at first," I soothed him, "though it doesn't do to show it." And little by little I got the story out of him.

While James had always been wallowing in the stuff, Holtzinger was a local product who'd only lately come into the real thing. He'd had a little business here in St. Louis and just about made ends meet when an uncle cashed in his chips somewhere and left little Augie the pile.

Now Holtzinger had acquired a fiancée and was building a big house. When it was finished, they'd be married and move into it. And one furnishing he demanded was a ceratopsian head over the fireplace. Those are the ones with the big horned heads with a parrot beak and a frill over the neck, you know. You have to think twice about collecting them, because if you put a seven-foot *Triceratops* head into a small living room, there's apt to be no room left for anything else.

We were talking about this when in came a girl: a small girl in her twenties, quite ordinary-looking, and crying.

"Augie!" she cried. "You can't! You mustn't! You'll be killed!" She grabbed him round the knees and said to me:

"Mr. Rivers, you mustn't take him! He's all I've got! He'll never stand the hardships!"

"My dear young lady," I said, "I should hate to cause you distress, but it's up to Mr. Holtzinger to decide whether he wishes to retain my services."

"It's no use, Claire," said Holtzinger. "I'm going, though I'll probably hate every minute of it."

"What's that, old boy?" I said. "If you hate it, why go? Did you lose a bet, or something?"

"No," said Holtzinger. "It's this way. Uh—I'm a completely undistinguished kind of guy. I'm not brilliant or big or strong or handsome. I'm just an ordinary Midwestern small businessman. You never even notice me at Rotary luncheons, I fit in so perfectly.

"But that doesn't say I'm satisfied. I've always hankered to go to far places and do big things. I'd like to be a glamorous, adventurous sort of guy. Like you, Mr. Rivers."

"Oh, come," I said. "Professional hunting may seem glamorous to you, but to me it's just a living."

He shook his head. "Nope. You know what I mean. Well, now I've got this legacy, I could settle down to play bridge and golf the rest of my life, and try to act like I wasn't bored. But I'm determined to do something with some color in it, once at least. Since there's no more real big-game hunting in the present, I'm gonna shoot a dinosaur and hang his head over my mantel if it's the last thing I do. I'll never be happy otherwise."

Well, Holtzinger and his girl argued, but he wouldn't give in. She made me swear to take the best care of her Augie and departed, sniffling.

When Holtzinger had left, who should come in but my vile-tempered friend Courtney James? He apologized for insulting me, though you could hardly say he groveled.

"I don't really have a bad temper," he said, "except when people won't coöperate with me. Then I sometimes get mad. But so long as they're coöperative I'm not hard to get along with."

I knew that by "coöperate" he meant to do whatever Courtney James wanted, but I didn't press the point. "How about Miss Bartram?" I asked.

"We had a row," he said. "I'm through with women. So, if there's no hard feelings, let's go on from where we left off."

"Very well," I said, business being business.

The Raja and I decided to make it a joint safari to

eighty-five million years ago: the Early Upper Cretaceous, or the Middle Cretaceous as some American geologists call it. It's about the best period for dinosaur in Missouri. You'll find some individual species a little larger in the Late Upper Cretaceous, but the period we were going to gives a wider variety.

Now, as to our equipment: The Raja and I each had a Continental .600, like the one I showed you, and a few smaller guns. At this time we hadn't worked up much capital and had no spare .600s to rent.

August Holtzinger said he would rent a gun, as he expected this to be his only safari, and there's no point in spending over a thousand dollars for a gun you'll shoot only a few times. But, since we had no spare .600s, his choice lay between buying one of those and renting one of our smaller pieces.

We drove into the country and set up a target to let him try the .600. Holtzinger heaved up the gun and let fly. He missed completely, and the kick knocked him flat on his back.

He got up, looking paler than ever, and handed me back the gun, saying: "Uh—I think I'd better try something smaller."

When his shoulder stopped hurting, I tried him out on the smaller rifles. He took a fancy to my Winchester 70, chambered for the .375 magnum cartridge. This is an excellent all-round gun—perfect for the big cats and bears, but a little light for elephant and definitely light for dinosaur. I should never have given in, but I was in a hurry, and it might have taken months to have a new .600 made to order for him. James already had a gun, a Holland & Holland .500 double express, which is almost in a class with the .600.

Both sahibs had done a bit of shooting, so I didn't worry about their accuracy. Shooting dinosaur is not a matter of extreme accuracy, but of sound judgment and smooth coordination so you shan't catch twigs in the mechanism of your gun, or fall into holes, or climb a small tree that the dinosaur can pluck you out of, or blow your guide's head off.

People used to hunting mammals sometimes try to shoot a dinosaur in the brain. That's the silliest thing you can do, because dinosaur haven't got any. To be exact, they have a little lump of tissue the size of a tennis ball on the front end of their spines, and how are you going to hit that when it's imbedded in a six-foot skull?

The only safe rule with dinosaur is: always try for a heart shot. They have big hearts, over a hundred pounds in the largest species, and a couple of .600 slugs through the heart will slow them up, at least. The problem is to get the slugs through that mountain of meat around it.

Well, we appeared at Prochaska's laboratory one rainy morning: James and Holtzinger, the Raja and I, our herder Beauregard Black, three helpers, a cook, and twelve jacks.

The transition chamber is a little cubbyhole the size of a small lift. My routine is for the men with the guns to go first in case a hungry theropod is standing near the machine when it arrives. So the two sahibs, the Raja, and I crowded into the chamber with our guns and packs. The operator squeezed in after us, closed the door, and fiddled with his dials. He set the thing for April twenty-fourth, eighty-five million B.C., and pressed the red button. The lights went out, leaving the chamber lit by a little battery-operated lamp. James and Holtzinger looked pretty green, but that may have been the lighting. The Raja and I had been through all this before, so the vibration and vertigo didn't bother us.

The little spinning black hands of the dials slowed down and stopped. The operator looked at his ground-level gauge and turned the handwheel that raised the chamber so it shouldn't materialize underground. Then he pressed another button, and the door slid open.

No matter how often I do it, I get a frightful thrill out of stepping into a bygone era. The operator had raised the chamber a foot above the ground level, so I jumped down, my gun ready. The others came after.

"Right-ho," I said to the chamber wallah, and he closed the door. The chamber disappeared, and we looked around. There weren't any dinosaur in sight, nothing but lizards.

In this period, the chamber materializes on top of a rocky rise, from which you can see in all directions as far as the haze will let you. To the west, you see the arm of the Kansas Sea that reaches across Missouri and the big swamp around the bayhead where the sauropods live.

To the north is a low range that the Raja named the Janpur Hills, after the Indian kingdom his forebears once ruled. To the east, the land slopes up to a plateau, good for ceratopsians, while to the south is flat country with more sauropod swamps and lots of ornithopod: duckbill and iguanodont.

The finest thing about the Cretaceous is the climate: balmy like the South Sea Islands, but not so muggy as most Jurassic climates. It was spring, with dwarf magnolias in bloom all over.

A thing about this landscape is that it combines a fairly high rainfall with an open type of vegetation cover. That is, the grasses hadn't yet evolved to the point of forming solid carpets over all the open ground. So the ground is thick with laurel, sassafras, and other shrubs, with bare earth between. There are big thickets of palmettos and ferns. The trees round the hill are mostly cycads, standing singly and in copses. You'd call 'em palms. Down towards the Kansas Sea are more cycads and willows, while the uplands are covered with screw pine and ginkgoes.

Now, I'm no bloody poet—the Raja writes the stuff, not me—but I can appreciate a beautiful scene. One of the helpers had come through the machine with two of the jacks and was pegging them out, and I was looking through the haze and sniffing the air, when a gun went off behind me—*bang! bang!*

I whirled round, and there was Courtney James with his .500, and an ornithomime legging it for cover fifty yards away. The ornithomimes are medium-sized running dinosaurs, slender things with long necks and legs, like a cross between a lizard and an ostrich. This kind is about seven feet tall and weighs as much as a man. The beggar had wandered out of the nearest copse, and James gave him both barrels. Missed.

I was upset, as trigger-happy sahibs are as much a menace to their party as theropods. I yelled: "Damn it, you idiot! I thought you weren't to shoot without a word from me?"

"And who the hell are you to tell me when I'll shoot my own gun?" he said.

We had a rare old row until Holtzinger and the Raja got us calmed down. I explained:

"Look here, Mr. James, I've got reasons. If you shoot off all your ammunition before the trip's over, your gun won't be available in a pinch, as it's the only one of its caliber. If you empty both barrels at an unimportant target, what would happen if a big theropod charged before you could reload? Finally, it's not sporting to shoot everything in sight, just to hear the gun go off. Do you understand?"

"Yeah, I guess so," he said.

The rest of the party came through the machine, and we pitched our camp a safe distance from the materializing place. Our first task was to get fresh meat. For a twenty-one-day safari like this, we calculate our food requirements closely, so we can make out on tinned stuff and concentrates if we must, but we count on killing at least one piece of meat. When that's butchered, we go off on a short tour, stopping at four or five camping places to hunt and arriving back at base a few days before the chamber is due to appear.

Holtzinger, as I said, wanted a ceratopsian head, any kind. James insisted on just one head: a tyrannosaur. Then everybody'd think he'd shot the most dangerous game of all time.

Fact is, the tyrannosaur's overrated. He's more a carrion eater than an active predator, though he'll snap you up if he gets the chance. He's less dangerous than some of the other therapods—the flesh eaters, you know—

such as the smaller *Gorgosaurus* from the period we were in. But everybody's read about the tyrant lizard, and he does have the biggest head of the theropods.

The one in our period isn't the *rex,* which is later and a bit bigger and more specialized. It's the *trionyches,* with the forelimbs not quite so reduced, though they're still too small for anything but picking the brute's teeth after a meal.

When camp was pitched, we still had the afternoon. So the Raja and I took our sahibs on their first hunt. We had a map of the local terrain from previous trips.

The Raja and I have worked out a system for dinosaur hunting. We split into two groups of two men each and walk parallel from twenty to forty yards apart. Each group has a sahib in front and a guide following, telling him where to go. We tell the sahibs we put them in front so they shall have the first shot. Well, that's true, but another reason is they're always tripping and falling with their guns cocked, and if the guide were in front he'd get shot.

The reason for two groups is that if a dinosaur starts for one, the other gets a good heart shot from the side.

As we walked, there was the usual rustle of lizards scuttling out of the way: little fellows, quick as a flash and colored like all the jewels in Tiffany's, and big gray ones that hiss at you as they plod off. There were tortoises and a few little snakes. Birds with beaks full of teeth flapped off squawking. And always there was that marvelous mild Cretaceous air. Makes a chap want to take his clothes off and dance with vine leaves in his hair, if you know what I mean.

Our sahibs soon found that Mesozoic country is cut up into millions of nullahs—gullies, you'd say. Walking is one long scramble, up and down, up and down.

We'd been scrambling for an hour, and the sahibs were soaked with sweat and had their tongues hanging out, when the Raja whistled. He'd spotted a group of bonehead feeding on cycad shoots.

These are the troödonts, small ornithopods about the

size of men with a bulge on top of their heads that makes them look almost intelligent. Means nothing, because the bulge is solid bone. The males butt each other with these heads in fighting over the females.

These chaps would drop down on all fours, munch up a shoot, then stand up and look around. They're warier than most dinosaur, because they're the favorite food of the big theropods.

People sometimes assume that because dinosaur are so stupid, their senses must be dim, too. But it's not so. Some, like the sauropods, are pretty dim-sensed, but most have good smell and eyesight and fair hearing. Their weakness is that having no minds, they have no memories. Hence, out of sight, out of mind. When a big theropod comes slavering after you, your best defense is to hide in a nullah or behind a bush, and if he can neither see you nor smell you he'll just wander off.

We skulked up behind a patch of palmetto downwind from the bonehead. I whispered to James:

"You've had a shot already today. Hold your fire until Holtzinger shoots, and then shoot only if he misses or if the beast is getting away wounded."

"Uh-huh," said James.

We separated, he with the Raja and Holtzinger with me. This got to be our regular arrangement. James and I got on each other's nerves, but the Raja's a friendly, sentimental sort of bloke nobody can help liking.

We crawled round the palmetto patch on opposite sides, and Holtzinger got up to shoot. You daren't shoot a heavy-caliber rifle prone. There's not enough give, and the kick can break your shoulder.

Holtzinger sighted round the last rew fronds of palmetto. I saw his barrel wobbling and waving. Then he lowered his gun and tucked it under his arm to wipe his glasses.

Off went James's gun, both barrels again.

The biggest bonehead went down, rolling and thrashing. The others ran away on their hindlegs in great leaps, their heads jerking and their tails sticking up behind.

"Put your gun on safety," I said to Holtzinger, who'd started forward. By the time we got to the bonehead, James was standing over it, breaking open his gun and blowing out the barrels. He looked as smug as if he'd come into another million and was asking the Raja to take his picture with his foot on the game.

I said: "I thought you were to give Holtzinger the first shot?"

"Hell, I waited," he said, "and he took so long I thought he must have gotten buck fever. If we stood around long enough, they'd see us or smell us."

There was something in what he said, but his way of saying it put my monkey up. I said: "If that sort of thing happens once more, we'll leave you in camp the next time we go out."

"Now, gentlemen," said the Raja. "After all, Reggie, these aren't experienced hunters."

"What now?" said Holtzinger. "Haul him back ourselves or send out the men?"

"We'll sling him under the pole," I said. "He weighs under two hundred."

The pole was a telescoping aluminium carrying pole I had in my pack, with padded yokes on the ends. I brought it because, in such eras, you can't count on finding saplings strong enough for proper poles on the spot.

The Raja and I cleaned our bonehead to lighten him and tied him to the pole. The flies began to light on the offal by thousands. Scientists say they're not true flies in the modern sense, but they look and act like flies. There's one huge four-winged carrion fly that flies with a distinctive deep thrumming note.

The rest of the afternoon we sweated under that pole, taking turn about. The lizards scuttled out of the way, and the flies buzzed round the carcass.

We got to camp just before sunset, feeling as if we could eat the whole bonehead at one meal. The boys had the camp running smoothly, so we sat down for our tot of whiskey, feeling like lords of creation, while the cook broiled bonehead steaks.

Holtzinger said: "Uh—if I kill a ceratopsian, how do we get his head back?"

I explained: "If the ground permits, we lash it to the patent aluminium roller frame and sled it in."

"How much does a head like that weigh?" he asked.

"Depends on the age and the species," I told him. "The biggest weigh over a ton, but most run between five hundred and a thousand pounds."

"And all the ground's rough like it was today?"

"Most of it," I said. "You see, it's the combination of the open vegetation cover and the moderately high rainfall. Erosion is frightfully rapid."

"And who hauls the head on its little sled?"

"Everybody with a hand," I said. "A big head would need every ounce of muscle in this party. On such a job there's no place for side."

"Oh," said Holtzinger. I could see he was wondering whether a ceratopsian head would be worth the effort.

The next couple of days we trekked round the neighborhood. Nothing worth shooting; only a herd of ornithomimes, which went bounding off like a lot of ballet dancers. Otherwise there were only the usual lizards and pterosaurs and birds and insects. There's a big lace-winged fly that bites dinosaurs, so, as you can imagine, its beak makes nothing of a human skin. One made Holtzinger leap and dance like a Red Indian when it bit him through his shirt. James joshed him about it, saying:

"What's all the fuss over one little bug?"

The second night, during the Raja's watch, James gave a yell that brought us all out of our tents with rifles. All that had happened was that a dinosaur tick had crawled in with him and started drilling under his armpit. Since it's as big as your thumb even when it hasn't fed, he was understandably startled. Luckily he got it before it had taken its pint of blood. He'd pulled Holtzinger's leg pretty hard about the fly bite, so now Holtzinger repeated the words:

"What's all the fuss over one little bug, buddy?"

James squashed the tick underfoot with a grunt, not much liking to be hoist by his own what-d'you-call-it.

We packed up and started on our circuit. We meant to take the sahibs first to the sauropod swamp, more to see the wildlife than to collect anything.

From where the transition chamber materializes, the sauropod swamp looks like a couple of hours' walk, but it's really an all-day scramble. The first part is easy, as it's downhill and the brush isn't heavy. Then, as you get near the swamp, the cycads and willows grow so thickly that you have to worm your way among them.

I led the party to a sandy ridge on the border of the swamp, as it was pretty bare of vegetation and afforded a fine view. When we got to the ridge, the sun was about to go down. A couple of crocs slipped off into the water. The sahibs were so tired that they flopped down in the sand as if dead.

The haze is thick round the swamp, so the sun was deep red and weirdly distorted by the atmospheric layers. There was a high layer of clouds reflecting the red and gold of the sun, too, so altogether it was something for the Raja to write one of his poems about. A few little pterosaur were wheeling overhead like bats.

Beauregard Black got a fire going. We'd started on our steaks, and that pagoda-shaped sun was just slipping below the horizon, and something back in the trees was making a noise like a rusty hinge, when a sauropod breathed out in the water. They're the really big ones, you know. If Mother Earth were to sigh over the misdeeds of her children, it would sound like that.

The sahibs jumped up, shouting: "Where is he? Where is he?"

I said: "That black spot in the water, just to the left of that point."

They yammered while the sauropod filled its lungs and disappeared. "Is that all?" said James. "Won't we see any more of him?"

Holtzinger said: "I read that they never come out of the water because they're too heavy to walk."

"No," I explained. "They can walk perfectly well and often do, for egg-laying and moving from one swamp to another. But most of the time they spend in the water, like hippopotamus. They eat eight hundred pounds of soft swamp plants a day, all through those little heads. So they wander about the bottoms of lakes and swamps, chomping away, and stick their heads up to breathe every quarter-hour or so. It's getting dark, so this fellow will soon come out and lie down in the shallows to sleep."

"Can we shoot one?" demanded James.

"I wouldn't," said I.

"Why not?"

I said: "There's no point in it, and it's not sporting. First, they're almost invulnerable. They're even harder to hit in the brain than other dinosaurs because of the way they sway their heads about on those long necks. Their hearts are too deeply buried to reach unless you're awfully lucky. Then, if you kill one in the water, he sinks and can't be recovered. If you kill one on land, the only trophy is that little head. You can't bring the whole beast back because he weighs thirty tons or more, and we've got no use for thirty tons of meat."

Holtzinger said: "That museum in New York got one."

"Yes," said I. "The American Museum of Natural History sent a party of forty-eight to the Early Cretaceous with a fifty-caliber machine gun. They killed a sauropod and spent two solid months skinning it and hacking the carcass apart and dragging it to the time machine. I know the chap in charge of that project, and he still has nightmares in which he smells decomposing dinosaur. They had to kill a dozen big theropods attracted by the stench, so they had them lying around and rotting, too. And the theropods ate three men of the party despite the big gun."

Next morning, we were finishing breakfast when one of the helpers said: "Look, Mr. Rivers, up there!"

He pointed along the shoreline. There were six big crested duckbill, feeding in the shallows. They were the kind called *Parasaurolophus,* with a long spike sticking out the back of their heads and a web of skin connecting this with the back of their necks.

"Keep your voices down!" I said. The duckbill, like the other ornithopods, are wary beasts because they have neither armor nor weapons. They feed on the margins of lakes and swamps, and when a gorgosaur rushes out of the trees they plunge into deep water and swim off. Then when *Phobosuchus*, the supercrocodile, goes for them in the water, they flee to the land. A hectic sort of life, what?

Holtzinger said: "Uh—Reggie! I've been thinking over what you said about ceratopsian heads. If I could get one of those yonder, I'd be satisfied. It would look big enough in my house, wouldn't it?"

"I'm sure of it, old boy," I said. "Now look here. We could detour to come out on the shore near here, but we should have to plow through half a mile of muck and brush, and they'd hear us coming. Or we can creep up to the north end of this sandspit, from which it's three or four hundred yards—a long shot but not impossible. Think you could do it?"

"Hm," said Holtzinger. "With my scope sight and a sitting position—okay, I'll try it."

"You stay here, Court," I said to James. "This is Augie's head, and I don't want any argument over your having fired first."

James grunted while Holtzinger clamped his scope to his rifle. We crouched our way up the spit, keeping the sand ridge between us and the duckbill. When we got to the end where there was no more cover, we crept along on hands and knees, moving slowly. If you move slowly enough, directly toward or away from a dinosaur, it probably won't notice you.

The duckbill continued to grub about on all fours, every few seconds rising to look round. Holtzinger eased himself into the sitting position, cocked his piece, and aimed through his scope. And then—

Bang! bang! went a big rifle back at the camp.

Holtzinger jumped. The duckbills jerked their heads

up and leaped for the deep water, splashing like mad. Holtzinger fired once and missed. I took one shot at the last duckbill before it vanished too, but missed. The .600 isn't built for long ranges.

Holtzinger and I started back toward the camp, for it had struck us that our party might be in theropod trouble.

What had happened was that a big sauropod had wandered down past the camp underwater, feeding as it went. Now, the water shoaled about a hundred yards offshore from our spit, halfway over to the swamp on the other side. The sauropod had ambled up the slope until its body was almost all out of water, weaving its head from side to side and looking for anything green to gobble. This is a species of *Alamosaurus,* which looks much like the well-known *Brontosaurus* except that it's bigger.

When I came in sight of the camp, the sauropod was turning round to go back the way it had come, making horrid groans. By the time we reached the camp, it had disappeared into deep water, all but its head and twenty feet of neck, which wove about for some time before they vanished into the haze.

When we came up to the camp, James was arguing with the Raja. Holtzinger burst out:

"You crummy bastard! That's the second time you've spoiled my shots."

"Don't be a fool," said James. "I couldn't let him wander into the camp and stamp everything flat."

"There was no danger of that," said the Raja. "You can see the water is deep offshore. It's just that our trigger-happee Mr. James cannot see any animal without shooting."

I added: "If it did get close, all you needed to do was throw a stick of firewood at it. They're perfectly harmless."

This wasn't strictly true. When the Comte de Lautrec ran after one for a close shot, the sauropod looked back at him, gave a flick of its tail, and took off the Comte's head as neatly as if he'd been axed in the tower. But, as a rule, they're inoffensive enough.

"How was I to know?" yelled James, turning purple. "You're all against me. What the hell are we on this miserable trip for, except to shoot things? Call yourselves hunters, but I'm the only one who hits anything!"

I got pretty wrothy and said he was just an excitable young skite with more money than brains, whom I should never have brought along.

"If that's how you feel," he said, "give me a burro and some food, and I'll go back to the base by myself. I won't pollute your pure air with my presence!"

"Don't be a bigger ass than you can help," I said. "What you propose is quite impossible."

"Then I'll go alone!" He grabbed his knapsack, thrust a couple of tins of beans and an opener into it, and started off with his rifle.

Beauregard Black spoke up: "Mr. Rivers, we cain't let him go off like that. He'll git lost and starve, or be et by a theropod."

"I'll fetch him back," said the Raja, and started after the runaway.

He caught up with James as the latter was disappearing into the cycads. We could see them arguing and waving their hands in the distance. After a while, they started back with arms around each other's necks like old school pals.

This shows the trouble we get into if we make mistakes in planning such a do. Having once got back in time, we had to make the best of our bargain.

I don't want to give the impression, however, that Courtney James was nothing but a pain in the rump. He had good points. He got over these rows quickly and next day would be as cheerful as ever. He was helpful with the general work of the camp, at least when he felt like it. He sang well and had an endless fund of dirty stories to keep us amused.

We stayed two more days at that camp. We saw crocodile, the small kind, and plenty of sauropod—as many as five at once—but no more duckbill. Nor any of those fifty-foot supercrocodiles.

So, on the first of May, we broke camp and headed north toward the Janpur Hills. My sahibs were beginning to harden up and were getting impatient. We'd been in the Cretaceous a week, and no trophies.

We saw nothing to speak of on the next leg, save a glimpse of a gorgosaur out of range and some tracks indicating a whopping big iguanodont, twenty-five or thirty feet high. We pitched camp at the base of the hills.

We'd finished off the bonehead, so the first thing was to shoot fresh meat. With an eye to trophies, too, of course. We got ready the morning of the third, and I told James:

"See here, old boy, no more of your tricks. The Raja will tell you when to shoot."

"Uh-huh, I get you," he said, meek as Moses.

We marched off, the four of us, into the foothills. There was a good chance of getting Holtzinger his ceratopsian. We'd seen a couple on the way up, but mere calves without decent horns.

As it was hot and sticky, we were soon panting and sweating. We'd hiked and scrambled all morning without seeing a thing except lizards, when I picked up the smell of carrion. I stopped the party and sniffed. We were in an open glade cut up by those little dry nullahs. The nullahs ran together into a couple of deeper gorges that cut through a slight depression choked with denser growth, cycad, and screw pine. When I listened, I heard the thrum of carrion flies.

"This way," I said. "Something ought to be dead—ah, here it is!"

And there it was: the remains of a huge ceratopsian lying in a little hollow on the edge of the copse. Must have weighed six or eight ton alive; a three-horned variety, perhaps the penultimate species of *Triceratops*. It was hard to tell, because most of the hide on the upper surface had been ripped off, and many bones had been pulled loose and lay scattered about.

Holtzinger said: "Oh, shucks! Why couldn't I have gotten to him before he died? That would have been a darned fine head."

I said: "On your toes, chaps. A theropod's been at this carcass and is probably nearby."

"How d'you know?" said James, with sweat running off his round red face. He spoke in what was for him a low voice, because a nearby theropod is a sobering thought to the flightiest.

I sniffed again and thought I could detect the distinctive rank odor of theropod. I couldn't be sure, though, because the carcass stank so strongly. My sahibs were turning green at the sight and smell of the cadaver. I told James:

"It's seldom that even the biggest theropod will attack a full-grown ceratopsian. Those horns are too much for them. But they love a dead or dying one. They'll hang round a dead ceratopsian for weeks, gorging and then sleeping off their meals for days at a time. They usually take cover in the heat of the day anyhow, because they can't stand much direct hot sunlight. You'll find them lying in copses like this or in hollows, wherever there's shade."

"What'll we do?" asked Holtzinger.

"We'll make our first cast through this copse, in two pairs as usual. Whatever you do, don't get impulsive or panicky."

I looked at Courtney James, but he looked right back and merely checked his gun.

"Should I still carry this broken?" he asked.

"No, close it, but keep the safety on till you're ready to shoot," I said. "We'll keep closer than usual, so we shall be in sight of each other. Start off at that angle, Raja; go slowly, and stop to listen between steps."

We pushed through the edge of the copse, leaving the carcass but not its stench behind us. For a few feet, you couldn't see a thing.

It opened out as we got in under the trees, which

shaded out some of the brush. The sun slanted down through the trees. I could hear nothing but the hum of insects and the scuttle of lizards and the squawks of toothed birds in the treetops. I thought I could be sure of the theropod smell, but told myself that might be imagination. The theropod might be any of several species. large or small, and the beast itself might be anywhere within a half-mile's radius.

"Go on," I whispered to Holtzinger. I could hear James and the Raja pushing ahead on my right and see the palm fronds and ferns lashing about as they disturbed them. I suppose they were trying to move quietly, but to me they sounded like an earthquake in a crockery shop.

"A little closer!" I called.

Presently, they appeared slanting in toward me. We dropped into a gully filled with ferns and scrambled up the other side. Then we found our way blocked by a big clump of palmetto.

"You go round that side; we'll go round this," I said. We started off, stopping to listen and smell. Our positions were the same as on that first day, when James killed the bonehead.

We'd gone two-thirds of the way round our half of the palmetto when I heard a noise ahead on our left. Holtzinger heard it too, and pushed off his safety. I put my thumb on mine and stepped to one side to have a clear field of fire.

The clatter grew louder. I raised my gun to aim at about the height of a big theropod's heart. There was a movement in the foliage—and a six-foot-high bonehead stepped into view, walking solemnly across our front and jerking its head with each step like a giant pigeon.

I heard Holtzinger let out a breath and had to keep myself from laughing. Holtzinger said: "Uh—"

Then that damned gun of James's went off, *bang! bang!* I had a glimpse of the bonehead knocked arsy-varsy with its tail and hindlegs flying.

"Got him!" yelled James. "I drilled him clean!" I heard him run forward.

"Good God, if he hasn't done it again!" I said.

Then there was a great swishing of foliage and a wild yell from James. Something heaved up out of the shrubbery, and I saw the head of the biggest of the local flesh eaters, *Tyrannosaurus trionyches* himself.

The scientists can insist that *rex* is the bigger species, but I'll swear this blighter was bigger than any *rex* ever hatched. It must have stood twenty feet high and been fifty feet long. I could see its big bright eye and six-inch teeth and the big dewlap that hangs down from its chin to its chest.

The second of the nullahs that cut through the copse ran athwart our path on the far side of the palmetto clump. Perhaps it was six feet deep. The tyrannosaur had been lying in this, sleeping off its last meal. Where its back stuck up above the ground level, the ferns on the edge of the nullah masked it. James had fired both barrels over the theropod's head and woke it up. Then the silly ass ran forward without reloading. Another twenty feet and he'd have stepped on the tyrannosaur.

James, naturally, stopped when this thing popped up in front of him. He remembered that he'd fired both barrels and that he'd left the Raja too far behind for a clear shot.

At first, James kept his nerve. He broke open his gun, took two rounds from his belt, and plugged them into the barrels. But, in his haste to snap the gun shut, he caught his hand between the barrels and the action. The painful pinch so startled James that he dropped his gun. Then he went to pieces and bolted.

The Raja was running up with his gun at high port, ready to snap it to his shoulder the instant he got a clear view. When he saw James running headlong toward him, he hesitated, not wishing to shoot James by accident. The latter plunged ahead, blundered into the Raja, and sent them both sprawling among the ferns. The tyrannosaur collected what little wits it had and stepped forward to snap them up.

And how about Holtzinger and me on the other side of the palmettos? Well, the instant James yelled and the tyrannosaur's head appeared, Holtzinger darted forward like a rabbit. I'd brought my gun up for a shot at the tyrannosaur's head, in hope of getting at least an eye; but, before I could find it in my sights, the head was out of sight behind the palmettos. Perhaps I should have fired at hazard, but all my experience is against wild shots.

When I looked back in front of me, Holtzinger had already disappeared round the curve of the palmetto clump. I'd started after him when I heard his rifle and the click of the bolt between shots: *bang*—click-click—*bang*—click-click, like that.

He'd come up on the tyrannosaur's quarter as the brute started to stoop for James and the Raja. With his muzzle twenty feet from the tyrannosaur's hide, Holtzinger began pumping .375s into the beast's body. He got off three shots when the tyrannosaur gave a tremendous booming grunt and wheeled round to see what was stinging it. The jaws came open, and the head swung round and down again.

Holtzinger got off one more shot and tried to leap to one side. As he was standing on a narrow place between the palmetto clump and the nullah, he fell into the nullah. The tyrannosaur continued its lunge and caught him. The jaws went *chomp,* and up came the head with poor Holtzinger in them, screaming like a damned soul.

I came up just then and aimed at the brute's face, but then realized that its jaws were full of my sahib and I should be shooting him, too. As the head went on up like the business end of a big power shovel, I fired a shot at the heart. The tyrannosaur was already turning away, and I suspect the ball just glanced along the ribs. The beast took a couple of steps when I gave it the other barrel in the jack. It staggered on its next step but kept on. Another step, and it was nearly out of sight among the trees, when the Raja fired twice. The stout fellow had untangled himself from James, got up, picked up his gun, and let the tyrannosaur have it.

The double wallop knocked the brute over with a tremendous crash. It fell into a dwarf magnolia, and I saw one of its huge birdlike hindlegs waving in the midst of a shower of pink-and-white petals. But the tyrannosaur got up again and blundered off without even dropping its victim. The last I saw of it was Holtzinger's legs dangling out one side of its jaws (he'd stopped screaming) and its big tail banging against the tree trunks as it swung from side to side.

The Raja and I reloaded and ran after the brute for all we were worth. I tripped and fell once, but jumped up again and didn't notice my skinned elbow till later. When we burst out of the copse, the tyrannosaur was already at the far end of the glade. We each took a quick shot but probably missed, and it was out of sight before we could fire again.

We ran on, following the tracks and spatters of blood, until we had to stop from exhaustion. Never again did we see that tyrannosaur. Their movements look slow and ponderous, but with those tremendous legs they don't have to step very fast to work up considerable speed.

When we'd got our breath, we got up and tried to track the tyrannosaur, on the theory that it might be dying and we should come up to it. But, though we found more spoor, it faded out and left us at a loss. We circled round, hoping to pick it up, but no luck.

Hours later, we gave up and went back to the glade.

Courtney James was sitting with his back against a tree, holding his rifle and Holtzinger's. His right hand was swollen and blue where he'd pinched it, but still usable. His first words were:

"Where the hell have you two been?"

I said: "We've been occupied. The late Mr. Holtzinger. Remember?"

"You shouldn't have gone off and left me; another of those things might have come along. Isn't it bad enough to lose one hunter through your stupidity without risking another one?"

I'd been preparing a warm wigging for James, but his attack so astonished me that I could only bleat: "What? *We* lost . . . ?"

"Sure," he said. "You put us in front of you, so if anybody gets eaten it's us. You send a guy up against these animals undergunned. You—"

"You Goddamn' stinking little swine!" I said. "If you hadn't been a blithering idiot and blown those two barrels, and then run like the yellow coward you are, this never would have happened. Holtzinger died trying to save your worthless life. By God, I wish he'd failed! He was worth six of a stupid, spoiled, muttonheaded bastard like you—"

I went on from there. The Raja tried to keep up with me, but ran out of English and was reduced to cursing James in Hindustani.

I could see by the purple color on James's face that I was getting home. He said: "Why, you—" and stepped forward and sloshed me one in the face with his left fist.

It rocked me a bit, but I said: "Now then, my lad, I'm glad you did that! It gives me a chance I've been waiting for. . . ."

So I waded into him. He was a good-sized bod, but between my sixteen stone and his sore right hand he had no chance. I got a few good ones home, and down he went.

"Now get up!" I said. "And I'll be glad to finish off!"

James raised himself to his elbows. I got set for more fisticuffs, though my knuckles were skinned and bleeding already. James rolled over, snatched his gun, and scrambled up, swinging the muzzle from one to the other of us.

"You won't finish anybody off!" he panted through swollen lips. "All right, put your hands up! Both of you!"

"Do not be an idiot," said the Raja. "Put that gun away!"

"Nobody treats me like that and gets away with it!"

"There's no use murdering us," I said. "You'd never get away with it."

"Why not? There won't be much left of you after one of these hits you. I'll just say the tyrannosaur ate you, too. Nobody could prove anything. They can't hold you for a murder eighty-five million years old. The statute of limitations, you know."

"You fool, you'd never make it back to the camp alive!" I shouted.

"I'll take a chance—" began James, setting the butt of his .500 against his shoulder, with the barrels pointed at my face. Looked like a pair of bleeding vehicular tunnels.

He was watching me so closely that he lost track of the Raja for a second. My partner had been resting on one knee, and now his right arm came up in a quick bowling motion with a three-pound rock. The rock bounced off James's head. The .500 went off. The ball must have parted my hair, and the explosion jolly well near broke my eardrums. Down went James again.

"Good work, old chap!" I said, gathering up James's gun.

"Yes," said the Raja thoughtfully, as he picked up the rock he'd thrown and tossed it. "Doesn't quite have the balance of a cricket ball, but it is just as hard."

"What shall we do now?" I said. "I'm inclined to leave the beggar here unarmed and let him fend for himself."

The Raja gave a little sigh. "It's a tempting thought, Reggie, but we really cannot, you know. Not done."

"I suppose you're right," I said. "Well, let's tie him up and take him back to camp."

We agreed there was no safety for us unless we kept James under guard every minute until we got home. Once a man has tried to kill you, you're a fool if you give him another chance.

We marched James back to camp and told the crew what we were up against. James cursed everybody.

We spent three dismal days combing the country for that tyrannosaur, but no luck. We felt it wouldn't have been cricket not to make a good try at recovering Holtzinger's remains. Back at our main camp, when it wasn't raining, we collected small reptiles and things for our scientific friends. The Raja and I discussed the question of legal proceedings against Courtney James, but decided there was nothing we could do in that direction.

When the transition chamber materialized, we fell over one another getting into it. We dumped James, still tied, in a corner, and told the chamber operator to throw the switches.

While we were in transition, James said: "You two should have killed me back there."

"Why?" I said. "You don't have a particularly good head."

The Raja added: "Wouldn't look at all well over a mantel."

"You can laugh," said James, "but I'll get you some day. I'll find a way and get off scot-free."

"My dear chap!" I said. "If there were some way to do it, I'd have you charged with Holtzinger's death. Look, you'd best leave well enough alone."

When we came out in the present, we handed him his empty gun and his other gear, and off he went without a word. As he left, Holtzinger's girl, that Claire, rushed up crying:

"Where is he? Where's August?"

There was a bloody heartrending scene, despite the Raja's skill at handling such situations.

We took our men and beasts down to the old laboratory building that the university has fitted up as a serai for such expeditions. We paid everybody off and found we were broke. The advance payments from Holtzinger and James didn't cover our expenses, and we should have precious little chance of collecting the rest of our fees either from James or from Holtzinger's estate.

And speaking of James, d'you know what that blighter was doing? He went home, got more ammunition, and came back to the university. He hunted up Professor Prochaska and asked him:

"Professor, I'd like you to send me back to the Cretaceous for a quick trip. If you can work me into your schedule right now, you can just about name your own price. I'll offer five thousand to begin with. I want to go to April twenty-third, eighty-five million B.C."

Prochaska answered: "Why do you wish to go back again so soon?"

"I lost my wallet in the Cretaceous," said James. "I figure if I go back to the day before I arrived in that era on my last trip, I'll watch myself when I arrived on that trip and follow myself around till I see myself lose the wallet."

"Five thousand is a lot for a wallet," said the professor.

"It's got some things in it I can't replace," said James.

"Well," said Prochaska, thinking. "The party that was supposed to go out this morning has telephoned that they would be late, so perhaps I can work you in. I have always wondered what would happen when the same man occupied the same stretch of time twice."

So James wrote out a check, and Prochaska took him to the chamber and saw him off. James's idea, it seems, was to sit behind a bush a few yards from where the transition chamber would appear and pot the Raja and me as we emerged.

Hours later, we'd changed into our street clothes and phoned our wives to come and get us. We were standing on Forsythe Boulevard waiting for them when there was a loud crack, like an explosion, and a flash of light not fifty feet from us. The shock wave staggered us and broke windows.

We ran toward the place and got there just as a bobby and several citizens came up. On the boulevard, just off the kerb, lay a human body. At least, it had been that, but it looked as if every bone in it had been pulverized and every blood vessel burst, so it was hardly more than a slimy mass of pink protoplasm. The clothes it had been wearing were shredded, but I recognized an H. & H. .500 double-barreled express rifle. The wood was scorched and the metal pitted, but it was Courtney James's gun. No doubt whatever.

Skipping the investigations and the milling about that

ensued, what had happened was this: nobody had shot at us as we emerged on the twenty-fourth, and that couldn't be changed. For that matter, the instant James started to do anything that would make a visible change in the world of eighty-five million B.C., such as making a footprint in the earth, the space-time forces snapped him forward to the present to prevent a paradox. And the violence of the passage practically tore him to bits.

Now that this is better understood, the professor won't send anybody to a period less than five thousand years prior to the time that some time traveler has already explored, because it would be too easy to do some act, like chopping down a tree or losing some durable artifact, that would affect the later world. Over longer periods, he tells me, such changes average out and are lost in the stream of time.

We had a rough time after that, with the bad publicity and all, though we did collect a fee from James's estate. Luckily for us, a steel manufacturer turned up who wanted a mastodon's head for his den.

I understand these things better now, too. The disaster hadn't been wholly James's fault. I shouldn't have taken him when I knew what a spoiled, unstable sort of bloke he was. And if Holtzinger could have used a really heavy gun, he'd probably have knocked the tyrannosaur down, even if he didn't kill it, and so have given the rest of us a chance to finish it.

So, Mr. Seligman, that's why I won't take you to that period to hunt. There are plenty of other eras, and if you look them over I'm sure you'll find something to suit you. But not the Jurassic or the Cretaceous. You're just not big enough to handle a gun for dinosaur.

The Emperor's Fan

IN THE FIFTEENTH year of his reign, Tsotuga the Fourth, Emperor of Kuromon, sat in the Forbidden Chamber of his Proscribed Palace, in his imperial city of Chingun. He played a game of Sachi with his crony, Reiro the beggar.

The pieces on one side were carved from single emeralds; those on the other, from single rubies. The board was of squares of onyx and gold. The many shelves and taborets in the room were crowded with small art objects. There were knickknacks of gold and silver, of ivory and ebony, of porcelain and pewter, of jasper and jade, of chrysoprase and chalcedony.

In a silken robe embroidered with lilies in silver thread and lotuses in golden thread, Tsotuga sat on a semithrone—a chair of gilded mahogany, the arms of which were carved in the form of diamond-eyed dragons. The Emperor was plainly well fed, and within the hour he had been bathed and perfumed. Yet, although he had just won a game, Emperor Tsotuga was not happy.

"The trouble with you, chum," said Reiro the beggar, "is that, not having enough real dangers to worry about, you make up imaginary ones."

The Emperor took no offense. The purpose of the Forbidden Chamber was to afford him a place where he could treat and be treated by his crony as if they were ordinary human beings, without the court's stifling formality.

Nor was it an accident that Reiro was a beggar. As such, he would never try to intrigue against or murder his imperial friend in order to seize the throne.

Although a fairly competent ruler, Tsotuga was not a man of much personal charm. He was in fact rather dull save when, as sometimes happened, he lost his temper. Then he might visit dire dooms on those about him. After he had calmed down, Tsotuga would regret his injustice and might even pension the victim's dependents. He honestly tried to be just but lacked the self-control and objectivity to do so.

Reiro got along with the Emperor well enough. While the beggar cared nothing for art, save when he could filch and sell a piece of it, he was glad to listen to the Emperor's endless tales of his collection in return for the sumptuous repasts he enjoyed. Reiro had gained twenty pounds since he had become intimate with the Emperor.

"Oh, yes?" said Tsotuga. "That is easy for you to say. You are not nightly haunted by your father's ghost, threatening dreadful doom."

Reiro shrugged. "You knew the risk when you had the old man poisoned. It is all in the game, pal. For your pay, I would cheerfully submit to any number of nightmares. How does old Haryo look in these dreams?"

"The same old tyrant. I had to slay him—you know that—ere he ruined the Empire. But have a care with that flapping tongue."

"Nought I hear here goes beyond these walls. Anyway, if you think Haryo's fate be not widely known, you do but befool yourself."

"I daresay it is suspected. But then, foul play is always suspected when an emperor dies. As said Dauhai to the timorous bird, every twig is a serpent.

"Still," continued the Emperor, "that solves not my problem. I wear mail beneath my robe. I sleep on a mattress floating in a pool of quicksilver. I have given up futtering my women, lest whilst I lie in their arms, some conspirator steal up and dagger me. The Empress, I can tell you, mislikes this abstinence. But still Haryo threatens and prophesies, and the warnings of a ghost are not to be flouted. I need some impregnable magical defense. That idiot Koxima does nought but fumigate and exorcise, which may drive out the demons but fails to blunt the steel of human foes. Have you any counsel, Ragbag?"

Reiro scratched. "There is a dark, beak-nosed, round-eyed old he-witch, hight Ajendra, lately come to Chingun from Mulvan. He gains a scanty living by selling love potions and finding lost bangles in trances. He claims to have a magical weapon of such power that none can stand against it."

"What is its nature?"

"He will not say."

"If he have so puissant a device, why is he not a king?"

"How could he make himself ruler? He is too old to lead an army in battle. Besides, he says that the holy order to which he belongs—all Mulvanian wizards call themselves holy men, be they never such rascals—forbids the use of this armament save in self-defense."

"Has anybody seen it?"

"Nay, chum, but rumor whispers that Ajendra has used it."

"Yes? And then what?"

"Know you a police spy named Nanka?"

The Emperor frowned. "Meseems—there was something about such a man who disappeared. It is supposed that the low company he kept at last learnt of his occupation and did him in."

The beggar chuckled. "Close, but not in the gold. This Nanka was a scoundrel of deepest dye, who supplemented his earnings as an informer by robbery and extortion. He skated into Ajendra's hut with the simple, wholesome intention of breaking the old man's neck and seizing Ajendra's rumored weapon."

"Hm. Well?"

"Well, Nanka never came out. A patrolman of the regular police found Ajendra sitting cross-legged in meditation and no sign of the erstwhile spy. Since Nanka was large and the hovel small, the corpse could not have been hidden. As it is said, the digger of pitfalls shall at last fall into one of his own."

"Hm," said Tsotuga. "I must look into this. Enough Sachi for the nonce. You must let me show you my latest acquisition!"

Reiro groaned inside and braced himself for an hour's lecture on the history and beauty of some antique bibelot. The thought of the palatial cookery, however, stiffened his resolve.

"Now, where did I put that little widget?" said Tsotuga, tapping his forehead with his folded fan.

"What is it, chum?" asked the beggar.

"A topaz statuette of the goddess Amarasupi, from the Jumbon Dynasty. Oh, curse my bowels with ulcers! I grow more absentminded day by day."

"Good thing your head is permanently affixed to the rest of you! As the wise Ashuziri said, hope is a charlatan, sense a bungler, and memory a traitor."

"I distinctly remember," muttered the Emperor, "telling myself to put it in a special place where I should be sure to remember it. But now I cannot recall the special place."

"The Proscribed Palace must have ten thousand special places," said Reiro. "That is the advantage of being poor. One has so few possessions that one need never wonder where they are."

"Almost you tempt me to change places with you, but my duty forbids. Damn, damn, what did I with that silly thing? Oh, well, let us play another game instead. You take the red this time, I the green."

Two days later, Emperor Tsotuga sat on his throne of audience, wearing his towering crown of state. This plumed and winged headgear, bedight with peacock feathers and precious stones, weighed over ten pounds. It even had a secret compartment. Because of its weight, Tsotuga avoided wearing it whenever he felt that he decently could.

The usher led in Ajendra. The Mulvanian magician was a tall, gaunt, bent old man, who supported himself on a stick. Save for the long white beard flowing down from his wrinkled, mahogany-hued face, he was brown all over, from dirty brown bulbous turban and dirty brown robe to dirty brown bare feet. His monotone contrasted with the golds and vermilions and greens and blues and purples of the Chamber of Audience.

In a cracked voice, speaking Kuromonian with an accent, Ajendra went through the formal greeting: "This wretched worm humbly abases himself before Thine ineffable Majesty!" The wizard began, slowly and painfully, to get down on hands and knees.

The Emperor motioned him up, saying, "In respect for your years, old man, we will omit the prostration. Simply tell us about this invincible weapon of yours."

"Your Imperial Majesty is too kind to this unworthy wretch. Sees Your Majesty this?"

From his ragged sleeve, the Mulvanian produced a large painted fan. Like the others present, Ajendra kept his gaze averted from the Emperor's face, on the pretense that one who looked the ruler full in the face would be blinded by his awful glory.

"This," continued Ajendra, "was made for the king of the Gwoling Islands by the noted wizard Tsunjing. By a series of chances too long to bore Your imperial Majesty with, it came into the unworthy hands of this inferior person."

At least, thought Tsotuga, the fellow had learnt the polite forms of Kuromonian address. Many Mulvanians were informal to the point of rudeness. Aloud he said, "It looks like any other fan. What is its power?"

"Simple, O Superior One. Any living thing that you fan with it disappears."

"Oho!" exclaimed the Emperor. "So that is what befell the missing Nanka!"

Ajendra looked innocent. "This loathsome reptile does not understand Your divine Majesty."

"Never mind. Whither go the victims!"

"One theory of my school is that they are translated to a higher dimension, coexistent with this one. Another holds that they are dispersed into constituent atoms, which, however, retain such mutual affinities that they can be reassembled when the signal for recall is—"

"Mean you that you can reverse the effect and fetch back the vanished beings?"

"Aye, Superhuman Sire. One folds the fan and taps one's wrists and forehead according to a simple code, and presto! there is the evanished one. Would Your Majesty see a demonstration? There is no danger to the demonstratee, since this humble person can bring him back instanter."

"Very well, good wizard. Just be careful not to wave that thing at us. On whom propose you to try it?"

Ajendra looked about the Chamber of Audience. There was a stir amongst ushers, guardsmen, and officials. Light winked on gilded armor and glowed on silken robes as each tried to make himself inconspicuous behind a pillar or another courtier.

"Who will volunteer?" asked the Emperor. "You, Dzakusan?"

The Prime Minister prostrated himself. "Great Emperor, live forever! This lump of iniquity has not been well lately. Moreover, he has nine children to support. He humbly begs Your Supremacy to excuse him."

Similar questions to other functionaries produced similar responses. At length Ajendra said, "If this lowly one may make a suggestion to Your Magnificence, it might be better to try it first on a beast—say, a dog or a cat."

"Aha!" said Tsotuga. "Just the thing. We know the animal, too. Surakai, fetch that cursed dog belonging to the Empress—you know, that yapping little monstrosity."

The messenger departed on his roller skates. Soon he was back, leading on a leash a small woolly white dog, which barked incessantly.

"Go ahead," said the Emperor.

"This negligible person hears and obeys," said Ajendra, opening the fan.

The dog's yelp was cut off as the draft from the fan struck it. Surakai trailed an empty leash. The courtiers started and murmured.

"By the Heavenly Bureaucrats!" exclaimed the Emperor. "That is impressive. Now bring the creature back. Fear not if you fail. The thing has bitten us twice, so the Empire will not fall if it remain in that other dimension."

Ajendra produced from his other sleeve a small codex, whose pages he thumbed. Then he held a reading glass to his eye. "Here it is," he said. " 'Dog. Two left, three right, one to head.' "

Having folded the fan, Ajendra, holding it in his right hand, rapped his left wrist twice. Transferring the fan to his left hand, he then tapped his right wrist thrice and his forehead once. Instantly the dog reappeared. Yapping, it fled under the throne.

"Very good," said the Emperor. "Leave the creature where it is. What is that, a code book?"

"Aye, supreme sire. It lists all the categories of organic beings subject to the fan's power."

"Well, let us try it on a human being—an expendable one. Mishuho, have we a condemned criminal handy?"

"Live forever, Incomparable One!" said the Minister of Justice. "We have a murderer due to lose his head tomorrow. Shall this miserable creature fetch him?"

The murderer was fetched. Ajendra fanned him out of existence and tapped him back again.

"Whew!" said the murderer. "This contemptible one must have suffered a dizzy spell."

"Where were you whilst you were vanished?" said the Emperor.

"I knew not that I was vanished, great Emperor!" said the murderer. "I felt dizzy and seemed to lose my wits for an instant—and then here I was, back in the Proscribed Palace."

"Well, you disappeared, all right. In consideration of his services to the state, Mishuho, commute his sentence to twenty-five lashes and turn him loose. Now, Doctor Ajendra!"

"Aye, Ruler of the World?"

"What are the limitations of your fan? Does it run out of charge and have to be resorceled?"

"Nay, Exalted One. At least, its power has not weakened in the centuries since Tsunjing made it."

"Does it work on a large animal, say, a horse or an elephant?"

"It does better than that. When the grandson of the Gwoling king for whom it was made, Prince Wangerr, met a dragon on Banshou Island, he swept the monster out of existence with three mighty strokes of the fan."

"Hm. Quite powerful enough, it seems. Now, good Ajendra, suppose you bring back that police spy, Nanka, on whom you employed your arts a few days ago!"

The Mulvanian shot a glance at the Emperor's face. Some courtiers murmured at this breach of decorum, but Tsotuga seemed not to notice. The wizard evidently satisfied himself that the ruler knew whereof he spoke. Ajendra thumbed through his book until he came to "Spy." Then he tapped his left wrist four times and his forehead twice.

A big, burly man in beggar's rags materialized. Nanka was still wearing the roller skates on which he had entered Ajendra's hut. Unprepared as he was for this appearance, his feet flew out from under him. He fell heavily on his back, cracking his head on the red-white-and-black tessellated marble floor. The Emperor laughed heartily, and the courtiers allowed themselves discreet smiles.

As the informer, red with rage and astonishment, climbed to his feet, Tsotuga said, "Mishuho, give him ten lashes for trying to rob a subject. Tell him that next time it will be his head—if not the boiling oil. Take him away. Well now, worthy wizard, what would you have for your device and its code book?"

"Ten thousand golden dragons," said Ajendra, "and an escort to my own country."

"Hm. Is that not a lot for a holy ascetic?"

"It is not for myself that this humble being asks," said the Mulvanian. "I would build and endow a temple to my favorite gods in my native village. There I shall pass my remaining days in meditation on the Thatness of the All."

"A meritorious project," said Tsotuga. "Let it be done. Chingitu, see that Doctor Ajendra has a trustworthy escort to Mulvan. Have them get a letter from the King of Kings testifying that they delivered Ajendra safely and did not murder him for his gold along the way."

"This despicable one hears and obeys," said the Minister of War.

For the next month, things went smoothly at court. The Emperor kept his temper. No one, knowing of the magical fan that the testy monarch carried, cared to provoke him. Even Empress Nasako, although furious at her husband's callous use of her dog, kept her sharp tongue sheathed. Tsotuga remembered where he had hidden the statuette of Amarasupi and so for a time was almost happy.

But, as said the philosopher Dauhai back in the Jumbon Dynasty, everything passes away. The day came when, in the Emperor's study, Minister of Finance Yaebu tried to explain the workings of that marvelous new invention, paper money. The Emperor demanded to know why he could not simply abolish all taxes, thus pleasing the people, and pay the government's bills with newly printed currency notes. Tsotuga was irascible as a result of having mislaid another of his prized antique gimcracks.

"But, Your Divine Majesty!" wailed Yaebu. "That was tried in Gwoling half a century ago! The value of the notes dropped to nought. None would offer aught for sale, since none wished to accept worthless paper. They had to go back to barter."

"We should think a few heads on poles would have fixed that," growled Tsotuga.

"The then king of Gwoling tried that, too," said

Yaebu. "It accomplished nought; the markets remained empty of goods. City folk starved. . . ."

The argument continued while the Emperor, who had little head for economics, became more and more restless, bored, and impatient. Ignoring these signs, Yaebu persisted in his arguments.

At last the Emperor exploded, "Curse your arse with boils, Yaebu! We will show you how to keep saying 'nay' and 'however' and 'impossible' to your sovran! Begone, sirrah!"

Tsotuga whipped out his fan, snapped it open, and fanned a blast of air at Yaebu. The minister vanished.

Hm, mused Tsotuga, *it really does work. Now I must fetch Yaebu back, for I did not really mean to destroy the faithful fellow. It is just that he irritates me so with his everlasting "if's" and "but's" and "can't's." Let me see, where did I put that code book? I remember hiding it in a special place where I could be sure of finding it again. But where?*

The Emperor looked first in the deep, baggy sleeves of his embroidered silken robe, which in Kuromon served the office of pockets. It was not there.

Then the Emperor rose from his business throne and went to the imperial wardrobe, where a hundred-odd robes hung from pegs. There were silken robes for official use, thin for summer and quilted for winter. There were woolen robes for outdoor winter use and cotton robes for outdoor summer use. They were dyed scarlet and emerald, saffron and azure, cream and violet, and all the other colors in the dyers' armory.

Tsotuga went down the line, feeling in the sleeves of each robe. A tireman hurried in, saying, "O Divine Autocrat, permit this filthy beggar to relieve you of this menial chore!"

Tsotuga: "Nay, good Shakatabi; we entrust this task to none but ourselves."

Laboriously, Tsotuga continued down the line until he had examined all the robes. Then he began the rounds of the Proscribed Palace, pulling out the drawers of desks and dressers, poking into cubbyholes, and shouting for the keys to chests and strongboxes.

After several hours, exhaustion forced the Emperor to desist. Falling into the semithrone of the Forbidden Chamber, he struck the gong. When the room was jampacked with servants, he said: "We, Tsotuga the Fourth, offer a reward of a hundred golden dragons to him who finds the missing code book that goes with our miraculous fan!"

That day, the Proscribed Palace saw a great scurrying and searching. Scores of felt-slippered servants shuffled about, opening, poking, prying, and peering. When night fell, the book had not been found.

Beshrew me! said Tsotuga to himself. *Poor Yaebu is lost unless we find the accursed book. I must be more careful with that fan.*

Again, as spring advanced, things went smoothly for a while. But the day came when Tsotuga was rollerskating about the paths of the palace gardens with Minister of War Chingitu. Questioned sharply about the recent defeat of the Kuromonian army by the nomads of the steppes, Chingitu offered excuses that Tsotuga knew to be mendacious. Away went Tsotuga's temper. "The real reason," roared the Emperor, "is that your cousin, the Quartermaster-General, has been grafting and filling posts with his worthless relatives, so that our soldiers were ill armed! And you know it! Take that!"

A wave of the fan, and no more Chingitu. In like manner, shortly thereafter, perished Prime Minister Dzakusan.

The want of properly appointed ministers soon made itself felt. Tsotuga could not personally supervise all the hundreds of bureaucrats in the now-headless departments. These civil servants devoted themselves more and more to feuding, loafing, nepotism, and peculation. Conditions were bad in Kuromon anyway, because of the inflation brought about by Tsotuga's paper-money scheme. The government was fast becoming a shambles.

"You must pull yourself together, lord," said Empress Nasako, "ere the pirates of the Gwoling Archipelago and the brigands from the steppes divide Kuromon between them, as a man divides an orange."

"But what in the name of the fifty-seven major deities shall I do?" cried Tsotuga. "Curse it, if I had that code book, I could bring back Yaebu, who would straighten out this financial mess."

"Oh, forget the book. If I were you, I should burn that magical fan ere it got me into more trouble."

"You are out of your mind, woman! Never!"

Nasako sighed. "As the sage Zuiku said: Who would use a tiger for a watchdog to guard his wealth will soon need neither wealth nor watchdog. At least appoint a new prime minister to bring order out of this chaos."

"I have gone over the list of possible candidates, but every one has a black mark against him. One was connected with that faction that conspired my assassination nine years ago. Another was accused of grafting, although it was never proved. Still another is ailing—"

"Is Zamben of Jompei on your list?"

"I have never heard of him. Who is he?"

"The supervisor of roads and bridges in Jade Mountain Province. They say he has made an excellent record there."

"How know you about him?" snapped the Emperor suspiciously.

"He is a cousin of my first lady-in-waiting. She has long urged his virtues upon me. I brushed her suit aside, knowing my lord's dislike of letting my ladies exploit their position by abetting their kinsmen's interests. In your present predicament, though, you could do worse than look the fellow over."

"Very well, I will."

Thus it happened that Zamben of Jompei became prime minister. The former supervisor of roads and bridges was younger by a decade than the Emperor. He was a handsome, cheerful, charming, rollicking person who made himself popular with the court, save for those determined to hate the favorite of the moment. Tsotuga thought Zamben was rather too lighthearted and lacking in respect for the labyrinthine etiquette. But Zamben proved an able administrator who soon had the vast governmental machine running smoothly.

But it is said that the thatcher's roof is the leakiest in the village. What the Emperor did not know was that Zamben and Empress Nasako were secret lovers. They had been before Zamben's elevation. Circumstances made it hard to consummate their passion, save rarely in one of Nasako's summer pavilions in the hills.

In the Proscribed Palace, it was even harder. The palace swarmed with menials who would be glad to carry tales. The amorous pair had to resort to stratagems. Nasako announced that she had to be left entirely alone in a summer house to compose a poem. The versatile Zamben wrote the poem for her as evidence before he hid himself in the summer house in advance of her arrival.

"That was worth waiting for," said the Empress, donning her garments. "That fat old fool Tsotuga has not touched me in a year, and a full-blooded woman like me needs frequent stoking. He has not even futtered his pretty young concubines, albeit he is not yet fifty."

"Why? Is he prematurely senile?"

"Nay, it is his fear of assassination. For a while, he tried doing it in the seated position, so that he could keep looking about for possible assailants. But since he insisted on wearing his armor, it proved too awkward to please anyone. So he gave it up altogether."

"Well, the thought of a stab in the back is depressing to more than just a man's spirit. If—which the gods forfend—an accident should befall His divine Majesty—"

"How?" said Nasako. "No assassin dares approach him whilst he has that fan."

"Where does he put it at night?"

"Under his pillow, and he sleeps clutching it. It would take a winged demon to get at him anyway, floating in that pool of quicksilver."

"A hard-driven crossbow bolt, shot from beyond the fan's range—"

"Nay, he is too well guarded to let an arbalester get within range, and he even sleeps in his mail."

"Well, we shall see," said Zamben. "Meanwhile, Nako, how would my love like another?"

"What a man you are!" cried Nasako, beginning to cast off her just-donned garments.

During the next two months, the court noted that Zamben, not content with being the second most powerful man in the Empire, had also ingratiated himself with the Emperor. He did so well as to oust Reiro the beggar from his position as Emperor's crony. Zamben even became an expert on the history of art, the better to admire Tsotuga's prized gewgaws.

The favorite-haters at court muttered that for an emperor to make a personal friend of a minister was a violation of sound method. Not only was the mystical balance among the Five Elements upset, but also Zamben might entertain usurpatory notions, which his friendship might enable him to put into effect. But none dared to broach the subject to the explosive-tempered Tsotuga. They shrugged, saying, "After all, it is the Empress's duty to warn him. If she cannot, what chance have we?"

Zamben went his smiling way, smoothly running the government by day and fraternizing with the Emperor by night.

At last came his opportunity. The Emperor was toying with his fan over a game of Sachi. Zamben dropped a piece—an elephant—on the floor so that it rolled under the table.

"Let me get it," said Tsotuga. "It is on my side."

As he bent to fumble for the piece, he dropped his fan. He straightened up holding the piece, to find Zamben holding the fan out to him. Tsotuga snatched it back. "Excuse my discourtesy," said the Emperor, "but I am fain not to let that thing out of my hands. It was stupid of me not to have put it away ere reaching for your elephant. It is still your move."

Days later, in the summer house, Empress Nasako asked, "Did you get it?"

"Aye," replied Zamben. "It was no trick to hand him the duplicate."

"Then what are you waiting for? Fan the old fool away!"

"Tut, tut, my sweet. I must assure the loyalty of my partisans. It is said that he who would swallow a pumpkin with one bite shall reap the reward of his gluttony. Besides, I have scruples."

"Oh, pish-tush! Are you just a pillow-warrior, strong in the yard but weak in the sword arm?"

"Nay, but I am a careful man who avoids offending the gods or biting off more than he can chew. Hence I would fan away only one who tried to do me ill. Knowing your imperial spouse, madam, I am sure he will soon force me to defend myself."

The evening came when Zamben, whose skill at Sachi had never seemed remarkable, suddenly beat the Emperor five games in a row.

"Curse you!" bawled Tsotuga as he lost his fifth king. "Have you been taking lessons? Or were you more skilled all along than you seemed?"

Zamben grinned and spread his hands. "The Divine Bureaucrats must have guided my moves."

"You—you—" Tsotuga choked with rage. "We will show you how to mock your emperor! Begone from the world!"

The Emperor whipped out his fan and fanned, but Zamben failed to disappear. Tsotuga fanned some more. "Curse it, has this thing lost its charge?" said Tsotuga. "Unless it be not the real—"

His sentence was cut off as Zamben, opening the true magical fan, swept the Emperor out of existence. Later, Zamben explained to the Empress, "I knew that when he found that his fan did not work, he would suspect a substitution. So there was nought to do but use the real one."

"What shall we tell the court and the people?"

"I have thought all that out. We will give out that, plagued by the summer's heat, in an absentminded moment he fanned himself."

"Would it work that way?"

"I know not; who were so rash as to try it? In any case, after a decent interval of mourning, I shall expect you to carry out your end of the bargain."

"Right willingly, my love."

Thus it came to pass that the widowed Empress wedded Zamben of Jompei, after the latter had, at her demand, put away his two previous wives. The minister acquired the courtesy title of "Emperor" but not the full powers of that office. Technically he was the consort of the Dowager Empress and guardian of and regent for the heir.

As to what would happen when the fourteen-year-old Prince Wakumba reached his majority, Zamben did not worry. He was sure that, whatever betid, he could charm the young Emperor into continuing his power and perquisites.

He thought of having the Prince murdered but quickly put that plan aside. For one thing, he feared that Nasako would have him killed in turn, for her supporters far outnumbered his. He had a hard enough task just keeping on good terms with her. She was disillusioned to find that in her new husband she had obtained, not an ever-panting satyr, but merely an ambitious politician so immersed in political maneuvers, administrative details, and religious rituals that he had little time and strength left over for stoking her fires. When she complained, he spoke of his "essential new project."

"What is that?" she demanded.

"I will not," he said, "waste more time in searching for that code book. Instead, I shall reconstruct the code by trial and error."

"How?"

"I shall try combinations of raps and note what I get each time. In the centuries that the fan has existed, hundreds of beings must have been fanned away."

The next day Zamben, flanked by six heavily armed palace guards, sat in the Chamber of Audience, which had been cleared of all others save two secretaries. Zamben tapped his left wrist once. A beggar appeared on the floor before him.

The beggar screamed with terror and fainted. When the man had been revived, it was found that he had been fanned out of existence more than a century before, in a fishing village on the shore of the ocean. He was astounded suddenly to find himself in a palace.

Zamben commanded, "Write: one tap on left wrist, beggar. Give him one golden dragon and show him out."

Two taps on the left wrist produced a swineherd, and so it was recorded. During the day, persons of all sorts were rapped into existence. Once a leopard appeared, snarling. Two guardsmen rushed upon it, but it sprang out the open window and vanished.

Some combinations of raps failed to bring results. Either they were not connected with victims of any definite kind, or no beings of that kind had ever been fanned away and not recalled.

"All right so far," said Zamben to the Empress that night.

"What if your experiments bring back Tsotuga?"

"By the fifty-seven major deities, I had not thought of that! An emperor, I suppose, needs a combination of many taps to bring him back. The instant I see him, I will fan him back to limbo."

"Have a care! I am sure that fan will sooner or later bring evil upon him who uses it."

"Fear not; I shall be cautious."

The next day, the experiments continued and the secretaries' lists of formulae lengthened. Three taps each on left wrist, right wrist, and forehead produced the missing Finance Minister Yaebu, much shaken.

Following Yaebu came an ass and a fuller. When the ass had been captured and led out, and the fuller had been soothed and sent away with his fee, Zamben tapped his left and right wrists each three times and his forehead four times.

There was a rush of displaced air. Filling most of the Chamber of Audience was a dragon. Zamben, his jaw sagging, started to rise. The dragon roared and roared, and the guards fled clattering.

Through Zamben's mind flashed a tale he had heard about the fan. Centuries before, it had saved the Gwolling prince, Wangerr, from a dragon on Banshou Island. This must be the same . . .

Zamben began to open the fan, but astonishment and terror had paralyzed him a few seconds too long. The great, scaly head swooped; the jaws slammed shut.

The only person left in the chamber was one of the secretaries, cowering behind the throne. This man heard a single scream. Then the dragon hunched itself out the window with a crashing of broken window frame and—since the aperture was still too small for it—of a goodly part of the wall. The scribe peeked around the throne to see the scaly tail vanishing through the jagged gap that yawned where the window had been, and a cloud of brick and plaster dust filling the Chamber of Audience.

Yaebu and Nasako became co-regents. Lacking a man, the lusty Dowager Empress took up with a handsome groom from the imperial stables, half her age but well equipped to pleasure her, having no thoughts to distract him from his lectual duties. Yaebu, a conservative family man with no lust for exalted adultery, became prime minister. He ran the Empire in a somewhat hesitant, bumbling way but not unsuccessfully.

Since there was no emperor, even a nominal one, young Prince Wakumba had to be enthroned forthwith. After the day-long ceremony, the lad slowly pulled off the plumed and winged crown of state. He complained, "This thing seems even heavier than usual." He poked about inside it.

Yaebu hovered anxiously, murmuring, "Have a care, my liege! Watch out that you harm not that holy headgear!"

Something went *spung,* and a metal flap snapped up inside the crown.

"Here is that secret compartment," said Wakumba, "with a—what is this?—a book in it. By the fifty-seven divinities, this must be that code book that Dad was hunting!"

"Let me see!" cried Yaebu and Nasako together.

"That is it, all right. But since the dragon ate the fan along with my stepfather, the book is of no use. Let it be put in the archives with other curios."

Nasako said, "We must ask Koxima to make another magical fan, so that the book shall again be useful."

It is not, however, recorded that the court wizard of Kuromon ever succeeded in this endeavor. For aught I know, the code book still reposes peacefully in the Kuromonian archives in Chingun, and those who, like Tsotuga and Dzakusan, were fanned away and never brought back, still await their deliverance.

Two Yards of Dragon

EUDORIC DAMBERTSON, ESQUIRE, rode home from his courting of Lusina, daughter of the enchanter Baldonius, with a face as long as an olifant's nose. Eudoric's sire, Sir Dambert, said:

"Well, how fared thy suit, boy? Ill, eh?"

"I—" began Eudoric.

"I told you 'twas an asinine notion, eh? Was I not right? When Baron Emmerhard has more daughters than he can count, any one of which would fetch a pretty parcel of land with her, eh? Well, why answerest not?"

"I—" said Eudoric.

"Come on, lad, speak up!"

"How can he, when ye talk all the time?" said Eudoric's mother, the Lady Aniset.

"Oh," said Sir Dambert. "Your pardon, son. Moreover and furthermore, as I've told you, an ye were Emmerhard's son-in-law, he'd use his influence to get you your spurs. Here ye be, a strapping youth of three-and-twenty, not yet knighted. 'Tis a disgrace to our lineage."

"There are no wars toward, to afford opportunity for deeds of knightly dought," said Eudoric.

"Aye, 'tis true. Certes, we all hail the blessings of peace, which the wise governance of our sovran emperor hath given us for lo these thirteen years. Howsomever, to perform a knightly deed, our young men must needs waylay banditti, disperse rioters, and do suchlike fribbling feats."

As Sir Dambert paused, Eudoric interjected, "Sir, that problem now seems on its way to solution."

"How meanest thou?"

"If you'll but hear me, Father! Doctor Baldonius has set me a task, ere he'll bestow Lusina on me, which should fit me for knighthood in any jurisdiction."

"And that is?"

"He's fain to have two square yards of dragon hide. Says he needs 'em for his magical mummeries."

"But there have been no dragons in these parts for a century or more!"

"True; but, quoth Baldonius, the monstrous reptiles still abound far to eastward, in the lands of Pathenia and Pantorozia. Forsooth, he's given me a letter of introduction to his colleague, Doctor Raspiudus, in Pathenia."

"What?" cried the Lady Aniset. "Thou, to set forth on some year-long journey to parts unknown, where, 'tis said, men hop on a single leg or have faces in their bellies? I'll not have it! Besides, Baldonius may be privy wizard to Baron Emmerhard, but 'tis not to be denied that he is of no gentle blood."

"Well," said Eudoric, "so who was gentle when the Divine Pair created the world?"

"Our forebears were, I'm sure, whate'er were the case with those of the learned Doctor Baldonius. You young people are always full of idealistic notions. Belike thou'lt fall into heretical delusions, for I hear that the Easterlings have not the true religion. They falsely believe that God is one, instead of two as we truly understand."

"Let's not wander into the mazes of theology," said Sir Dambert, his chin in his fist. "To be sure, the paynim Southrons believe that God is three, an even more pernicious notion than that of the Easterlings."

"An I meet God in my travels, I'll ask him the truth o't," said Eudoric.

"Be not sacrilegious, thou impertinent whelp! Still

and all and notwithstanding, Doctor Baldonius were a man of influence to have in the family, be his origin never so humble. Methinks I could prevail upon him to utter spells to cause my crops, my neat, and my villeins to thrive, whilst casting poxes and murrains on my enemies. Like that caitiff Rainmar, eh? What of the bad seasons we've had? The God and Goddess know we need all the supernatural help we can get to keep us from penury. Else we may some fine day awaken to find that we've lost the holding to some greasy tradesman with a purchased title, with pen for lance and tally sheet for shield."

"Then I have your leave, sire?" cried Eudoric, a broad grin splitting his square, bronzed young face.

The Lady Aniset still objected, and the argument raged for another hour. Eudoric pointed out that it was not as if he were an only child, having two younger brothers and a sister. In the end, Sir Dambert and his lady agreed to Eudoric's quest, provided he return in time to help with the harvest, and take a manservant of their choice.

"Whom have you in mind?" asked Eudoric.

"I fancy Jillo the trainer," said Sir Dambert.

Eudoric groaned. "That old mossback, ever canting and haranguing me on the duties and dignities of my station?"

"He's but a decade older than ye," said Sir Dambert. "Moreover and furthermore, ye'll need an older man, with a sense of order and propriety, to keep you on the path of a gentleman. Class loyalty above all, my boy! Young men are wont to swallow every new idea that flits past, like a frog snapping at flies. Betimes they find they've engulfed a wasp, to their scathe and dolor."

"He's an awkward wight, Father, and not overbrained."

"Aye, but he's honest and true, no small virtues in our degenerate days. In my sire's time there was none of this newfangled saying the courteous 'ye' and 'you' even to mere churls and scullions. 'Twas always 'thou' and "thee.' "

"How you do go on, Dambert dear," said the Lady Aniset.

"Aye, I ramble. 'Tis the penalty of age. At least, Eudoric, the faithful Jillo knows horses and will keep your beasts in prime fettle." Sir Dambert smiled. "Moreover and furthermore, if I know Jillo Godmarson, he'll be glad to get away from his nagging wife for a spell."

So Eudoric and Jillo set forth to eastward, from the knight's holding of Arduen, in the barony of Zurgau, in the county of Treveria, in the kingdom of Locania, in the New Napolitanian Empire. Eudoric—of medium height, powerful build, dark, with square-jawed but otherwise undistinguished features—rode his palfrey and led his mighty destrier Morgrim. The lank, lean Jillo bestrode another palfrey and led a sumpter mule. Morgrim was piled with Eudoric's panoply of plate, carefully nested into a compact bundle and lashed down under a canvas cover. The mule bore the rest of their supplies.

For a fortnight they wended uneventfully through the duchies and counties of the Empire. When they reached lands where they could no longer understand the local dialects, they made shift with Helladic, the tongue of the Old Napolitanian Empire, which lettered men spoke everywhere.

They stopped at inns where inns were to be had. For the first fortnight, Eudoric was too preoccupied with dreams of his beloved Lusina to notice the tavern wenches. After that, his urges began to fever him, and he bedded one in Zerbstat, to their mutual satisfaction. Thereafter, however, he forebore, not as a matter of sexual morals but as a matter of thrift.

When benighted on the road, they slept under the stars—or, as befell them on the marches of Avaria, under a rain-dripping canopy of clouds. As they bedded down in the wet, Eudoric asked his companion:

"Jillo, why did you not remind me to bring a tent?"

Jillo sneezed. "Why, sir, come rain, come snow, I never thought that so sturdy a springald as ye be would ever need one. The heroes in the romances never travel with tents."

"To the nethermost hell with heroes of the romances! They go clattering around on their destriers for a thousand cantos. Weather is ever fine. Food, shelter, and a change of clothing appear, as by magic, whenever desired. Their armor never rusts. They suffer no tisics and fluxes. They pick up no fleas or lice at the inns. They're never swindled by merchants, for none does aught so vulgar as buying and selling."

"If ye'll pardon me, sir," said Jillo, "that were no knightly way to speak. It becomes not your station."

"Well, to the nethermost hells with my station, too! Wherever these paladins go, they find damsels in distress to rescue, or have other agreeable, thrilling, and sanitary adventures. What adventures have we had? The time we fled from robbers in the Turonian Forest. The time I fished you out of the Albis half drowned. The time we ran out of food in the Asciburgi Mountains and had to plod fodderless over those hair-raising peaks for three days on empty stomachs."

"The Divine Pair do but seek to try the mettle of a valorous aspirant knight, sir. Ye should welcome these petty adversities as a chance to prove your manhood."

Eudoric made a rude noise with his mouth. "That for my manhood! Right now, I'd fainer have a stout roof overhead, a warm fire before me, and a hot repast in my belly. An ever I go on such a silly jaunt again, I'll find one of those versemongers—like that troubadour, Landwin of Kromnitch, that visited us yesteryear—and drag him along, to show him how little real adventures are like those of the romances. And if he fall into the Albis, he may drown, for all of me. Were it not for my darling Lusina—"

Eudoric lapsed into gloomy silence, punctuated by sneezes.

They plodded on until they came to the village of Liptai, on the border of Pathenia. After the border guards had questioned and passed them, they walked their animals down the deep mud of the main street. Most of the slatternly houses were of logs or of crudely hewn planks, innocent of paint.

"Heaven above!" said Jillo. "Look at that, sir!"

"That" was a gigantic snail shell, converted into a small house.

"Knew you not of the giant snails of Pathenia?" asked Eudoric. "I've read of them in Doctor Baldonius' encyclopedia. When full grown, they—or rather their shells—are ofttimes used for dwellings in this land."

Jillo shook his head. " 'Twere better had ye spent more of your time on your knightly exercises and less on reading. Your sire hath never learnt his letters, yet he doth his duties well enow."

"Times change, Jillo. I may not clang rhymes so featly as Doctor Baldonius, or that ass Landwin of Kromnitch; but in these days a stroke of the pen were oft more fell than the slash of a sword. Here's a hostelry that looks not too slummocky. Do you dismount and inquire within as to their tallage."

"Why, sir?"

"Because I am fain to know, ere we put our necks in the noose! Go ahead. An I go in, they'll double the scot at sight of me."

When Jillo came out and quoted prices, Eudoric said, "Too dear. We'll try the other."

"But, Master! Mean ye to put us in some flea-bitten hovel, like that which we suffered in Bitava?"

"Aye. Didst not prate to me on the virtues of petty adversity in strengthening one's knightly mettle?"

" 'Tis not that, sir."

"What, then?"

"Why, when better quarters are to be had, to make do with the worse were an insult to your rank and station. No gentleman—"

"Ah, here we are!" said Eudoric. "Suitably squalid, too! You see, good Jillo, I did but yestere'en count our money, and lo! more than half is gone, and our journey not yet half completed."

"But, noble Master, no man of knightly mettle would

so debase himself as to tally his silver, like some baseborn commercial—"

"Then I must needs lack true knightly mettle. Here we be!"

For a dozen leagues beyond Liptai rose the great, dense Motolian Forest. Beyond the forest lay the provincial capital of Velitchovo. Beyond Velitchovo, the forest thinned out *gradatim* to the great grassy plains of Pathenia. Beyond Pathenia, Eudoric had been told, stretched the boundless deserts of Pantorozia, over which a man might ride for months without seeing a city.

Yes, the innkeeper told him, there were plenty of dragons in the Motolian Forest. "But fear them not," said Kasmar in broken Helladic. "From being hunted, they have become wary and even timid. An ye stick to the road and move yarely, they'll pester you not unless ye surprise or corner one."

"Have any dragons been devouring maidens fair lately?" asked Eudoric.

Kasmar laughed. "Nay, good Master. What were maidens fair doing, traipsing round the woods to stir up the beasties? Leave them be, I say, and they'll do the same by you."

A cautious instinct warned Eudoric not to speak of his quest. After he and Jillo had rested and had renewed their equipment, they set out, two days later, into the Motolian Forest. They rode for a league along the Velitchovo road. Then Eudoric, accoutered in full plate and riding Morgrim, led his companion off the road into the woods to southward. They threaded their way among the trees, ducking branches, in a wide sweep around. Steering by the sun, Eudoric brought them back to the road near Liptai.

The next day they did the same, except that their circuit was to the north of the highway.

After three more days of this exploration, Jillo became restless. "Good Master, what do we, circling round and about so bootlessly? The dragons dwell farther east, away from the haunts of men, they say."

"Having once been lost in the woods," said Eudoric, "I would not repeat the experience. Therefore do we scout our field of action, like a general scouting a future battlefield."

" 'Tis an arid business," said Jillo with a shrug. "But then, ye were always one to see further into a millstone than most."

At last, having thoroughly committed the byways of the nearer forest to memory, Eudoric led Jillo farther east. After casting about, they came at last upon the unmistakable tracks of a dragon. The animal had beaten a path through the brush, along which they could ride almost as well as on the road. When they had followed this track for above an hour, Eudoric became aware of a strong, musky stench.

"My lance, Jillo!" said Eudoric, trying to keep his voice from rising with nervousness.

The next bend in the path brought them into full view of the dragon, a thirty-footer facing them on the trail.

"Ha!" said Eudoric. "Meseems 'tis a mere cockadrill, albeit longer of neck and of limb than those that dwell in the rivers of Agisymba—if the pictures in Doctor Baldonius' books lie not. Have at thee, vile worm!"

Eudoric counched his lance and put spurs to Morgrim. The destrier bounded forward.

The dragon raised its head and peered this way and that, as if it could not see well. As the hoofbeats drew nearer, the dragon opened its jaws and uttered a loud, hoarse, groaning bellow.

At that, Morgrim checked his rush with stiffened forelegs, spun ponderously on his haunches, and veered off the trail into the woods. Jillo's palfrey bolted likewise, but in another direction. The dragon set out after Eudoric at a shambling trot.

Eudoric had not gone fifty yards when Morgrim passed close aboard a massive old oak, a thick limb of which jutted into their path. The horse ducked beneath the bough. The branch caught Eudoric across the breastplate, flipped him backwards over the high cantle of his saddle, and swept him to earth with a great clatter.

Half stunned, he saw the dragon trot closer and closer—and then lumber past him, almost within arm's length, and disappear on the trail of the fleeing horse. The next that Eudoric knew, Jillo was bending over him, crying:

"Alas, my poor heroic Master! Be any bones broke, sir?"

"All of them, methinks," groaned Eudoric. "What's befallen Morgrim?"

"That I know not. And look at this dreadful dent in your beauteous cuirass!"

"Help me out of the thing. The dent pokes most sorely into my ribs. The misadventures I suffer for my dear Lusina!"

"We must get your breastplate to a smith to have it hammered out and filed smooth again."

"Fiends take the smiths! They'd charge half the cost of a new one. I'll fix it myself, if I can find a flat rock to set it on and a big stone wherewith to pound it."

"Well, sir," said Jillo, "ye were always a good man of your hands. But the mar will show, and that were not suitable for one of your quality."

"Thou mayst take my quality and stuff it!" cried Eudoric. "Canst speak of nought else? Help me up, pray." He got slowly to his feet, wincing, and limped a few steps.

"At least," he said, "nought seems fractured. But I misdoubt I can walk back to Liptai."

"Oh, sir, that were not to be thought of! Me allow you to wend afoot whilst I ride? Fiends take the thought!" Jillo unhitched the palfrey from the tree to which he had tethered it and led it to Eudoric.

"I accept your courtesy, good Jillo, only because I must. To plod the distance afoot were but a condign punishment for so bungling my charge. Give me a boost, will you?" Eudoric grunted as Jillo helped him into the saddle.

"Tell me, sir," said Jillo, "why did the beast ramp on past you without stopping to devour you as ye lay helpless? Was't that Morgrim promised a more bounteous repast? Or that the monster feared that your plate would give him a disorder of the bowels?"

"Meseems 'twas neither. Marked you how gray and milky appeared its eyes? According to Doctor Baldonius' book, dragons shed their skins from time to time, like serpents. This one neared the time of its skin change, wherefore the skin over its eyeballs had become thickened and opaque, like glass of poor quality. Therefore it could not plainly discern objects lying still, and pursued only those that moved."

They got back to Liptai after dark. Both were barely able to stagger, Eudoric from his sprains and bruises and Jillo footsore from the unaccustomed three-league hike.

Two days later, when they had recovered, they set out on the two palfreys to hunt for Morgrim. "For," Eudoric said, "that nag is worth more in solid money than all the rest of my possessions together."

Eudoric rode unarmored save for a shirt of light mesh mail, since the palfrey could not carry the extra weight of the plate all day at a brisk pace. He bore his lance and sword, however, in case they should again encounter a dragon.

They found the site of the previous encounter, but no sign either of the dragon or of the destrier. Eudoric and Jillo tracked the horse by its prints in the soft mold for a few bowshots, but then the slot faded out on harder ground.

"Still, I misdoubt Morgrim fell victim to the beast," said Eudoric. "He could show clean heels to many a steed of lighter build, and from its looks the dragon was no courser."

After hours of fruitless searching, whistling, and calling, they returned to Liptai. For a small fee, Eudoric was allowed to post a notice in Helladic on the town notice board, offering a reward for the return of his horse.

No word, however, came of the sighting of Morgrim. For all that Eudoric could tell, the destrier might have run clear to Velitchovo.

"You are free with advice, good Jillo," said Eudoric. "Well, rede me this riddle. We've established that our steeds will bolt from the sight and smell of dragon, for which I blame them little. Had we all the time in the world, we could doubtless train them to face the monsters, beginning with a stuffed dragon, and then, perchance, one in a cage in some monarch's menagerie. But our lucre dwindles like the snow in spring. What's to do?"

"Well, if the nags won't stand, needs we must face the worms on foot," said Jillo.

"That seems to me to throw away our lives to no good purpose, for these vasty lizards can outrun and outturn us and are well harnessed to boot. Barring the luckiest of lucky thrusts with the spear—as, say, into the eye or down the gullet—that fellow we erst encountered could make one mouthful of my lance and another of me."

"Your knightly courage were sufficient defense, sir. The Divine Pair would surely grant victory to the right."

"From all I've read of battles and feuds," said Eudoric, "methinks the Holy Couple's attention oft strays elsewhither when they should be deciding the outcome of some mundane fray."

"That is the trouble with reading; it undermines one's faith in the True Religion. But ye could be at least as well armored as the dragon, in your panoply of plate."

"Aye, but then poor Daisy could not bear so much weight to the site—or, at least, bear it thither and have breath left for a charge. We must be as chary of our beasts' welfare as of our own, for without them 'tis a long walk back to Treveria. Nor do I deem that we should like to pass our lives in Liptai."

"Then, sir, we could pack the armor on the mule, for you to do on in dragon country."

"I like it not," said Eudoric. "Afoot, weighted down by that lobster's habit, I could move no more spryly than a tortoise. 'Twere small comfort to know that if the dragon ate me, he'd suffer indigestion afterward."

Jillo sighed. "Not the knightly attitude, sir, if ye'll pardon my saying so."

"Say what you please, but I'll follow the course of what meseems were common sense. What we need is a brace of those heavy steel crossbows for sieges. At close range, they'll punch a hole in a breastplate as 'twere a sheet of papyrus."

"They take too long to crank up," said Jillo. "By the time ye've readied your second shot, the battle's over."

"Oh, it would behoove us to shoot straight the first time; but better one shot that pierces the monster's scales than a score that bounce off. Howsomever, we have these fell little hand catapults not, and they don't make them in this barbarous land."

A few days later, while Eudoric still fretted over the lack of means to his goal, he heard a sudden sound like a single thunderclap from close at hand. Hastening out from Kasmar's Inn, Eudoric and Jillo found a crowd of Pathenians around the border guard's barracks.

In the drill yard, the guard was drawn up to watch a man demonstrate a weapon. Eudoric, whose few words of Pathenian were not up to conversation, asked among the crowd for somebody who could speak Helladic. When he found one, he learned that the demonstrator was a Pantorozian. The man was a stocky, snub-nosed fellow in a bulbous fur hat, a jacket of coarse undyed wool, and baggy trousers tucked into soft boots.

"He says the device was invented by the Sericans," said the villager. "They live half a world away, across the Pantorozian deserts. He puts some powder into that thing, touches a flame to it, and *boom!* it spits a leaden ball through the target as neatly as you please."

The Pantorozian demonstrated again, pouring black powder from the small end of a horn down his brass barrel. He placed a wad of rag over the mouth of the tube, then a leaden ball, and pushed both ball and wad down the tube with a rod. He poured a pinch of powder into a hole on the upper side of the tube near its rear, closed end.

Then he set a forked rest in the ground before him, rested the barrel in the fork, and took a small torch that a guardsman handed him. He pressed the wooden stock of the device against his shoulder, sighted along the tube, and with his free hand touched the torch to the touchhole. Ffft, *bang!* A cloud of smoke, and another hole appeared in the target.

The Pantorozian spoke with the captain of the guard, but they were too far for Eudoric to hear, even if he could have understood their Pathenian. After a while, the Pantorozian picked up his tube and rest, slung his bag of powder over his shoulder, and walked with downcast air to a cart hitched to a shade tree.

Eudoric approached the man, who was climbing into his cart. "God den, fair sir!" began Eudoric, but the Pantorozian spread his hands with a smile of incomprehension.

"Kasmar!" cried Eudoric, sighting the innkeeper in the crowd. "Will you have the goodness to interpret for me and this fellow?"

"He says," said Kasmar, "that he started out with a wainload of these devices and has sold all but one. He hoped to dispose of his last one in Liptai, but our gallant Captain Boriswaf will have nought to do with it."

"Why?" asked Eudoric. "Meseems 'twere a fell weapon in practiced hands."

"That is the trouble, quoth Master Vlek. Boriswaf says that should so fiendish a weapon come into use, 'twill utterly extinguish the noble art of war, for all men will down weapons and refuse to fight rather than face so devilish a device. Then what should he, a lifelong soldier, do for his bread? Beg?"

"Ask Master Vlek where he thinks to pass the night."

"I have already persuaded him to lodge with us, Master Eudoric."

"Good, for I would fain have further converse with him."

Over dinner, Eudoric sounded out the Pantorozian on the price he asked for his device. Acting as translator, Kasmar said, "If ye strike a bargain on this, I should get ten per centum as a broker's commission, for ye were helpless without me."

Eudoric got the gun, with thirty pounds of powder and a bag of leaden balls and wadding, for less than half of what Vlek had asked of Captain Boriswaf. As Vlek explained, he had not done badly on this peddling trip and was eager to get home to his wives and children.

"Only remember," he said through Kasmar, "overcharge it not, lest it blow apart and take your head off. Press the stock firmly against your shoulder, lest it knock you on your arse like a mule's kick. And keep fire away from the spare powder, lest it explode all at once and blast you to gobbets."

Later, Eudoric told Jillo, "That deal all but wiped out our funds."

"After the tradesmanlike way ye chaffered that barbarian down?"

"Aye. The scheme had better work, or we shall find ourselves choosing betwixt starving and seeking employment as collectors of offal or diggers of ditches. Assuming, that is, that in this reeky place they even bother to collect offal."

"Master Eudoric!" said Jillo. "Ye would not really lower yourself to accept menial wage labor?"

"Sooner than starve, aye. As Helvolius the philosopher said, no rider wears sharper spurs than Necessity."

"But if 'twere known at home, they'd hack off your gilded spurs, break your sword over your head, and degrade you to base varlet!"

"Well, till now I've had no knightly spurs to hack off, but only the plain silvered ones of an esquire. For the rest, I count on you to see that they don't find out. Now go to sleep and cease your grumbling."

The next day found Eudoric and Jillo deep into the Motolian Forest. At the noonday halt, Jillo kindled a fire. Eudoric made a small torch of a stick whose end was wound with a rag soaked in bacon fat. Then he loaded the device as he had been shown how to do and fired three balls at a mark on a tree. The third time, he hit the mark squarely, although the noise caused the palfreys frantically to tug and rear.

They remounted and went on to where they had met the dragon. Jillo rekindled the torch, and they cast up and down the beast's trail. For two hours they saw no wildlife save a fleeing sow with a farrow of piglets and several huge snails with boulder-sized shells.

Then the horses became unruly. "Methinks they scent our quarry," said Eudoric.

When the riders themselves could detect the odor and the horses became almost unmanageable, Eudoric and Jillo dismounted.

"Tie the nags securely," said Eudoric. " 'Twould never do to slay our beast and then find that our horses had fled, leaving us to drag this land cockadrill home afoot."

As if in answer, a deep grunt came from ahead. While Jillo secured the horses, Eudoric laid out his new equipment and methodically loaded his piece.

"Here it comes," said Eudoric. "Stand by with that torch. Apply it not ere I give the word!"

The dragon came in sight, plodding along the trail and swinging its head from side to side. Having just shed its skin, the dragon gleamed in a reticular pattern of green and black, as if it had been freshly painted. Its great, golden, slit-pupiled eyes were now keen.

The horses screamed, causing the dragon to look up and speed its approach.

"Ready?" said Eudoric, setting the device in its rest.

"Aye, sir. Here goeth!" Without awaiting further command, Jillo applied the torch to the touchhole.

With a great boom and a cloud of smoke, the device discharged, rocking Eudoric back a pace. When the smoke cleared, the dragon was still rushing upon them, unharmed.

"Thou idiot!" screamed Eudoric. "I told thee not to give fire until I commanded! Thou hast made me miss it clean!"

"I'm s-sorry, sir. I was palsied with fear. What shall we do now?"

"Run, fool!" Dropping the device, Eudoric turned and fled.

Jillo also ran. Eudoric tripped over a root and fell sprawling. Jillo stopped to guard his fallen master and turned to face the dragon. As Eudoric scrambled up, Jillo hurled the torch at the dragon's open maw.

The throw fell just short of its target. It happened, however, that the dragon was just passing over the bag of black powder in its charge. The whirling torch, descending in its flight beneath the monster's head, struck this sack.

BOOM!

When the dragon hunters returned, they found the dragon writhing in its death throes. Its whole underside had been blown open, and blood and guts spilled out.

"Well!" said Eudoric, drawing a long breath. "That is enough knightly adventure to last me for many a year. Fall to; we must flay the creature. Belike we can sell that part of the hide that we take not home ourselves."

"How do ye propose to get it back to Liptai? Its hide alone must weigh in the hundreds."

"We shall hitch the dragon's tail to our two nags and lead them, dragging it behind. 'Twill be a weary swink, but we must needs recover as much as we can to recoup our losses."

An hour later, blood-spattered from head to foot, they were still struggling with the vast hide. Then, a man in forester's garb, with a large gilt medallion on his breast, rode up and dismounted. He was a big, rugged-looking man with a rat-trap mouth.

"Who slew this beast, good my sirs?" he inquired.

Jillo spoke: "My noble master, the squire Eudoric Dambertson here. He is the hero who hath brought this accursed beast to book."

"Be that sooth?" said the man to Eudoric.

"Well, ah," said Eudoric, "I must not claim much credit for the deed."

"But ye were the slayer, yea? Then, sir, ye are under arrest."

"What? But wherefore?"

"Ye shall see." From his garments, the stranger produced a length of cord with knots at intervals. With this he measured the dragon from nose to tail. Then the man stood up again.

"To answer your question, on three grounds: *imprimis,* for slaying a dragon out of lawful season; *secundus,* for slaying a dragon below the minimum size permitted; and *tertius,* for slaying a female dragon, which is protected the year round."

"You say this is a female?"

"Aye, 'tis as plain as the nose on your face."

"How does one tell with dragons?"

"Know, knave, that the male hath small horns behind the eyes, the which this specimen patently lacks."

"Who are you, anyway?" demanded Eudoric.

"Senior game warden Voytsik of Prath, at your service. My credentials." The man fingered his medallion. "Now, show me your licenses, pray!"

"Licenses?" said Eudoric blankly.

"Hunting licenses, oaf!"

"None told us that such were required, sir," said Jillo.

"Ignorance of the law is no prctext; ye should have asked. That makes four counts of illegality."

Eudoric said, "But why—why in the name of the God and Goddess—"

"Pray, swear not by your false, heretical deities."

"Well, why should you Pathenians wish to preserve these monstrous reptiles?"

"*Imprimis,* because their hides and other parts have

commercial value, which would perish were the whole race extirpated. *Secundus,* because they help to maintain the balance of nature by devouring the giant snails, which otherwise would issue forth nightly from the forest in such numbers as to strip bare our crops, orchards, and gardens and reduce our folk to hunger. And *tertius,* because they add a picturesque element to the landscape, thus luring foreigners to visit our land and spend their gold therein. Doth that explanation satisfy you?"

Eudoric had a fleeting thought of assaulting the stranger and either killing him or rendering him helpless while Eudoric and Jillo salvaged their prize. Even as he thought, three more tough-looking fellows, clad like Voytsik and armed with crossbows, rode out of the trees and formed up behind their leader.

"Now come along, ye two," said Voytsik.

"Whither?" asked Eudoric.

"Back to Liptai. On the morrow, we take the stage to Velitchovo, where your case will be tried."

"Your pardon, sir; we take the what?"

"The stagecoach."

"What's that, good my sir?"

"By the only God, ye must come from a barbarous land indeed! Ye shall see. Now come along, lest we be benighted in the woods."

The stagecoach made a regular round trip between Liptai and Velitchovo thrice a sennight. Jillo made the journey sunk in gloom, Eudoric kept busy viewing the passing countryside and, when opportunity offered, asking the driver about his occupation: pay, hours, fares, the cost of the vehicle, and so forth. By the time the prisoners reached their destination, both stank mightily because they had had no chance to wash the dragon's blood from their blood-soaked garments.

As they neared the capital, the driver whipped up his team to a gallop. They rattled along the road beside the muddy river Pshora until the river made a bend. Then they thundered across the planks of a bridge.

Velitchovo was a real city, with a roughly paved

main street and an onion-domed, brightly colored cathedral of the One God. In a massively timbered municipal palace, a bewhiskered magistrate asked, "Which of you two aliens truly slew the beast?"

"The younger, hight Eudoric," said Voytsik.

"Nay, Your Honor, 'twas I!" said Jillo.

"That is not what he said when we came upon them red-handed from their crime," said Voytsik. "This lean fellow plainly averred that his companion had done the deed, and the other denied it not."

"I can explain that," said Jillo. "I am the servant of the most worshipful squire Eudoric Dambertson of Arduen. We set forth to slay the creature, thinking this a noble and heroic deed that should redound to our glory on earth and our credit in Heaven. Whereas we both had a part in the act, the fatal stroke was delivered by your humble servant here. Howsomever, wishing like a good servant for all the glory to go to my master, I gave him the full credit, not knowing that this credit should be counted as blame."

"What say ye to that, Master Eudoric?" asked the judge.

"Jillo's account is essentially true," said Eudoric. "I must, however, confess that my failure to slay the beast was due to mischance and not want of intent."

"Methinks they utter a pack of lies to confuse the court," said Voytsik. "I have told Your Honor of the circumstance of their arrest, whence ye may judge how matters stand."

The judge put his fingertips together. "Master Eudoric," he said, "ye may plead innocent, or as incurring sole guilt, or as guilty in company with your servant. I do not think that you can escape some guilt, since Master Jillo, being your servant, acted under your orders. Ye be therefore responsible for his acts and at the very least a fautor of dragocide."

"What happens if I plead innocent?" said Eudoric.

"Why, in that case, an ye can find an attorney, ye shall be tried in due course. Bail can plainly not be allowed to foreign travelers, who can so easily slip through the law's fingers."

"In other words, I needs must stay in jail until my case comes up. How long will that take?"

"Since our calendar be crowded, 'twill be at least a year and a half. Whereas, an ye plead guilty, all is settled in a trice."

"Then I plead sole guilt," said Eudoric.

"But, dear Master—" wailed Jillo.

"Hold thy tongue, Jillo. I know what I do."

The judge chuckled. "An old head on young shoulders, I perceive. Well, Master Eudoric, I find you guilty on all four counts and amerce you the wonted fine, which is one hundred marks on each count."

"Four hundred marks!" exclaimed Eudoric. "Our total combined wealth at this moment amounts to fourteen marks and thirty-seven pence, plus some items of property left with Master Kasmar in Liptai."

"So, ye'll have to serve out the corresponding prison term, which comes to one mark a day—unless ye can find someone to pay the balance of the fine for you. Take him away, jailer."

"But, Your Honor!" cried Jillo, "what shall I do without my noble master? When shall I see him again?"

"Ye may visit him any day during the regular visiting hours. It were well if ye brought him somewhat to eat, for our prison fare is not of the daintiest."

At the first visiting hour, when Jillo pleaded to be allowed to share Eudoric's sentence, Eudoric said, "Be not a bigger fool than thou canst help! I took sole blame so that ye should be free to run mine errands; whereas had I shared my guilt with you, we had both been mewed up here. Here, take this letter to Doctor Raspiudus; seek him out and acquaint him with our plight. If he be in sooth a true friend of our own Doctor Baldonius, belike he'll come to our rescue."

Doctor Raspiudus was short and fat, with a bushy white beard to his waist. "Ah, dear old Baldonius!" he cried in good Helladic. "I mind me of when we were lads together at the Arcane College of Saalingen University! Doth he still string verses together?"

"Aye, that he does," said Eudoric.

"Now, young man, I daresay that your chiefest desire is to get out of this foul hole, is't not?"

"That, *and* to recover our three remaining animals and other possessions left behind in Liptai, *and* to depart with the two square yards of dragon hide that I've promised to Doctor Baldonius, with enough money to see us home."

"Methinks all these matters were easily arranged, young sir. I need only your power of attorney to enable me to go to Liptai, recover the objects in question, and return hither to pay your fine and release you. Your firearm is, I fear, lost to you, having been confiscated by the law."

" 'Twere of little use without a new supply of the magical powder," said Eudoric. "Your plan sounds splendid. But, sir, what do you get out of this?"

The enchanter rubbed his hands together. "Why, the pleasure of favoring an old friend—and also the chance to acquire a complete dragon hide for my own purposes. I know somewhat of Baldonius' experiments. An he can do thus and so with two yards of dragon, I can surely do more with a score."

"How will you obtain this dragon hide?"

"By now the foresters will have skinned the beast and salvaged the other parts of monetary worth, all of which will be put up at auction for the benefit of the kingdom. And I shall bid them in." Raspiudus chuckled. "When the other bidders know against whom they bid, I think not that they'll force the price up very far."

"Why can't you get me out of here now and then go to Liptai?"

Another chuckle. "My dear boy, first I must see that all is as ye say in Liptai. After all, I have only your word that ye be in sooth the Eudoric Dambertson of whom Baldonius writes. So bide ye in patience a few days more. I'll see that ye be sent better aliment than the slop they serve here. And now, pray, your authorization. Here are pen and ink."

To keep from starvation, Jillo got a job as a paver's helper and worked in hasty visits to the jail during his lunch hour. When a fortnight had passed without word from Doctor Raspiudus, Eudoric told Jillo to go to the wizard's home for an explanation.

"They turned me away at the door," reported Jillo. "They told me that the learned doctor had never heard of us."

As the import of this news sank in, Eudoric cursed and beat the wall in his rage. "That filthy, treacherous he-witch! He gets me to sign that power of attorney; then, when he has my property in his grubby paws, he conveniently forgets about us! By the God and Goddess, if ever I catch him—"

"Here, here, what's all this noise?" said the jailer. "Ye disturb the other prisoners."

When Jillo explained the cause of his master's outrage, the jailer laughed. "Why, everyone knows that Raspiudus is the worst skinflint and treacher in Velitchovo! Had ye asked me, I'd have warned you."

"Why has none of his victims slain him?" asked Eudoric.

"We are a law-abiding folk, sir. We do not permit private persons to indulge their feuds on their own, and we have some *most* ingenious penalties for homicide."

"Mean ye," said Jillo, "that amongst you Pathenians a gentleman may not avenge an insult by the gage of battle?"

"Of course not! We are not bloodthirsty barbarians."

"Ye mean there are no true gentlemen amongst you," sniffed Jillo.

"Then, Master Tiolkhof," said Eudoric, calming himself by force of will, "am I stuck here for a year and more?"

"Aye, but ye may get time off for good behavior at the end—three or four days, belike."

When the jailer had gone, Jillo said, "When ye get

out, Master, ye must needs uphold your honor by challenging this runagate to the trial of battle, to the death."

Eudoric shook his head. "Heard you not what Tiolkhof said? They deem dueling barbarous and boil the duelists in oil, or something equally entertaining. Anyway, Raspiudus could beg off on grounds of age. We must, instead, use what wits the Holy Couple gave us. I wish now that I'd sent you back to Liptai to fetch our belongings and never meddled with his rolypoly sorcerer."

"True, but how could ye know, dear Master? I should probably have bungled the task in any case, what with my ignorance of the tongue and all."

After another fortnight, King Vladmor of Pathenia died. When his son Yogor ascended the throne, he declared a general amnesty for all crimes lesser than murder. Thus Eudoric found himself out in the street again, but without horse, armor, weapons, or money beyond a few marks.

"Jillo," he said that night in their mean little cubicle, "we must needs get into Raspiudus' house somehow. As we saw this afternoon, 'tis a big place with a stout, high wall around it."

"An ye could get a supply of that black powder, we could blast a breach in the wall."

"But we have no such stuff, nor means of getting it, unless we raid the royal armory, which I do not think we can do."

"Then how about climbing a tree near the wall and letting ourselves down by ropes inside the wall from a convenient branch?"

"A promising plan, *if* there were such an overhanging tree. But there isn't, as you saw as well as I when we scouted the place. Let me think. Raspiudus must have supplies borne into his stronghold from time to time. I misdoubt his wizardry is potent enough to conjure foodstuffs out of air."

"Mean ye that we should gain entrance as, say, a brace of chicken farmers with eggs to sell?"

"Just so. But nay, that won't do. Raspiudus is no

fool. Knowing of this amnesty that enlarged me, he'll be on the watch for such a trick. At least, so should I be, in his room, and I credit him with no less wit than mine own. . . . I have it! What visitor would logically be likely to call upon him now, whom he will not have seen for many a year and whom he would hasten to welcome?"

"That I know not, sir."

"Who would wonder what had become of us and, detecting our troubles in his magical scryglass, would follow upon our track by uncanny means?"

"Oh, ye mean Doctor Baldonius!"

"Aye. My whiskers have grown nigh as long as his since last I shaved. And we're much of a size."

"But I never heard that your old tutor could fly about on an enchanted broomstick, as some of the mightiest magicians are said to do."

"Belike he can't, but Doctor Raspiudus wouldn't know that."

"Mean ye," said Jillo, "that ye've a mind to play Doctor Baldonius? Or to have me play him? The latter would never do."

"I know it wouldn't, good my Jillo. You know not the learned patter proper to wizards and other philosophers."

"Won't Raspiudus know you, sir? As ye say he's a shrewd old villain."

"He's seen me but once, in that dark, dank cell, and that for a mere quarter hour. You he's never seen at all. Methinks I can disguise myself well enough to befool him—unless you have a better notion."

"Alack, I have none! Then what part shall I play?"

"I had thought of going in alone."

"Nay, sir, dismiss the thought! Me let my master risk his mortal body and immortal soul in a witch's lair without my being there to help him?"

"If you help me the way you did by touching off that firearm whilst our dragon was out of range—"

"Ah, but who threw the torch and saved us in the end? What disguise shall I wear?"

"Since Raspiudus knows you not, there's no need for any. You shall be Baldonius' servant, as you are mine."

"Ye forget, sir, that if Raspiudus knows me not, his gatekeepers might. Forsooth, they're likely to recall me because of the noisy protests I made when they barred me out."

"Hm. Well, you're too old for a page, too lank for a bodyguard, and too unlearned for a wizard's assistant. I have it! You shall go as my concubine!"

"Oh, Heaven above, sir, not that! I am a normal man! I should never live it down!"

To the massive gate before Raspiudus' house came Eudoric, with a patch over one eye, and his beard, uncut for a month, dyed white. A white wig cascaded down from under his hat. He presented a note, in a plausible imitation of Baldonius' hand, to the gatekeeper:

> Doctor Baldonius of Treveria presents his compliments to his old friend and colleague Doctor Raspiudus of Velitchovo, and begs the favor of an audience to discuss the apparent disappearance of two young protégés of his.

A pace behind, stooping to disguise his stature, slouched a rouged and powdered Jillo in woman's dress. If Jillo was a homely man, he made a hideous woman, at least as far as his face could be seen under the headcloth. Nor was his beauty enhanced by the dress, which Eudoric had stitched together out of cheap cloth. The garment looked like what it was: the work of a rank amateur at dressmaking.

"My master begs you to enter," said the gatekeeper.

"Why, dear old Baldonius!" cried Raspiudus, rubbing his hands together. "Ye've not changed a mite since those glad, mad days at Saalingen! Do ye still string verses?"

"Ye've withstood the ravages of time well yourself, Raspiudus," said Eudoric, in an imitation of Baldonius' voice. " 'As fly the years, the geese fly north in spring; Ah, would the years, like geese, return awing!' "

Raspiudus roared with laughter, patting his paunch. "The same old Baldonius! Made ye that one up?"

Eudoric made a deprecatory motion. "I am a mere poetaster; but had not the higher wisdom claimed my allegiance, I might have made my mark in poesy."

"What befell your poor eye?"

"My own carelessness in leaving a corner of a pentacle open. The demon got in a swipe of his claws ere I could banish him. But now, good Raspiudus, I have a matter to discuss whereof I told you in my note."

"Yea, yea, time enow for that. Be ye weary from the road? Need ye baths? Aliment? Drink?"

"Not yet, old friend. We have but now come from Velitchovo's best hostelry."

"Then let me show you my house and grounds. Your lady . . . ?"

"She'll stay with me. She speaks nought but Treverian and fears being separated from me among strangers. A mere swineherd's chick, but a faithful creature. At my age, that is of more moment than a pretty face."

Presently, Eudoric was looking at his and Jillo's palfreys and their sumpter mule in Raspiudus' stables. Eudoric made a few hesitant efforts, as if he were Baldonius seeking his young friends, to inquire after their disappearance. Each time Raspiudus smoothly turned the question aside, promising enlightenment later.

An hour later, Raspiudus was showing off his magical sanctum. With obvious interest, Eudoric examined a number of squares of dragon hide spread out on a workbench. He asked:

"Be this the integument of one of those Pathenian dragons, whereof I have heard?"

"Certes, good Baldonius. Are they extinct in your part of the world?"

"Aye. 'Twas for that reason that I sent my young friend and former pupil, of whom I'm waiting to tell you, eastward to fetch me some of this hide for use in my work. How does one cure this hide?"

"With salt, and—*unh!*"

Raspiudus collapsed, Eudoric having just struck him on the head with a short bludgeon that he whisked out of his voluminous sleeves.

"Bind and gag him and roll him behind the bench!" said Eudoric.

"Were it not better to cut his throat, sir?" said Jillo.

"Nay. The jailer told us that they have ingenious ways of punishing homicide, and I have no wish to prove them by experiment."

While Jillo bound the unconscious Raspiudus, Eudoric chose two pieces of dragon hide, each about a yard square. He rolled them together into a bundle and lashed them with a length of rope from inside his robe. As an afterthought, he helped himself to the contents of Raspiudus' purse. Then he hoisted the roll of hide to his shoulder and issued from the laboratory. He called to the nearest stableboy.

"Doctor Raspiudus," he said, "asks that ye saddle up those two nags." He pointed. "Good saddles, mind you! Are the animals well shod?"

"Hasten, sir," muttered Jillo. "Every instant we hang about here—"

"Hold thy peace! The appearance of haste were the surest way to arouse suspicion." Eudoric raised his voice. "Another heave on that girth, fellow! I am not minded to have my aged bones shattered by a tumble into the roadway."

Jillo whispered, "Can't we recover the mule and your armor, to boot?"

Eudoric shook his head. "Too risky," he murmured. "Be glad if we get away with whole skins."

When the horses had been saddled to his satisfaction, he said, "Lend me some of your strength in mounting, youngster." He groaned as he swung awkwardly into the saddle. "A murrain on thy master, to send us off on this footling errand—me that hasn't sat a horse in years! Now hand me that accursed roll of hide. I thank thee, youth; here's a little for thy trouble. Run ahead and tell the gatekeeper to have his portal well opened. I fear that if this beast pulls up of a sudden, I shall go flying over its head!"

A few minutes later, when they had turned a corner and were out of sight of Raspiudus' house, Eudoric said, "Now trot!"

"If I could but get out of this damned gown," muttered Jillo. "I can't ride decently in it."

"Wait till we're out of the city gate."

When Jillo had shed the offending garment, Eudoric said, "Now ride, man, as never before in your life!"

They pounded off on the Liptai road. Looking back, Jillo gave a screech. "There's a thing flying after us! It looks like a giant bat!"

"One of Raspiudus' sendings," said Eudoric. "I knew he'd get loose. Use your spurs! Can we but gain the bridge. . . ."

They fled at a mad gallop. The sending came closer and closer, until Eudoric thought he could feel the wind of its wings.

Then their hooves thundered across the bridge over the Pshora.

"Those things will not cross running water," said Eudoric, looking back. "Slow down, Jillo. These nags must bear us many leagues, and we must not founder them at the start."

". . . so here we are," Eudoric told Doctor Baldonius.

"Ye've seen your family, lad?"

"Certes. They thrive, praise to the Divine Pair. Where's Lusina?"

"Well—ah—ahem—the fact is, she is not here."

"Oh? Then where?"

"Ye put me to shame, Eudoric. I promised you her hand in return for the two yards of dragon hide. Well, ye've fetched me the hide, at no small effort and risk, but I cannot fulfill my side of the bargain."

"Wherefore?"

"Alas! My undutiful daughter ran off with a strolling player last summer, whilst ye were chasing dragons—or perchance 'twas the other way round. I'm right truly sorry. . . ."

Eudoric frowned silently for an instant, then said, "Fret not, esteemed Doctor. I shall recover from the wound—provided, that is, that you salve it by making up my losses in more materialistic fashion."

Baldonius raised bushy gray brows. "So? Ye seem not so grief-stricken as I should have expected, to judge from the lover's sighs and tears wherewith ye parted from the jade last spring. Now ye'll accept money instead?"

"Aye, sir. I admit that my passion had somewhat cooled during our long separation. Was it likewise with her? What said she of me?"

"Aye, her sentiments did indeed change. She said you were too much an opportunist altogether to please her. I would not wound your feelings. . . ."

Eudoric waved a deprecatory hand. "Continue, pray. I have been somewhat toughened by my months in the rude, rough world, and I am interested."

"Well, I told her she was being foolish; that ye were a shrewd lad who, an ye survived the dragon hunt, would go far. But her words were: 'That is just the trouble, Father. He is too shrewd to be very lovable.' "

"Hmph," grunted Eudoric. "As one might say: I am a man of enterprise, thou art an opportunist, he is a conniving scoundrel. 'Tis all in the point of view. Well, if she perfers the fools of this world, I wish her joy of them. As a man of honor, I would have wedded Lusina had she wished. As things stand, trouble is saved all around."

"To you, belike, though I misdoubt my headstrong lass'll find the life of an actor's wife a bed of violets:

'Who'd wed on a whim is soon filled to the brim
Of worry and doubt, till he longs for an out.
So if ye would wive, beware of the gyve
Of an ill-chosen mate; 'tis a harrowing fate.'

But enough of that. What sum had ye in mind?"

"Enough to cover the cost of my good destrier Morgrim and my panoply of plate, together with lance and sword, plus a few other chattels and incidental expenses of travel. Fifteen hundred marks should cover the lot."

"Fif-teen *hundred!* Whew! I could ne'er afford—nor are these moldy patches of dragon hide worth a fraction of the sum."

Eudoric sighed and rose. "You know what you can afford, good my sage." He picked up the roll of dragon hide. "Your colleague Doctor Calporio, wizard to the Count of Treveria, expressed a keen interest in this material. In fact, he offered me more than I have asked of you, but I thought it only honorable to give you the first chance."

"What!" cried Baldonius. "That mountebank, charlatan, that faker? Misusing the hide and not deriving a tenth of the magical benefits from it that I should? Sit down, Eudoric; we will dicuss these things."

An hour's haggling got Eudoric his fifteen hundred marks. Baldonius said, "Well, praise the Divine Couple that's over. And now, beloved pupil, what are your plans?"

"Would ye believe it, Doctor Baldonius," said Jillo, "that my poor, deluded master is about to disgrace his lineage and betray his class by a base commercial enterprise?"

"Forsooth, Jillo? What's this?"

"He means my proposed coach line," said Eudoric.

"Good Heaven, what's that?"

"My plan to run a carriage on a weekly schedule for Zurgau to Kromnitch, taking all who can pay the fare, as they do in Pathenia. We can't let the heathen Easterlings get ahead of us."

"What an extraordinary idea! Need ye a partner?"

"Thanks, but nay. Baron Emmerhard has already thrown in with me. He's promised me my knighthood in exchange for the partnership."

"There is no nobility anymore," said Jillo.

Eudoric grinned. "Emmerhard said much the same

sort of thing, but I convinced him that anything to do with horses is a proper pursuit for a gentleman. Jillo, you can spell me at driving the coach, which will make you a gentleman, too!"

Jillo sighed. "Alas! The true spirit of knighthood is dying in this degenerate age. Woe is me that I should live to see the end of chivalry! How much did ye think of paying me, sir?"

The Little Green Men

Ah, little green fellows from Venus
Or some other planet afar:
From Mars or Calypso or, maybe,
A world of an alien star!

According to bestselling authors—
Blavatsky to von Däniken—
They taught us the skills that were needed
To make super-apes into men.

They guided our faltering footsteps
From savagery into the dawns
Of burgeoning civilization
With cities and writing and bronze.

By them were the Pyramids builded;
They reared the first temples in Hind;
Drew lines at Peruvian Nazca
To uplift the poor Amerind.

With all of these wonders they gave us
It's sad these divine astronauts
Revealed not the answers to questions
That foil our most rational thoughts.

Such puzzles as riches and paupers,
  The problems of peace and of war,
Relations between the two sexes,
  Or crime and chastisement therefor.

So when we feel dim and defeated
  By problems immune to attack,
Let's send out a prayer electronic:
  "O little green fellows, come back!"

Author's Afterword

WHEN PEOPLE ASK me how I came to be a writer, I tell them: I lost my job.

It was in 1938 when I was working in New York as editor on a trade journal. The publisher decided to cut costs by firing the two most junior editors.

I had done some writing. I had been active on my college paper, *The California Tech,* serving one year as editor. As an employee of the International Correspondence Schools of Scranton, I had co-authored (with the late Alf K. Berle) a textbook on inventions and patents. I was trained as an engineer; but, graduating in the early thirties when the great Depression was on and engineers were being fired everywhere, I had to make do with jobs in technical editing and education.

When I lived in Scranton, my friend and college roommate, Dr. John D. Clark, was job-hunting in New York. He was then a more faithful reader of the science-fiction magazines than I. To keep on eating, John wrote a couple of science-fiction stories, on whose plotting I helped him on weekend visits. He sent them to *Astounding Stories* (then edited by F. Orlin Tremaine) and, to our delighted surprise, sold them.

So, thought I, if he can, why not I? I wrote a couple and sold them, too. I also started collaborating with P.

Schuyler Miller on the novel that eventually became *Genus Homo.*

When I made my first sales, I thought: Whee! Why hasn't somebody told me about this? It sure beats working! When I got fired from the Fowler-Becker Publishing Company, I reasoned that if I could make so much money by writing for five hours a week, for fifty hours I could make ten times as much.

There is a fallacy there, since one soon runs into a law of diminishing returns. But I tried it, found I did about as well financially as I had been doing, and discovered that I preferred to be my own boss. Save for the Second World War and a few temporary jobs, I have been at it ever since.

The first story herein, "Hyperpilosity," is one of those two first stories that I wrote in Scranton. (There was one other, an amateurish little caveman tale eventually published in the short-lived magazine of historical adventure, *Golden Fleece.*) The next two items were composed after I had moved back to New York. The dates of the others you can get from the copyright page.

John W. Campbell replaced F. Orlin Tremaine as editor of *Astrounding Stories* (soon changed to *Astounding Science Fiction*) at about the time I broke into that magazine. Campbell taught me much of what I think I know about fiction writing—he, and my longtime collaborator Fletcher Pratt, and the Bread Loaf Writers Conference in 1941, which I attended as a Fellow.

The article "Language for Time Travelers" made a bit of a stir, I suppose, because nobody in the science-fiction field had given the matter of future languages much serious thought. I had made a hobby of phonetics and knew at least something about linguistic evolution, when my contemporaries were equipping their heroes for strange milieu by endowing them with telepathy or electronic translators or some such easy solution. Seventeen years later, I went over the same ground in another article, written in the light of fuller knowledge: "How to Talk Futurian" (*Fantasy and Science Fiction,* October 1957).

"The Command" had no special inspiration, unless one counts visits to the Central Park Zoo. It was the first of a series of four sequels. I learned the hard way that each story of a series must top its predecessor or it will look less good. In this case, the series ran down; Johnny Black starts out by saving the world and ends up saving his boss's job. It should have been the other way around, but that would have meant planning the whole series in advance. This would have been wise, but I did not then know that.

"Employment" reflects a longtime interest in paleontology. As a high-school student, I intended to be a paleontologist. This ambition dismayed my mother, who was sure that the occupation would not provide the income and social position that she thought desirable. My father offered a sensible compromise: that I should get an engineering degree and so be able to earn a living. (He did not foresee the effect of the Depression on the engineering profession.) Then, if I still wished to go into pure science, it would be time enough to get the advanced training required.

As things turned out, I was never able to practice real engineering until the Hitlerian War and never to practice paleontology at all. I have consoled myself by writing books and articles on prehistoric life and putting paleontological elements into a few of my stories.

"Employment," by the way, is my only story published under a pseudonym. Campbell demanded it because, in that issue of *Astounding,* he was running the first installment of my long article "Design for Life," and there is a tabu against letting an author's name appear more than once on the contents page. So I chose "Lyman R. Lyon," the name of a great-grandfather. L.R.L. was a big man in upstate New York around the time of the Civil War. He once horsewhipped his brother Caleb, an eccentric politician-adventurer, in the streets of Rome, New York. Walter Edmonds fictionalized the incident in his novel *The Big Barn* (Little, Brown, 1930). My great-aunt used to protest that Edmonds had made her father (as "Ralph Wilder") much more of a hick than he really was. He was, she would have you know, an educated, cultivated man. . . .

Otherwise I have practically not used pseudonyms. With a bogus-sounding name like mine, who needs one? When I started writing fiction, readers wrote in asking who this "L. Sprague de Camp" *really* was. Was he Henry Kuttner? Or L. Ron Hubbard? It took them a while to accept the idea that such a person existed.

"The Merman" is set in the old New York City Aquarium, a converted fort at the southern tip of Manhattan. I knew the place well but did not foresee that Robert Moses would demolish the structure and build a new aquarium at Coney Island, more than an hour by subway from Manhattan. So easily are prophetic stories dated by events!

"The Gnarly Man" has a little story. In December 1938, P. Schuyler Miller came from his home in Schenectady to New York for a meeting of the American Anthropological Association and other learned societies. I had just returned to New York after a year in Scranton and met Schuyler. I mentioned that I had been playing with an idea for a story about an immortal Neanderthal man. That's funny, said Schuy; he had been toying with the same idea.

For a while, we played Alphonse and Gaston: You write it! No, *you* write it! At last we agreed that we should both write it whenever we got around to it. Schuyler urged me to write my story first, since he was busy with other things. In addition, he generously gave me anthropological information on the man of Neanderthal. The result was "The Gnarly Man," followed a year and a half later by Schuyler's "Old Man Mulligan" in *Astounding*.

If I were writing the story today, I should diminish the physical differences between Aloysius and modern men, in accordance with modern anthropological research. These differences were exaggerated in the literature available in 1938 because the first nearly complete Neanderthal skeleton found, the man of La Chapelle-aux-Saints, was that of an arthritic old man, who could not help his slouching, shambling posture.

Biographies of writers usually make much of the connection between the writer's experiences and his fiction. John Livingston Lowes wrote a celebrated book, *The Road to Xanadu,* tracing everything in Coleridge's poems to things that Coleridge had read.

Actually, most fictions are composites of things the writer has experienced, seen, heard about, and read, put together in various combinations to make a new sequence of imaginary events. A writer may get all the material for one story from the library, while for another he uses his own life, with himself (thinly disguised) as protagonist. In the latter case, we may speak of the story as autobiographical. We should not, however, use the term if a story contains merely a few elements from the writer's own life amid many elements from other sources.

Compared to vicarious experience, personal experience is generally more useful to a writer. With many experiences, such as being in love, or in a battle, or in a storm at sea, or in a surgical operation, no amount of research will give one quite the feel of the experience that going through it will.

The trouble is that a writer does not live long enough to have all the experiences that he may wish to use in his stories. The man who spends a lifetime at one occupation and then writes a novel based on his experience may produce a good story but is likely to prove a one-book author. So a practicing writer must pad out his personal experience with vicarious experience. This he does by reading, talking with others, or even watching documentaries on television. Reading is the most fruitful source, but it all helps.

One can sometimes fool knowledgeable readers by research. An early story of mine, "The Blue Giraffe," was set in South Africa, where I had never been. You can imagine how pleased I was when a South African reader wrote to say that I must have once lived "in this sunny land of ours."

The mistake that some writers make is to think one can convincingly describe an exotic milieu from a mere smattering of knowledge, such as one gains by reading others' fiction laid in that milieu, with *neither* personal experience nor intensive research. A weakness of Robert E. Howard as a writer was that he wrote stories laid in Afghanistan and other oriental lands without ever having been out of the American Southwest. Hence he admitted that his fictional Orientals were merely "Englishmen and Irishmen in turbans and sandals."

If personal experience is impossible, then one must hole up in the library and dig like a mole, noting every aspect of the milieu in question: weather, topography, fauna, flora, custom, costume, language, and so on. Of course, no amount of research guarantees the writer against any mistakes. In *Lest Darkness Fall,* laid in sixth-century Rome, I caused one of my characters to say a few words in Gothic. A scholarly reader wrote to point out that I had made this Goth use the nominative case where he should have used the vocative!

Like others, I have used my own experiences in my fiction. Naturally, as I have lived longer, I have had more experiences to draw upon. Since most of the present stories are relatively old—more than half go back before the Hitlerian War—their content of personal experience is smaller than in many later pieces.

"Nothing in the Rules" was suggested by a swimming meet at the YMCA where I lived for a while in New York. In "The Hardwood Pile" and "The Reluctant Shaman," I leaned on my firsthand knowledge of the Adirondacks, where my father was in business and where I spent much of my boyhood and youth. There I have hiked, climbed, ridden, hunted, fished, worked in a sawmill and on a survey gang, and even prospected by airplane for uranium. The story was written long before the New York Central Railroad abandoned its Adirondack Division and became part of the Penn Central.

"The Guided Man" uses some of my trade-journal experience. Other stories, not represented here, have used other bits out of my own past. I drew on my correspondence-school days for the fantasy novelette "Mr. Arson" and on my war service in a Naval research center for my historical novel, *The Arrows of Hercules*. Recently I have drawn upon my travels for the backgrounds of some of my Willy Newbury stories, and on my experience as a guidee on many guided tours for my new Krishna novel, *The Hostage of Zir*.

The story that comes the nearest to being autobiographical is "Judgment Day," in which several incidents are taken straight out of my boyhood. It was, as you can infer, not a very pleasant one. Many other elements of the story, such as the narrator's parents and wife, are imaginary. From what colleagues tell me, this boyhood must have been fairly typical for a writer. Boys who are more athletic, extroverted, boisterous, and mischievous to begin with are, I suppose, less likely to take up the scrivener's solitary trade.

This collection is skewed in another way. Twenty years ago, with "Aristotle and the Gun," I took a vacation from writing science fiction *sensu stricto* for over a decade and a half. In the interim I was busy with historical novels, nonfiction books (popularizations of science and history, biography, and miscellaneous works), and fantasy stories, many of them collaborative tales in the Conan saga. Lately I have been getting back to science fiction proper, with a couple of novels in press. As a result, of my eighty-odd books, about half are fiction and half nonfiction. Of the works of fiction, deducting the five historical novels, about half the remainder are science fiction and half fantasy.

A standard problem of writers is that as they get along in years, they find that their writing techniques become sharpened but their ideas come with more difficulty. As a wise editor once said, fiction is the only trade that gets harder with practice. The reason is that when you conceive an idea and exploit it in a story, that idea is used up. You cannot (or rather, you had better not) use the same idea in the next story. Readers and editors soon catch on to the fact that you are repeating yourself. Therefore you have to dig up a new idea, and for each successive story idea you have to dig deeper and deeper into your unconscious.

Well, I do not think I have yet run out of ideas. In fact, the ideas are still far ahead of the time available to get them on paper. I do, though, think that I have learned a few things in the last forty years about composing English prose. When I reread some of my early stories, I shudder: awkward sentences, ill-chosen expressions, disregard of rhythm, erratic punctuation, and so forth. Now, if I could have as simple and powerful an idea right now, how much more felicitously I could express it. . . .

But the river of time flows one way only. I agree, at least in part, with George Washington when he said: "We ought not to look back, unless it is to derive useful lessons from past errors." So I hope there will be many more stories where these came from, and that readers will like them even better than they did their predecessors.

L. Sprague de Camp
Villanova, Pennsylvania
June, 1977